CHILDREN PLAYING
BEFORE A
STATUE OF HERCULES

EDITED AND INTRODUCED BY
DAVID SEDARIS

SIMON & SCHUSTER PAPERBACKS

New York   London   Toronto   Sydney

SIMON & SCHUSTER PAPERBACKS
Rockefeller Center
1230 Avenue of the Americas
New York, NY 10020

Permissions acknowledgments appear on page 343.

First Simon & Schuster paperback edition 2005

SIMON & SCHUSTER PAPERBACKS and colophon are registered trademarks
of Simon & Schuster, Inc.

For information about special discounts for bulk purchases,
please contact Simon & Schuster Special Sales at
1-800-456-6798 or business@simonandschuster.com.

Designed by Ruth Lee-Mui

Manufactured in the United States of America

10 9 8 7 6 5

Library of Congress Catalog Card Number: 2005042532

ISBN 0-7432-7394-X

CONTENTS

CONTENTS

CHILDREN PLAYING

BEFORE A

STATUE OF HERCULES

INTRODUCTION

David Sedaris

✷ ✷ ✷

One afternoon, in the middle of a particularly boring grammar lesson, my seventh-grade English teacher set aside her book and took nominations for the best song on WKIX, our local Top 40 radio station. It was her way of getting the circulation back into our arms, and it worked like a charm. For the first time that year, all hands were in the air, not just at head level but well above it, and waving, as if they held flags. There was no "right answer" to a question of personal taste, or so I thought until she eventually called on me, and I announced that "Indiana Wants Me" was not only the best song in the Top 40 but possibly the best song ever. The phrase "in the history of all time" may have been used, but what I remember is not my recommendation so much as the silence that followed it, an absence of agreement I can only describe as deafening.

The person in front of me, a guy named Teetsil, turned around in his seat. "'Indiana Wants Me'?"

"Now, now," the teacher said, "to each his own."

Teetsil said that was fine or whatever. "But 'Indiana Wants Me'? He's got to be kidding."

I wasn't close friends with Teetsil, no one was, but on hearing his disapproval, I decided that maybe my choice wasn't all it was cracked up to be. I thought I'd enjoyed it as a grim little narrative, the confession of a man who was wanted for murder in the exotic Midwest. The singer's voice was tinged with regret, more country than pop, and that, too, I liked, or thought I had. At the end of the song, the authorities pulled up, and you could hear them in the background shouting into their megaphones: "This is the police. You are surrounded. Give yourself up." It was, I thought, a classy touch.

The first time I heard it, I was hooked, and then I bought the 45 and played it over and over again. The song satisfied me on every level, but if nobody else liked it, I guessed that I didn't, either. "What I meant," I said, "is that I *don't* like 'Indiana Wants Me.' My sister does, she plays it all the time, but me, I can't stand it."

"Then what *do* you like?" the teacher asked, and I saw the same expression our cat had when torturing a mole.

I looked at Teetsil, who'd named something by the Rolling Stones, and then at the girl across the aisle who liked the Carpenters.

"Everything," I announced, "I like everything."

"Everything but 'Indiana Wants Me'?"

"Yes," I said. "Everything but that."

That evening, alone in my room, I found that I was too ashamed to listen to my record, or even to look at it, really. It reminded me of my wretched eagerness to please, and would now have to be banished, hidden in the closet and then thrown away. This was a loss but not a total one, as at least I had learned a lesson. From this point on, whenever someone asked my opinion, I would turn the question around, and then proceed accordingly. If the person I was with loved game shows and Deep Purple, then so would I, and if I was caught contradicting myself—watching or listening to something I'd sworn to have hated—I would claim to be doing research, or to be enjoying the thing for its very badness. You could do this, I learned, and people would forgive you, consider you interesting, even. The downside was that it led to crummy gifts: Mitch Miller records, heads made from coconuts, campy stuff thought to be "a hoot," or, if it was extra lame, "a hoot and a half."

My own tastes I kept to myself, and in time they became hazy. If everyone I knew could agree on the same thing, I might have settled into a particular genre, but my friends were all over the place. And so opinionated! At college in the mountains of North Carolina, I claimed to love bluegrass and *The Prophet*. Then on weekends, I'd come home to the Andrews Sisters and back issues of wrestling magazines. Another college, a better one in Ohio, and I was all for Huey Newton, vegetarian meat loaf, Muddy Waters.

After dropping out, I fell in with a group of avant-gardists—that's what we called ourselves, and very seriously. Now came records that sounded as if they had ended, the thup, thup, thup of a needle having run its course. I pretended to like plays with no plots, books in which characters had no names, no faces, no reason to get out of bed.

Nothing changed until I left North Carolina and moved to Odell, Oregon, where I had no friends and no hopes of making any. There was a small public library in the neighboring town, and on my first visit, I picked up a neglected copy of *Ulysses,* hoping it might impress the woman behind the checkout desk. She stamped the card, and when I saw that she was not going to react one way or another, I returned to the stacks in search of a second book. It could be anything I wanted, but what was that, exactly? Having spent my life trying to fit the will of others, I was unable to distinguish between what I enjoyed and what I thought I should enjoy.

Like a lot of beginning readers, I wanted a mirror. The story of a twenty-one-year-old apple picker who lived in a trailer would have been perfect, but this was a small library, and when I found nothing that reflected me precisely, I broadened my category and defined myself as a wayfarer. This left me with *Ulysses* and *The Odyssey,* neither of which I actually read.

On my next trip to the library, I defined myself as just a guy and picked up something a bit more inviting, *Babbitt,* I think it was. Sinclair Lewis led to Sherwood Anderson and other names I vaguely recalled from high school: John Steinbeck, Richard Wright, D. H. Lawrence—authors who weren't so bad as long as you didn't have to write papers about them. After a bout of Ernest Hemingway, I once again broadened my definition and saw myself as a human being, able to relate to anything as long as there weren't detectives in it. I had nothing against mysteries, far from it, but because they're so often published in large type, I decided to save them for my golden years, which began when I turned forty-five.

When apple-picking season ended, I got a job in a packing plant and gravitated toward short stories, which I could read during my break and reflect upon for the remainder of my shift. A good one would take me out of myself and then stuff me back in, outsized, now, and uneasy with the fit. This led to a kind of trance that made the dullest work, the dullest life, bearable.

I was in Oregon only four months, but it was long enough to develop a habit, and with it, a certain confidence in my opinion. It was based on nothing formal or complicated—I just knew when something affected me and caused me to see the world in a different way. Back in Raleigh, I dug in to the public library, which was vast compared to the one in Hood River. The one in Chicago was bigger still, and I staggered around it like a zombie.

As I started to write myself, I began to read stories differently, harder. Margins were marked with comments, and memorable passages were underlined, then copied down. I wanted to sense what it must have been like to write these words for the first time, so I would type them hesitantly, pretending that they had just come to me. Once, before leaving on vacation, I copied an entire page from an Alice Munro story and left it in my typewriter, hoping a burglar might come upon it and mistake her words for my own. That an intruder would spend his valuable time reading, that he might be impressed by the description of a crooked face, was something I did not question, as I believed, and still do, that stories can save you. In my head are memorized passages, suitable for every occasion, and if those don't work, I'm heartened by the very possibility of writing—the thought that someone could create something as hypnotic to me as "Half a Grapefruit" or "Revelation," or anything else in this collection. Look what's possible, I think. Look at what people have managed to do!

In selecting stories for this anthology, I chose things that have stuck with me over the years, and that I turn to again and again. Some of them—the Richard Yates, the Flannery O'Connor, the Tobias Wolff—remind me to be careful, to stop judging people, to be a better person. Others, like "Interpreter of Maladies," bring me news from a world I never imagined, and others still leave me shaken no matter how often I read them, "The Girl with the Blackened Eye," for instance, when the narrator claims that her life would not be any different had she not been abducted at the age of fifteen. That's such a bodacious thing to say.

I don't purposely seek out humor, but when it falls in my lap and is equal parts funny and tragic, I am delighted, hence the Dorothy Parker, the Amy Hempel, the Jincy Willett, and the short

Frank Gannon story I read years ago in *Harper's*. Lorrie Moore is somehow beyond humor, off the laugh meter and into an area that has no name. This particular story is from *Birds of America,* the closest you can get to a perfect book.

While I'm an honest enthusiast, I'm not very good at explaining why I like what I like. Most often I come off sounding like a stoned teenager ("It's got, like, monkeys in it and everything"). I included the Patricia Highsmith story because it is quiet, built on what I think of as old-fashioned description, and I like "The Garden Party" for much the same reason. I read it in high school, but it didn't really hit me until I listened to it on a Caedmon audio collection. A lot of people pooh-pooh them as laziness, but I love a good book on tape, the pleasure of being read to. I first heard Akhil Sharma on *The Best American Short Stories 1998,* and then I went and read his novel, *An Obedient Father,* which is sublime.

I'm a big fan of anthologies, and I count on them to expose me to authors I otherwise might have missed, people like Charles Baxter, Tim Johnston, and Jean Thompson, whom I first read in a book called *Matters of Life and Death,* edited by Tobias Wolff. Most of these stories have already been collected in one place or another, but I saw that as no reason to exclude them. Books fall in and out of print, and were I to select, say, a less satisfying Richard Yates sample, a newcomer might not realize how magnificent he is, might not be persuaded to read *Liars in Love,* or his great, sad masterpiece, *Revolutionary Road.* My hope with this anthology is that you'll use it as a springboard and seek out everything these authors have written. Then you'll see how difficult it was to choose one Tobias Wolff story, one Alice Munro story, and so on down the line. It's the writers who make it hard. Them and their damned excellence.

While corraling my favorite stories was a joy, titling the collection was a pain in the ass. I was searching under rocks, considering puns, when I came across an Adriaen van der Werff at the Alte

Pinakothek, an art museum in Munich. As a painting, *Children Playing Before a Statue of Hercules* didn't do much for me, but I loved the title and realized that in terms of this anthology, it actually made a good deal of sense. The authors in this book are huge to me, and I am a comparative midget, scratching around in their collective shadow. "Pint-sized Fanatic Bowing Before Statues of Hercules" might have been more concise, but people don't paint things like that, and besides, it doesn't sound as good.

There are plenty more Herculai where these came from, but there are only so many you can include in a fourteen-dollar book, so a lot of them were left out. Those who are gathered here, though, I would defend to my death. When it comes to music and movies, I'm still the same coward I was in the seventh grade. "You liked that?" someone will say, and I'll take it all back, just as I did with "Indiana Wants Me." With stories, though, I feel more self-assured, almost bullyish. I'm ready to pick fights for these writers, step outside, fight dirty, and if I'm beaten down, I'll be like that knight in the Monty Python movie, armless and legless, a determined stump shouting, "Come back here, you. I'm not finished yet."

OH, JOSEPH, I'M SO TIRED

Richard Yates

★ ★ ★

When Franklin D. Roosevelt was President-elect there must have been sculptors all over America who wanted a chance to model his head from life, but my mother had connections. One of her closest friends and neighbors, in the Greenwich Village courtyard where we lived, was an amiable man named Howard Whitman who had recently lost his job as a reporter on the *New York Post*. And one of Howard's former colleagues from the *Post* was now employed in the press office of Roosevelt's New York headquarters. That would make it easy for her to get in—or, as she said, to get an entrée—and she was confident she could take it from there. She was confident about everything she did in those days, but it never quite disguised a terrible need for support and approval on every side.

She wasn't a very good sculptor. She had been working at it for only three years, since breaking up her marriage to my father, and there was still something stiff and amateurish about her pieces. Before the Roosevelt project her specialty had been "garden figures"—a life-size little boy whose legs turned into the legs of a goat at the knees and another who knelt among ferns to play the pipes of Pan; little girls who trailed chains of daisies from their upraised arms or walked beside a spread-winged goose. These fanciful children, in plaster painted green to simulate weathered bronze, were arranged on homemade wooden pedestals to loom around her studio and to leave a cleared space in the middle for the modeling stand that held whatever she was working on in clay.

Her idea was that any number of rich people, all of them gracious and aristocratic, would soon discover her: they would want her sculpture to decorate their landscaped gardens, and they would want to make her their friend for life. In the meantime, a little nationwide publicity as the first woman sculptor to "do" the President-elect certainly wouldn't hurt her career.

And, if nothing else, she had a good studio. It was, in fact, the best of all the studios she would have in the rest of her life. There were six or eight old houses facing our side of the courtyard, with their backs to Bedford Street, and ours was probably the showplace of the row because the front room on its ground floor was two stories high. You went down a broad set of brick steps to the tall front windows and the front door; then you were in the high, wide, light-flooded studio. It was big enough to serve as a living room too, and so along with the green garden children it contained all the living-room furniture from the house we'd lived in with my father in the suburban town of Hastings-on-Hudson, where I was born. A second-floor balcony ran along the far end of the studio, with two small bedrooms and a tiny bathroom tucked away up-stairs; beneath that, where the ground floor continued through to the Bedford Street side, lay the only part of the apartment that might let you know we didn't have much money. The ceiling was very low and it was always dark in there; the small windows looked out underneath an iron sidewalk grating, and the bottom of that street cavity was thick with strewn garbage. Our roach-infested kitchen was barely big enough for a stove and sink that were never clean, and for a brown wooden icebox with its dark, ever-melting block of ice; the rest of that area was our dining room, and not even the amplitude of the old Hastings dining-room table could brighten it. But our Majestic radio was in there too, and that made it a cozy place for my sister, Edith, and me: we liked the children's programs that came on in the late afternoons.

We had just turned off the radio one day when we went out into the studio and found our mother discussing the Roosevelt project with Howard Whitman. It was the first we'd heard of it, and we must have interrupted her with too many questions because she said, "Edith? Billy? That's enough, now. I'll tell you all about this later. Run out in the garden and play."

She always called the courtyard "the garden," though nothing grew there except a few stunted city trees and a patch of grass that never had a chance to spread. Mostly it was bald earth, interrupted here and there by brick paving, lightly powdered with soot and scattered with the droppings of dogs and cats. It may have been six or eight houses long, but it was only two houses wide, which gave it a hemmed-in, cheerless look; its only point of interest was a di-lapidated marble fountain, not much bigger than a birdbath, which stood near our house. The original idea of the fountain was that water would drip evenly from around the rim of its upper tier and tinkle into its lower basin, but age had unsettled it; the water spilled in a single ropy stream from the only inch of the upper tier's rim that stayed clean. The lower basin was deep enough to soak your feet in on a hot day, but there wasn't much pleasure in that because the underwater part of the marble was coated with brown scum.

My sister and I found things to do in the courtyard every day, for all of the two years we lived there, but that was only because Edith was an imaginative child. She was eleven at the time of the Roosevelt project, and I was seven.

"Daddy?" she asked in our father's office uptown one afternoon. "Have you heard Mommy's doing a head of President Roosevelt?"

"Oh?" He was rummaging in his desk, looking for something he'd said we might like.

"She's going to take his measurements and stuff here in New York," Edith said, "and then after the Inauguration, when the sculpture's done, she's going to take it to Washington and present it to him in the White House." Edith often told one of our parents about the other's more virtuous activities; it was part of her long, hopeless effort to bring them back together. Many years later she told me she thought she had never recovered, and never would, from the shock of their breakup: she said Hastings-on-Hudson remained the happiest time of her life, and that made me envious because I could scarcely remember it at all.

"Well," my father said. "That's really something, isn't it." Then he found what he'd been looking for in the desk and said, "Here we go; what do you think of these?" They were two fragile perforated sheets of what looked like postage stamps, each stamp bearing the insignia of an electric lightbulb in vivid white against a yellow background, and the words "More light."

My father's office was one of many small cubicles on the twenty-third floor of the General Electric building. He was an assistant regional sales manager in what was then called the Mazda Lamp Division—a modest job, but good enough to have allowed him to rent into a town like Hastings-on-Hudson in better times—and these "More light" stamps were souvenirs of a recent sales convention. We told him the stamps were neat—and they were—but expressed some doubt as to what we might do with them.

"Oh, they're just for decoration," he said. "I thought you could paste them into your schoolbooks, or—you know—whatever you want. Ready to go?" And he carefully folded the sheets of stamps and put them in his inside pocket for safekeeping on the way home.

Between the subway exit and the courtyard, somewhere in the West Village, we always walked past a vacant lot where men stood huddled around weak fires built of broken fruit crates and trash, some of them warming tin cans of food held by coat-hanger wire over the flames. "Don't stare," my father had said the first time. "All those men are out of work, and they're hungry."

"Daddy?" Edith inquired. "Do you think Roosevelt's good?"

"Sure I do."

"Do you think all the Democrats are good?"

"Well, most of 'em, sure."

Much later I would learn that my father had participated in local Democratic Party politics for years. He had served some of his political friends—men my mother described as dreadful little Irish people from Tammany Hall—by helping them to establish Mazda Lamp distributorships in various parts of the city. And he loved their social gatherings, at which he was always asked to sing.

"Well, of course, you're too young to remember Daddy's singing," Edith said to me once after his death in 1942.

"No, I'm not; I remember."

"But I mean really remember," she said. "He had the most beautiful tenor voice I've ever heard. Remember 'Danny Boy'?"

"Sure."

"Ah, God, that was something," she said, closing her eyes. "That was really—that was really something."

When we got back to the courtyard that afternoon, and back into the studio, Edith and I watched our parents say hello to each other. We always watched that closely, hoping they might drift into conversation and sit down together and find things to laugh about, but they never did. And it was even less likely than usual that day because my mother had a guest—a woman named Sloane Cabot who was her best friend in the courtyard, and who greeted my father with a little rush of false, flirtatious enthusiasm.

"How've you been, Sloane?" he said. Then he turned back to his former wife and said, "Helen? I hear you're planning to make a bust of Roosevelt."

"Well, not a bust," she said. "A head. I think it'll be more effective if I cut it off at the neck."

"Well, good. That's fine. Good luck with it. Okay, then." He gave his whole attention to Edith and me. "Okay. See you soon. How about a hug?"

And those hugs of his, the climax of his visitation rights, were unforgettable. One at a time we would be swept up and pressed hard into the smells of linen and whiskey and tobacco; the warm rasp of his jaw would graze one cheek and there would be a quick moist kiss near the ear; then he'd let us go.

He was almost all the way out of the courtyard, almost out in the street, when Edith and I went racing after him.

"Daddy! Daddy! You forgot the stamps!"

He stopped and turned around, and that was when we saw he was crying. He tried to hide it—he put his face nearly into his armpit as if that might help him search his inside pocket—but there is no way to disguise the awful bloat and pucker of a face in tears.

"Here," he said. "Here you go." And he gave us the least convincing smile I had ever seen. It would be good to report that we stayed and talked to him—that we hugged him again—but we were too embarrassed for that. We took the stamps and ran home without looking back.

"Oh, aren't you excited, Helen?" Sloane Cabot was saying. "To be meeting him, and talking to him and everything, in front of all those reporters?"

"Well, of course," my mother said, "but the important thing is to get the measurements right. I hope there won't be a lot of photographers and silly interruptions."

Sloane Cabot was some years younger than my mother, and strikingly pretty in a style often portrayed in what I think are called Art Deco illustrations of that period: straight dark bangs, big eyes, and a big mouth. She too was a divorced mother, though her former husband had vanished long ago and was referred to only as "that bastard" or "that cowardly son of a bitch." Her only child was a boy of Edith's age named John, whom Edith and I liked enormously.

The two women had met within days of our moving into the courtyard, and their friendship was sealed when my mother solved the problem of John's schooling. She knew a Hastings-on-Hudson family who would appreciate the money earned from taking in a boarder, so John went up there to live and go to school, and came home only on weekends. The arrangement cost more than Sloane could comfortably afford, but she managed to make ends meet and was forever grateful.

Sloane worked in the Wall Street district as a private secretary. She talked a lot about how she hated her job and her boss, but the good part was that her boss was often out of town for extended periods: that gave her time to use the office typewriter in pursuit of her life's ambition, which was to write scripts for the radio.

She once confided to my mother that she'd made up both of her names: "Sloane" because it sounded masculine, the kind of name a woman alone might need for making her way in the world, and "Cabot" because—well, because it had a touch of class. Was there anything wrong with that?

"Oh, Helen," she said. "This is going to be wonderful for

you. If you get the publicity—if the papers pick it up, and the newsreels—you'll be one of the most interesting personalities in America."

Five or six people were gathered in the studio on the day my mother came home from her first visit with the President-elect.

"Will somebody get me a drink?" she asked, looking around in mock helplessness. "Then I'll tell you all about it."

And with the drink in her hand, with her eyes as wide as a child's, she told us how a door had opened and two big men had brought him in.

"Big men," she insisted. "Young, strong men, holding him up under the arms, and you could see how they were straining. Then you saw this *foot* come out, with these awful metal braces on the shoe, and then the *other* foot. And he was sweating, and he was panting for breath, and his face was—I don't know—all bright and tense and horrible." She shuddered.

"Well," Howard Whitman said, looking uneasy, "he can't help being crippled, Helen."

"Howard," she said impatiently, "I'm only trying to tell you how *ugly* it was." And that seemed to carry a certain weight. If she was an authority on beauty—on how a little boy might kneel among ferns to play the pipes of Pan, for example—then surely she had earned her credentials as an authority on ugliness.

"*Any*way," she went on, "they got him into a chair, and he wiped most of the sweat off his face with a handkerchief—he was still out of breath—and after a while he started talking to some of the other men there; I couldn't follow that part of it. Then finally he turned to me with this smile of his. Honestly, I don't know if I can describe that smile. It isn't something you can see in the newsreels; you have to be there. His eyes don't change at all, but the corners of his mouth go up as if they're being pulled by puppet strings. It's a frightening smile. It makes you think: this could be a dangerous man. This could be an evil man. Well anyway, we started talking, and I spoke right up to him. I said, 'I didn't vote for you, Mr. President.' I said, 'I'm a good Republican and I voted for President Hoover.' He said, 'Why are you here, then?' or something like that, and I said, 'Because you have a very interesting head.' So he gave me the smile again and he said, 'What's interesting about it?' And I said, 'I like the bumps on it.'"

By then she must have assumed that every reporter in the room was writing in his notebook, while the photographers got their flashbulbs ready; tomorrow's papers might easily read:

GAL SCULPTOR TWITS FDR
ABOUT "BUMPS" ON HEAD

At the end of her preliminary chat with him she got down to business, which was to measure different parts of his head with her calipers. I knew how that felt: the cold, trembling points of those clay-encrusted calipers had tickled and poked me all over during the times I'd served as model for her fey little woodland boys.

But not a single flashbulb went off while she took and recorded the measurements, and nobody asked her any questions; after a few nervous words of thanks and goodbye she was out in the corridor again among all the hopeless, craning people who couldn't get in. It must have been a bad disappointment, and I imagine she tried to make up for it by planning the triumphant way she'd tell us about it when she got home.

"Helen?" Howard Whitman inquired, after most of the other visitors had gone. "Why'd you tell him you didn't vote for him?"

"Well, because it's true. I *am* a good Republican; you know that."

She was a storekeeper's daughter from a small town in Ohio; she had probably grown up hearing the phrase "good Republican" as an index of respectability and clean clothes. And maybe she had come to relax her standards of respectability, maybe she didn't even care much about clean clothes anymore, but "good Republican" was worth clinging to. It would be helpful when she met the customers for her garden figures, the people whose low, courteous voices would welcome her into their lives and who would almost certainly turn out to be Republicans too.

"I believe in the aristocracy!" she often cried, trying to make herself heard above the rumble of voices when her guests were discussing Communism, and they seldom paid her any attention. They liked her well enough: she gave parties with plenty of liquor, and she was an agreeable hostess if only because of her touching eagerness to please; but in any talk of politics she was like a shrill, exasperating child. She believed in the aristocracy.

She believed in God too, or at least in the ceremony of St. Luke's Episcopal Church, which she attended once or twice a year. And she believed in Eric Nicholson, the handsome middle-aged Englishman who was her lover. He had something to do with the American end of a British chain of foundries: his company cast ornamental objects into bronze and lead. The cupolas of college and high-school buildings all over the East, the lead casement windows for Tudor-style homes in places like Scarsdale and Bronxville— these were some of the things Eric Nicholson's firm had accomplished. He was always self-deprecating about his business, but ruddy and glowing with its success.

My mother had met him the year before, when she'd sought help in having one of her garden figures cast into bronze, to be "placed on consignment" with some garden-sculpture gallery from which it would never be sold. Eric Nicholson had persuaded her that lead would be almost as nice as bronze and much cheaper; then he'd asked her out to dinner, and that evening changed our lives.

Mr. Nicholson rarely spoke to my sister or me, and I think we were both frightened of him, but he overwhelmed us with gifts. At first they were mostly books—a volume of cartoons from *Punch,* a partial set of Dickens, a book called *England in Tudor Times* containing tissue-covered color plates that Edith liked. But in the summer of 1933, when our father arranged for us to spend two weeks with our mother at a small lake in New Jersey, Mr. Nicholson's gifts became a cornucopia of sporting goods. He gave Edith a steel fishing rod with a reel so intricate that none of us could have figured it out even if we'd known how to fish, a wicker creel for carrying the fish she would never catch, and a sheathed hunting knife to be worn at her waist. He gave me a short ax whose head was encased in a leather holster and strapped to my belt—I guess this was for cutting firewood to cook the fish—and a cumbersome net with a handle that hung from an elastic shoulder strap, in case I should be called upon to wade in and help Edith land a tricky one. There was nothing to do in that New Jersey village except take walks, or what my mother called good hikes; and every day, as we plodded out through the insect-humming weeds in the sun, we wore our full regalia of useless equipment.

That same summer Mr. Nicholson gave me a three-year subscription to *Field & Stream,* and I think that impenetrable magazine was the least appropriate of all his gifts because it kept coming in the mail for such a long, long time after everything else had changed for us: after we'd moved out of New York to Scarsdale, where Mr. Nicholson had found a house with a low rent, and after he had abandoned my mother in that house—with no warning—to return to England and to the wife from whom he'd never really been divorced.

But all that came later; I want to go back to the time between Franklin D. Roosevelt's election and his Inauguration, when his head was slowly taking shape on my mother's modeling stand.

Her original plan had been to make it life-size, or larger than life-size, but Mr. Nicholson urged her to scale it down for economy in the casting, and so she made it only six or seven inches high. He persuaded her too, for the second time since he'd known her, that lead would be almost as nice as bronze.

She had always said she didn't mind at all if Edith and I watched her work, but we had never much wanted to; now it was a little more interesting because we could watch her sift through many photographs of Roosevelt cut from newspapers until she found one that would help her execute a subtle plane of cheek or brow.

But most of our day was taken up with school. John Cabot might go to school in Hastings-on-Hudson, for which Edith would always yearn, but we had what even Edith admitted was the next best thing: we went to school in our bedroom.

During the previous year my mother had enrolled us in the public school down the street, but she'd begun to regret it when we came home with lice in our hair. Then one day Edith came home accused of having stolen a boy's coat, and that was too much. She withdrew us both, in defiance of the city truant officer, and pleaded with my father to help her meet the cost of a private school. He refused. The rent she paid and the bills she ran up were already taxing him far beyond the terms of the divorce agreement; he was in debt; surely she must realize he was lucky even to have a job. Would she ever learn to be reasonable?

It was Howard Whitman who broke the deadlock. He knew of an inexpensive, fully accredited mail-order service called the Calvert School, intended mainly for the homes of children who were invalids. The Calvert School furnished weekly supplies of books and materials and study plans; all she would need was some-one in the house to administer the program and to serve as a tutor. And someone like Bart Kampen would be ideal for the job.

"The skinny fellow?" she asked. "The Jewish boy from Holland or wherever it is?"

"He's very well educated, Helen," Howard told her. "And he speaks fluent English, and he'd be very conscientious. And he could certainly use the money."

We were delighted to learn that Bart Kampen would be our tutor. With the exception of Howard himself, Bart was probably our favorite among the adults around the courtyard. He was twenty-eight or so, young enough so that his ears could still turn red when he was teased by children; we had found that out in teasing him once or twice about such matters as that his socks didn't match. He was tall and very thin and seemed always to look startled except when he was comforted enough to smile. He was a violinist, a Dutch Jew who had emigrated the year before in the hope of joining a symphony orchestra, and eventually of launching a concert career. But the symphonies weren't hiring then, nor were lesser orchestras, so Bart had gone without work for a long time. He lived alone in a room on Seventh Avenue, not far from the courtyard, and people who liked him used to worry that he might not have enough to eat. He owned two suits, both cut in a way that must have been stylish in the Netherlands at the time: stiff, heavily padded shoulders and a nipped-in waist; they would probably have looked better on someone with a little more meat on his bones. In shirtsleeves, with the cuffs rolled back, his hairy wrists and forearms looked even more fragile than you might have expected, but his long hands were shapely and strong enough to suggest authority on the violin.

"I'll leave it entirely up to you, Bart," my mother said when he asked if she had any instructions for our tutoring. "I know you'll do wonders with them."

A small table was moved into our bedroom, under the window, and three chairs placed around it. Bart sat in the middle so that he could divide his time equally between Edith and me. Big, clean, heavy brown envelopes arrived in the mail from the Calvert School once a week, and when Bart slid their fascinating contents onto the table it was like settling down to begin a game.

Edith was in the fifth grade that year—her part of the table was given over to incomprehensible talk about English and History and Social Studies—and I was in the first. I spent my mornings asking Bart to help me puzzle out the very opening moves of an education.

"Take your time, Billy," he would say. "Don't get impatient with this. Once you have it you'll see how easy it is, and then you'll be ready for the next thing."

At eleven each morning we would take a break. We'd go downstairs and out to the part of the courtyard that had a little grass. Bart would carefully lay his folded coat on the sidelines, turn back his shirt cuffs, and present himself as ready to give what he called airplane rides. Taking us one at a time, he would grasp one wrist and one ankle; then he'd whirl us off our feet and around and around, with himself as the pivot, until the courtyard and the buildings and the city and the world were lost in the dizzying blur of our flight.

After the airplane rides we would hurry down the steps into the studio, where we'd usually find that my mother had set out a tray bearing three tall glasses of cold Ovaltine, sometimes with cookies on the side and sometimes not. I once overheard her telling Sloane Cabot she thought the Ovaltine must be Bart's first nourishment of the day—and I think she was probably right, if only because of the way his hand would tremble in reaching for his glass. Sometimes she'd forget to prepare the tray and we'd crowd into the kitchen and fix it ourselves; I can never see a jar of Ovaltine on a grocery shelf without remembering those times. Then it was back upstairs to school again. And during that year, by coaxing and prodding and telling me not to get impatient, Bart Kampen taught me to read.

It was an excellent opportunity for showing off. I would pull books down from my mother's shelves—mostly books that were the gifts of Mr. Nicholson—and try to impress her by reading mangled sentences aloud.

"That's wonderful, dear," she would say. "You've really learned to read, haven't you."

Soon a white-and-yellow "More light" stamp was affixed to every page of my Calvert First Grade Reader, proving I had mas-

tered it, and others were accumulating at a slower rate in my arithmetic workbook. Still other stamps were fastened to the wall beside my place at the school table, arranged in a proud little
white-and-yellow thumb-smudged column that rose as high as I
could reach.

"You shouldn't have put your stamps on the wall," Edith said.

"Why?"

"Well, because they'll be hard to take off."

"Who's going to take them off?"

That small room of ours, with its double function of sleep and
learning, stands more clearly in my memory than any other part of
our home. Someone should probably have told my mother that a
girl and boy of our ages ought to have separate rooms, but that
never occurred to me until much later. Our cots were set foot-to-
foot against the wall, leaving just enough space to pass alongside
them to the school table, and we had some good conversations as
we lay waiting for sleep at night. The one I remember best was the
time Edith told me about the sound of the city.

"I don't mean just the loud noises," she said, "like the siren going by just now, or those car doors slamming, or all the laughing
and shouting down the street; that's just close-up stuff. I'm talking
about something else. Because you see there are millions and millions of people in New York—more people than you can possibly
imagine, ever—and most of them are doing something that makes
sound. Maybe talking, or playing the radio, maybe closing doors,
maybe putting their forks down on their plates if they're having
dinner, or dropping their shoes if they're going to bed—and because there are so many of them, all those little sounds add up and
come together in a kind of burn. But it's so faint—so very, very
faint—that you can't hear it unless you listen very carefully for a
long time."

"Can you hear it?" I asked her.

"Sometimes. I listen every night, but I can only hear it sometimes. Other times I fall asleep. Let's be quiet now, and just listen. See if you can hear it, Billy."

And I tried hard, closing my eyes as if that would help, opening my mouth to minimize the sound of my breathing, but in the end I had to tell her I'd failed. "How about you?" I asked.

"Oh, I heard it," she said. "Just for a few seconds, but I heard it. You'll hear it too, if you keep trying. And it's worth waiting for. When you hear it, you're hearing the whole city of New York."

The high point of our week was Friday afternoon, when John Cabot came home from Hastings. He exuded health and normality; he brought fresh suburban air into our bohemian lives. He even transformed his mother's small apartment, while he was there, into an enviable place of rest between vigorous encounters with the world. He subscribed to both *Boys' Life* and *Open Road for Boys,* and these seemed to me to be wonderful things to have in your house, if only for the illustrations. John dressed in the same heroic way as the boys shown in those magazines, corduroy knickers with ribbed stockings pulled taut over his muscular calves. He talked a lot about the Hastings high-school football team, for which he planned to try out as soon as he was old enough, and about Hastings friends whose names and personalities grew almost as familiar to us as if they were friends of our own. He taught us invigorating new ways to speak, like saying "What's the diff?" instead of "What's the difference?" And he was better even than Edith at finding new things to do in the courtyard.

You could buy goldfish for ten or fifteen cents apiece in Woolworth's then, and one day we brought home three of them to keep in the fountain. We sprinkled the water with more Woolworth's granulated fish food than they could possibly need, and we named them after ourselves: "John," "Edith," and "Billy." For a week or two Edith and I would run to the fountain every morning, before Bart came for school, to make sure they were still alive and to see if they had enough food, and to watch them.

"Have you noticed how much bigger Billy's getting?" Edith asked me. "He's huge. He's almost as big as John and Edith now. He'll probably be bigger than both of them."

Then one weekend when John was home he called our attention to how quickly the fish could turn and move. "They have better reflexes than humans," he explained. "When they see a shadow in the water, or anything that looks like danger, they get away faster than you can blink. Watch." And he sank one hand into the water to make a grab for the fish named Edith, but she evaded him and fled. "See that?" he asked. "How's that for speed? Know something? I bet you could shoot an arrow in there, and they'd get away in time. Wait." To prove his point he ran to his mother's apartment and came back with the handsome bow and arrow he had made at summer camp (going to camp every summer was another admirable thing about John); then he knelt at the rim of the fountain like the picture of an archer, his bow steady in one strong hand and the feathered end of his arrow tight against the bowstring in the other. He was taking aim at the fish named Billy. "Now, the velocity of this arrow," he said in a voice weakened by his effort, "is probably more than a car going eighty miles an hour. It's probably more like an airplane, or maybe even more than that. Okay; watch."

The fish named Billy was suddenly floating dead on the surface, on his side, impaled a quarter of the way up the arrow with parts of his pink guts dribbled along the shaft.

I was too old to cry, but something had to be done about the shock and rage and grief that filled me as I ran from the fountain, heading blindly for home, and halfway there I came upon my mother. She stood looking very clean, wearing a new coat and dress I'd never seen before and fastened to the arm of Mr. Nicholson. They were either just going out or just coming in—I didn't care which—and Mr. Nicholson frowned at me (he had told me more than once that boys of my age went to boarding school in

England), but I didn't care about that either. I bent my head into her waist and didn't stop crying until long after I'd felt her hands stroking my back, until after she had assured me that goldfish didn't cost much and I'd have another one soon, and that John was sorry for the thoughtless thing he'd done. I had discovered, or rediscoverd, that crying is a pleasure—that it can be a pleasure beyond all reckoning if your head is pressed in your mother's waist and her hands are on your back, and if she happens to be wearing clean clothes.

There were other pleasures. We had a good Christmas Eve in our house that year, or at least it was good at first. My father was there, which obliged Mr. Nicholson to stay away, and it was nice to see how relaxed he was among my mother's friends. He was shy, but they seemed to like him. He got along especially well with Bart Kampen.

Howard Whitman's daughter, Molly, a sweet-natured girl of about my age, had come in from Tarrytown to spend the holidays with him, and there were several other children whom we knew but rarely saw. John looked very mature that night in a dark coat and tie, plainly aware of his social responsibilities as the oldest boy.

After a while, with no plan, the party drifted back into the dining-room area and staged an impromptu vaudeville. Howard started it: he brought the tall stool from my mother's modeling stand and sat his daughter on it, facing the audience. He folded back the opening of a brown paper bag two or three times and fitted it onto her head; then he took off his suit coat and draped it around her backwards, up to the chin; he went behind her, crouched out of sight, and worked his hands through the coat sleeves so that when they emerged they appeared to be hers. And the sight of a smiling little girl in a paper-bag hat, waving and gesturing with huge, expressive hands, was enough to make everyone laugh. The big hands wiped her eyes and stroked her chin and pushed her hair behind her ears; then they elaborately thumbed her nose at us.

Next came Sloane Cabot. She sat very straight on the stool with her heels hooked over the rungs in such a way as to show her good legs to their best advantage, but her first act didn't go over.

"Well," she began, "I was at work today—you know my office is on the fortieth floor—when I happened to glance up from my typewriter and saw this big old man sort of crouched on the ledge outside the window, with a white beard and a funny red suit. So I ran to the window and opened it and said, 'Are you all right?' Well, it was Santa Claus, and he said, 'Of course I'm all right; I'm used to high places. But listen, miss: can you direct me to number seventy-five Bedford Street?'"

There was more, but our embarrassed looks must have told her we knew we were being condescended to; as soon as she'd found a way to finish it she did so quickly. Then, after a thoughtful pause, she tried something else that turned out to be much better.

"Have you children ever heard the story of the first Christmas?" she asked. "When Jesus was born?" And she began to tell it in the kind of hushed, dramatic voice she must have hoped might be used by the narrators of her more serious radio plays.

" ...And there were still many miles to go before they reached Bethlehem," she said, "and it was a cold night. Now, Mary knew she would very soon have a baby. She even knew, because an angel had told her, that her baby might one day be the savior of all mankind. But she was only a young girl"—here Sloane's eyes glistened, as if they might be filling with tears—"and the traveling had exhausted her. She was bruised by the jolting gait of the donkey and she ached all over, and she thought they'd never, ever get there, and all she could say was 'Oh, Joseph, I'm so tired.'"

The story went on through the rejection at the inn, and the birth in the stable, and the manger, and the animals, and the arrival of the three kings; when it was over we clapped a long time because Sloane had told it so well.

"Daddy?" Edith asked. "Will you sing for us?"

"Oh well, thanks, honey," he said, "but no; I really need a piano for that. Thanks anyway."

The final performer of the evening was Bart Kampen, persuaded by popular demand to go home and get his violin. There was no surprise in discovering that he played like a professional, like something you might easily hear on the radio; the enjoyment came from watching how his thin face frowned over the chin rest, empty of all emotion except concern that the sound be right. We were proud of him.

Some time after my father left a good many other adults began to arrive, most of them strangers to me, looking as though they'd already been to several other parties that night. It was very late, or rather very early Christmas morning, when I looked into the kitchen and saw Sloane standing close to a bald man I didn't know. He held a trembling drink in one hand and slowly massaged her shoulder with the other; she seemed to be shrinking back against the old wooden icebox. Sloane had a way of smiling that allowed little wisps of cigarette smoke to escape from between her almost-closed lips while she looked you up and down, and she was doing that. Then the man put his drink on top of the icebox and took her in his arms, and I couldn't see her face anymore.

Another man, in a rumpled brown suit, lay unconscious on the dining-room floor. I walked around him and went into the studio, where a good-looking young woman stood weeping wretchedly and three men kept getting in each other's way as they tried to comfort her. Then I saw that one of the men was Bart, and I watched while he outlasted the other two and turned the girl away toward the door. He put his arm around her and she nestled her head in his shoulder; that was how they left the house.

Edith looked jaded in her wrinkled party dress. She was reclining in our old Hastings-on-Hudson easy chair with her head tipped back and her legs flung out over both the chair's arms, and John sat cross-legged on the floor near one of her dangling feet.

They seemed to have been talking about something that didn't interest either of them much, and the talk petered out altogether when I sat on the floor to join them.

"Billy," she said, "do you realize what time it is?"

"What's the diff?" I said.

"You should've been in bed hours ago. Come on. Let's go up."

"I don't feel like it."

"Well," she said, "I'm going up, anyway," and she got laboriously out of the chair and walked away into the crowd.

John turned to me and narrowed his eyes unpleasantly. "Know something?" he said. "When she was in the chair that way I could see everything."

"Huh?"

"I could see everything. I could see the crack, and the hair. She's beginning to get hair."

I had observed these features of my sister many times—in the bathtub, or when she was changing her clothes—and hadn't found them especially remarkable; even so, I understood at once how remarkable they must have been for him. If only he had smiled in a bashful way we might have laughed together like a couple of regular fellows out of *Open Road for Boys,* but his face was still set in that disdainful look.

"I kept looking and looking," he said, "and I had to keep her talking so she wouldn't catch on, but I was doing fine until you had to come over and ruin it."

Was I supposed to apologize? That didn't seem right, but nothing else seemed right either. All I did was look at the floor.

When I finally got to bed there was scarcely time for trying to hear the elusive sound of the city—I had found that a good way to keep from thinking of anything else—when my mother came blundering in. She'd had too much to drink and wanted to lie down, but instead of going to her own room she got into bed with me. "Oh," she said. "Oh, my boy. Oh, my boy." It was a narrow cot and there was no way to make room for her; then suddenly she retched, bolted to her feet, and ran for the bathroom, where I heard her vomiting. And when I moved over into the part of the bed she had occupied my face recoiled quickly, but not quite in time, from the slick mouthful of puke she had left on her side of the pillow.

For a month or so that winter we didn't see much of Sloane because she said she was "working on something big. Something really big." When it was finished she brought it to the studio, looking tired but prettier than ever, and shyly asked if she could read it aloud.

"Wonderful," my mother said. "What's it about?"

"That's the best part. It's about us. All of us. Listen."

Bart had gone for the day and Edith was out in the courtyard by herself—she often played by herself—so there was nobody for an audience but my mother and me. We sat on the sofa and Sloane arranged herself on the tall stool, just as she'd done for telling the Bethlehem story.

"There is an enchanted courtyard in Greenwich Village," she read "It's only a narrow patch of brick and green among the irregular shapes of very old houses, but what makes it enchanted is that the people who live in it, or near it, have come to form an enchanted circle of friends.

"None of them have enough money and some are quite poor, but they believe in the future; they believe in each other, and in themselves.

"There is Howard, once a top reporter on a metropolitan daily newspaper. Everyone knows Howard will soon scale the journalistic heights again, and in the meantime he serves as the wise and humorous sage of the courtyard.

"There is Bart, a young violinist clearly destined for virtuosity on the concert stage, who just for the present must graciously accept all lunch and dinner invitations in order to survive.

"And there is Helen, a sculptor whose charming works will

someday grace the finest gardens in America, and whose studio is the favorite gathering place for members of the circle."

There was more like that, introducing other characters, and toward the end she got around to the children. She described my sister as "a lanky, dreamy tomboy," which was odd—I had never thought of Edith that way—and she called me "a sad-eyed seven-year-old philosopher," which was wholly baffling. When the introduction was over she paused a few seconds for dramatic effect and then went into the opening episode of the series, or what I suppose would be called the "pilot."

I couldn't follow the story very well—it seemed to be mostly an excuse for bringing each character up to the microphone for a few lines apiece—and before long I was listening only to see if there would be any lines for the character based on me. And there were, in a way. She announced my name—"Billy"—but then instead of speaking she put her mouth through a terrible series of contortions, accompanied by funny little bursts of sound, and by the time the words came out I didn't care what they were. It was true that I stuttered badly—I wouldn't get over it for five or six more years—but I hadn't expected anyone to put it on the radio.

"Oh, Sloane, that's marvelous," my mother said when the reading was over. "That's really exciting."

And Sloane was carefully stacking her typed pages in the way she'd probably been taught to do in secretarial school, blushing and smiling with pride. "Well," she said, "it probably needs work, but I do think it's got a lot of potential."

"It's perfect," my mother said. "Just the way it is."

Sloane mailed the script to a radio producer and he mailed it back with a letter typed by some radio secretary, explaining that her material had too limited an appeal to be commercial. The radio public was not yet ready, he said, for a story of Greenwich Village life.

Then it was March. The new President promised that the only

31

thing we had to fear was fear itself, and soon after that his head came packed in wood and excelsior from Mr. Nicholson's foundry.

It was a fairly good likeness. She had caught the famous lift of the chin—it might not have looked like him at all if she hadn't— and everyone told her it was fine. What nobody said was that her original plan had been right, and Mr. Nicholson shouldn't have interfered: it was too small. It didn't look heroic. If you could have hollowed it out and put a slot in the top, it might have made a serviceable bank for loose change.

The foundry had burnished the lead until it shone almost silver in the highlights, and they'd mounted it on a sturdy little base of heavy black plastic. They had sent back three copies: one for the White House presentation, one to keep for exhibition purposes, and an extra one. But the extra one soon toppled to the floor and was badly damaged—the nose mashed almost into the chin—and my mother might have burst into tears if Howard Whitman hadn't made everyone laugh by saying it was now a good portrait of Vice President Garner.

Charlie Hines, Howard's old friend from the *Post* who was now a minor member of the White House staff, made an appointment for my mother with the President late on a weekday morning. She arranged for Sloane to spend the night with Edith and me; then she took an evening train down to Washington, carrying the sculpture in a cardboard box, and stayed at one of the less expensive Washington hotels. In the morning she met Charlie Hines in some crowded White House anteroom, where I guess they disposed of the cardboard box, and he took her to the waiting room outside the Oval Office. He sat with her as she held the naked head in her lap, and when their turn came he escorted her in to the President's desk for the presentation. It didn't take long. There were no reporters and no photographers.

Afterwards Charlie Hines took her out to lunch, probably because he'd promised Howard Whitman to do so. I imagine it wasn't a first-class restaurant, more likely some bustling, no-nonsense place favored by the working press, and I imagine they had trouble making conversation until they settled on Howard, and on what a shame it was that he was still out of work.

"No, but do you know Howard's friend Bart Kampen?" Charlie asked. "The young Dutchman? The violinist?"

"Yes, certainly," she said. "I know Bart."

"Well, Jesus, there's *one* story with a happy ending, right? Have you heard about that? Last time I saw Bart he said, 'Charlie, the Depression's over for me,' and he told me he'd found some rich, dumb, crazy woman who's paying him to tutor her kids."

I can picture how she looked riding the long, slow train back to New York that afternoon. She must have sat staring straight ahead or out the dirty window, seeing nothing, her eyes round and her face held in a soft shape of hurt. Her adventure with Franklin D. Roosevelt had come to nothing. There would be no photographs or interviews or feature articles, no thrilling moments of newsreel coverage; strangers would never know of how she'd come from a small Ohio town, or of how she'd nurtured her talent through the brave, difficult, one-woman journey that had brought her to the attention of the world. It wasn't fair.

All she had to look forward to now was her romance with Eric Nicholson, and I think she may have known even then that it was faltering—his final desertion came the next fall.

She was forty-one, an age when even romantics must admit that youth is gone, and she had nothing to show for the years but a studio crowded with green plaster statues that nobody would buy. She believed in the aristocracy, but there was no reason to suppose the aristocracy would ever believe in her.

And every time she thought of what Charlie Hines had said about Bart Kampen—oh, how hateful; oh, how hateful—the humiliation came back in wave on wave, in merciless rhythm to the clatter of the train.

She made a brave show of her homecoming, though nobody was there to greet her but Sloane and Edith and me. Sloane had fed us, and she said, "There's a plate for you in the oven, Helen," but my mother said she'd rather just have a drink instead. She was then at the onset of a long battle with alcohol that she would ultimately lose; it must have seemed bracing that night to decide on a drink instead of dinner. Then she told us "all about" her trip to Washington, managing to make it sound like a success. She talked of how thrilling it was to be actually inside the White House; she repeated whatever small, courteous thing it was that President Roosevelt had said to her on receiving the head. And she had brought back souvenirs: a handful of note-size White House stationery for Edith, and a well-used briar pipe for me. She explained that she'd seen a very distinguished-looking man smoking the pipe in the waiting room outside the Oval Office; when his name was called he had knocked it out quickly into an ashtray and left it there as he hurried inside. She had waited until she was sure no one was looking; then she'd taken the pipe from the ashtray and put it in her purse. "Because I knew he must have been somebody important," she said. "He could easily have been a member of the Cabinet, or something like that. Anyway, I thought you'd have a lot of fun with it." But I didn't. It was too heavy to hold in my teeth and it tasted terrible when I sucked on it; besides, I kept wondering what the man must have thought when he came out of the President's office and found it gone.

Sloane went home after a while, and my mother sat drinking alone at the dining-room table. I think she hoped Howard Whitman or some of her other friends might drop in, but nobody did. It was almost our bedtime when she looked up and said, "Edith? Run out in the garden and see if you can find Bart."

He had recently bought a pair of bright tan shoes with crepe soles. I saw those shoes trip rapidly down the dark brick steps beyond the windows—he seemed scarcely to touch each step in his buoyancy—and then I saw him come smiling into the studio, with

Edith closing the door behind him. "Helen!" he said. "You're back!"

She acknowledged that she was back. Then she got up from the table and slowly advanced on him, and Edith and I began to realize we were in for something bad.

"Bart," she said, "I had lunch with Charlie Hines in Washington today."

"Oh?"

"And we had a very interesting talk. He seems to know you very well."

"Oh, not really; we've met a few times at Howard's, but we're not really—"

"And he said you'd told him the Depression was over for you because you'd found some rich, dumb, crazy woman who was paying you to tutor her kids. Don't interrupt me."

But Bart clearly had no intention of interrupting her. He was backing away from her in his soundless shoes, retreating past one stiff green garden child after another. His face looked startled and pink.

"I'm not a rich woman, Bart," she said, bearing down on him. "And I'm not dumb. And I'm not crazy. And I can recognize ingratitude and disloyalty and sheer, rotten viciousness and *lies* when they're thrown in my face."

My sister and I were halfway up the stairs, jostling each other in our need to hide before the worst part came. The worst part of these things always came at the end, after she'd lost all control and gone on shouting anyway.

"I want you to get out of my house, Bart," she said. "And I don't ever want to see you again. And I want to tell you something. All my life I've hated people who say 'Some of my best friends are Jews.' Because *none* of my friends are Jews, or ever will be. Do you understand me? *None* of my friends are Jews, or ever will be."

The studio was quiet after that. Without speaking, avoiding

35

each other's eyes, Edith and I got into our pajamas and into bed. But it wasn't more than a few minutes before the house began to ring with our mother's raging voice all over again, as if Bart had somehow been brought back and made to take his punishment twice.

" ...And I said, '*None* of my friends are Jews, or ever will be....' "

She was on the telephone, giving Sloane Cabot the highlights of the scene, and it was clear that Sloane would take her side and comfort her. Sloane might know how the Virgin Mary felt on the way to Bethlehem, but she also knew how to play my stutter for laughs. In a case like this she would quickly see where her allegiance lay, and it wouldn't cost her much to drop Bart Kampen from her enchanted circle.

When the telephone call came to an end at last there was silence downstairs until we heard her working with the ice pick in the icebox: she was making herself another drink.

There would be no more school in our room. We would probably never see Bart again—or if we ever did, he would probably not want to see us. But our mother was ours; we were hers; and we lived with that knowledge as we lay listening for the faint, faint sound of millions.

GRYPHON

Charles Baxter

On Wednesday afternoon, between the geography lesson on ancient Egypt's hand-operated irrigation system and an art project that involved drawing a model city next to a mountain, our fourth-grade teacher, Mr. Hibler, developed a cough. This cough began with a series of muffled throat-clearings and progressed to propulsive noises contained within Mr. Hibler's closed mouth. "Listen to him," Carol Peterson whispered to me. "He's gonna blow up." Mr. Hibler's laughter—dazed and infrequent—sounded a bit like his cough, but as we worked on our model cities we would look up, thinking he was enjoying a joke, and see Mr. Hibler's face turning red, his cheeks puffed out. This was not laughter. Twice he bent over, and his loose tie, like a plumb line, hung down straight from his neck as he exploded himself into a Kleenex. He would excuse himself, then go on coughing. "I'll bet you a dime," Carol Peterson whispered, "we get a substitute tomorrow."

Carol sat at the desk in front of mine and was a bad person—when she thought no one was looking she would blow her nose on notebook paper, then crumple it up and throw it into the wastebasket—but at times of crisis she spoke the truth. I knew I'd lose the dime.

"No deal," I said.

When Mr. Hibler stood us in formation at the door just prior to the final bell, he was almost incapable of speech. "I'm sorry, boys and girls," he said. "I seem to be coming down with something."

"I hope you feel better tomorrow, Mr. Hibler," Bobby Kryzanowicz, the faultless brown-noser, said, and I heard Carol Peterson's evil giggle. Then Mr. Hibler opened the door and we walked out to the buses, a clique of us starting noisily to hawk and laugh as soon as we thought we were a few feet beyond Mr. Hibler's earshot.

★ ★ ★

Since Five Oaks was a rural community, and in Michigan, the supply of substitute teachers was limited to the town's unemployed community college graduates, a pool of about four mothers. These ladies fluttered, provided easeful class days, and nervously covered material we had mastered weeks earlier. Therefore it was a surprise when a woman we had never seen came into the class the next day, carrying a purple purse, a checkerboard lunchbox, and a few books. She put the books on one side of Mr. Hibler's desk and the lunchbox on the other, next to the Voice of Music phonograph.

Three of us in the back of the room were playing with Heever, the chameleon that lived in a terrarium and on one of the plastic drapes, when she walked in.

She clapped her hands at us. "Little boys," she said, "why are you bent over together like that?" She didn't wait for us to answer. "Are you tormenting an animal? Put it back. Please sit down at your desks. I want no cabals this time of the day." We just stared at her. "Boys," she repeated, "I asked you to sit down."

I put the chameleon in his terrarium and felt my way to my desk, never taking my eyes off the woman! With white and green chalk, she had started to draw a tree on the left side of the black-board. She didn't look usual. Furthermore, her tree was outsized, disproportionate, for some reason.

"This room needs a tree," she said, with one line drawing the suggestion of a leaf. "A large, leafy, shady, deciduous . . . oak."

Her fine, light hair had been done up in what I would learn years later was called a chignon, and she wore gold-rimmed glasses whose lenses seemed to have the faintest blue tint. Harold Knardahl, who sat across from me, whispered, "Mars," and I nodded slowly, savoring the imminent weirdness of the day. The substitute drew another branch with an extravagant arm gesture, then turned around and said, "Good morning. I don't believe I said good morning to all of you yet."

Facing us, she was no special age—an adult is an adult—but her face had two prominent lines, descending vertically from the sides of her mouth to her chin. I knew where I had seen those lines before: *Pinocchio*. They were marionette lines. "You may stare at me," she said to us, as a few more kids from the last bus came into the room, their eyes fixed on her, "for a few more seconds, until the bell rings. Then I will permit no more staring. Looking I will permit. Staring, no. It is impolite to stare, and a sign of bad breeding. You cannot make a social effort while staring."

Harold Knardahl did not glance at me, or nudge, but I heard

him whisper "Mars" again, trying to get more mileage out of his single joke with the kids who had just come in.

When everyone was seated, the substitute teacher finished her tree, put down her chalk fastidiously on the phonograph, brushed her hands, and faced us. "Good morning," she said. "I am Miss Ferenczi, your teacher for the day. I am fairly new to your community, and I don't believe any of you know me. I will therefore start by telling you a story about myself."

While we settled back, she launched into her tale. She said her grandfather had been a Hungarian prince; her mother had been born in some place called Flanders, had been a pianist, and had played concerts for people Miss Ferenczi referred to as "crowned heads." She gave us a knowing look. "Grieg," she said, "the Norwegian master, wrote a concerto for piano that was . . ."—she paused—"my mother's triumph at her debut concert in London." Her eyes searched the ceiling. Our eyes followed. Nothing up there but ceiling tile. "For reasons that I shall not go into, my family's fortunes took us to Detroit, then north to dreadful Saginaw, and now here I am in Five Oaks, as your substitute teacher, for today, Thursday, October the eleventh. I believe it will be a good day: all the forecasts coincide. We shall start with your reading lesson. Take out your reading book. I believe it is called *Broad Horizons,* or something along those lines."

Jeannie Vermeesch raised her hand. Miss Ferenczi nodded at her. "Mr. Hibler always starts the day with the Pledge of Allegiance," Jeannie whined.

"Oh, does he? In that case," Miss Ferenczi said, "you must know it *very* well by now, and we certainly need not spend our time on it. No, no allegiance pledging on the premises today, by my reckoning. Not with so much sunlight coming into the room. A pledge does not suit my mood." She glanced at her watch. "Time *is* flying. Take out *Broad Horizons.*"

★ ★ ★

She disappointed us by giving us an ordinary lesson, complete with vocabulary and drills, comprehension questions, and recitation. She didn't seem to care for the material, however. She sighed every few minutes and rubbed her glasses with a frilly handkerchief that she withdrew, magician-style, from her left sleeve.

After reading we moved on to arithmetic. It was my favorite time of the morning, when the lazy autumn sunlight dazzled its way through ribbons of clouds past the windows on the east side of the classroom and crept across the linoleum floor. On the playground the first group of children, the kindergartners, were running on the quack grass just beyond the monkey bars. We were doing multiplication tables. Miss Ferenczi had made John Wazny stand up at his desk in the front row. He was supposed to go through the tables of six. From where I was sitting, I could smell the Vitalis soaked into John's plastered hair. He was doing fine until he came to six times eleven and six times twelve. "Six times eleven," he said, "is sixty-eight. Six times twelve is . . ." He put his fingers to his head, quickly and secretly sniffed his fingertips, and said, " . . . seventy-two." Then he sat down.

"Fine," Miss Ferenczi said. "Well now. That was very good."

"Miss Ferenczi!" One of the Eddy twins was waving her hand desperately in the air. "Miss Ferenczi! Miss Ferenczi!"

"Yes?"

"John said that six times eleven is sixty-eight and you said he was right!"

"*Did* I?" She gazed at the class with a jolly look breaking across her marionette's face. "Did I say that? Well, what *is* six times eleven?"

"It's sixty-six!"

She nodded. "Yes. So it is. But, and I know some people will not entirely agree with me, at some times it is sixty-eight."

"When? When is it sixty-eight?"

We were all waiting.

"In higher mathematics, which you children do not yet under-stand, six times eleven can be considered to be sixty-eight." She laughed through her nose. "In higher mathematics numbers are ... more fluid. The only thing a number does is contain a certain amount of something. Think of water. A cup is not the only way to measure a certain amount of water, is it?" We were staring, shaking our heads. "You could use saucepans or thimbles. In either case, the water *would be the same*. Perhaps," she started again, "it would be better for you to think that six times eleven is sixty-eight only when I am in the room."

"Why is it sixty-eight," Mark Poole asked, "when you're in the room?"

"Because it's more interesting that way," she said, smiling very rapidly behind her blue-tinted glasses. "Besides, I'm your substitute teacher, am I not?" We all nodded. "Well, then, think of six times eleven equals sixty-eight as a substitute fact."

"A substitute fact?"

"Yes." Then she looked at us carefully. "Do you think," she asked, "that anyone is going to be hurt by a substitute fact?"

We looked back at her.

"Will the plants on the windowsill be hurt?" We glanced at them. There were sensitive plants thriving in a green plastic tray, and several wilted ferns in small clay pots. "Your dogs and cats, or your moms and dads?" She waited. "So," she concluded, "what's the problem?"

"But it's wrong," Janice Weber said, "isn't it?"

"What's your name, young lady?"

"Janice Weber."

"And you think it's wrong, Janice?"

"I was just asking."

"Well, all right. You were just asking. I think we've spent enough time on this matter by now, don't you, class? You are free to think what you like. When your teacher, Mr. Hibler, returns, six times eleven will be sixty-six again, you can rest assured. And it will be that for the rest of your lives in Five Oaks. Too bad, eh?" She raised her eyebrows and glinted herself at us. "But for now, it wasn't. So much for that. Let us go on to your assigned problems for today, as painstakingly outlined, I see, in Mr. Hibler's lesson plan. Take out a sheet of paper and write your names on the upper left-hand corner."

For the next half hour we did the rest of our arithmetic problems. We handed them in and then went on to spelling, my worst subject. Spelling always came before lunch. We were taking spelling dictation and looking at the clock. "Thorough," Miss Ferenczi said. "Boundary." She walked in the aisles between the desks, holding the spelling book open and looking down at our papers. "Balcony." I clutched my pencil. Somehow, the way she said those words, they seemed foreign, misvoweled and misconsonanted. I stared down at what I had spelled. *Balconie.* I turned the pencil upside down and erased my mistake. *Balconey.* That looked better, but still incorrect. I cursed the world of spelling and tried erasing it again and saw the paper beginning to wear away. *Balkony.* Suddenly I felt a hand on my shoulder.

"I don't like that word either," Miss Ferenczi whispered, bent over, her mouth near my ear. "It's ugly. My feeling is, if you don't like a word, you don't have to use it." She straightened up, leaving behind a slight odor of Clorets.

At lunchtime we went out to get our trays of sloppy joes, peaches in heavy syrup, coconut cookies, and milk, and brought them back to the classroom, where Miss Ferenczi was sitting at the desk, eating a brown sticky thing she had unwrapped from tightly rubber-banded waxed paper. "Miss Ferenczi," I said, raising my hand. "You don't have to eat with us. You can eat with the other teachers. There's a teacher's lounge," I ended up, "next to the principal's office."

"No, thank you," she said. "I prefer it here."

"We've got a room monitor," I said. "Mrs. Eddy." I pointed to where Mrs. Eddy, Joyce and Judy's mother, sat silently at the back of the room, doing her knitting.

"That's fine," Miss Ferenczi said. "But I shall continue to eat here, with you children. I prefer it," she repeated.

"How come?" Wayne Razmer asked without raising his hand.

"I talked to the other teachers before class this morning," Miss Ferenczi said, biting into her brown food. "There was a great rattling of the words for the fewness of the ideas. I didn't care for their brand of hilarity. I don't like ditto-machine jokes."

"Oh," Wayne said.

"What's that you're eating?" Maxine Sylvester asked, twitching her nose. "Is it food?"

"It most certainly *is* food. It's a stuffed fig. I had to drive almost down to Detroit to get it. I also brought some smoked sturgeon. And this," she said, lifting some green leaves out of her lunchbox, "is raw spinach, cleaned this morning."

"Why're you eating raw spinach?" Maxine asked.

"It's good for you," Miss Ferenczi said. "More stimulating than soda pop or smelling salts." I bit into my sloppy joe and stared blankly out the window. An almost invisible moon was faintly silvered in the daytime autumn sky. "As far as food is concerned," Miss Ferenczi was saying, "you have to shuffle the pack. Mix it up. Too many people eat . . . well, never mind."

"Miss Ferenczi," Carol Peterson said, "what are we going to do this afternoon?"

"Well," she said, looking down at Mr. Hibler's lesson plan, "I see that your teacher, Mr. Hibler, has you scheduled for a unit on the Egyptians." Carol groaned. "Yessss," Miss Ferenczi continued, "that is what we will do: the Egyptians. A remarkable people. Almost as remarkable as the Americans. But not quite." She lowered her head, did her quick smile, and went back to eating her spinach.

✷ ✷ ✷

After noon recess we came back into the classroom and saw that Miss Ferenczi had drawn a pyramid on the blackboard close to her oak tree. Some of us who had been playing baseball were messing around in the back of the room, dropping the bats and gloves into the playground box, and Ray Schontzeler had just slugged me when I heard Miss Ferenczi's high-pitched voice, quavering with emotions. "Boys," she said, "come to order right this minute and take your seats. I do not wish to waste a minute of class time. Take out your geography books." We trudged to our desks and, still sweating, pulled out *Distant Lands and Their People*. "Turn to page forty-two." She waited for thirty seconds, then looked over at Kelly Munger. "Young man," she said, "why are you still fossicking in your desk?"

Kelly looked as if his foot had been stepped on. "Why am I what?"

"Why are you . . . burrowing in your desk like that?"

"I'm lookin' for the book, Miss Ferenczi."

Bobby Kryzanowicz, the faultless brown-noser who sat in the first row by choice, softly said, "His name is Kelly Munger. He can't ever find his stuff. He always does that."

"I don't care what his name is, especially after lunch," Miss Ferenczi said. *"Where is your book?"*

"I just found it." Kelly was peering into his desk and with both hands pulled at the book, shoveling along in front of it several pencils and crayons, which fell into his lap and then to the floor.

"I hate a mess," Miss Ferenczi said. "I hate a mess in a desk or a mind. It's . . . unsanitary. You wouldn't want your house at home to look like your desk at school, now, would you?" She didn't wait for an answer. "I should think not. A house at home should be as neat as human hands can make it. What were we talking about? Egypt. Page forty-two. I note from Mr. Hibler's lesson plan that you have been discussing the modes of Egyptian irrigation. Interesting, in my view, but not so interesting as what we are about to cover. The pyramids, and Egyptian slave labor. A plus on one side, a minus on the other." We had our books open to page forty-two, where there was a picture of a pyramid, but Miss Ferenczi wasn't looking at the book. Instead, she was staring at some object just outside the window.

"Pyramids," Miss Ferenczi said, still looking past the window. "I want you to think about pyramids. And what was inside. The bodies of the pharaohs, of course, and their attendant treasures. Scrolls. Perhaps," Miss Ferenczi said, her face gleeful but unsmiling, "these scrolls were novels for the pharaohs, helping them to pass the time in their long voyage through the centuries. But then, I am joking." I was looking at the lines on Miss Ferenczi's skin. "Pyramids," Miss Ferenczi went on, "were the repositories of special cosmic powers. The nature of a pyramid is to guide cosmic energy forces into a concentrated point. The Egyptians knew that; we have generally forgotten it. Did you know," she asked, walking to the side of the room so that she was standing by the coat closet, "that George Washington had Egyptian blood, from his grandmother? Certain features of the Constitution of the United States are notable for their Egyptian ideas."

Without glancing down at the book, she began to talk about the movement of souls in Egyptian religion. She said that when people die, their souls return to earth in the form of carpenter ants or walnut trees, depending on how they behaved—"well or ill"— in life. She said that the Egyptians believed that people act the way they do because of magnetism produced by tidal forces in the solar system, forces produced by the sun and by its "planetary ally," Jupiter. Jupiter, she said, was a planet, as we had been told, but had "certain properties of stars." She was speaking very fast. She said that the Egyptians were great explorers and conquerors. She said that the greatest of all the conquerors, Genghis Khan, had had forty horses and forty young women killed on the site of his grave. We listened. No one tried to stop her. "I myself have been in Egypt," she said, "and have witnessed much dust and many brutalities." She said that an old man in Egypt who worked for a circus had personally shown her an animal in a cage, a monster, half bird and half lion. She said that this monster was called a gryphon and that she had heard about them but never seen them until she traveled to the outskirts of Cairo. She wrote the word out on the blackboard in large capital letters: GRYPHON. She said that Egyptian astronomers had discovered the planet Saturn but had not seen its rings. She said that the Egyptians were the first to discover that dogs, when they are ill, will not drink from rivers, but wait for rain, and hold their jaws open to catch it.

✷ ✷ ✷

"She lies."

We were on the school bus home. I was sitting next to Carl Whiteside, who had bad breath and a huge collection of marbles. We were arguing. Carl thought she was lying. I said she wasn't, probably.

"I didn't believe that stuff about the bird," Carl said, "and what she told us about the pyramids? I didn't believe that, either. She didn't know what she was talking about."

"Oh yeah?" I had liked her. She was strange. I thought I could nail him. "If she was lying," I said, "what'd she say that was a lie?"

"Six times eleven isn't sixty-eight. It isn't ever. It's sixty-six, I know for a fact."

"She said so. She admitted it. What else did she lie about?"

"I don't know," he said. "Stuff."

"What stuff?"

"Well." He swung his legs back and forth. "You ever see an animal that was half lion and half bird?" He crossed his arms. "It sounded real fakey to me."

"It could happen," I said. I had to improvise, to outrage him. "I read in this newspaper my mom bought in the IGA about this scientist, this mad scientist in the Swiss Alps, and he's been putting genes and chromosomes and stuff together in test tubes, and he combined a human being and a hamster." I waited, for effect. "It's called a humster."

"You never." Carl was staring at me, his mouth open, his terrible bad breath making its way toward me. "What newspaper was it?"

"*The National Enquirer,*" I said, "that they sell next to the cash registers." When I saw his look of recognition, I knew I had him. "And this mad scientist," I said, "his name was, um, Dr. Frankenbush." I realized belatedly that this name was a mistake and waited for Carl to notice its resemblance to the name of the other famous mad master of permutations, but he only sat there.

"A man and a hamster?" He was staring at me, squinting, his mouth opening in distaste. "Jeez. What'd it look like?"

★ ★ ★

When the bus reached my stop, I took off down our dirt road and ran up through the backyard, kicking the tire swing for good luck. I dropped my books on the back steps so I could hug and kiss our dog, Mr. Selby. Then I hurried inside. I could smell brussels sprouts cooking, my unfavorite vegetable. My mother was washing other vegetables in the kitchen sink, and my baby brother was hollering in his yellow playpen on the kitchen floor.

"Hi, Mom," I said, hopping around the playpen to kiss her. "Guess what?"

"I have no idea."

"We had this substitute today, Miss Ferenczi, and I'd never seen her before, and she had all these stories and ideas and stuff."

"Well. That's good." My mother looked out the window in front of the sink, her eyes on the pine woods west of our house. That time of the afternoon her skin always looked so white to me. Strangers always said my mother looked like Betty Crocker, framed by the giant spoon on the side of the Bisquick box. "Listen, Tommy," she said. "Would you please go upstairs and pick your clothes off the floor in the bathroom, and then go outside to the shed and put the shovel and ax away that your father left outside this morning?"

"She said that six times eleven was sometimes sixty-eight!" I said. "And she said she once saw a monster that was half lion and half bird." I waited. "In Egypt."

"Did you hear me?" my mother asked, raising her arm to wipe her forehead with the back of her hand. "You have chores to do."

"I know," I said. "I was just telling you about the substitute."

"It's very interesting," my mother said, quickly glancing down at me, "and we can talk about it later when your father gets home. But right now you have some work to do."

"Okay, Mom." I took a cookie out of the jar on the counter and was about to go outside when I had a thought. I ran into the living room, pulled out a dictionary next to the TV stand, and opened it to the Gs. After five minutes I found it. *Gryphon:* variant of griffin. *Griffin:* "a fabulous beast with the head and wings of an eagle and the body of a lion." Fabulous was right. I shouted with triumph and ran outside to put my father's tools in their proper places.

✷ ✷ ✷

Miss Ferenczi was back the next day, slightly altered. She had pulled her hair down and twisted it into pigtails, with red rubber bands holding them tight one inch from the ends. She was wearing a green blouse and pink scarf, making her difficult to look at for a full class day. This time there was no pretense of doing a reading lesson or moving on to arithmetic. As soon as the bell rang, she simply began to talk.

She talked for forty minutes straight. There seemed to be less connection between her ideas, but the ideas themselves were, as the dictionary would say, fabulous. She said she had heard of a huge jewel, in what she called the antipodes, that was so brilliant that when light shone into it at a certain angle it would blind whoever was looking at its center. She said the biggest diamond in the world was cursed and had killed everyone who owned it, and that by a trick of fate it was called the Hope Diamond. Diamonds are magic, she said, and this is why women wear them on their fingers, as a sign of the magic of womanhood. Men have strength, Miss Ferenczi said, but no true magic. That is why men fall in love with women but women do not fall in love with men: they just love being loved. George Washington had died because of a mistake he made about a diamond. Washington was not the first *true* President, but she didn't say who was. In some places in the world, she said, men and women still live in the trees and eat monkeys for breakfast. Their doctors are magicians. At the bottom of the sea are creatures thin as pancakes who have never been studied by scientists because when you take them up to air, the fish explode.

There was not a sound in the classroom, except for Miss Ferenczi's voice, and Donna DeShano's coughing. No one even went to the bathroom.

Beethoven, she said, had not been deaf; it was a trick to make himself famous, and it worked. As she talked, Miss Ferenczi's pigtails swung back and forth. There are trees in the world, she said, that eat meat: their leaves are sticky and close up on bugs like hands. She lifted her hands and brought them together, palm to palm. Venus, which most people think is the next closest planet to the sun, is not always closer, and, besides, it is the planet of greatest mystery because of its thick cloud cover. "I know what lies underneath those clouds," Miss Ferenczi said, and waited. After the silence, she said, "Angels. Angels live under those clouds." She said that angels were not invisible to everyone and were in fact smarter than most people. They did not dress in robes as was often claimed but instead wore formal evening clothes, as if they were about to attend a concert. Often angels *do* attend concerts and sit in the aisles, where, she said, most people pay no attention to them. She said the most terrible angel had the shape of the Sphinx. "There is no running away from that one," she said. She said that unquenchable fires burn just under the surface of the earth in Ohio, and that the baby Mozart fainted dead away in his cradle when he first heard the sound of a trumpet. She said that someone named Narzim al Harrardim was the greatest writer who ever lived. She said that planets control behavior, and anyone conceived during a solar eclipse would be born with webbed feet.

"I know you children like to hear these things," she said, "these secrets, and that is why I am telling you all this." We nodded. It was better than doing comprehension questions for the readings in *Broad Horizons*.

"I will tell you one more story," she said, "and then we will have to do arithmetic." She leaned over, and her voice grew soft. "There is no death," she said. "You must never be afraid. Never. That which is, cannot die. It will change into different earthly and unearthly elements, but I know this as sure as I stand here in front of you, and I swear it: you must not be afraid. I have seen this truth with these eyes. I know it because in a dream God kissed me. Here." And she pointed with her right index finger to the side of her head, below the mouth where the vertical lines were carved into her skin.

★ ★ ★

Absentmindedly we all did our arithmetic problems. At recess the class was out on the playground, but no one was playing. We were all standing in small groups, talking about Miss Ferenczi. We didn't know if she was crazy, or what. I looked out beyond the playground, at the rusted cars piled in a small heap behind a clump of sumac, and I wanted to see shapes there, approaching me.

★ ★ ★

On the way home, Carl sat next to me again. He didn't say much, and I didn't either. At last he turned to me. "You know what she said about the leaves that close up on bugs?"

"Huh?"

"The leaves," Carl insisted. "The meat-eating plants. I know it's true. I saw it on television. The leaves have this icky glue that the plants have got smeared all over them and the insects can't get off 'cause they're stuck. I saw it." He seemed demoralized. "She's tellin' the truth."

"Yeah."

"You think she's seen all those angels?"

I shrugged.

"I don't think she has," Carl informed me. "I think she made that part up."

"There's a tree," I suddenly said. I was looking out the window at the farms along County Road H. I knew every barn, every broken windmill, every fence, every anhydrous ammonia tank by heart. "There's a tree that's . . . that I've seen . . ."

"Don't you try to do it," Carl said. "You'll just sound like a jerk."

★ ★ ★

I kissed my mother. She was standing in front of the stove. "How was your day?" she asked.

"Fine."

"Did you have Miss Ferenczi again?"

"Yeah."

"Well?"

"She was fine. Mom," I asked, "can I go to my room?"

"No," she said, "not until you've gone but to the vegetable garden and picked me a few tomatoes." She glanced at the sky. "I think it's going to rain. Skedaddle and do it now. Then you come back inside and watch your brother for a few minutes while I go upstairs. I need to clean up before dinner." She looked down at me. "You're looking a little pale, Tommy." She touched the back of her hand to my forehead and I felt her diamond ring against my skin. "Do you feel all right?"

"I'm fine," I said, and went out to pick the tomatoes.

✷ ✷ ✷

Coughing mutedly, Mr. Hibler was back the next day, slipping lozenges into his mouth when his back was turned at forty-five-minute intervals and asking us how much of his prepared lesson plan Miss Ferenczi had followed. Edith Atwater took the responsibility for the class of explaining to Mr. Hibler that the substitute hadn't always done exactly what he, Mr. Hibler, would have done, but we had worked hard even though she talked a lot. About what? he asked. All kinds of things, Edith said. I sort of forgot. To our relief, Mr. Hibler seemed not at all interested in what Miss Ferenczi had said to fill the day. He probably thought it was woman's talk: unserious and not suited for school. It was enough that he had a pile of arithmetic problems from us to correct.

For the next month, the sumac turned a distracting red in the field, and the sun traveled toward the southern sky, so that its rays reached Mr. Hibler's Halloween display on the bulletin board in the back of the room, fading the pumpkin head scarecrow from orange to tan. Every three days I measured how much farther the sun had moved toward the southern horizon by making small marks with my black Crayola on the north wall, ant-sized marks only I knew were there.

And then in early December, four days after the first permanent snowfall, she appeared again in our classroom. The minute she came in the door, I felt my heart begin to pound. Once again, she was different: this time, her hair hung straight down and seemed hardly to have been combed. She hadn't brought her lunchbox with her, but she was carrying what seemed to be a small box. She greeted all of us and talked about the weather. Donna DeShano had to remind her to take her overcoat off.

When the bell to start the day finally rang, Miss Ferenczi looked out at all of us and said, "Children, I have enjoyed your company in the past, and today I am going to reward you." She held up the small box. "Do you know what this is?" She waited. "Of course you don't. It is a tarot pack."

Edith Atwater raised her hand. "What's a tarot pack, Miss Ferenczi?"

"It is used to tell fortunes," she said. "And that is what I shall do this morning. I shall tell your fortunes, as I have been taught to do."

"What's fortune?" Bobby Kryzanowicz asked.

"The future, young man. I shall tell you what your future will be. I can't do your whole future, of course. I shall have to limit myself to the five-card system, the wands, cups, swords, pentacles, and the higher arcanes. Now who wants to be first?"

There was a long silence. Then Carol Peterson raised her hand.

"All right," Miss Ferenczi said. She divided the pack into five smaller packs and walked back to Carol's desk, in front of mine. "Pick one card from each one of these packs," she said. I saw that Carol had a four of cups and a six of swords, but I couldn't see the other cards. Miss Ferenczi studied the cards on Carol's desk for a minute. "Not bad," she said. "I do not see much higher education. Probably an early marriage. Many children. There's something bleak and dreary here, but I can't tell what. Perhaps just the tasks of a housewife life. I think you'll do very well, for the most part." She smiled at Carol, a smile with a certain lack of interest. "Who wants to be next?"

Carl Whiteside raised his hand slowly.

"Yes," Miss Ferenczi said, "let's do a boy." She walked over to where Carl sat. After he picked his five cards, she gazed at them for a long time. "Travel," she said. "Much distant travel. You might go into the army. Not too much romantic interest here. A late marriage, if at all. But the sun in your major arcana, that's a very good card." She giggled. "You'll have a happy life."

Next I raised my hand. She told me my future. She did the

same with Bobby Kryzanowicz, Kelly Munger, Edith Atwater, and Kim Foor. Then she came to Wayne Razmer. He picked his five cards, and I could see that the death card was one of them.

"What's your name?" Miss Ferenczi asked.

"Wayne."

"Well, Wayne," she said, "you will undergo a great metamorphosis, a change, before you become an adult. Your earthly element will no doubt leap higher, because you seem to be a sweet boy. This card, this nine of swords, tells me of suffering and desolation. And this ten of wands, well, that's a heavy load."

"What about this one?" Wayne pointed at the death card.

"It means, my sweet, that you will die soon." She gathered up the cards. We were all looking at Wayne. "But do not fear," she said. "It is not really death. Just change. Out of your earthly shape." She put the cards on Mr. Hibler's desk. "And now, let's do some arithmetic."

✷ ✷ ✷

At lunchtime Wayne went to Mr. Faegre, the principal, and informed him of what Miss Ferenczi had done. During the noon recess, we saw Miss Ferenczi drive out of the parking lot in her rusting green Rambler American. I stood under the slide, listening to the other kids coasting down and landing in the little depressive bowls at the bottom. I was kicking stones and tugging at my hair right up to the moment when I saw Wayne come out to the playground. He smiled, the dead fool, and with the fingers of his right hand he was showing everyone how he had told on Miss Ferenczi.

I made my way toward Wayne, pushing myself past two girls from another class. He was watching me with his little pinhead eyes.

"You told," I shouted at him. "She was just kidding."

"She shouldn't have," he shouted back. "We were supposed to be doing arithmetic."

"She just scared you," I said. "You're a chicken. You're a chicken, Wayne. You are. Scared of a little card," I singsonged.

Wayne fell at me, his two fists hammering down on my nose. I gave him a good one in the stomach and then I tried for his head. Aiming my fist, I saw that he was crying. I slugged him.

"She was right," I yelled. "She was always right! She told the truth!" Other kids were whooping. "You were just scared, that's all!"

And then large hands pulled at us, and it was my turn to speak to Mr. Faegre.

✷ ✷ ✷

In the afternoon Miss Ferenczi was gone, and my nose was stuffed with cotton clotted with blood, and my lip had swelled, and our class had been combined with Mrs. Mantei's sixth-grade class for a crowded afternoon science unit on insect life in ditches and swamps. I knew where Mrs. Mantei lived: she had a new house trailer just down the road from us, at the Clearwater Park. She was no mystery. Somehow she and Mr. Bodine, the other fourth-grade teacher, had managed to fit forty-five desks into the room. Kelly Munger asked if Miss Ferenczi had been arrested, and Mrs. Mantei said no, of course not. All that afternoon, until the buses came to pick us up, we learned about field crickets and two-striped grasshoppers, water bugs, cicadas, mosquitoes, flies, and moths. We learned about insects' hard outer shell, the exoskeleton, and the usual parts of the mouth, including the labrum, mandible, maxilla, and glossa. We learned about compound eyes, and the four-stage metamorphosis from egg to larva to pupa to adult. We learned something, but not much, about mating. Mrs. Mantei drew, very skillfully, the internal anatomy of the grasshopper on the blackboard. We learned about the dance of the honeybee, directing other bees in the hive to pollen. We found out about which insects were pests to man, and which were not. On lined white pieces of paper we made lists of insects we might actually see, then a list of insects too small to be clearly visible, such as fleas; Mrs. Mantei said that our assignment would be to memorize these lists for the next day, when Mr. Hibler would certainly return and test us on our knowledge.

INTERPRETER OF MALADIES

Jhumpa Lahiri

★ ★ ★

At the tea stall Mr. and Mrs. Das bickered about who should take Tina to the toilet. Eventually Mrs. Das relented when Mr. Das pointed out that he had given the girl her bath the night before. In the rearview mirror Mr. Kapasi watched as Mrs. Das emerged slowly from his bulky white Ambassador, dragging her shaved, largely bare legs across the backseat. She did not hold the little girl's hand as they walked to the restroom.

They were on their way to see the Sun Temple at Konarak. It was a dry, bright Saturday, the mid-July heat tempered by a steady ocean breeze, ideal weather for sightseeing. Ordinarily Mr. Kapasi would not have stopped so soon along the way, but less than five minutes after he'd picked up the family that morning in front of Hotel Sandy Villa, the little girl had complained. The first thing Mr. Kapasi had noticed when he saw Mr. and Mrs. Das, standing with their children under the portico of the hotel, was that they were very young, perhaps not even thirty. In addition to Tina they had two boys, Ronny and Bobby, who appeared very close in age and had teeth covered in a network of flashing silver wires. The family looked Indian but dressed as foreigners did, the children in stiff, brightly colored clothing and caps with translucent visors. Mr. Kapasi was accustomed to foreign tourists; he was assigned to them regularly because he could speak English. Yesterday he had driven an elderly couple from Scotland, both with spotted faces and fluffy white hair so thin it exposed their sunburnt scalps. In comparison, the tanned, youthful faces of Mr. and Mrs. Das were all the more striking. When he'd introduced himself, Mr. Kapasi had pressed his palms together in greeting, but Mr. Das squeezed hands like an American so that Mr. Kapasi felt it in his elbow. Mrs. Das, for her part, had flexed one side of her mouth, smiling dutifully at Mr. Kapasi, without displaying any interest in him.

As they waited at the tea stall, Ronny, who looked like the older of the two boys, clambered suddenly out of the backseat, intrigued by a goat tied to a stake in the ground.

"Don't touch it," Mr. Das said. He glanced up from his paperback tour book, which said "INDIA" in yellow letters and looked as if it had been published abroad. His voice, somehow tentative and a little shrill, sounded as though it had not yet settled into maturity.

"I want to give it a piece of gum," the boy called back as he trotted ahead.

Mr. Das stepped out of the car and stretched his legs by squatting briefly to the ground. A clean-shaven man, he looked exactly like a magnified version of Ronny. He had a sapphire blue visor, and was dressed in shorts, sneakers, and a T-shirt. The camera slung around his neck, with an impressive telephoto lens and numerous buttons and markings, was the only complicated thing he wore. He frowned, watching as Ronny rushed toward the goat, but appeared to have no intention of intervening. "Bobby, make sure that your brother doesn't do anything stupid."

"I don't feel like it," Bobby said, not moving. He was sitting in the front seat beside Mr. Kapasi, studying a picture of the elephant god taped to the glove compartment.

"No need to worry," Mr. Kapasi said. "They are quite tame." Mr. Kapasi was forty-six years old, with receding hair that had gone completely silver, but his butterscotch complexion and his unlined brow, which he treated in spare moments to dabs of lotus-oil balm, made it easy to imagine what he must have looked like at an earlier age. He wore gray trousers and a matching jacket-style shirt, tapered at the waist, with short sleeves and a large pointed collar, made of a thin but durable synthetic material. He had specified both the cut and the fabric to his tailor—it was his preferred uniform for giving tours because it did not get crushed during his long hours behind the wheel. Through the windshield he watched as Ronny circled around the goat, touched it quickly on its side, then trotted back to the car.

"You left India as a child?" Mr. Kapasi asked when Mr. Das had settled once again into the passenger seat.

"Oh, Mina and I were both born in America," Mr. Das announced with an air of sudden confidence. "Born and raised. Our parents live here now, in Assansol. They retired. We visit them every couple years." He turned to watch as the little girl ran toward the car, the wide purple bows of her sundress flopping on her narrow brown shoulders. She was holding to her chest a doll with yellow hair that looked as if it had been chopped, as a punitive measure, with a pair of dull scissors. "This is Tina's first trip to India, isn't it, Tina?"

"I don't have to go to the bathroom anymore," Tina announced.

"Where's Mina?" Mr. Das asked.

Mr. Kapasi found it strange that Mr. Das should refer to his wife by her first name when speaking to the little girl. Tina pointed to where Mrs. Das was purchasing something from one of the shirtless men who worked at the tea stall. Mr. Kapasi heard one of the shirtless men sing a phrase from a popular Hindi love song as Mrs. Das walked back to the car, but she did not appear to understand the words of the song, for she did not express irritation, or embarrassment, or react in any other way to the man's declarations.

He observed her. She wore a red-and-white-checkered skirt that stopped above her knees, slip-on shoes with a square wooden heel, and a close-fitting blouse styled like a man's undershirt. The blouse was decorated at chest-level with a calico appliqué in the shape of a strawberry. She was a short woman, with small hands like paws, her frosty pink fingernails painted to match her lips, and was slightly plump in her figure. Her hair, shorn only a little longer than her husband's, was parted far to one side. She was wearing large dark brown sunglasses with a pinkish tint to them, and carried a big straw bag, almost as big as her torso, shaped like a bowl, with a water bottle poking out of it. She walked slowly, carrying some puffed rice tossed with peanuts and chili peppers in a large packet made from newspapers. Mr. Kapasi turned to Mr. Das.

"Where in America do you live?"

"New Brunswick, New Jersey."

"Next to New York?"

"Exactly. I teach middle school there."

"What subject?"

"Science. In fact, every year I take my students on a trip to the Museum of Natural History in New York City. In a way we have a lot in common, you could say, you and I. How long have you been a tour guide. Mr. Kapasi?"

"Five years."

Mrs. Das reached the car. "How long's the trip?" she asked, shutting the door.

"About two and a half hours," Mr. Kapasi replied.

At this Mrs. Das gave an impatient sigh, as if she had been traveling her whole life without pause. She fanned herself with a folded Bombay film magazine written in English.

"I thought that the Sun Temple is only eighteen miles north of Puri," Mr. Das said, tapping on the tour book.

"The roads to Konarak are poor. Actually it is a distance of fifty-two miles," Mr. Kapasi explained.

Mr. Das nodded, readjusting the camera strap where it had begun to chafe the back of his neck.

Before starting the ignition, Mr. Kapasi reached back to make sure the cranklike locks on the inside of each of the back doors were secured. As soon as the car began to move the little girl began to play with the lock on her side, clicking it with some effort forward and backward, but Mrs. Das said nothing to stop her. She sat a bit slouched at one end of the backseat, not offering her puffed rice to anyone. Ronny and Tina sat on either side of her, both snapping bright green gum.

"Look," Bobby said as the car began to gather speed. He pointed with his finger to the tall trees that lined the road. "Look."

"Monkeys!" Ronny shrieked. "Wow!"

They were seated in groups along the branches, with shining black faces, silver bodies, horizontal eyebrows, and crested heads. Their long gray tails dangled like a series of ropes among the leaves. A few scratched themselves with black leathery hands, or swung their feet, staring as the car passed.

"We call them the hanuman," Mr. Kapasi said. "They are quite common in the area."

As soon as he spoke, one of the monkeys leaped into the middle of the road, causing Mr. Kapasi to brake suddenly. Another bounced onto the hood of the car, then sprang away. Mr. Kapasi beeped his horn. The children began to get excited, sucking in their breath and covering their faces partly with their hands. They had never seen monkeys outside of a zoo, Mr. Das explained. He asked Mr. Kapasi to stop the car so that he could take a picture.

While Mr. Das adjusted his telephoto lens, Mrs. Das reached into her straw bag and pulled out a bottle of colorless nail polish, which she proceeded to stroke on the tip of her index finger.

The little girl stuck out a hand. "Mine too. Mommy, do mine too."

"Leave me alone," Mrs. Das said, blowing on her nail and turning her body slightly. "You're making me mess up."

The little girl occupied herself by buttoning and unbuttoning a pinafore on the doll's plastic body.

"All set," Mr. Das said, replacing the lens cap.

The car rattled considerably as it raced along the dusty road, causing them all to pop up from their seats every now and then, but Mrs. Das continued to polish her nails. Mr. Kapasi eased up on the accelerator, hoping to produce a smoother ride. When he reached for the gearshift the boy in front accommodated him by swinging his hairless knees out of the way. Mr. Kapasi noted that this boy was slightly paler than the other children. "Daddy, why is the driver sitting on the wrong side in this car, too?" the boy asked.

"They all do that here, dummy." Ronny said.

"Don't call your brother a dummy," Mr. Das said. He turned to Mr. Kapasi. "In America, you know . . . it confuses them."

"Oh yes, I am well aware," Mr. Kapasi said. As delicately as he could, he shifted gears again, accelerating as they approached a hill in the road. "I see it on *Dallas,* the steering wheels are on the left-hand side."

"What's *Dallas?*" Tina asked, banging her now naked doll on the seat behind Mr. Kapasi.

"It went off the air," Mr. Das explained. "It's a television show."

They were all like siblings, Mr. Kapasi thought as they passed a row of date trees. Mr. and Mrs. Das behaved like an older brother and sister, not parents. It seemed that they were in charge of the children only for the day; it was hard to believe they were regularly responsible for anything other than themselves. Mr. Das tapped on his lens cap, and his tour book, dragging his thumbnail occasionally across the pages so that they made a scraping sound. Mrs. Das continued to polish her nails. She had still not removed her sunglasses. Every now and then Tina renewed her plea that she wanted her nails done, too, and so at one point Mrs. Das flicked a drop of polish on the little girl's finger before depositing the bottle back inside her straw bag.

"Isn't this an air-conditioned car?" she asked, still blowing on her hand. The window on Tina's side was broken and could not be rolled down.

"Quit complaining," Mr. Das said. "It isn't so hot."

"I told you to get a car with air-conditioning," Mrs. Das continued. "Why do you do this, Raj, just to save a few stupid rupees. What are you saving us, fifty cents?"

Their accents sounded just like the ones Mr. Kapasi heard on American television programs, though not like the ones on *Dallas.*

"Doesn't it get tiresome, Mr. Kapasi, showing people the same thing every day?" Mr. Das asked, rolling down his own window all the way. "Hey, do you mind stopping the car? I just want to get a shot of this guy."

Mr. Kapasi pulled over to the side of the road as Mr. Das took a picture of a barefoot man, his head wrapped in a dirty turban, seated on top of a cart of grain sacks pulled by a pair of bullocks. Both the man and the bullocks were emaciated. In the backseat Mrs. Das gazed out another window, at the sky, where nearly transparent clouds passed quickly in front of one another.

"I look forward to it, actually," Mr. Kapasi said as they continued on their way. "The Sun Temple is one of my favorite places. In that way it is a reward for me. I give tours on Fridays and Saturdays only. I have another job during the week."

"Oh? Where?" Mr. Das asked.

"I work in a doctor's office."

"You're a doctor?"

"I am not a doctor. I work with one. As an interpreter."

"What does a doctor need an interpreter for?"

"He has a number of Gujarati patients. My father was Gujarati, but many people do not speak Gujarati in this area, including the doctor. And so the doctor asked me to work in his office, interpreting what the patients say."

"Interesting. I've never heard of anything like that," Mr. Das said.

Mr. Kapasi shrugged. "It is a job like any other."

"But so romantic," Mrs. Das said dreamily, breaking her extended silence. She lifted her pinkish-brown sunglasses and arranged them on top of her head like a tiara. For the first time, her eyes met Mr. Kapasi's in the rearview mirror: pale, a bit small, their gaze fixed but drowsy.

Mr. Das craned to look at her. "What's so romantic about it?"

"I don't know. Something." She shrugged, knitting her brows together for an instant. "Would you like a piece of gum, Mr. Kapasi?" she asked brightly. She reached into her straw bag and handed him a small square wrapped in green-and-white-striped paper. As soon as Mr. Kapasi put the gum in his mouth a thick sweet liquid burst onto his tongue.

"Tell us more about your job, Mr. Kapasi," Mrs. Das said.

"What would you like to know, madame?"

"I don't know," she shrugged, munching on some puffed rice and licking the mustard oil from the corners of her mouth. "Tell us a typical situation." She settled back in her seat, her head tilted in a patch of sun, and closed her eyes. "I want to picture what happens."

"Very well. The other day a man came in with a pain in his throat."

"Did he smoke cigarettes?"

"No. It was very curious. He complained that he felt as if there were long pieces of straw stuck in his throat. When I told the doctor he was able to prescribe the proper medication."

"That's so neat."

"Yes," Mr. Kapasi agreed after some hesitation.

"So these patients are totally dependent on you," Mrs. Das said. She spoke slowly, as if she were thinking aloud. "In a way, more dependent on you than the doctor."

"How do you mean? How could it be?"

"Well, for example, you could tell the doctor that the pain felt like a burning, not straw. The patient would never know what you had told the doctor, and the doctor wouldn't know that you had told the wrong thing. It's a big responsibility."

"Yes, a big responsibility you have there, Mr. Kapasi," Mr. Das agreed.

Mr. Kapasi had never thought of his job in such complimentary terms. To him it was a thankless occupation. He found nothing noble in interpreting people's maladies, assiduously translating the symptoms of so many swollen bones, countless cramps of bellies and bowels, spots on people's palms that changed color, shape, or size. The doctor, nearly half his age, had an affinity for bell-bottom trousers and made humorless jokes about the Congress party. Together they worked in a stale little infirmary where Mr. Kapasi's smartly tailored clothes clung to him in the heat, in spite of the blackened blades of a ceiling fan churning over their heads.

The job was a sign of his failings. In his youth he'd been a devoted scholar of foreign languages, the owner of an impressive collection of dictionaries. He had dreamed of being an interpreter for diplomats and dignitaries, resolving conflicts between people and nations, settling disputes of which he alone could understand both sides. He was a self-educated man. In a series of notebooks, in the evenings before his parents settled his marriage, he had listed the common etymologies of words, and at one point in his life he was confident that he could converse, if given the opportunity, in English, French, Russian, Portuguese, and Italian, not to mention Hindi, Bengali, Orissi, and Gujarati. Now only a handful of European phrases remained in his memory, scattered words for things like saucers and chairs. English was the only non-Indian language he spoke fluently anymore. Mr. Kapasi knew it was not a re-markable talent. Sometimes he feared that his children knew better English than he did, just from watching television. Still, it came in handy for the tours.

He had taken the job as an interpreter after his first son, at the age of seven, contracted typhoid—that was how he had first made the acquaintance of the doctor. At the time Mr. Kapasi had been teaching English in a grammar school, and he bartered his skills as an interpreter to pay the increasingly exorbitant medical bills. In the end the boy had died one evening in his mother's arms, his limbs burning with fever, but then there was the funeral to pay for, and the other children who were born soon enough, and the newer, bigger house, and the good schools and tutors, and the fine shoes and the television, and the countless other ways he tried to console his wife and to keep her from crying in her sleep, and so when the doctor offered to pay him twice as much as he earned at the grammar school, he accepted. Mr. Kapasi knew that his wife had little regard for his career as an interpreter. He knew it reminded her of the son she'd lost, and that she resented the other lives he helped, in his own small way, to save. If ever she referred to his position, she used the phrase "doctor's assistant," as if the process of interpretation were equal to taking someone's temperature, or changing a bedpan. She never asked him about the patients who came to the doctor's office, or said that his job was a big responsibility.

For this reason it flattered Mr. Kapasi that Mrs. Das was so in-trigued by his job. Unlike his wife, she had reminded him of its in-tellectual challenges. She had also used the word "romantic." She did not behave in a romantic way toward her husband, and yet she had used the word to describe him. He wondered if Mr. and Mrs. Das were a bad match, just as he and his wife were. Perhaps they, too, had little in common apart from three children and a decade of their lives. The signs he recognized from his own marriage were there—the bickering, the indifference, the protracted silences. Her sudden interest in him, an interest she did not express in either her husband or her children, was mildly intoxicating. When Mr. Kapasi thought once again about how she had said "romantic," the feeling of intoxication grew.

He began to check his reflection in the rearview mirror as he drove, feeling grateful that he had chosen the gray suit that morning and not the brown one, which tended to sag a little in the knees. From time to time he glanced through the mirror at Mrs. Das. In addition to glancing at her face he glanced at the strawberry between her breasts, and the golden-brown hollow in her throat. He decided to tell Mrs. Das about another patient, and another: the young woman who had complained of a sensation of raindrops in her spine, the gentleman whose birthmark had begun to sprout hairs. Mrs. Das listened attentively, stroking her hair with a small plastic brush that resembled an oval bed of nails, asking more questions, for yet another example. The children were quiet, intent on spotting more monkeys in the trees, and Mr. Das was absorbed by his tour book, so it seemed like a private conversation between Mr. Kapasi and Mrs. Das. In this manner the next half hour passed, and when they stopped for lunch at a roadside restaurant that sold fritters and omelette sandwiches, usually something Mr. Kapasi looked forward to on his tours so that he could sit in peace and enjoy some hot tea, he was disappointed. As the Das family settled together under a magenta umbrella fringed with white and orange tassels, and placed their orders with one of the waiters who marched about in tricornered caps, Mr. Kapasi reluctantly headed toward a neighboring table.

"Mr. Kapasi, wait. There's room here," Mrs. Das called out. She gathered Tina onto her lap, insisting that he accompany them. And so, together, they had bottled mango juice and sandwiches and plates of onions and potatoes deep-fried in graham-flour batter. After finishing two omelette sandwiches Mr. Das took more pictures of the group as they ate.

"How much longer?" he asked Mr. Kapasi as he paused to load a new roll of film in the camera.

"About half an hour more."

By now the children had gotten up from the table to look at more monkeys perched in a nearby tree, so there was a considerable space between Mrs. Das and Mr. Kapasi. Mr. Das placed the camera to his face and squeezed one eye shut, his tongue exposed at one corner of his mouth. "This looks funny. Mina, you need to lean in closer to Mr. Kapasi."

She did. He could smell a scent on her skin, like a mixture of whiskey and rose water. He worried suddenly that she could smell his perspiration, which he knew had collected beneath the synthetic material of his shirt. He polished off his mango juice in one gulp and smoothed his silver hair with his hands. A bit of the juice dripped onto his chin. He wondered if Mrs. Das had noticed.

She had not. "What's your address, Mr. Kapasi?" she inquired, fishing for something inside her straw bag.

"You would like my address?"

"So we can send you copies," she said. "Of the pictures." She handed him a scrap of paper which she had hastily ripped from a page of her film magazine. The blank portion was limited, for the narrow strip was crowded by lines of text and a tiny picture of a hero and heroine embracing under a eucalyptus tree.

The paper curled as Mr. Kapasi wrote his address in clear, careful letters. She would write to him, asking about his days interpreting at the doctor's office, and he would respond eloquently, choosing only the most entertaining anecdotes, ones that would make her laugh out loud as she read them in her house in New Jersey. In time she would reveal the disappointment of her marriage, and he his. In this way their friendship would grow, and flourish. He would possess a picture of the two of them, eating fried onions under a magenta umbrella, which he would keep, he decided, safely tucked between the pages of his Russian grammar. As his mind raced, Mr. Kapasi experienced a mild and pleasant shock. It was similar to a feeling he used to experience long ago when, after months of translating with the aid of a dictionary, he would finally read a passage from a French novel, or an Italian sonnet, and understand the words, one after another, unencumbered by his own efforts. In those moments Mr. Kapasi used to believe that all was right with the world, that all struggles were rewarded, that all of life's mistakes made sense in the end. The promise that he would hear from Mrs. Das now filled him with the same belief.

When he finished writing his address Mr. Kapasi handed her the paper, but as soon as he did so he worried that he had either misspelled his name, or accidentally reversed the numbers of his postal code. He dreaded the possibility of a lost letter, the photograph never reaching him, hovering somewhere in Orissa, close but ultimately unattainable. He thought of asking for the slip of paper again, just to make sure he had written his address accurately, but Mrs. Das had already dropped it into the jumble of her bag.

✷ ✷ ✷

They reached Konarak at two-thirty. The temple, made of sandstone, was a massive pyramid-like structure in the shape of a chariot. It was dedicated to the great master of life, the sun, which struck three sides of the edifice as it made its journey each day across the sky. Twenty-four giant wheels were carved on the north and south sides of the plinth. The whole thing was drawn by a team of seven horses, speeding as if through the heavens. As they approached, Mr. Kapasi explained that the temple had been built between A.D. 1243 and 1255, with the efforts of twelve hundred artisans, by the great ruler of the Ganga dynasty, King Narasimhadeva the First, to commemorate his victory against the Muslim army.

"It says the temple occupies about a hundred and seventy acres of land," Mr. Das said, reading from his book.

"It's like a desert," Ronny said, his eyes wandering across the sand that stretched on all sides beyond the temple.

"The Chandrabhaga River once flowed one mile north of here. It is dry now," Mr. Kapasi said, turning off the engine.

They got out and walked toward the temple, posing first for pictures by the pair of lions that flanked the steps. Mr. Kapasi led them next to one of the wheels of the chariot, higher than any human being, nine feet in diameter.

" 'The wheels are supposed to symbolize the wheel of life,' " Mr. Das read. " 'They depict the cycle of creation, preservation, and achievement of realization.' Cool." He turned the page of his book. " 'Each wheel is divided into eight thick and thin spokes, dividing the day into eight equal parts. The rims are carved with designs of birds and animals, whereas the medallions in the spokes are carved with women in luxurious poses, largely erotic in nature.' "

What he referred to were the countless friezes of entwined naked bodies, making love in various positions, women clinging to the necks of men, their knees wrapped eternally around their lovers' thighs. In addition to these were assorted scenes from daily life, of hunting and trading, of deer being killed with bows and arrows and marching warriors holding swords in their hands.

It was no longer possible to enter the temple, for it had filled with rubble years ago, but they admired the exterior, as did all the tourists Mr. Kapasi brought there, slowly strolling along each of its sides. Mr. Das trailed behind, taking pictures. The children ran ahead, pointing to figures of naked people, intrigued in particular by the Nagamithunas, the half-human, half-serpentine couples who were said, Mr. Kapasi told them, to live in the deepest waters of the sea. Mr. Kapasi was pleased that they liked the temple, pleased especially that it appealed to Mrs. Das. She stopped every three or four paces, staring silently at the carved lovers, and the processions of elephants, and the topless female musicians beating on two-sided drums.

Though Mr. Kapasi had been to the temple countless times, it occurred to him, as he, too, gazed at the topless women, that he had never seen his own wife fully naked. Even when they had made love she kept the panels of her blouse hooked together, the string of her petticoat knotted around her waist. He had never admired the backs of his wife's legs the way he now admired those of Mrs. Das, walking as if for his benefit alone. He had, of course, seen plenty of bare limbs before, belonging to the American and European ladies who took his tours. But Mrs. Das was different. Unlike the other women, who had an interest only in the temple, and kept their noses buried in a guidebook, or their eyes behind the lens of a camera, Mrs. Das had taken an interest in him.

Mr. Kapasi was anxious to be alone with her, to continue their private conversation, yet he felt nervous to walk at her side. She was lost behind her sunglasses, ignoring her husband's requests that she pose for another picture, walking past her children as if they were strangers. Worried that he might disturb her, Mr. Kapasi walked ahead, to admire, as he always did, the three life-sized bronze avatars of Surya, the sun god, each emerging from its own niche on the temple facade to greet the sun at dawn, noon, and evening. They wore elaborate headdresses, their languid, elongated eyes closed, their bare chests draped with carved chains and amulets. Hibiscus petals, offerings from previous visitors, were strewn at their gray-green feet. The last statue, on the northern wall of the temple, was Mr. Kapasi's favorite. This Surya had a tired expression, weary after a hard day of work, sitting astride a horse with folded legs. Even his horse's eyes were drowsy. Around his body were smaller sculptures of women in pairs, their hips thrust to one side.

"Who's that?" Mrs. Das asked. He was startled to see that she was standing beside him.

"He is the Astachala-Surya," Mr. Kapasi said. "The setting sun."

"So in a couple of hours the sun will set right here?" She slipped a foot out of one of her square-heeled shoes, rubbed her toes on the back of her other leg.

"That is correct."

She raised her sunglasses for a moment, then put them back on again. "Neat."

Mr. Kapasi was not certain exactly what the word suggested, but he had a feeling it was a favorable response. He hoped that Mrs. Das had understood Surya's beauty, his power. Perhaps they would discuss it further in their letters. He would explain things to her, things about India, and she would explain things to him about America. In its own way this correspondence would fulfill his dream, of serving as an interpreter between nations. He looked at her straw bag, delighted that his address lay nestled among its contents. When he pictured her so many thousands of miles away he plummeted, so much so that he had an overwhelming urge to wrap his arms around her, to freeze with her, even for an instant, in an embrace witnessed by his favorite Surya. But Mrs. Das had already started walking.

"When do you return to America?" he asked, trying to sound placid.

"In ten days."

He calculated: a week to settle in, a week to develop the pictures, a few days to compose her letter, two weeks to get to India by air. According to his schedule, allowing room for delays, he would hear from Mrs. Das in approximately six weeks' time.

* * *

The family was silent as Mr. Kapasi drove them back, a little past four-thirty, to Hotel Sandy Villa. The children had bought miniature granite versions of the chariot's wheels at a souvenir stand, and they turned them round in their hands. Mr. Das continued to read his book. Mrs. Das untangled Tina's hair with her brush and divided it into two little ponytails.

Mr. Kapasi was beginning to dread the thought of dropping them off. He was not prepared to begin his six-week wait to hear from Mrs. Das. As he stole glances at her in the rearview mirror, wrapping elastic bands around Tina's hair, he wondered how he might make the tour last a little longer. Ordinarily he sped back to Puri using a shortcut, eager to return home, scrub his feet and hands with sandalwood soap, and enjoy the evening newspaper and a cup of tea that his wife would serve him in silence. The thought of that silence, something to which he'd long been resigned, now oppressed him. It was then that he suggested visiting the hills at Udayagiri and Khandagiri, where a number of monastic dwellings were hewn out of the ground, facing one another across a defile. It was some miles away, but well worth seeing, Mr. Kapasi told them.

"Oh yeah, there's something mentioned about it in this book," Mr. Das said. "Built by a Jain king or something."

"Shall we go, then?" Mr. Kapasi asked. He paused at a turn in the road. "It's to the left."

Mr. Das turned to look at Mrs. Das. Both of them shrugged.

"Left, left," the children chanted.

Mr. Kapasi turned the wheel, almost delirious with relief. He did not know what he would do or say to Mrs. Das once they arrived at the hills. Perhaps he would tell her what a pleasing smile she had. Perhaps he would compliment her strawberry shirt, which he found irresistibly becoming. Perhaps, when Mr. Das was busy taking a picture, he would take her hand.

He did not have to worry. When they got to the hills, divided by a steep path thick with trees, Mrs. Das refused to get out of the car. All along the path, dozens of monkeys were seated on stones, as well as on the branches of the trees. Their hind legs were stretched out in front and raised to shoulder level, their arms resting on their knees.

"My legs are tired," she said, sinking low in her seat. "I'll stay here."

"Why did you have to wear those stupid shoes?" Mr. Das said. "You won't be in the pictures."

"Pretend I'm there."

"But we could use one of these pictures for our Christmas card this year. We didn't get one of all five of us at the Sun Temple. Mr. Kapasi could take it."

"I'm not coming. Anyway, those monkeys give me the creeps."

"But they're harmless," Mr. Das said. He turned to Mr. Kapasi. "Aren't they?"

"They are more hungry than dangerous," Mr. Kapasi said. "Do not provoke them with food, and they will not bother you."

Mr. Das headed up the defile with the children, the boys at his side, the little girl on his shoulders. Mr. Kapasi watched as they crossed paths with a Japanese man and woman, the only other tourists there, who paused for a final photograph, then stepped into a nearby car and drove away. As the car disappeared out of view some of the monkeys called out, emitting soft whooping sounds, and then walked on their flat black hands and feet up the path. At one point a group of them formed a little ring around Mr. Das and the children. Tina screamed in delight. Ronny ran in circles around his father. Bobby bent down and picked up a fat stick on the ground. When he extended it, one of the monkeys approached him and snatched it, then briefly beat the ground.

"I'll join them," Mr. Kapasi said, unlocking the door on his side. "There is much to explain about the caves."

"No. Stay a minute," Mrs. Das said. She got out of the backseat and slipped in beside Mr. Kapasi. "Raj has his dumb book, anyway." Together, through the windshield, Mrs. Das and Mr. Kapasi watched as Bobby and the monkey passed the stick back and forth between them.

"A brave little boy," Mr. Kapasi commented.

"It's not so surprising," Mrs. Das said.

"No?"

"He's not his."

"I beg your pardon?"

"Raj's. He's not Raj's son."

Mr. Kapasi felt a prickle on his skin. He reached into his shirt pocket for the small tin of lotus-oil balm he carried with him at all times, and applied it to three spots on his forehead. He knew that Mrs. Das was watching him, but he did not turn to face her. Instead he watched as the figures of Mr. Das and the children grew smaller, climbing up the steep path, pausing every now and then for a picture, surrounded by a growing number of monkeys.

"Are you surprised?" The way she put it made him choose his words with care.

"It's not the type of thing one assumes," Mr. Kapasi replied slowly. He put the tin of lotus-oil balm back in his pocket.

"No, of course not. And no one knows, of course. No one at all. I've kept it a secret for eight whole years." She looked at Mr. Kapasi, tilting her chin as if to gain a fresh perspective. "But now I've told you."

Mr. Kapasi nodded. He felt suddenly parched, and his forehead was warm and slightly numb from the balm. He considered asking Mrs. Das for a sip of water, then decided against it.

"We met when we were very young," she said. She reached into her straw bag in search of something, then pulled out a packet of puffed rice. "Want some?"

"No, thank you."

She put a fistful in her mouth, sank into the seat a little, and looked away from Mr. Kapasi, out the window on her side of the car. "We married when we were still in college. We were in high school when he proposed. We went to the same college, of course. Back then we couldn't stand the thought of being separated, not for a day, not for a minute. Our parents were best friends who lived in the same town. My entire life I saw him every weekend, either at our house or theirs. We were sent upstairs to play together while our parents joked about our marriage. Imagine! They never caught us at anything, though in a way I think it was all more or less a setup. The things we did those Friday and Saturday nights, while our parents sat downstairs drinking tea . . . I could tell you stories, Mr. Kapasi."

As a result of spending all her time in college with Raj, she continued, she did not make many close friends. There was no one to confide in about him at the end of a difficult day, or to share a passing thought or a worry. Her parents now lived on the other side of the world, but she had never been very close to them, anyway. After marrying so young she was overwhelmed by it all, having a child so quickly, and nursing, and warming up bottles of milk and testing their temperature against her wrist while Raj was at work, dressed in sweaters and corduroy pants, teaching his students about rocks and dinosaurs. Raj never looked cross or harried, or plump as she had become after the first baby.

Always tired, she declined invitations from her one or two college girlfriends, to have lunch or shop in Manhattan. Eventually the friends stopped calling her, so that she was left at home all day with the baby, surrounded by toys that made her trip when she walked or wince when she sat, always cross and tired. Only occasionally did they go out after Ronny was born, and even more rarely did they entertain. Raj didn't mind; he looked forward to coming home from teaching and watching television and bouncing Ronny on his knee. She had been outraged when Raj told her that a Punjabi friend, someone whom she had once met but did not remember, would be staying with them for a week for some job interviews in the New Brunswick area.

Bobby was conceived in the afternoon, on a sofa littered with rubber teething toys, after the friend learned that a London pharmaceutical company had hired him, while Ronny cried to be freed from his playpen. She made no protest when the friend touched the small of her back as she was about to make a pot of coffee, then pulled her against his crisp navy suit. He made love to her swiftly, in silence, with an expertise she had never known, without the meaningful expressions and smiles Raj always insisted on afterward. The next day Raj drove the friend to JFK. He was married now, to a Punjabi girl, and they lived in London still, and every year they exchanged Christmas cards with Raj and Mina, each couple tucking photos of their families into the envelopes. He did not know that he was Bobby's father. He never would.

"I beg your pardon, Mrs. Das, but why have you told me this information?" Mr. Kapasi asked when she had finally finished speaking, and had turned to face him once again.

"For God's sake, stop calling me Mrs. Das. I'm twenty-eight. You probably have children my age."

"Not quite." It disturbed Mr. Kapasi to learn that she thought of him as a parent. The feeling he had had toward her, that had made him check his reflection in the rearview mirror as they drove, evaporated a little.

"I told you because of your talents." She put the packet of puffed rice back into her bag without folding over the top.

"I don't understand," Mr. Kapasi said.

"Don't you see? For eight years I haven't been able to express this to anybody, not to friends, certainly not to Raj. He doesn't even suspect it. He thinks I'm still in love with him. Well, don't you have anything to say?"

"About what?"

"About what I've just told you. About my secret, and about how terrible it makes me feel. I feel terrible looking at my children, and at Raj, always terrible. I have terrible urges, Mr. Kapasi, to throw things away. One day I had the urge to throw everything I own out the window, the television, the children, everything. Don't you think it's unhealthy?"

He was silent.

"Mr. Kapasi, don't you have anything to say? I thought that was your job."

"My job is to give tours, Mrs. Das."

"Not that. Your other job. As an interpreter."

"But we do not face a language barrier. What need is there for an interpreter?"

"That's not what I mean. I would never have told you otherwise. Don't you realize what it means for me to tell you?"

"What does it mean?"

"It means that I'm tired of feeling so terrible all the time. Eight years, Mr. Kapasi, I've been in pain eight years. I was hoping you could help me feel better, say the right thing. Suggest some kind of remedy."

He looked at her, in her red plaid skirt and strawberry T-shirt, a woman not yet thirty, who loved neither her husband nor her children, who had already fallen out of love with life. Her confession depressed him, depressed him all the more when he thought of Mr. Das at the top of the path, Tina clinging to his shoulders, taking pictures of ancient monastic cells cut into the hills to show his students in America, unsuspecting and unaware that one of his sons was not his own. Mr. Kapasi felt insulted that Mrs. Das should ask him to interpret her common, trivial little secret. She did not resemble the patients in the doctor's office, those who came glassy-eyed and desperate, unable to sleep or breathe or urinate with ease, unable, above all, to give words to their pains. Still, Mr. Kapasi believed it was his duty to assist Mrs. Das. Perhaps he ought to tell her to confess the truth to Mr. Das. He would explain that honesty was the best policy. Honesty, surely, would help her feel better, as she'd put it. Perhaps he would offer to preside over the discussion, as a mediator. He decided to begin with the most obvious question, to get to the heart of the matter, and so he asked, "Is it really pain you feel, Mrs. Das, or is it guilt?"

She turned to him and glared, mustard oil thick on her frosty pink lips. She opened her mouth to say something, but as she glared at Mr. Kapasi some certain knowledge seemed to pass before her eyes, and she stopped. It crushed him; he knew at that moment that he was not even important enough to be properly insulted. She opened the car door and began walking up the path, wobbling a little on her square wooden heels, reaching into her straw bag to eat handfuls of puffed rice. It fell through her fingers, leaving a zigzagging trail, causing a monkey to leap down from a tree and devour the little white grains. In search of more, the monkey began to follow Mrs. Das. Others joined him, so that she was soon being followed by about half a dozen of them, their velvety tails dragging behind.

Mr. Kapasi stepped out of the car. He wanted to holler, to alert her in some way, but he worried that if she knew they were behind her, she would grow nervous. Perhaps she would lose her balance. Perhaps they would pull at her bag or her hair. He began to jog up the path, taking a fallen branch in his hand to scare away the monkeys. Mrs. Das continued walking, oblivious, trailing grains of puffed rice. Near the top of the incline, before a group of cells fronted by a row of squat stone pillars, Mr. Das was kneeling on the ground, focusing the lens of his camera. The children stood under the arcade, now hiding, now emerging from view.

"Wait for me," Mrs. Das called out. "I'm coming."

Tina jumped up and down. "Here comes Mommy!"

"Great," Mr. Das said without looking up. "Just in time. We'll get Mr. Kapasi to take a picture of the five of us."

Mr. Kapasi quickened his pace, waving his branch so that the monkeys scampered away, distracted, in another direction.

"Where's Bobby?" Mrs. Das asked when she stopped.

Mr. Das looked up from the camera. "I don't know. Ronny, where's Bobby?"

Ronny shrugged. "I thought he was right here."

"Where is he?" Mrs. Das repeated sharply. "What's wrong with all of you?"

They began calling his name, wandering up and down the path a bit. Because they were calling, they did not initially hear the boy's screams. When they found him, a little farther down the path under a tree, he was surrounded by a group of monkeys, over a dozen of them, pulling at his T-shirt with their long black fingers. The puffed rice Mrs. Das had spilled was scattered at his feet, raked over by the monkeys' hands. The boy was silent, his body frozen, swift tears running down his startled face. His bare legs were dusty and red with welts from where one of the monkeys struck him repeatedly with the stick he had given to it earlier.

"Daddy, the monkey's hurting Bobby," Tina said.

Mr. Das wiped his palms on the front of his shorts. In his nervousness he accidentally pressed the shutter on his camera; the whirring noise of the advancing film excited the monkeys, and the one with the stick began to beat Bobby more intently. "What are we supposed to do? What if they start attacking?"

"Mr. Kapasi," Mrs. Das shrieked, noticing him standing to one side. "Do something, for God's sake, do something!"

Mr. Kapasi took his branch and shooed them away, hissing at the ones that remained, stomping his feet to scare them. The animals retreated slowly, with a measured gait, obedient but unintimidated. Mr. Kapasi gathered Bobby in his arms and brought him back to where his parents and siblings were standing. As he carried him he was tempted to whisper a secret into the boy's ear. But Bobby was stunned, and shivering with fright, his legs bleeding slightly where the stick had broken the skin. When Mr. Kapasi delivered him to his parents, Mr. Das brushed some dirt off the boy's T-shirt and put the visor on him the right way. Mrs. Das reached into her straw bag to find a bandage which she taped over the cut on his knee. Ronny offered his brother a fresh piece of gum. "He's fine. Just a little scared, right, Bobby?" Mr. Das said, patting the top of his head.

"God, let's get out of here," Mrs. Das said. She folded her arms across the strawberry on her chest. "This place gives me the creeps."

"Yeah. Back to the hotel, definitely," Mr. Das agreed.

"Poor Bobby," Mrs. Das said. "Come here a second. Let Mommy fix your hair." Again she reached into her straw bag, this time for her hairbrush, and began to run it around the edges of the translucent visor. When she whipped out the hairbrush, the slip of paper with Mr. Kapasi's address on it fluttered away in the wind. No one but Mr. Kapasi noticed. He watched as it rose, carried higher and higher by the breeze, into the trees where the monkeys now sat, solemnly observing the scene below. Mr. Kapasi observed it too, knowing that this was the picture of the Das family he would preserve forever in his mind.

THE GARDEN PARTY

Katherine Mansfield

★ ★ ★

And after all the weather was ideal. They could not have had a more perfect day for a garden party if they had ordered it. Windless, warm, the sky without a cloud. Only the blue was veiled with a haze of light gold, as it is sometimes in early summer. The gardener had been up since dawn, mowing the lawns and sweeping them, until the grass and the dark flat rosettes where the daisy plants had been seemed to shine. As for the roses, you could not help feeling they understood that roses are the only flowers that impress people at garden parties; the only flowers that everybody is certain of knowing. Hundreds, yes, literally hundreds, had come out in a single night; the green bushes bowed down as though they had been visited by archangels.

Breakfast was not yet over before the men came to put up the marquee.

"Where do you want the marquee put, Mother?"

"My dear child, it's no use asking me. I'm determined to leave everything to you children this year. Forget I am your mother. Treat me as an honored guests."

But Meg could not possibly go and supervise the men. She had washed her hair before breakfast, and she sat drinking her coffee in a green turban, with a dark wet curl stamped on each cheek. Jose, the butterfly, always came down in a silk petticoat and a kimono jacket.

"You'll have to go, Laura; you're the artistic one."

Away Laura flew, still holding her piece of bread-and-butter. It's so delicious to have an excuse for eating out of doors, and besides, she loved having to arrange things; she always felt she could do it so much better than anybody else.

Four men in their shirt-sleeves stood grouped together on the garden path. They carried staves covered with rolls of canvas, and they had big tool-bags slung on their backs. They looked impressive. Laura wished now that she was not holding that piece of bread-and-butter, but there was nowhere to put it, and she couldn't possibly throw it away. She blushed and tried to look severe and even a little bit short-sighted as she came up to them.

"Good morning," she said, copying her mother's voice. But that sounded so fearfully affected that she was ashamed, and stammered like a little girl, "Oh—er—have you come—is it about the marquee?"

"That's right, miss," said the tallest of the men, a lanky, freckled fellow, and he shifted his tool-bag, knocked back his straw hat and smiled down at her. "That's about it."

His smile was so easy, so friendly, that Laura recovered. What nice eyes he had, small, but such a dark blue! And now she looked at the others, they were smiling too. "Cheer up, we won't bite," their smile seemed to say. How very nice workmen were! And what a beautiful morning! She mustn't mention the morning; she must be business-like. The marquee.

"Well, what about the lily-lawn? Would that do?"

And she pointed to the lily-lawn with the hand that didn't hold the bread-and-butter. They turned, they stared in the direction. A little fat chap thrust out his under-lip, and the tall fellow frowned.

"I don't fancy it," said he. "Not conspicuous enough. You see, with a thing like a marquee," and he turned to Laura in his easy way, "you want to put it somewhere where it'll give you a bang slap in the eye, if you follow me."

Laura's upbringing made her wonder for a moment whether it was quite respectful of a workman to talk to her of bangs slap in the eye. But she did quite follow him.

"A corner of the tennis-court," she suggested. "But the band's going to be in one corner."

"H'm, going to have a band, are you?" said another of the workmen. He was pale. He had a haggard look as his dark eyes scanned the tennis-court. What was he thinking?

"Only a very small band," said Laura gently. Perhaps he wouldn't mind so much if the band was quite small. But the tall fellow interrupted.

"Look here, miss, that's the place. Against those trees. Over there. That'll do fine."

Against the karakas. Then the karaka-trees would be hidden. And they were so lovely, with their broad, gleaming leaves, and their clusters of yellow fruit. They were like trees you imagined growing on a desert island, proud, solitary, lifting their leaves and fruits to the sun in a kind of silent splendor. Must they be hidden by a marquee?

They must. Already the men had shouldered their staves and were making for the place. Only the tall fellow was left. He bent down, pinched a sprig of lavender, put his thumb and forefinger to his nose and snuffed up the smell. When Laura saw that gesture she forgot all about the karakas in her wonder at him caring for things like that—caring for the smell of lavender. How many men that she knew would have done such a thing. Oh, how extraordinarily nice workmen were, she thought. Why couldn't she have workmen for friends rather than the silly boys she danced with and who came to Sunday night supper? She would get on much better with men like these.

It's all the fault, she decided, as the tall fellow drew something on the back of an envelope, something that was to be looped up or left to hang, of these absurd class distinctions. Well, for her part, she didn't feel them. Not a bit, not an atom . . . And now there came the chock-chock of wooden hammers. Someone whistled, someone sang out, "Are you right there, matey?" "Matey!" The friendliness of it, the—the— Just to prove how happy she was, just to show the tall fellow how at home she felt, and how she despised stupid conventions, Laura took a big bite of her bread-and-butter as she stared at the little drawing. She felt just like a work-girl.

"Laura, Laura, where are you? Telephone, Laura!" a voice cried from the house.

"Coming!" Away she skimmed, over the lawn, up the path, up the steps, across the veranda, and into the porch. In the hall her father and Laurie were brushing their hats ready to go to the office.

"I say, Laura," said Laurie very fast, "you might just give a squiz at my coat before this afternoon. See if it wants pressing."

"I will," said she. Suddenly she couldn't stop herself. She ran at Laurie and gave him a small, quick squeeze. "Oh, I do love parties, don't you?" gasped Laura.

"Ra-ther," said Laurie's warm, boyish voice, and he squeezed his sister too, and gave her a gentle push. "Dash off to the telephone, old girl."

The telephone. "Yes, yes; oh yes. Kitty? Good morning, dear.

Come to lunch? Do, dear. Delighted of course. It will only be a very scratch meal—just the sandwich crusts and broken meringue-shells and what's left over. Yes, isn't it a perfect morning? Your white? Oh, I certainly should. One moment—hold the line. Mother's calling." And Laura sat back. "What, Mother? Can't hear."

Mrs. Sheridan's voice floated down the stairs. "Tell her to wear that sweet hat she had on last Sunday."

"Mother says you're to wear that *sweet* hat you had on last Sunday. Good. One o'clock. Bye-bye."

Laura put back the receiver, flung her arms over her head, took a deep breath, stretched and let them fall. "Huh," she sighed, and the moment after the sigh she sat up quickly. She was still, listening. All the doors in the house seemed to be open. The house was alive with soft, quick steps and running voices. The green baize door that led to the kitchen regions swung open and shut with a muffled thud. And now there came a long, chuckling absurd sound. It was the heavy piano being moved on its stiff castors. But the air! If you stopped to notice, was the air always like this? Little faint winds were playing chase in at the tops of the windows, out at the doors. And there were two tiny spots of sun, one on the inkpot, one on a silver photograph frame, playing too. Darling little spots. Especially the one on the inkpot lid. It was quite warm. A warm little silver star. She could have kissed it.

The front door bell pealed, and there sounded the rustle of Sadie's print skirt on the stairs. A man's voice murmured; Sadie answered, careless, "I'm sure I don't know. Wait. I'll ask Mrs. Sheridan."

"What is it, Sadie?" Laura came into the hall.

"It's the florist, Miss Laura."

It was, indeed. There, just inside the door, stood a wide, shallow tray full of pots of pink lilies. No other kind. Nothing but lilies—canna lilies, big pink flowers, wide open, radiant, almost frighteningly alive on bright crimson stems.

"O-oh, Sadie!" said Laura, and the sound was like a little moan.

She crouched down as if to warm herself at that blaze of lilies; she felt they were in her fingers, on her lips, growing in her breast.

"It's some mistake," she said faintly. "Nobody ever ordered so many. Sadie, go and find Mother."

But at that moment Mrs. Sheridan joined them.

"It's quite right," she said calmly. "Yes, I ordered them. Aren't they lovely?" She pressed Laura's arm. "I was passing the shop yesterday, and I saw them in the window. And I suddenly thought for once in my life I shall have enough canna lilies. The garden party will be a good excuse."

"But I thought you said you didn't mean to interfere," said Laura. Sadie had gone. The florist's man was still outside at his van. She put her arm round her mother's neck and gently, very gently, she bit her mother's ear.

"My darling child, you wouldn't like a logical mother, would you? Don't do that. Here's the man."

He carried more lilies still, another whole tray.

"Bank them up, just inside the door, on both sides of the porch, please," said Mrs. Sheridan. "Don't you agree, Laura?"

"Oh, I *do*, Mother."

In the drawing-room Meg, Jose and good little Hans had at last succeeded in moving the piano.

"Now, if we put this chesterfield against the wall and move everything out of the room except the chairs, don't you think?"

"Quite."

"Hans, move these tables into the smoking-room, and bring a sweeper to take these marks off the carpet and—one moment, Hans—" Jose loved giving orders to the servants, and they loved obeying her. She always made them feel they were taking part in some drama. "Tell Mother and Miss Laura to come here at once."

"Very good, Miss Jose."

She turned to Meg. "I want to hear what the piano sounds like, just in case I'm asked to sing this afternoon. Let's try over 'This Life Is Weary.'"

Pom! Ta-ta-ta *Tee*-ta! The piano burst out so passionately that Jose's face changed. She clasped her hands. She looked mournfully and enigmatically at her mother and Laura as they came in.

> *This Life is Wee*-ary,
> A Tear—a Sigh.
> A Love that *Chan*-ges,
> This Life is *Wee*-ary,
> A Tear—a Sigh.
> A Love that *Chan*-ges,
> And then . . . Goodbye!

But at the word "goodbye," and although the piano sounded more desperate than ever, her face broke into a brilliant, dreadfully unsympathetic smile.

"Aren't I in good voice, Mummy?" she beamed.

> *This Life is Wee*-ary,
> Hope comes to Die.
> A Dream—a *Wa*-kening.

But now Sadie interrupted them. "What is it, Sadie?"

"If you please, m'm, Cook says have you got the flags for the sandwiches?"

"The flags for the sandwiches, Sadie?" echoed Mrs. Sheridan dreamily. And the children knew by her face that she hadn't got them. "Let me see." And she said to Sadie firmly, "Tell Cook I'll let her have them in ten minutes."

Sadie went.

"Now, Laura," said her mother quickly, "come with me into the smoking-room. I've got the names somewhere on the back of an envelope. You'll have to write them out for me. Meg, go upstairs this minute and take that wet thing off your head. Jose, run and finish dressing this instant. Do you hear me, children, or shall I have to tell your father when he comes home tonight? And—and, Jose, pacify Cook if you do go into the kitchen, will you? I'm terrified of her this morning."

The envelope was found at last behind the dining-room clock, though how it had got there Mrs. Sheridan could not imagine.

"One of you children must have stolen it out of my bag, because I remember vividly—cream-cheese and lemon-curd. Have you done that?"

"Yes."

"Egg and—" Mrs. Sheridan held the envelope away from her. "It looks like mice. It can't be mice, can it?"

"Olive, pet," said Laura, looking over her shoulder.

"Yes, of course, olive. What a horrible combination it sounds. Egg and olive."

They were finished at last, and Laura took them off to the kitchen. She found Jose there pacifying the cook, who did not look at all terrifying.

"I have never seen such exquisite sandwiches," said Jose's rapturous voice. "How many kinds did you say there were, Cook? Fifteen?"

"Fifteen, Miss Jose."

"Well, Cook, I congratulate you."

Cook swept up crusts with the long sandwich knife, and smiled broadly.

"Godber's has come," announced Sadie, issuing out of the pantry. She had seen the man pass the window.

That meant the cream puffs had come. Godber's were famous for their cream puffs. Nobody ever thought of making them at home.

"Bring them in and put them on the table, my girl," ordered Cook.

Sadie brought them in and went back to the door. Of course Laura and Jose were far too grown up to really care about such things. All the same, they couldn't help agreeing that the puffs looked very attractive. Very. Cook began arranging them, shaking off the extra icing sugar.

"Don't they carry one back to all one's parties?" said Laura.

"I suppose they do," said practical Jose, who never liked to be carried back. "They look beautifully light and feathery, I must say."

"Have one each, my dears," said Cook in her comfortable voice. "Yer ma won't know."

Oh, impossible. Fancy cream puffs so soon after breakfast. The very idea made one shudder. All the same, two minutes later Jose and Laura were licking their fingers with that absorbed inward look that only comes from whipped cream.

"Let's go into the garden, out by the back way," suggested Laura. "I want to see how the men are getting on with the marquee. They're such awfully nice men."

But the back door was blocked by Cook, Sadie, Godber's man and Hans.

Something had happened.

"Tuk-ruk-tuk," clucked Cook like an agitated hen. Sadie had her hand clapped to her cheek as though she had toothache. Hans's face was screwed up in the effort to understand. Only Godber's man seemed to be enjoying himself; it was his story.

"What's the matter? What's happened?"

"There's been a horrible accident," said Cook. "A man killed."

"A man killed! Where? How? When?"

But Godber's man wasn't going to have his story snatched from under his very nose.

"Know those little cottages just below here, miss?" Know them? Of course she knew them. "Well, there's a young chap living there, name of Scott, a carter. His horse shied at a traction-engine, corner of Hawke Street this morning, and he was thrown out on the back of his head. Killed."

"Dead!" Laura stared at Godber's man.

"Dead when they picked him up," said Godber's man with relish. "They were taking the body home as I come up here." And he said to the cook, "He's left a wife and five little ones."

"Jose, come here." Laura caught hold of her sister's sleeve and dragged her through the kitchen to the other side of the green baize door. There she paused and leaned against it. "Jose!" she said, horrified, "however are we going to stop everything?"

"Stop everything, Laura!" cried Jose in astonishment. "What do you mean?"

"Stop the garden party, of course." Why did Jose pretend?

But Jose was still more amazed. "Stop the garden party? My dear Laura, don't be so absurd. Of course we can't do anything of the kind. Nobody expects us to. Don't be so extravagant."

"But we can't possibly have a garden party with a man dead just outside the front gate."

That really was extravagant, for the little cottages were in a lane to themselves at the very bottom of a steep rise that led up to the house. A broad road ran between. True, they were far too near. They were the greatest possible eyesore, and they had no right to be in that neighborhood at all. They were little mean dwellings painted a chocolate brown. In the garden patches there was nothing but cabbage stalks, sick hens and tomato cans. The very smoke coming out of their chimneys was poverty-stricken. Little rags and shreds of smoke, so unlike the great silvery plumes that uncurled from the Sheridans' chimneys. Washerwomen lived in the lane and sweeps and a cobbler, and a man whose house-front was studded all over with minute birdcages. Children swarmed. When the Sheridans were little they were forbidden to set foot there because of the revolting language and of what they might catch. But since they were grown up, Laura and Laurie on their prowls sometimes walked through. It was disgusting and sordid. They came out with a shudder. But still one must go everywhere; one must see everything. So through they went.

"And just think of what the band would sound like to that poor woman," said Laura.

"Oh, Laura!" Jose began to be seriously annoyed. "If you're going to stop a band playing every time someone has an accident, you'll lead a very strenuous life. I'm every bit as sorry about it as you. I feel just as sympathetic." Her eyes hardened. She looked at her sister just as she used to when they were little and fighting together. "You won't bring a drunken workman back to life by being sentimental," she said softly.

"Drunk! Who said he was drunk?" Laura turned furiously on Jose. She said just as they had used to say on those occasions, "I'm going straight up to tell Mother."

"Do, dear," cooed Jose.

"Mother, can I come into your room?" Laura turned the big glass doorknob.

"Of course, child. Why, what's the matter? What's given you such a color?" And Mrs. Sheridan turned round from her dressing-table. She was trying on a new hat.

"Mother, a man's been killed," began Laura.

"*Not* in the garden?" interrupted her mother.

"No, no!"

"Oh, what a fright you gave me!" Mrs. Sheridan sighed with relief, and took off the big hat and held it on her knees.

"But listen, Mother," said Laura. Breathless, half-choking, she told the dreadful story. "Of course, we can't have our party, can we?" she pleaded. "The band and everybody arriving. They'd hear us, Mother; they're nearly neighbors!"

To Laura's astonishment her mother behaved just like Jose; it was harder to bear because she seemed amused. She refused to take Laura seriously.

"But, my dear child, use your common sense. It's only by accident we've heard of it. If someone had died there normally—and I can't understand how they keep alive in those poky little holes—we should still be having our party, shouldn't we?"

Laura had to say yes to that, but she felt it was all wrong. She sat down on her mother's sofa and pinched the cushion frill.

"Mother, isn't it really terribly heartless of us?" she asked.

"Darling!" Mrs. Sheridan got up and came over to her, carrying the hat. Before Laura could stop her, she had popped it on. "My child!" said her mother, "the hat is yours. It's made for you. It's much too young for me. I have never seen you look such a picture. Look at yourself!" And she held up her hand-mirror.

"But, mother," Laura began again. She couldn't look at herself; she turned aside.

This time Mrs. Sheridan lost patience just as Jose had done.

"You are being very absurd, Laura," she said coldly. "People like that don't expect sacrifices from us. And it's not very sympathetic to spoil everybody's enjoyment as you're doing now."

"I don't understand," said Laura, and she walked quickly out of the room into her own bedroom. There, quite by chance, the first thing she saw was this charming girl in the mirror, in her black hat trimmed with gold daisies, and a long black velvet ribbon. Never had she imagined she could look like that. Is Mother right? she thought. And now she hoped her mother was right. Am I being extravagant? Perhaps it was extravagant. Just for a moment she had another glimpse of that poor woman and those little children, and the body being carried into the house. But it all seemed blurred, unreal, like a picture in the newspaper. I'll remember it again after the party's over, she decided. And somehow that seemed quite the best plan . . .

Lunch was over by half-past one. By half-past two they were all ready for the fray. The green-coated band had arrived and was established in a corner of the tennis-court.

"My dear!" trilled Kitty Maitland, "aren't they too like frogs for words? You ought to have arranged them round the pond with the conductor in the middle on a leaf."

Laurie arrived and hailed them on his way to dress. At the sight of him Laura remembered the accident again. She wanted to tell him. If Laurie agreed with the others, then it was bound to be all right. And she followed him into the hall.

"Laurie!"

"Hallo!" He was half-way upstairs, but when he turned round and saw Laura he suddenly puffed out his cheeks and goggled his eyes at her. "My word, Laura! You do look stunning," said Laurie. "What an absolutely topping hat!"

Laura said faintly, "Is it?" and smiled up at Laurie, and didn't tell him after all.

Soon after that people began coming in streams. The band struck up; the hired waiters ran from the house to the marquee. Wherever you looked there were couples strolling, bending to the flowers, greeting, moving on over the lawn. They were like bright birds that had alighted in the Sheridans' garden for this one afternoon, on their way to—where? Ah, what happiness it is to be with people who all are happy, to press hands, press cheeks, smile into eyes.

"Darling Laura, how well you look!"

"What a becoming hat, child!"

"Laura, you look quite Spanish. I've never seen you look so striking."

And Laura, glowing, answered softly, "Have you had tea? Won't you have an ice? The passion-fruit ices really are rather special." She ran to her father and begged him. "Daddy darling, can't the band have something to drink?"

And the perfect afternoon slowly ripened, slowly faded, slowly its petals closed.

"Never a more delightful garden party ..." "The greatest success ..." "Quite the most ..."

Laura helped her mother with the goodbyes. They stood side by side in the porch till it was all over.

"All over, all over, thank heaven," said Mrs. Sheridan. "Round up the others, Laura. Let's go and have some fresh coffee. I'm exhausted. Yes, it's been very successful. But oh, these parties, these parties! Why will you children insist on giving parties!" And they all of them sat down in the deserted marquee.

"Have a sandwich, Daddy dear. I wrote the flag."

"Thanks." Mr. Sheridan took a bite and the sandwich was gone. He took another. "I suppose you didn't hear of a beastly accident that happened today?" he said.

"My dear," said Mrs. Sheridan, holding up her hand, "we did. It nearly ruined the party. Laura insisted we should put it off."

"Oh, Mother!" Laura didn't want to be teased about it.

"It was a horrible affair all the same," said Mr. Sheridan. "The chap was married too. Lived just below in the lane, and leaves a wife and half a dozen kiddies, so they say."

An awkward little silence fell. Mrs. Sheridan fidgeted with her cup. Really, it was very tactless of Father . . .

Suddenly she looked up. There on the table were all those sandwiches, cakes, puffs, all uneaten, all going to be wasted. She had one of her brilliant ideas.

"I know," she said. "Let's make up a basket. Let's send that poor creature some of this perfectly good food. At any rate, it will be the greatest treat for the children. Don't you agree? And she's sure to have neighbors calling in and so on. What a point to have it all ready prepared. Laura!" She jumped up. "Get me the big basket out of the stairs cupboard."

"But, Mother, do you really think it's a good idea?" said Laura.

Again, how curious, she seemed to be different from them all. To take scraps from their party. Would the poor woman really like that?

"Of course! What's the matter with you today? An hour or two ago you were insisting on us being sympathetic, and now—"

Oh well! Laura ran for the basket. It was filled, it was heaped by her mother.

"Take it yourself, darling," said she. "Run down just as you are. No, wait, take the arum lilies too. People of that class are so impressed by arum lilies."

"The stems will ruin her lace frock," said practical Jose.

So they would. Just in time. "Only the basket, then. And, Laura!"—her mother followed her out of the marquee—"don't on any account—"

"What, Mother?"

No, better not put such ideas into the child's head! "Nothing! Run along."

It was just growing dusky as Laura shut their garden gates. A big dog ran by like a shadow. The road gleamed white, and down below in the hollow the little cottages were in deep shade. How quiet it seemed after the afternoon. Here she was going down the hill to somewhere where a man lay dead, and she couldn't realize it. Why couldn't she? She stopped a minute. And it seemed to her that kisses, voices, tinkling spoons, laughter, the smell of crushed grass were somehow inside her. She had no room for anything else. How strange! She looked up at the pale sky, and all she thought was, Yes, it was the most successful party.

Now the broad road was crossed. The lane began, smoky and dark. Women in shawls and men's tweed caps hurried by. Men hung over the palings; the children played in the doorways. A low hum came from the mean little cottages. In some of them there was a flicker of light, and a shadow, crab-like, moved across the window. Laura bent her head and hurried on. She wished now she had put on a coat. How her frock shone! And the big hat with the velvet streamer—if only it was another hat! Were the people looking at her? They must be. It was a mistake to have come; she knew all along it was a mistake. Should she go back even now?

No, too late. This was the house. It must be. A dark knot of people stood outside. Beside the gate an old, old woman with a crutch sat in a chair, watching. She had her feet on a newspaper. The voices stopped as Laura drew near. The group patted. It was as though she was expected, as though they had known she was coming here.

Laura was terribly nervous. Tossing the velvet ribbon over her shoulder, she said to a woman standing by, "Is this Mrs. Scott's house?" and the woman, smiling queerly, said, "It is, my lass."

Oh, to be away from this! She actually said, "Help me, God," as she walked up the tiny path and knocked. To be away from those staring eyes, or to be covered up in anything, one of those women's shawls even. I'll just leave the basket and go, she decided. I shan't even wait for it to be emptied.

Then the door opened. A little woman in black showed in the gloom.

Laura said, "Are you Mrs. Scott?" But to her horror the woman answered, "Walk in please, miss," and she was shut in the passage.

"No," said Laura, "I don't want to come in. I only want to leave this basket. Mother sent—"

The little woman in the gloomy passage seemed not to have heard her. "Step this way, please, miss," she said in an oily voice, and Laura followed her.

She found herself in a wretched little low kitchen, lighted by a smoky lamp. There was a woman sitting before the fire.

"Em," said the little creature who had let her in. "Em! It's a young lady." She turned to Laura. She said meaningly, "I'm 'er sister, miss. You'll excuse 'er, won't you?"

"Oh, but of course!" said Laura. "Please, please don't disturb her. I—I only want to leave—"

But at that moment the woman at the fire turned round. Her face, puffed up, red, with swollen eyes and swollen lips, looked terrible. She seemed as though she couldn't understand why Laura was there. What did it mean? Why was this stranger standing in the kitchen with a basket? What was it all about? And the poor face puckered up again.

"All right, my dear," said the other. "I'll thenk the young lady."

And again she began, "You'll excuse her, miss, I'm sure," and her face, swollen too, tried an oily smile.

Laura only wanted to get out, to get away. She was back in the passage. The door opened. She walked straight through into the bedroom, where the dead man was lying.

"You'd like a look at 'im, wouldn't you?" said Em's sister, and she brushed past Laura over to the bed. "Don't be afraid, my lass"—and now her voice sounded fond and sly, and fondly she drew down the sheet—" 'e looks a picture. There's nothing to show. Come along, my dear."

Laura came.

There lay a young man, fast asleep—sleeping so soundly, so deeply, that he was far, far away from them both. Oh, so remote, so peaceful. He was dreaming. Never wake him up again. His head was sunk in the pillow, his eyes were closed; they were blind under the closed eyelids. He was given up to his dream. What did garden parties and baskets and lace frocks matter to him? He was far from all those things. He was wonderful, beautiful. While they were laughing and while the band was playing, this marvel had come to the lane. Happy . . . happy . . . All is well, said that sleeping face. This is just as it should be. I am content.

But all the same you had to cry, and she couldn't go out of the room without saying something to him. Laura gave a loud childish sob.

"Forgive my hat," she said.

And this time she didn't wait for Em's sister. She found her way out of the door, down the path, past all those dark people. At the corner of the lane she met Laurie.

He stepped out of the shadow. "Is that you, Laura?"

"Yes."

"Mother was getting anxious. Was it all right?"

"Yes, quite. Oh, Laurie!" She took his arm, she pressed up against him.

"I say, you're not crying, are you?" asked her brother.

Laura shook her head. She was.

Laurie put his arm round her shoulder. "Don't cry," he said in his warm, loving voice. "Was it awful?"

"No," sobbed Laura. "It was simply marvelous. But, Laurie—" She stopped, she looked at her brother. "Isn't life," she stammered, "isn't life—" But what life was she couldn't explain. No matter. He quite understood.

"*Isn't* it, darling?" said Laurie.

HALF A GRAPEFRUIT

Alice Munro

✷ ✷ ✷

Rose wrote the Entrance, she went across the bridge, she went to high school.

There were four large clean windows along the wall. There were new fluorescent lights. The class was Health and Guidance, a new idea. Boys and girls mixed until after Christmas, when they got on to Family Life. The teacher was young and optimistic. She wore a dashing red suit that flared out over the hips. She went up and down, up and down the rows, making everybody say what they had for breakfast, to see if they were keeping Canada's Food Rules.

Differences soon became evident, between town and country.

"Fried potatoes."

"Bread and corn syrup."

"Tea and porridge."

"Tea and bread."

"Tea and fried eggs and cottage roll."

"Raisin pie."

There was some laughing, the teacher making ineffectual scolding faces. She was getting to the town side of the room. A rough sort of segregation was maintained, voluntarily, in the classroom. Over here people claimed to have eaten toast and marmalade, bacon and eggs, Corn Flakes, even waffles and syrup. Orange juice, said a few.

Rose had stuck herself on to the back of a town row. West Hanratty was not represented, except by her. She was wanting badly to align herself with towners, against her place of origin, to attach herself to those waffle-eating coffee-drinking aloof and knowledgeable possessors of breakfast nooks.

"Half a grapefruit," she said boldly. Nobody else had thought of it.

As a matter of fact Flo would have thought eating grapefruit for breakfast as bad as drinking champagne. They didn't even sell grapefruit in the store. They didn't go in much for fresh fruit. A few spotty bananas, small unpromising oranges. Flo believed, as many country people did, that anything not well cooked was bad for the stomach. For breakfast they too had tea and porridge. Puffed Rice in the summertime. The first morning the Puffed Rice, light as pollen, came spilling into the bowl, was as festive, as encouraging a time as the first day walking on the hard road without rubbers or the first day the door could be left open in the lovely, brief time between frost and flies.

Rose was pleased with herself for thinking of the grapefruit and with the way she had said it, in so bold, yet so natural, a voice.

Her voice could go dry altogether in school, her heart could roll itself up into a thumping ball and lodge in her throat, sweat could plaster her blouse to her arms, in spite of Mum. Her nerves were calamitous.

She was walking home across the bridge a few days later, and she heard someone calling. Not her name but she knew it was meant for her, so she softened her steps on the boards, and listened. The voices were underneath her, it seemed, though she could look down through the cracks and see nothing but fast-running water. Somebody must be hidden down by the pilings. The voices were wistful, so delicately disguised she could not tell if they were boys' or girls'.

"Half-a-grapefruit!"

She would hear that called, now and again, for years, called out from an alley or a dark window. She would never let on she heard, but would soon have to touch her face, wipe the moisture away from her upper lip. We sweat for our pretensions.

It could have been worse. Disgrace was the easiest thing to come by. High school life was hazardous, in that harsh clean light, and nothing was ever forgotten. Rose could have been the girl who lost the Kotex. That was probably a country girl, carrying the Kotex in her pocket or in the back of her notebook, for use later in the day. Anybody who lived at a distance might have done that. Rose herself had done it. There was a Kotex dispenser in the girls' washroom but it was always empty, would swallow your dimes but disgorge nothing in return. There was the famous pact made by two country girls to seek out the janitor at lunchtime, ask him to fill it. No use.

"Which one of you is the one that needs it?" he said. They fled. They said his room under the stairs had an old grimy couch in it, and a cat's skeleton. They swore to it.

That Kotex must have fallen on the floor, maybe in the cloakroom, then been picked up and smuggled somehow into the trophy case in the main hall. There it came to public notice. Folding and carrying had spoiled its fresh look, rubbed its surface, so that it was possible to imagine it had been warmed against the body. A great scandal. In morning assembly, the Principal made reference to a disgusting object. He vowed to discover, expose, flog and expel the culprit who had put it on view. Every girl in the school was denying knowledge of it. Theories abounded. Rose was afraid that she might be a leading candidate for ownership, so was relieved when responsibility was fixed on a big sullen country girl named Muriel Mason, who wore slub rayon housedresses to school, and had B.O.

"You got the rag on today, Muriel?" boys would say to her now, would call after her.

"If I was Muriel Mason I would want to kill myself," Rose heard a senior girl say to another on the stairs. "I *would* kill myself." She spoke not pityingly but impatiently.

Every day when Rose got home she would tell Flo about what went on in school. Flo enjoyed the episode of the Kotex, would ask about fresh developments. Half-a-grapefruit she never got to hear about. Rose would not have told her anything in which she did not play a superior, an onlooker's part. Pitfalls were for others, Flo and Rose agreed. The change in Rose, once she left the scene, crossed the bridge, changed herself into chronicler, was remarkable. No nerves anymore. A loud skeptical voice, some hip-swinging in a red and yellow plaid skirt, more than a hint of swaggering.

Flo and Rose had switched roles. Now Rose was the one bringing stories home, Flo was the one who knew the names of the characters and was waiting to hear.

Horse Nicholson, Del Fairbridge, Runt Chesterton. Florence Dodie, Shirley Pickering, Ruby Carruthers. Flo waited daily for news of them. She called them Jokers.

"Well, what did those jokers get up to today?"

They would sit in the kitchen, the door wide open to the store in case any customers came in, and to the stairs in case her father called. He was in bed. Flo made coffee or she told Rose to get a couple of Cokes out of the cooler.

This is the sort of story Rose brought home:

Ruby Carruthers was a slutty sort of girl, a redhead with a bad squint. (One of the great differences between then and now, at least in the country, and places like West Hanratty, was that squints and walleyes were let alone, teeth overlapped or protruded any way they liked.) Ruby Carruthers worked for the Bryants, the hardware people; she did housework for her board and stayed in the house when they went away, as they often did, to the horse races or the hockey games or to Florida. One time when she was there alone three boys went over to see her. Del Fairbridge, Horse Nicholson, Runt Chesterton.

"To see what they could get," Flo put in. She looked at the ceiling and told Rose to keep her voice down. Her father would not tolerate this sort of story.

Del Fairbridge was a good-looking boy, conceited, and not very clever. He said he would go into the house and persuade Ruby to do it with him, and if he could get her to do it with all three of them, he would. What he didn't know was that Horse Nicholson had already arranged with Ruby to meet him under the veranda.

"Spiders in there, likely," said Flo. "I guess they don't care."

While Del was wandering around the dark house looking for her, Ruby was under the veranda with Horse, and Runt who was in on the whole plan was sitting on the veranda steps keeping watch, no doubt listening attentively to the bumping and the breathing.

Presently Horse crawled out and said he was going into the house to find Del, not to enlighten him but to see how the joke was working, this being the most important part of the proceedings, as far as Horse was concerned. He found Del eating marshmallows in the pantry and saying Ruby Carruthers wasn't fit to piss on, he could do better any day, and he was going home.

Meanwhile Runt had crawled under the veranda and got to work on Ruby.

"Jesus Murphy!" said Flo.

Then Horse came out of the house and Runt and Ruby could hear him overhead, walking on the veranda. Said Ruby, who is that? And Runt said, oh, that's only Horse Nicholson. *Then who the hell are you?* said Ruby.

Jesus Murphy!

Rose did not bother with the rest of the story, which was that Ruby got into a bad mood, sat on the veranda steps with the dirt from underneath all over her clothes and in her hair, refused to smoke a cigarette or share a package of cupcakes (now probably rather squashed) that Runt had swiped from the grocery store where he worked after school. They teased her to tell them what was the matter and at last she said, "I think I got a right to know who I'm doing it with."

"She'll get what she deserves," said Flo philosophically. Other people thought so too. It was the fashion, if you picked up any of Ruby's things, by mistake, particularly her gym suit or running shoes, to go and wash your hands, so you wouldn't risk getting V.D.

Upstairs Rose's father was having a coughing fit. These fits were desperate, but they had become used to them. Flo got up and went to the bottom of the stairs. She listened there until the fit was over.

"That medicine doesn't help him one iota," she said. "That doctor couldn't put a Band-Aid on straight." To the end, she blamed all Rose's father's troubles on medicines, doctors.

"If you ever got up to any of that with a boy it would be the end of you," she said. "I mean it."

Rose flushed with rage and said she would die first.

"I hope so," Flo said.

* * *

Here is the sort of story Flo told Rose:

When her mother died, Flo was twelve, and her father gave her away. He gave her to a well-to-do farming family who were to work her for her board and send her to school. But most of the time they did not send her. There was too much work to be done. They were hard people.

"If you were picking apples and there was one left on the tree you would have to go back and pick over every tree in the entire orchard. The same when you were out picking up stones in the field. Leave one and you had to do the whole field again."

The wife was the sister of a bishop. She was always careful of her skin, rubbing it with Hinds Honey and Almond. She took a high tone with everybody and was sarcastic and believed that she had married down.

"But she was good-looking," said Flo, "and she gave me one thing. It was a long pair of satin gloves, they were a light brown color. Fawn. They were lovely. I never meant to lose them but I did."

Flo had to take the men's dinner to them in the far field. The husband opened it up and said, "Why is there no pie in this dinner?"

"If you want any pie you can make it yourself," said Flo, in the exact words and tone of her mistress when they were packing the dinner. It was not surprising that she could imitate that woman so well; she was always doing it, even practicing at the mirror. It *was* surprising she let it out then.

The husband was amazed, but recognized the imitation. He marched Flo back to the house and demanded of his wife if that was what she had said. He was a big man, and very bad-tempered. No, it is not true, said the bishop's sister, that girl is nothing but a troublemaker and a liar. She faced him down, and when she got Flo alone she hit her such a clout that Flo was knocked across the room into a cupboard. Her scalp was cut. It healed in time without stitches (the bishop's sister didn't get the doctor, she didn't want talk), and Flo had the scar still.

She never went back to school after that.

Just before she was fourteen she ran away. She lied about her age and got a job in the glove factory, in Hanratty. But the bishop's sister found out where she was, and every once in a while would come to see her. We forgive you, Flo. You ran away and left us but we still think of you as our Flo and our friend. You are welcome to come out and spend a day with us. Wouldn't you like a day in the country? It's not very healthy in the glove factory, for a young person. You need the air. Why don't you come and see us? Why don't you come today?

And every time Flo accepted this invitation it would turn out that there was a big fruit preserving or chili sauce making in progress, or they were wallpapering or spring-cleaning, or the threshers were coming. All she ever got to see of the country was where she threw the dishwater over the fence. She never could understand why she went or why she stayed. It was a long way, to turn around and walk back to town. And they were such a helpless outfit on their own. The bishop's sister put her preserving jars away dirty. When you brought them up from the cellar there would be bits of mold growing in them, clots of fuzzy rotten fruit on the bottom. How could you help but be sorry for people like that?

When the bishop's sister was in the hospital, dying, it happened that Flo was in there too. She was in for her gallbladder operation, which Rose could just remember. The bishop's sister heard that Flo was there and wanted to see her. So Flo let herself be hoisted into a wheelchair and wheeled down the hall, and as soon as she laid eyes on the woman in the bed—the tall, smooth-skinned woman all bony and spotted now, drugged and cancerous—she began an overwhelming nosebleed, the first and last she ever suffered in her life. The red blood was whipping out of her, she said, like streamers.

She had the nurses running for help up and down the hall. It seemed as if nothing could stop it. When she lifted her head it shot right on the sick woman's bed, when she lowered her head it streamed down on the floor. They had to put her in ice packs, finally. She never got to say good-bye to the woman in the bed.

"I never did say good-bye to her."

"Would you want to?"

"Well yes," said Flo. "Oh yes. I would."

✳ ✳ ✳

Rose brought a pile of books home every night. Latin, Algebra, Ancient and Medieval History, French, Geography. *The Merchant of Venice, A Tale of Two Cities, Shorter Poems, Macbeth.* Flo expressed hostility to them as she did toward all books. The hostility seemed to increase with a book's weight and size, the darkness and gloominess of its binding and the length and difficulty of the words in its title. *Shorter Poems* enraged her, because she opened it and found a poem that was five pages long.

She made rubble out of the titles. Rose believed she deliberately mispronounced. Ode came out Odd and Ulysses had a long shh in it, as if the hero was drunk.

Rose's father had to come downstairs to go to the bathroom. He hung on to the banister and moved slowly but without halting. He wore a brown wool bathrobe with a tasseled tie. Rose avoided looking at his face. This was not particularly because of the alterations his sickness might have made, but because of the bad opinion of herself she was afraid she would find written there. It was for him she brought the books, no doubt about it, to show off to him. And he did look at them, he could not walk past any book in the world without picking it up and looking at its title. But all he said was, "Look out you don't get too smart for your own good."

Rose believed he said that to please Flo, in case she might be listening. She was in the store at the time. But Rose imagined that no matter where Flo was, he would speak as if she might be listening. He was anxious to please Flo, to anticipate her objections. He had made a decision, it seemed. Safety lay with Flo.

Rose never answered him back. When he spoke she automatically bowed her head, tightened her lips in an expression that was secretive, but carefully not disrespectful. She was circumspect. But all her need for flaunting, her high hopes for herself, her gaudy ambitions, were not hidden from him. He knew them all, and Rose was ashamed, just to be in the same room with him. She felt that she disgraced him, had disgraced him somehow from the time she was born, and would disgrace him still more thoroughly in the future. But she was not repenting. She knew her own stubbornness; she did not mean to change.

Flo was his idea of what a woman ought to be. Rose knew that, and indeed he often said it. A woman ought to be energetic, practical, clever at making and saving; she ought to be shrewd, good at bargaining and bossing and seeing through people's pretensions. At the same time she should be naive intellectually, childlike, contemptuous of maps and long words and anything in books, full of charming jumbled notions, superstitions, traditional beliefs.

"Women's minds are different," he said to Rose during one of the calm, even friendly periods, when she was a bit younger. Perhaps he forgot that Rose was, or would be, a woman herself. "They believe what they have to believe. You can't follow their thought." He was saying this in connection with a belief of Flo's, that wearing rubbers in the house would make you go blind. "But they can manage life some ways, that's their talent, it's not in their heads, there's something they are smarter at than a man."

So part of Rose's disgrace was that she was female but mistakenly so, would not turn out to be the right kind of woman. But there was more to it. The real problem was that she combined and carried on what he must have thought of as the worst qualities in himself. All the things he had beaten down, successfully submerged, in himself, had surfaced again in her, and she was showing no will to combat them. She mooned and daydreamed, she was vain and eager to show off; her whole life was in her head. She had not inherited the thing he took pride in, and counted on—his skill with his hands, his thoroughness and conscientiousness at any work; in fact she was unusually clumsy, slapdash, ready to cut corners. The sight of her slopping around with her hands in the dishpan, her thoughts a thousand miles away, her rump already bigger than Flo's, her hair wild and bushy; the sight of the large and indolent and self-absorbed fact of her seemed to fill him with irritation, with melancholy, almost with disgust.

All of which Rose knew. Until he had passed through the room she was holding herself still, she was looking at herself through his eyes. She too could hate the space she occupied. But the minute he was gone she recovered. She went back into her thoughts or to the mirror, where she was often busy these days, piling all her hair up on top of her head, turning part way to see the line of her bust, or pulling the skin to see how she would look with a slant, a very slight, provocative slant, to her eyes.

She knew perfectly well, too, that he had another set of feelings about her. She knew he felt pride in her as well as this nearly uncontrollable irritation and apprehension; the truth was, the final truth was, that he would not have her otherwise and willed her as she was. Or one part of him did. Naturally he had to keep denying this. Out of humility, he had to, and perversity. Perverse humility. And he had to seem to be in sufficient agreement with Flo.

Rose did not really think this through, or want to. She was as uneasy as he was, about the way their chords struck together.

✯ ✯ ✯

When Rose came home from school Flo said to her, "Well, it's a good thing you got here. You have to stay in the store."

Her father was going to London, to the Veterans' Hospital.

"Why?"

"Don't ask me. The doctor said."

"Is he worse?"

"*I* don't know. *I* don't know anything. That do-nothing doctor doesn't think so. He came this morning and looked him over and he says he's going. We're lucky, we got Billy Pope to run him down."

Billy Pope was a cousin of Flo's who worked in the butcher shop. He used actually to live at the slaughterhouse, in two rooms with cement floors, smelling naturally of tripe and entrails and live pig. But he must have had a home-loving nature; he grew geraniums in old tobacco cans, on the thick cement windowsills. Now he had the little apartment over the shop, and had saved his money and bought a car, an Oldsmobile. This was shortly after the war, when new cars made a special sensation. When he came to visit he kept wandering to the window and taking a look at it, saying something to call attention, such as, "She's light on the hay but you don't get the fertilizer out of her."

Flo was proud of him and the car.

"See, Billy Pope's got a big backseat, if your father needs to lay down."

"Flo!"

Rose's father was calling her. When he was in bed at first he very seldom called her, and then discreetly, apologetically even. But he had got past that, called her often, made up reasons, she said, to get her upstairs.

"How does he think he'll get along without me down there?" she said. "He can't let me alone five minutes." She seemed proud of this, although often she would make him wait; sometimes she would go to the bottom of the stairs and force him to call down further details about why he needed her. She told people in the store that he wouldn't let her alone for five minutes, and how she had to change his sheets twice a day. That was true. His sheets became soaked with sweat. Late at night she or Rose, or both of them, would be out at the washing machine in the woodshed. Sometimes, Rose saw, her father's underwear was stained. She would not want to look, but Flo held it up, waved it almost under Rose's nose, cried out, "Lookit that again!" and made clucking noises that were a burlesque of disapproval.

Rose hated her at these times, hated her father as well; his sickness; the poverty or frugality that made it unthinkable for them to send things to the laundry; the way there was not a thing in their lives they were protected from. Flo was there to see to that.

★ ★ ★

Rose stayed in the store. No one came in. It was a gritty, windy day, past the usual time for snow, though there hadn't been any. She could hear Flo moving around upstairs, scolding and encouraging, getting her father dressed, probably, packing his suitcase, looking for things. Rose had her schoolbooks on the counter and to shut out the household noises she was reading a story in her English book. It was a story by Katherine Mansfield, called "The Garden Party." There were poor people in that story. They lived along the lane at the bottom of the garden. They were viewed with compassion. All very well. But Rose was angry in a way that the story did not mean her to be. She could not really understand what she was angry about, but it had something to do with the fact that she was sure Katherine Mansfield was never obliged to look at stained underwear; her relatives might be cruel and frivolous but their accents would be agreeable; her compassion was floating on clouds of good fortune, deplored by herself, no doubt, but *despised* by Rose. Rose was getting to be a prig about poverty, and would stay that way for a long time.

She heard Billy Pope come into the kitchen and shout out cheerfully, "Well, I guess yez wondered where I was."

Katherine Mansfield had no relatives who said *yez*.

Rose had finished the story. She picked up *Macbeth*. She had memorized some speeches from it. She memorized things from Shakespeare, and poems, other than the things they had to memorize for school. She didn't imagine herself as an actress, playing Lady Macbeth on a stage, when she said them. She imagined herself *being* her, being Lady Macbeth.

"I come on foot," Billy Pope was shouting up the stairs. "I had to take her in." He assumed everyone would know he meant the car. "I don't know what it is. I can't idle her, she stalls on me. I didn't want to go down to the city with anything running not right. Rose home?"

Billy Pope had been fond of Rose ever since she was a little girl. He used to give her a dime, and say, "Save up and buy yourself some corsets." That was when she was flat and thin. His joke.

He came into the store.

"Well Rose, you bein a good girl?"

She barely spoke to him.

"You goin at your schoolbooks? You want to be a school-teacher?"

"I might." She had no intention of being a schoolteacher. But it was surprising how people would let you alone, once you admitted to that ambition.

"This is a sad day for you folks here," said Billy Pope in a lower voice.

Rose lifted her head and looked at him coldly.

"I mean, your dad goin down to the hospital. They'll fix him up, though. They got all the equipment down there. They got the good doctors."

"I doubt it," Rose said. She hated that too, the way people hinted at things and then withdrew, that slyness. Death and sex were what they did that about.

"They'll fix him and get him back by spring."

"Not if he has lung cancer," Rose said firmly. She had never said that before and certainly Flo had not said it.

Billy Pope looked as miserable and ashamed for her as if she had said something very dirty.

"Now that isn't no way for you to talk. You don't talk that way. He's going to be coming downstairs and he could of heard you."

There is no denying the situation gave Rose pleasure, at times. A severe pleasure, when she was not too mixed up in it, washing the sheets or listening to a coughing fit. She dramatized her own part in it, saw herself clear-eyed and unsurprised, refusing all deceptions, young in years but old in bitter experience of life. In such spirit she had said *lung cancer.*

Billy Pope phoned the garage. It turned out that the car would not be fixed until suppertime. Rather than set out then, Billy Pope would stay overnight, sleeping on the kitchen couch. He and Rose's father would go down to the hospital in the morning.

"There don't need to be any great hurry, I'm not going to jump for *him,*" said Flo, meaning the doctor. She had come into the store to get a can of salmon, to make a loaf. Although she was not going anywhere and had not planned to, she had put on stockings, and a clean blouse and skirt.

She and Billy Pope kept up a loud conversation in the kitchen while she got supper. Rose sat on the high stool and recited in her head, looking out the front window at West Hanratty, the dust scudding along the street, the dry puddle holes.

> Come to my woman's breasts.
> And take my milk for gall, you murdering ministers!

A jolt it would give them, if she yelled that into the kitchen.

At six o'clock she locked the store. When she went into the kitchen she was surprised to see her father there. She hadn't heard him. He hadn't been either talking or coughing. He was dressed in his good suit, which was an unusual color—a dark oily sort of green. Perhaps it had been cheap.

"Look at him all dressed up," Flo said. "He thinks he looks smart. He's so pleased with himself he wouldn't go back to bed."

Rose's father smiled unnaturally, obediently.

"How do you feel now?" Flo said.

"I feel all right."

"You haven't had a coughing spell, anyway."

Her father's face was newly shaved, smooth and delicate, like the animals they had once carved at school out of yellow laundry soap.

"Maybe I ought to get up and stay up."

"That's the ticket," Billy Pope said boisterously. "No more laziness. Get up and stay up. Get back to work."

There was a bottle of whiskey on the table. Billy Pope had brought it. The men drank it out of little glasses that had once held cream cheese. They topped it up with half an inch or so of water.

Brian, Rose's half brother, had come in from playing somewhere; noisy, muddy, with the cold smell of outdoors around him.

Just as he came in Rose said, "Can I have some?" nodding at the whiskey bottle.

"Girls don't drink that," Billy Pope said.

"Give you some and we'd have Brian whining after some," said Flo.

"Can I have some?" said Brian, whining, and Flo laughed uproariously, sliding her own glass behind the bread box. "See there?"

★ ★ ★

"There used to be people around in the old days that did cures," said Billy Pope at the supper table. "But you don't hear about none of them no more."

"Too bad we can't get hold of one of them right now," said Rose's father, getting hold of and conquering a coughing fit.

"There was the one faith healer I used to hear my dad talk about," said Billy Pope. "He had a way of talkin, he talked like the

Bible. So this deaf fellow went to him and he seen him and he cured him of his deafness. Then he says to him, 'Durst hear?'"

"Dost hear?" Rose suggested. She had drained Flo's glass while getting out the bread for supper, and felt more kindly disposed toward all her relatives.

"That's it. *Dost hear?* And the fellow said yes, he did. So the faith healer says then, *Dost believe?* Now maybe the fellow didn't understand what he meant. And he says, *What in?* So the faith healer he got mad, and he took away the fellow's hearing like that, and he went home deaf as he come."

Flo said that out where she lived when she was little, there was a woman who had second sight. Buggies, and later on, cars, would be parked to the end of her lane on Sundays. That was the day people came from a distance to consult with her. Mostly they came to consult her about things that were lost.

"Didn't they want to get in touch with their relations?" Rose's father said, egging Flo on as he liked to when she was telling a story. "I thought she could put you in touch with the dead."

"Well, most of them seen enough of their relations when they was alive."

It was rings and wills and livestock they wanted to know about; where had things disappeared to?

"One fellow I knew went to her and he had lost his wallet. He was a man that worked on the railway line. And she says to him, well, do you remember it was about a week ago you were working along the tracks and you come along near an orchard and you thought you would like an apple? So you hopped over the fence and it was right then you dropped your wallet, right then and there in the long grass. But a dog came along, she says, a dog picked it up and dropped it a ways further along the fence, and that's where you'll find it. Well, he'd forgot all about the orchard and climbing that fence and he was so amazed at her, he gave her a dollar. And he went and found his wallet in the very place she described. This is true, I knew him. But the money was all chewed up, it was all chewed up in shreds, and when he found that he was so mad he said he wished he never give her so much!"

"Now, you never went to her," said Rose's father. "You wouldn't put your faith in the like of that?" When he talked to Flo he often spoke in country phrases, and adopted the country habit of teasing, saying the opposite of what's true, or believed tô be true.

"No, I never went actually to ask her anything," Flo said. "But one time I went. I had to go over there and get some green onions. My mother was sick and suffering with her nerves and this woman sent word over, that she had some green onions was good for nerves. It wasn't nerves at all it was cancer, so what good they did I don't know."

Flo's voice climbed and hurried on, embarrassed that she had let that out.

"I had to go and get them. She had them pulled and washed and tied up for me, and she says, don't go yet, come on in the kitchen and see what I got for you. Well, I didn't know what, but I dasn't not do it. I thought she was a witch. We all did. We all did, at school. So I sat down in the kitchen and she went into the pantry and brought out a big chocolate cake and she cut a piece and give it to me. I had to sit and eat it. She sat there and watched me eat. All I can remember about her is her hands. They were great big red hands with big veins sticking up on them, and she'd be flopping and twisting them all the time in her lap. I often thought since, she ought to eat the green onions herself, she didn't have so good nerves either.

"Then I tasted a funny taste. In the cake. It was peculiar. I dasn't stop eating though. I ate and ate and when I finished it all up I said thank you and I tell you I got out of there. I walked all the way down the lane because I figured she was watching me, and when I got to the road I started to run. But I was still scared she was following after me, invisible or something, and she might read what was in my mind and pick me up and pound my brains out on the gravel. When I got home I just flung open the door and hollered, *Poison!* That's what I was thinking. I thought she made me eat a poisoned cake.

"All it was was moldy. That's what my mother said. The damp in her house and she would go for days without no visitors to eat it, in spite of the crowds she collected other times. She could have a cake sitting around too long a while.

"But I didn't think so. No. I thought I had ate poison and I was doomed. I went and sat in this sort of place I had in a corner of the granary. Nobody knew I had it. I kept all kinds of junk in there. I kept some chips of broken china and some velvet flowers. I remember them, they were off a hat that had got rained on. So I just sat there, and I waited."

Billy Pope was laughing at her. "Did they come and haul you out?"

"I forget. I don't think so. They would've had a hard time finding me. I was in behind all the feed bags. No. I don't know. I guess what happened in the end was I got tired out waiting and come out by myself."

"And lived to tell the tale," said Rose's father, swallowing the last word as he was overcome by a prolonged coughing fit. Flo said he shouldn't stay up any longer but he said he would just lie down on the kitchen couch, which he did. Flo and Rose cleared the table and washed the dishes, then for something to do they all—Flo and Billy Pope and Brian and Rose—sat around the table and played euchre. Her father dozed. Rose thought of Flo sitting in a corner of the granary with the bits of china and the wilted velvet flowers and whatever else was precious to her, waiting, in a gradually reduced state of terror, it must have been, and exaltation, and desire, to see how death would slice the day.

Her father was waiting. His shed was locked, his books would not be opened again, by him, and tomorrow was the last day he would wear shoes. They were all used to this idea, and in some ways they would be more disturbed if his death did not take place, than if it did. No one could ask what he thought about it. He would have treated such an inquiry as an impertinence, a piece of dramatizing, an indulgence. Rose believed he would have. She believed he was prepared for Westminster Hospital, the old soldiers' hospital, prepared for its masculine gloom, its yellowing curtains pulled around the bed, its spotty basins. And for what followed. She understood that he would never be with her more than at the present moment. The surprise to come was that he wouldn't be with her less.

✳ ✳ ✳

Drinking coffee, wandering around the blind green halls of the new high school, at the Centennial Year Reunion—she hadn't come for that, had bumped into it accidentally, so to speak, when she came home to see what was to be done about Flo—Rose met people who said, "Did you know Ruby Carruthers was dead? They took off the one breast and then the other but it was all through her, she died."

And people who said, "I saw your picture in a magazine, what was the name of that magazine, I have it at home."

The new high school had an auto mechanics' shop for training auto mechanics and a beauty parlor for training beauty parlor operators; a library; an auditorium; a gymnasium; a whirling fountain arrangement for washing your hands in the Ladies' Room. Also a functioning dispenser of Kotex.

Del Fairbridge had become an undertaker.

Runt Chesterton had become an accountant.

Horse Nicholson had made a lot of money as a contractor and had left that to go into politics. He had made a speech saying that what they needed was a lot more God in the classroom and a lot less French.

APPLAUSE, APPLAUSE

Jean Thompson

★ ★ ★

Poor Bernie, Ted thought, as rain thudded against the car like rotten fruit. Watching it stream and bubble on the windshield, he promised himself not to complain about it lest Bernie's feelings be hurt. He was anxious to impress this on his wife. Poor Bernie, he said aloud. Things never work out the way he plans.

His wife nodded. Ted could see from her unsmiling, preoccupied face that it would be difficult to coax her into a conspiracy. In fact, she was probably blaming him for it: his friend, his weekend, therefore, his rain. Look, Ted said. He went to so much trouble setting this up. I'd hate to have him think we weren't enjoying it, whatever happens.

Lee, his wife, turned her chin toward him. He used to call her the Siennese Madonna because of that narrow face, long cheeks and haughty blue eyes. Easy to see her reduced to two-dimensional paint. She had never heard of Sienna. Now she said, All right, I won't sulk. But I'll save the vivaciousness till later, OK?

He was a little hurt that she saw no need to be charming for him, but he said nothing. After all, she hadn't complained. He burrowed his hands in his pockets for warmth and looked out the smeared window.

The car was parked in a clearing of pebbled yellow clay. On all sides were dark sopping pine trees, impenetrable, suffocating. It made him a little dizzy to think of how limitless those trees were, how many square miles they covered. The clearing contained two gas pumps and a trading post that sold moccasins, orange pop, and insect repellent. If you turned your back on the building it was easy to believe the world contained only the pines and the implacable rain.

Poor Bernie. He wondered at what point the friends of one's youth acquire epithets. When do we begin to measure their achievements against their ambitions?

Ten years ago he and Bernie Doyle were in college. Ten years ago they sat in bars, Bernie's pipe smoke looped around their heads. Or perhaps on the broken-spined, cat-perfumed sofa that was always reincarnated in their succession of apartments. How they had talked: God, he had never talked that seriously, that openly, to a woman. Perhaps it was something one outgrew. Like the daydreams of the dusky, moody photographs that would appear on one's book jackets. The experimentation with names. Theodore Valentine? T. R. Valentine? T. Robert Valentine? The imaginary interviews. ("Valentine is a disarmingly candid, intensely personal man whose lean, somber features belie his formidable humor. The day I met him he wore an old black turtleneck, Levi's and sandals, a singularly unpretentious yet becoming costume . . .")

Yes, he had admitted all these fantasies to Bernie, and Bernie admitted he shared them. How vulnerable they had been to each other, still were, he supposed. Behind the naive vanities, the day-dreams, they had very badly wanted to be writers. Had wanted it without knowing at all what it was they wanted, their fervor mak-ing up for their ignorance. His older self was cooler, more non-committal, for he had learned that to publicize your goals means running the risk of falling short of them.

Ten years of letters, of extravagant alcoholic phone calls. The continual measure they took of each other. Their vanished precoc-ity, reluctantly cast aside at age twenty-five or so. Ten years which established Ted's increasingly self-conscious, increasingly offhand reports of publications, recognitions. Bernie had kept up for a few years, had even talked about getting a book together. After that he responded to Ted's letters with the same grave formula: he wasn't getting a lot done but he hoped to have more time soon. Ted was sure he'd given it up entirely. He knew how easy it was to let your discipline go slack. You had to drive yourself continually, not just to get the work done but to keep faith. Faith that what you were do-ing was worth the hideous effort you put into it. Easier, much eas-ier, to let it go. The whole process of writing was a road as quirky and blind as the one they had driven this morning to the heart of the Adirondacks, this weekend, and the epithet, Poor Bernie.

Was he himself a success? He wasn't able to say that, not yet at least. Three years ago a national magazine printed a story. The smaller quarterlies published him with some regularity, paid him less frequently. His was one of the names an extremely well-read person might frown at and say, Yes, I think I've heard of him. It was like being one of those Presidents no one can ever remember, Polk or Millard Fillmore. Of course you wanted more than that.

But he'd made progress. He hadn't given up. These were the

important things. And he dreaded the inevitable discussions with Bernie when their younger incarnations would stand in judgment of them. How could he manage to be both tactful and truthful, feeling as he did that uncomfortable mixture of protectiveness and contempt. Yes, he admitted it, the slightest touch of contempt . . .

Is this them? Lee asked as an orange VW station wagon, its rainslick paint lurid against the pines, slowed at the clearing. Ted squinted. Maybe . . . The car stopping. Yeah, I think so. The window on the passenger's side was rolled down and a woman's face bobbed and smiled at him. He had an impression of freckles, skin pink as soap. Paula? Ted grinned and pantomimed comprehension.

We're supposed to follow, he told Lee, and eased the car onto the road. Again the dripping trees closed over them. They were climbing now, trailing the VW along a tight spiral. It was impossible to see more than twenty yards ahead. At times they passed mailboxes, or shallow openings in the woods that indicated roads, but for the most part there was only the green-black forest, the thick pudding rain.

Where's that college he teaches at? asked Lee. Ted looked at her and tried to unravel the history of her thoughts for the last silent half hour. She still wore her languid, neutral expression. The Madonna attends a required meeting of the Ladies' Auxiliary.

Sixty miles away. No, farther. Eighty. It was another thing he wondered about, Bernie's precarious instructor job. Four sections of composition. Abortion, Pro and Con. My First Date. Topic sentences. Footnotes.

And he married one of his students?

Ted nodded. It was hard for him to imagine Bernie as a figure of authority or some little girl regarding him with the reverence and hysteria of student crushes. But it had happened.

Lee pointed. The VW's bumper was winking at them and Ted slowed, ready to turn. Now it was scarcely a road they followed but a dirt lane. Milder, deciduous trees interlaced above them and screened the rain somewhat. They rocked along the muddy ruts for half a mile.

Then the sudden end of the lane, the cabin of dark brown shingles with Bernie already waving from the porch. Ted was out of the car almost before it had stopped, was shaking Bernie's hand and saying something like Son of a gun, and grinning. Bernie said, Valentine, you lout, and reached up to pound him on the back.

The women drifted after them. Hey Paula, come shake hands with Ted. And this is Lee. Bernie, Paula. Ted found himself appraising Lee as she climbed the steps, took satisfaction in her length of leg, her severely beautiful face now softened with a smile. The four of them stood nodding at each other for a moment. Like two sets of dolls built to different scale, Ted thought, the Doyles so small, he and Lee an angular six inches taller. Furious exercise had kept Ted in shape, and he knew the faint line of sunburn under his eyes was becoming. He realized he was standing at attention, and cursed his vanity.

Bernie looked more than ever like a Swiss toymaker as imagined by Walt Disney. Small bones and white supple hands. His gray eyes unfocused behind rimless glasses. The ever-present pipe which, when inserted, drew his whole face into a preoccupied, constipated look. He had grown a dark manicured beard.

And Paula? He knew her to be at least twenty-four, but she could have passed for sweet eighteen. Snub little nose. Smiling mouth like the squiggle painted on a china doll. Green eyes in that pink transparent skin. Yes, she would be something to take notice of in a stuffy classroom.

Even as he absorbed and ordered his impressions the group broke, Bernie pushing the front door open, Paula talking about food. He followed Bernie into a paneled room and the damp, bone-deep cold that would accompany the whole weekend first seized him. He heard Lee's lightly inflected voice keeping her promise: What a lovely fireplace. We can tell ghost stories around it.

You bet, said Bernie, and squatted before it, poking the grate. There's even dry wood on the porch.

Looking at him, Ted experienced the uneasy process of having to square his observations with his memories. As if this were not really Bernie until he conformed with Ted's image of him. How long had it been, three years? He began to be more sure of himself as he noted familiar mannerisms surfacing. Bernie's solemnity; he discussed firewood in the same tone another man might use for religion. The deftness of his hands wielding the fireplace tools. Ted imagined him shaping chunks of pine into cuckoo clocks, bears, and monkeys . . .

Now stop that, he warned himself. It was a writer's curse, this verbal embroidery. Never seeing anything as it was, always analyzing and reformulating it. Maybe the entire habit of observation, the thing he trained himself in, was just a nervous tic, a compulsion. He shook his head and joined Lee in her exploration of the cabin.

The main room was high-ceilinged, dark. In hot weather he imagined its shadows would bless the skin, but now the bare floors made his feet ache with cold. There were two bedrooms, one on each side of the main room. The furniture was a mixture of wicker and raw wood. In the rear were a trim new kitchen and bathroom. They stepped out the back door and Ted whistled.

Even in the rain the blue-gray bowl of the lake freshened his eyes. Its irregular shoreline formed bays, coves, little tongues of land, all furred with silent pine. He could not see the opposite shore. There was an island just where he might have wished for one, a mound of brush and rock. The air smelled clean and thin.

Lee spoke to Bernie, who had joined them. It's incredible. Just too lovely.

Bernie grinned, as if the lake were a treat he had prepared especially for them. And Ted felt all his discomfort drop away as he saw his friend's happiness, his desire to make them happy. God bless

Bernie; he'd forget all this gloomy nonsense about artistic accomplishment. Are there many cabins up here? he asked.

Quite a few. But the lake is so big and the trees so thick we have a lot of privacy. He pointed with his pipe. There's the boathouse. And dock. No beach, I'm afraid, it's all mud.

They stood in the shelter of the porch, rain hanging like lace from the gutters. Then Lee said, Too cold out here for me, and they all went inside.

Paula was rummaging through groceries in the kitchen. Here, said Lee. Let me do something useful. A little cluster of polite words filled the air, Paula demurring, Lee insisting. Ted hoped that for once Lee would be graceful about helping in the kitchen, leave him and Bernie alone without getting sarcastic later about Man-Talk and Woman's Work. He tried to catch her eye but she was pulling her blonde hair into a knot and asking Paula about the mayonnaise.

Bernie offered him a beer and they drifted to the living room. Sitting down, Ted had a moment of apprehension, like the beginning of a job interview. Bernie frowned and coaxed his pipe into life. How often had he used it as a prop; Ted knew his shyness. At last the bowl reddened. So tell me, Bernie said. How goes it with you?

Ted realized how much he'd rehearsed his answer: Not too bad. But I'll never be rich.

Bernie chuckled. Poor but honest.

Poor but poor. With Lee's job we get by. And I do some free-lancing, write ad copy for a car dealer, that sort of thing. He shrugged. And how about you?

Ted was aware he had shifted too quickly, had seemed to brush off Bernie's question in an attempt to be polite, reciprocal. Damn. He'd have to watch that.

Ah, Bernie said. The pastoral life of a college instructor. It's like being a country priest, really, with your life revolving around the feast days. Registration. Final exams. Department meetings on First Fridays.

You're getting tired of it?

It's a job, Ted. Like anything else it has its ups and downs. Actually I'm glad it's not excessively glamorous. This way I don't feel tied to it, committed. I can stay fluid, you know?

What would you do instead?

Sell hardware. Open a museum. I don't know. Paula wants to work as a photographer. She's pretty good. And I wouldn't mind getting back to the writing. It's been simmering in me for a long time.

That hint of justification. Ted felt the same prepared quality in Bernie's answer as in his own. He risked his question: Have you been able to get anything done?

Any writing, you mean? Dribs and drabs. I decided what I needed was to remove myself from pressure, you know? Work at my own pace without worrying about marketing a finished product. Of course I know that's not the way you go about it.

Yeah. It's out of the typewriter and into the mails.

You still work on a schedule?

Absolutely. Seems to be the only way I get anything done. Lee covers for me. I have tantrums if the phone rings.

You must really throw yourself into the thing.

The implied sympathy, the chance to speak of his frustrations with someone who would understand them, was a luxury. Jesus, he said. You spend hours wrestling with yourself, trying to keep your vision intact, your intensity undiminished. Sometimes I have to stick my head under the tap to get my wits back. And for what? You know what publishing is like these days. Paper costs going up all the time. Nothing gets printed unless it can be made into a movie. Everything is media. Crooked politicians sell their unwritten memoirs for thousands. I've got a great idea for a novel. It's about a giant shark who's possessed by a demon while swimming in the Bermuda Triangle. And the demon talks in CB lingo, see? There'll be recipes in the back.

Bernie laughed and Ted continued. Then the quarterlies, the places you expect to publish serious writing. They're falling all over themselves trying to be trendy, avant-garde. If you write in sentence fragments and leave plenty of blank space on the page, you're in. Pretentiousness disguised as trailblazing. All the editors want to set themselves up as interpreters of a new movement. I hope they choke on their own jargon. Anti-meta-post-contemporary-surfictional literature. Balls.

He stopped for breath. I'm sorry, he said. Didn't mean to get carried away.

Not at all. It does me good to hear a tirade now and then. Reminds me of college, makes me feel ten years younger.

Still. He should not have spoken with such bitterness. It sounded like he was making excuses. Ted smiled, lightening his tone. The artist takes his lonely stand against the world.

As well he ought to. But really, Valentine, don't you get tired of beating your head against all that commercialism? Trying to compete with it? I mean, of course you do, but do you think it affects what you write?

Was it Bernie's solemnity that always made his questions sound so judgmental? Ted knew it was more than an issue of mannerisms. Bernie pondered things, thought them through; you respected his sincerity. Ted gave the only answer pride allowed: No, because the work can't exist in a vacuum. It has to get out there in the world, and reach people. Ted drained his beer and ventured to define the issue between them. You're saying it's better to be an Emily Dickinson, a violet by a mossy stone half-hidden to the eye, that sort of thing. Keep it in shoeboxes in the closet so you can remain uncorrupted.

Bernie turned his hands palms upward and managed to express dissent by spreading his white fingers. Just that it's possible to lose sight of what you set out to do. Even get too discouraged.

How quickly we've moved into position, Ted thought. Each of us defending our lives. He remembered his earlier resolution to speak tactfully, cushion any comparison between their accomplishments. And here was Bernie seeming to demand such comparison. How easy it would be to make some mention of his publications, play up some of the things he'd muted in his letters, insist on Bernie's paying tribute to them. He even admitted to himself that beneath everything he'd wanted his success acknowledged. Like the high school loser who dreams of driving to the class reunion in a custom-made sports car. As if only those who knew your earlier weakness could verify your success.

But he would not indulge himself. Partly because, like his earlier outburst, it would threaten to say too much, and partly because he wanted this meeting to be without friction. Couldn't they rediscover their younger, untried selves? It was a kind of nostalgia. So he said, I don't know, Bernie. You may be right. But the only way for me to accomplish anything is by competing with the market.

Bernie considered this, seemed to accept it as a final statement. He dumped his pipe into the fireplace. Ted noticed the beginning of a tonsure, a doorknob-sized patch of naked scalp. The sight enabled him to recapture all his tenderness. Shall we join the ladies? Bernie asked, rising.

They were sitting at the kitchen table with mugs of coffee. Well, Ted said, resting a hand on Lee's shoulder. I hope you haven't been bored. He meant it half as apology, half as warning: you'd better not be.

Au contraire, Lee answered. We've been trying to reconcile post-Hegelian dogma with Jamesian pragmatism. But she grinned.

And Paula said, Actually, we were telling raunchy jokes. Give us ten more minutes.

He liked her. Her pinkness, plumpness. Like a neat little bird, all smooth lines and down. Her round good-humored chin. And Lee seemed to be doing all right with her.

I think it's quit raining, said Bernie. If you've got sturdy enough shoes we could take a hike.

It was still very wet under the trees. A careless tug at a branch might flip cold rainbow-edged drops down your back. And the sky was gray as concrete. But they enjoyed the silence, the soft sucking ground matted with last year's needles. They perched on a fallen tree at the lake's edge and chunked stones into the crisp water. Bernie explained it was too early, too cool, for the black flies whose bites made bloody circles just beneath the skin.

How often do you get up here? Ted asked. Bernie told him about every other weekend when the weather was right. Ted launched into abundant, envious speech: they were lucky sons-of-bitches, did they know that back in Illinois there were only tame little man-made lakes, tidy parks, lines of Winnebagos like an elephant graveyard, right Lee? As if complimenting this part of Bernie's life might restore some balance between them.

They walked back single-file along the sunken trail. Ted was at the rear. Lee's blondeness looked whiter, milkier, out here. Perhaps it was the heaviness of the dark green air, like the light just before a thunderstorm which plays up contrasts. Bernie and Paula's heads were the same shade of sleek brown, slipping in and out of his vision. It struck him that once again he was observing and being conscious of himself as an observer. It was a habit he'd fallen into, not necessarily a bad one. But he'd been working very hard at the writing lately (Lee had insisted on this vacation; he rather begrudged the time spent away from his desk) and this heightened self-awareness was a sign of strain. As if he couldn't really escape his work or the persona that went with it.

The Artist's impressions of a walk in the woods. The Artist's view on viewing. The Artist on Art. How do you get your ideas for stories, Mr. Valentine? Well, I simply exploit everything I come into contact with. One ended, of course, by losing all spontaneity. You saw people as characters, sunsets as an excuse for similes—

Bernie called a warning over his shoulder just as Ted felt a drop of rain slide down his nose. They quickened their pace to a trot as the rain fell, first in fat splatters that landed as heavily as frogs, then finer, harder. By the time they reached the porch their clothes were dark and dripping.

Fire, said Bernie. Coffee and hot baths, said Paula. The movement, the busyness, cheered them as much as the dry clothes. When at last they sat on each side of the stone fireplace, the odor of smoke working into their skins and hair, they all felt the same sense of shelter.

Damn, said Bernie. I wanted to take you fishing. But he looked comfortable, his pipe bobbing in his mouth.

Maybe tomorrow, said Paula. The rain had polished her skin, now the fire was warming it, bringing out different tints: apricot, cameo. She and Bernie made a peaceful, domestic couple. He could imagine them sitting like this, on either side of the fire, for the next thirty years. The retired Swiss toymaker and his wife.

But was Bernie happy? Did he feel, as Ted would have in his place, a sense of failure, of goals having shrunk. You never knew. Or, this visit would probably not allow him to learn. The time was too short to break down much of the politeness that passed between them as guest and host. Recapturing their former intimacy, that intensity, seemed as difficult as remembering what virginity had felt like. They should have left the wives behind, just come up here for a messy bachelor weekend of drinking and cards. This impulse moved him to ask if anyone wanted a whiskey.

They did. He passed glasses, leaned back into his chair. Well, said Lee. It's too early to tell ghost stories.

Ted and I could talk about our misspent youth.

She wants something ghostly, Doyle, not ghastly.

Oh go ahead, Lee urged Bernie. Tell me something that can be used against him. She was at her most animated, perhaps from the first bite of the liquor. The Madonna is photographed for a Seagram's commercial. Go ahead, she repeated.

Tell her I was a football hero.

If you won't tell Paula about that indecent exposure thing.

Agreed. Ted gulped at his drink to induce the mood of nostalgia. One thing I'll always remember. You and me taking a bottle of strawberry wine up on the roof of the humanities building.

Did you really, said Paula.

We thought we were Bohemians, Bernie explained. Artistic, not ethnic.

We pretended it was absinthe.

A rooftop in Paris at the turn of the century.

I was James Joyce.

I was Oscar Wilde.

We were going to be paperback sensations.

We were full of shit.

I don't know, Ted objected. I mean, certainly we were naive. Who isn't at twenty? But you have to begin with wild idealism, dreams of glory. It's the raw fuel that gets you through the disappointments.

You mean the brute facts of editors, publishing.

Ted nodded. The manuscripts that come back stained with spaghetti sauce. The places that misspell your name. All the ambiguities of success. If we'd known what was actually involved in writing, we probably never would have attempted it.

When we leave here, Lee put in, we have to go to New York and talk with Ted's agent. You wouldn't believe the nastiness and wheeler-dealer stuff that goes on in that New York scene. It's like a court in Renaissance Italy. Intrigues within intrigues.

Bernie raised his eyebrows above the rims of his glasses. You have an agent now?

Yes. Since last November. He's trying to place the novel for me.

And you've finished the novel? Paula, do we have champagne? I've been hearing about this book for years.

Well, I've finished the draft. If it's accepted I'll no doubt have to do rewrites. Damn Lee for bringing up the agent; it would only make Bernie more aware of the gap between their achievements. He searched for some way to de-escalate things. You should be glad you've escaped all this messiness so far. Retained your youthful innocence.

The bottom log of the fire, which had been threatening to burn through, now collapsed. Red winking sparks flew up the black column of the chimney as the fire assumed a new pattern. Bernie squatted in front of it raking the embers into place. He spoke without turning around.

You know, I read that piece you had in—what was it—the one about the schizophrenic?

"The Lunatic." He sat up a little straighter in his chair, adopted the carefully pleasant expression with which he received criticism.

Ted was very happy with that piece, Lee informed everyone. And the magazine did a good production job. She beamed at him, sweetly proud of making a contribution to the discussion. He wished she hadn't spoken, had left him free to frame his reply after listening to Bernie. But she was only repeating what she'd heard him say.

That's it, "The Lunatic." I admire the language use, the control in the thing. The way you managed to milk images. But—

that terrible pause—

I felt there was a kind of slickness in the thing, almost glibness. I mean, you're talking about a man who's having a mental breakdown. And you treat that rather flippantly. Perhaps you intended it, but I wondered why.

There were a number of replies he could make. He settled for the most general: The story is something of a satire, Bernie. Think of all the literature that's dealt with madness. It's an extremely well-trodden path. You simply can't write about the subject straightforwardly anymore. People expect something new.

Bernie frowned and rubbed his jaw under the dense beard. Ted knew, watching him, that Bernie had thought his argument through. Had prepared it carefully, step by step, like he did everything.

I thought, Bernie continued, that your complaint against avant-garde fiction was its emphasis on form over content. Blank space on the page, tortured syntax, that sort of thing. The writing screaming for attention. Aren't you agreeing with them now? Saying, in effect, rather than exploring the individuality of this character or situation, I'll dress it up in a different package. Pretend not to take it seriously.

Both women were watching rather helplessly, as if they realized their little store of soothing words and social graces would be of no use. And the defense that came to Ted's mind (Nobody writes like Henry James anymore. Or, more crudely, Your aesthetic is out-dated) sounded like a small boy's taunts. So he said, I do take the character and situation seriously. That doesn't mean one can't ex-periment with form, depart from rigid storytelling conventions. Otherwise you wind up repeating what's already been done. Repeating yourself too.

Bernie shook his head. Again that gesture of judgment. I'm sorry, but I see it as a response to the market. The thing I was talk-ing about earlier. You tailor the writing to what the editors are buying. Maybe unconsciously. You're certainly not writing about the giant sharks. But it's still a form of corruption.

And what, in particular, is being corrupted?

I hope I can put this right. It's like, that increased self-consciousness, that authorial presence that's always thrusting itself between the reader and the page—see, I'm telling this story, you're reading it, I'll try to amuse you, watch this—is rather paralyzing. What you're doing, a general you (a parenthetical smile), is making disclaimers for the piece, covering your tracks. I'll play this a little tongue-in-cheek so I won't be called to account for it.

You might as well dispute abstraction in painting, Bernie. Form can't be entirely neglected in favor of content. Otherwise we might still be seeing those Victorian pictures of blind children and noble hounds.

It runs the danger of shallowness, Ted.

Well, I suppose the only way to avoid the dangers is not to write anything at all.

He hadn't realized how angry he was until he heard himself speak. Damn the whiskey, damn his own thin-skinned hatred of criticism. He was too quick to take things as insults. Now, having said the one unforgivable thing, there was no retreat. The four of them sat without looking at each other. Bernie plunged into a fury of pipe-cleaning, tamping, lighting, as another man might have cracked his knuckles. The rain filled the silence, gusting against the windows and shrinking the warmth of the fire.

Finally Paula said, I'm going to see what there is for dinner. Ted stood up as soon as she did, muttering about another drink. He paused in the kitchen only long enough to slosh the liquor in his glass. Paula opened the refrigerator and said, Hm, fried chicken maybe? He said, Fine and walked out the back door.

The rain had brought an early blue darkness. He could still make out the shoreline, the agitation of the lake as the rain pocked its surface. Far away on his left shone one point of light, a white feeble thing that he could not imagine indicated human companionship, laughter, warmth. Even though he stood under the ledge, moisture beaded his clothes like dew. He gave himself over completely to the melancholy of it all. The only consolation he could find was the thought that argument was a form of intimacy.

When he came back inside, both women were busy in the kitchen. Can I peel potatoes or something? he asked. They sat him at the kitchen table with a bowl of strawberries to hull. A little boy hiding behind women. He didn't want to go back to the living room where he knew Bernie would be sitting. Lee and Paula seemed determined to speak of nothing more serious than gravy making. He watched Lee as she moved between stove and sink, a little surprised at her vivacity. As if she had formed some alliance without his being aware of it. Her hair had dried in soft waves with a hint of fuzziness; a looser style than she usually wore. Although she spoke to him occasionally, she did not meet his eye. It didn't seem that she was avoiding him; rather, she was busy, he was extraneous, incidental . . .

But he was projecting his injured feeling onto her, his gloom and self-pity. Snap out of it, he told himself. You're going to be here another thirty-six hours.

That realization must have been shared, must have been what got them through the evening. The act of sitting down to food together restored some tenuous rhythm. Afterward Paula suggested Monopoly. They let the bright cardboard, the little mock triumphs and defeats, absorb them. Ted thought how harmless all greed and competition were when reduced to this scale, then he berated himself for facile irony.

At midnight Bernie yawned and said, I'm down to thirty dollars and Marvin Gardens. Somebody buy me out.

Who's ahead? Add it up, Paula suggested.

It turned out to be Ted, who felt hulking and foolish raking in his pile of paper money. Flimsy pastel trophies. He was duly congratulated. He did a parody of the young Lindbergh acknowledging cheers. Modestly tugging his forelock. The tycoon needs some rest, he said, and they all agreed.

Good night. Good night, and if you need extra blankets they're at the top of the closet. I'm sure we'll be fine. Bernie latched the door and said, Maybe it'll clear up tomorrow.

It took Ted a moment to realize he was speaking of the rain.

He waited until everyone was settled before he used the bathroom. No use risking more sprightly greetings. When he got back Lee was in bed, her fair hair spilling from the rolled sheets like corn silk.

He wanted her to start talking first, but her eyes were squeezed shut against the bedside lamp. Well, he said. Too neutral, inadequate.

Would you turn that light off?

He reached, produced darkness. She sighed and said, Much better. He lay for a moment accustoming himself to the black stillness, the smell of the rough pine boards. The mattress was sparse, lopsided. It seemed to have absorbed the dank cold of the cabin. He burrowed into its thin center. Then the even sound of Lee's breathing told him she was falling asleep. Almost angry, he shook her shoulder.

What? She was more irritated than sleepy.

Don't fall asleep. I wanted to talk to you.

Go ahead.

He waited a moment to control himself. You're not making it very easy.

She twisted inside the sheets until she rested on one elbow, facing him. All right, I'll make it easy. What the hell were you arguing about? I hate it when you start talking like that. All that rhetoric. You take it so seriously. Was any of it worth snapping at him like that?

Of course I take it seriously. He was accusing me of shallowness. Corruption.

Oh boy. Lee drawled her sarcasm. And you couldn't forget your literary reflexes for one minute.

No. I guess I couldn't.

Her hand emerged from the darkness and gave his shoulder a series of small tentative pats. Poor Ted. Her voice was kinder. The pats continued, light but persistent, as if a moth were battering itself against him. He supressed the impulse to brush it away.

Why poor Ted?

Because sometimes I think you don't enjoy what you're doing at all. The writing I mean. You get so upset.

Don't be silly.

I know. The Agony and the Ecstasy. She yawned. Well, I hope you two make up. They're nice folks.

Her lips, seeming disembodied in the blind darkness, found his chin, his mouth. Good night.

Good night.

He waited until she was asleep or pretending to be asleep. He got up, put on his pants and sweater, and padded into the kitchen. Turned on the fluorescent light over the sink.

Her cruelest words spoken in her softest voice. Her revenge, thinking or unthinking, for all the times he'd shut himself away from her. He'd had his work to do. His sulks and tantrums. His insistence on the loftiness of his purpose, the promise of his future. His monstrous self-importance. The whole edifice threatened.

He didn't enjoy it.

Of course you were gratified at the high points. The little recognitions and deference. Of course you made a point of bemoaning the labor involved. Saying it drove you mad with frustration. That was expected. But enjoyment? Where was the enjoyment?

The pines still rattled in the wind. The rain was a dim silver fabric without seam or edge, unrolling from the sky. He thought of walking into it, losing himself in all that fragrant blackness, in the thick gunmetal lake. Oh he was tired of his cleverness, his swollen sensitivity. Better to crouch under a rock in the rain and reduce yourself to nerve, skin, and muscle. But his self-consciousness would not allow this either. It told him it would be melodramatic, a petulant gesture. Bad form.

Something, some weight, passed over the floorboards behind him and he turned, his nostrils cocked. It was the ticklish perfume of pipe smoke that reached him first.

H'lo, he said, and Bernie's mouth curved around the polished wooden stem of his pipe. He managed to walk to where Ted was standing by the back door without seeming to advance in a straight line.

Foul weather, he said, nodding. He too had resumed his clothes.

I'll say. They watched the faint movement of water on water. Then Bernie said, Drink?

Sure.

While there was still tension perceptible in their cautious responses, in Bernie's stiff-wristed pouring of drinks, it seemed a formality. The simple fact of coming together like this was a promise of reconciliation. When Bernie was seated across from him, Ted began with the obvious. I'm sorry about tonight. I was way out of line.

I guess I provoked you, Ted. I'm jealous. I admit it.

And I am insecure and narcissistic.

Would it be too maudlin to wish we were kids again?

Ted shook his head. In some ways I think I'm still twenty. The prize student who's always fawning for approval, pats on the head.

You're too hard on yourself.

Yes, I am. He blinked at the checked tablecloth, trying to get his eyes to focus on its pattern.

And I'm not hard enough. Bernie smiled. Such confessions.

They're necessary. Who else can absolve us of our sordid pasts?

Now the room has the contours and atmosphere of all rooms in which people stay awake talking. The fluorescent light is grainy, staring. The clutter on the kitchen table—ketchup bottle, sagging butter dish, tin of Nestlé Quik, the rowdy crudded ashtray—the world is narrowed into these, a little universe that the eyes return to again and again. Now it begins, the sorting and testing of words. Remember that words are not symbols of other words. There are words which, when tinkered with, become honest representatives of the cresting blood, the fine living net of nerves. Define rain. Or even joy. It can be done.

I KNOW WHAT
I'M DOING ABOUT
ALL THE ATTENTION
I'VE BEEN GETTING

Frank Gannon

✷ ✷ ✷

Iwas really worried about what to wear. It was like an anvil on my brain, just beating and beating and never stopping. Earlier that afternoon I saw someone walk into a clothes store and come out with a package. I knew what was in that package.

NEW CLOTHES.

It was like, Somebody bought some clothes, why can't I have some clothes too?

I went into my closet and got down on all fours and started to breathe really heavy. I was *trying* not to get nervous. I nudged a pair

of brogans with my nose. Why not wear everything that's fallen off
the hangers? It was a desperate, Hans Arp type of gesture, but what
was left me? Yesterday I went to buy dog food in absolutely the
worst thing: green shorts, gray socks, white sneakers. A brown shirt
with the numeral "16" on the back. As soon as I walked into the
grocery store I knew right away: wrong, *wrong,* WRONG!

But what could I do? It was too late then. I was trapped. I went
through with it, but when I got to my car my heart was pounding
and my face was flushed. My throat was dry and my hair was wet.
My feet were bent and my back was twitchin'.

I'll *never* do that again.

I'm a quirky dresser. I'm absolutely fearless about what it is that
I believe in. My shirts are incognizant and my socks—you must be
completely *unaware* of my socks, that's, like, my approach to socks.
My pants can be wily or even dishonest on some days if I just get
up and feel that. But I have to feel it. When I wear a tie—and believe me, sometimes I really *wear* a tie—it can be porcine, strait-
laced, odious. I have a certain little-boy quality, but there's also that
big-fat-sweaty-guy thing in there too.

I've stopped taking myself so seriously. I can take a step back
and laugh at myself. Sometimes I can get a really big charge out of
what an absolute idiot I am. I'll have this big intellectual stumbling
block right in my way, and suddenly I'll realize, Hey, who put the
damn stumbling block there in the first place? That's right: Mister
Serious Artist Person!

Whoa, I just crack up when that happens. Actually I'm a real
easy laugher. I'll laugh at anybody who's being phony or preten-
tious. I'll laugh at anybody who's trying to make it the best they
know how. I'll laugh at anybody. Before I started getting all this attention, I was completely invisible. I could go where I wished and
do what I liked without fear of being seen because I was completely invisible. I'm not making this up or being metaphorical
here. I have the power to just completely turn off whatever it is in

human beings that causes us to reflect light on the visible spectrum. So some nights I just make myself completely invisible and go for a walk. It's just this *power* I have. It's not like it was my life's dream or anything.

Anyway, people seem impressed by it. People would come up to me at parties and ask me about it. It made my girlfriend so mad. It was like she was really jealous or something. She finally told me that I had to choose between her and my ability to turn off whatever it is that causes human bodies to reflect visible light. That pretty well did in the relationship.

We still lived together, but it was like I was a sterilized needle and she was a little sliver of wood stuck in your finger. We could both tell what was going to happen so we decided to end it.

Now I'm in a whole new place. That other, older part of my life seems like some sort of surrealist joke that a bunch of my old buddies got together and pulled on me. Like they all got behind the furniture and waited until they heard me drive up, then they all jumped out and hit me with that part of my life.

But now I have to deal with now. I need some help on my clothes, so I just go manic and call everybody I can think of. They give me a lot of advice, but ultimately I'm the person under the hammer. It is I who have to wear the clothes, not all these well-wishers and hangers-on. Not the current artist of the month. Not all these vapid, air-brained media types. It will be me putting on the pants. It will be me pulling up the socks. I know how to do this. I've been at it for quite a while. I dressed myself for a long time before anybody was paying attention, and I'll dress myself a long time after everybody's paying attention to the way somebody else dresses himself. I know how these things go.

So what do I do? First I admit that I don't know what to do. Then I tell myself that I'm not alone, nobody else knows what to do either.

Once I've got that out of the way, I can start.

First I get out a big baggy pair of boxer underwear that is sort of right on the line between a lime and a grassy green. Then I go with the socks. They're white, but get this: they have this really thick black ribbing about an inch down from the top. Then I go with some gray trousers that really don't have anything to say, but I know that and that's what I want. Then I can tell that it's time for a black T-shirt. Don't ask me why, that's just the way I'm feeling. I put on some white sneakers, tie them quickly, and walk right out the door without a second thought.

That night I mingled. Everything went well because everybody was thinking that I had *planned* to look that way all along.

There's nothing permanent about this. I know that now. Tomorrow I'll be faced with more problems, but they won't be today's problems, they'll be newer, different problems. I can deal with it. I know what I'm doing.

WHERE THE DOOR IS ALWAYS OPEN AND THE WELCOME MAT IS OUT

Patricia Highsmith

★ ★ ★

Riding home on the Third Avenue bus, sitting anxiously on the very edge of the seat she had captured, Mildred made rapid calculations for the hundredth time that day.

Her sister Edith was arriving from Cleveland at 6:10 at Penn Station. It was already 5:22, later than she had anticipated, because some letters Mr. Sweeney wanted sent out at the last minute had delayed her at the office. She would have only about twenty-two minutes at home to straighten anything that might have gotten unstraightened since last night's cleaning, lay the table and organize their delicatessen supper, and fix her face a bit before she left for Penn Station. It was lucky she'd done the marketing in her lunch hour. All the last half of the afternoon, though, she had watched the dark spot on the grocery bag grow bigger—the dill pickles leaking—and she'd been too busy at the office to drag all the things out and rearrange them. Now, with her firm, square hand over the wet place, she felt better.

The bus swayed to a stop, and she twisted and ducked her head to see a street marker. Only Thirty-sixth Street.

Dill pickles, pumpernickel bread, rollmops (maybe it was the rollmops leaking, not the pickles), liverwurst, salami, celery and garlic for the potato salad, coffee ring for dessert, and oranges for breakfast tomorrow. She'd found some gladiolas in her lunch hour, too, and their blossoms still looked as fresh as when she'd bought them. It seemed like everything, but she knew better than to think there wouldn't be *something* at the last minute she'd forgotten.

Edith's telegram last evening had taken her completely by surprise, but Mildred had just pitched in and cleaned everything, spent all last evening and early this morning at it, washing windows, cleaning out closets, as well as the usual dusting and sweeping and scouring. Her sister Edith was such a neat housekeeper herself, Mildred knew she would have to have things in apple pie order, if her sister was to take a good report back to their Cleveland relations. Well, at least none of the folks in Cleveland could say she'd lost her hospitality because she'd become a New Yorker. "The welcome mat is always out," Mildred had written many a time to friends and members of the family who showed any signs of coming to New York. Her guests were treated to a home-cooked meal—though she did depend on the delicatessen quite a bit, she supposed—and to every comfort she could offer for as long as they cared to stay. Edith probably wouldn't stay more than two or three days, though. She was just passing through on her way to Ithaca to visit her son Arthur and his wife.

She got off at Twenty-sixth Street. Five twenty-seven, said a clock in a hardware store window. She certainly would have to rush. Well, wasn't she always rushing? A lot Edith, with nothing but a household to manage, knew of a life as busy as hers!

Mildred's apartment house was a six-story redbrick building on Third Avenue over a delicatessen. The delicatessen's crowded window prompted her to go over everything again. The coleslaw! And milk, of course. How could she have forgotten?

There were two women ahead of her, their shopping bags full of empty bottles, and they chatted with Mr. Weintraub and had their items charged in the notebook he kept hanging by the cash register. Mildred shifted and trembled inwardly with impatience and frustration, regretted that neighborliness had such a price these days, but her tense smile was a pleasant one.

"Coleslaw and milk," repeated Mr. Weintraub. "Anything else?"

"No, that's all, thank you," Mildred said quickly, not wanting to delay the woman who had come in after her.

Some children playing tag on the sidewalk deliberately dragged an ash can into her path, but Mildred ignored them and fumbled for her keys. Necessity had taught her the trick of pushing the key with a thumb as she turned the knob with the same hand, a method she used even on those rare occasions when both arms were not full. She saw mail in her box, but she could get it later. No, it might be something from Edith. It was a beauty parlor advertisement and a postcard about a new dry-cleaning process for rugs.

"Plumber's upstairs, Miss Stratton," said the superintendent, who was on his way down.

"Oh? What's happened?"

"Nothing much. Woman above had her bowl run over, and the plumber thinks the trouble might be in your place."

"But I haven't—" It was quicker to suffer accusation, however, so she plodded up the stairs.

The door of her apartment was ajar. She went into a narrow room whose two close-set windows looked out on the avenue. Crossing her room, she felt a lift of pride at the unaccustomed orderliness of everything. On the coffee table lay the single careless touch: a program of the performance of *Hansel and Gretel* she had attended last Christmas in Brooklyn. She'd found it in cleaning the bookcase, and had put it out for Edith to see.

But the sight of the bathroom made her gasp. There were black smudges on everything, even on the frame of the mirror over the basin. What *didn't* plumbers and superintendents manage to touch, and weren't their hands always black!

"All fixed, ma'am. Here's what the trouble was." The plumber held up something barely recognizable as a toothbrush, and smiled. "Remember it?"

"No, I don't," she said, letting her parcels slide onto a kitchen chair. It wasn't *her* toothbrush, she was sure of that, but the less talk about it, the sooner he would leave.

While she waited to get at the bathroom, she spread her best tablecloth on the gateleg table in the kitchen, pulled the window shade down so the people in the kitchen three feet away across the air chute couldn't see in, then dashed the morning coffee grounds into the garbage pail and stuck the dirty coffeepot into the sink. Keeping one foot on the pedal of the garbage pail, she pivoted in a half-dozen directions, reached even the bag of groceries on the chair and began to unload it.

The closing of the door told her the plumber was gone, and crushing the last paper bag into the garbage—she generally saved them for old Sam the greengrocer, but there was no time now— she went into the bathroom and erased every black fingerprint with rag and scouring powder, and mopped up the floor as she backed her way out. In the minute she allowed for the floor to dry, she pushed off her medium-heeled oxfords at the closet door and stepped into identical newer oxfords. But their laces were tied from a hasty removal, too. She stooped down, and felt a dart over her bent knee. A run. She mustn't forget to change the stocking before she left for the station. Or had she another good stocking? Buying stockings was one of the errands she had intended to do today in her lunch hour.

Twenty-one minutes of six, she saw as she trotted into the bathroom. Eleven minutes before she ought to leave the house.

Even after the brisk scrubbing with a washrag, her squarish face looked as colorless as her short jacket of black and gray tweed. Her hair, of which the gray had recently gotten an edge over the brown, was naturally wavy, and now the more wiry gray hairs stood out from her head, making her look entirely gray, unfortunately, and giving her an air of harassed untidiness no matter what she did to correct it. But her eyes made up for the dullness of the rest of her face, she thought. Her round but rather small gray eyes still looked honest and kind, though sometimes there was a bewildered, almost frightened expression in them that shocked her. She saw it now. It was because she was hurrying so, she supposed. She must remember to look calm with Edith. Edith was so calm.

She daubed a spot of rouge on one cheek and was spreading it outward with timid strokes when the peal of the doorbell made her jump.

"Miss," said a frail voice in the semidarkness of the hall, "take a ten-cent chance on the St. Ant'ny School lottery Saturday May twenny-second?"

"No. No, child, I haven't time," Mildred said, closing the door. She hated to be harsh with the little tykes, but at seventeen minutes of six . . . .

As a matter of fact, the alarm clock shouldn't be out on the coffee table, she thought, it looked too much as if she slept on the living room couch, which of course she did. She put the clock in a bureau drawer.

For a moment, she stood in the center of the room with her

mind a complete blank. What should she do next? Why was her heart beating so fast? One would think she'd been running, or at least that she was terribly excited about something, and she wasn't really.

Maybe a bit of whiskey would help. Her father had always said a little nip was good when a person was under a strain, and she was under a slight strain, she supposed. After all, she hadn't seen Edith in nearly two years, not since she'd been to Cleveland on her vacation two summers ago.

Mr. Sweeney had given her the whiskey last Christmas, and she hadn't touched it since she made the eggnog Christmas Day for old Mrs. Chevlov upstairs. The bottle was still almost full. Cautiously, she poured an inch into a small glass that had once contained cheese, then added another half inch, and drank it off at a gulp to save time. The drink landed with a warm explosion inside her.

"Dear old Edith!" she said aloud, and smiled with anticipation.

The doorbell rang.

Those children again, she thought, they always tried twice. Absently, she plucked a piece of thread from the carpet, and rolled it between her thumb and forefinger, wondering if she should answer the door or not. Then the bell came again, with a rap besides, and she plunged toward it. It might be the plumber about something else.

"Miss, take a ten-cent chance on the St. Ant'ny—"

"No," Mildred said with a shudder. "No, thank you, children." But she found a coin in the pocket of her jacket and thrust it at them.

Then she dashed into the kitchen and set out plates, cups and saucers, and paper napkins in buffet style. It looked nice to have everything out, and would save considerable time later. She put the big mixing bowl for the potato salad on the left, and lined up beside it the smaller mixing bowl for the dressing, the salad oil, the vinegar, mustard, paprika, salt and pepper, the jar of stuffed olives—a little moldy, best wash them off—in a militarily straight row. The sugar bowl was low, she noticed, and lumpy, too. And only three minutes left! She hacked at the lumps in the bowl with a teaspoon, but not all of them would dislodge, so finally she gave it up and just added more sugar. Some of it spilled on the floor. She seized broom and dustpan and went after it. Her heart was pounding again. What on earth ailed her?

Thoughtfully, she took down the whiskey and poured another inch or two into the glass. Soothing sensations crept from her stomach in all directions, made their way even into her hands and feet. She swept up the sugar with renewed fortitude and patience, and whisked the remaining grains under the sink so they wouldn't crackle underfoot.

The kitchen curtains caught her eye for the first time in months, but she resolutely refused to worry about their streaks of black grit. A person was allowed *one* fault in a household, she thought.

As she pulled on her coat, it occurred to her she hadn't boiled the eggs for the salad, and she'd meant to do it the first thing when she came home. She put three eggs into a saucepan of water and turned the gas on high. At least she could start them in the few moments she'd be here, and turn them off as she went out the door.

Now. Had she keys? Money? Her hat. She snatched up her hat—a once-stiff pillbox of Persian lamb, much the same color as her hair—and pressed it on with the flat of her hand. Nice to have the kind of hats one didn't have to worry about being straight or crooked, she thought, but she allowed herself one glance in the hall mirror as she passed by, and it was enough to reveal one rouged cheek and one plain one. She hurried back into the bathroom, where the light was best.

It was six minutes to six when she flew downstairs.

She'd better take a taxi to the station after all. She regretted the extravagance, though she felt herself yielding to a gaiety and abandonment that had been plucking at her ever since she thought of taking a nip of whiskey. She didn't really care about eighty-five cents, a dollar with tip. A dollar was just a little more than one-hundredth of her weekly salary. Or a little more than one-thousandth? No, than one-hundredth, of course.

Crossing the lobby of Penn Station toward the information center, she felt the run in her stocking travel upward and was afraid to look. She'd forgotten to change it, but she wouldn't, really wouldn't have had time to look for a good stocking, even if she'd remembered. She could tell Edith she'd gotten the run hurrying to meet her. In fact, she thought brilliantly, Edith didn't have to know she'd been home at all, which would make her house and herself, after some apologies, look very nice indeed.

"Downstairs for incoming train information," the clerk told her.

Mildred trotted downstairs, and was referred to a blackboard, where she learned that the Cleveland Flyer would be twenty minutes late. Suddenly something collapsed in her, and she felt terribly tired. She started for a nearby bench, but she knew she was too restless to sit still. She wandered back upstairs. Her nervous system was not adjusted to waiting. She could wait in the office for Mr. Sweeney to finish a long telephone conversation and get back to whatever work they were doing together, but she could not wait on her own time—for an elevator, for a clerk in a department store, or on a line in the post office—without growing anxious and jumpy. Maybe another touch of whiskey would be a good idea, she thought, a leisurely one she could sip while she composed herself.

A big, softly lighted, pink and beige bar came into view almost immediately. And there were several women inside, she was relieved to see. Feeling strange and somehow very special, Mildred went in through the revolving door. Every table was in use, so she stood shyly behind two men at the bar, over whose shoulders she could see the barman now and then.

"Whiskey," she said, when the barman seemed to be looking at her.

"What kind?"

"Oh, it doesn't matter," she said cheerfully.

Everybody in the place seemed to be having such a good time, it was fun just to watch them. She never gave such places a thought, yet they were going full blast all over New York every evening, she supposed. It occurred to her she was probably a more sophisticated person than she realized.

She wondered if Edith still wore her hair in those stiff marcel waves. The last time she had seen Edith, she had looked like one of those dummies with wigs they have in beauty parlor windows. That wasn't a nice thing to think about one's sister, but Edith really had looked like them. For the first time now, Mildred realized that Edith was actually coming, that she would see her within minutes. She could hear Edith's slow voice as clearly as if she stood beside her, saying, "Well, that's fate, Millie," as she often did, and as she probably would say about her daughter Phyllis's marriage. Phyllis's husband was only nineteen and without a job, and, according to a letter Cousin John in Toledo had written her a few weeks ago, without ambition, either. "Well, that's fate," Edith would say by way of passing if off. "Parents can't boss their children anymore, once the children think they're grown." Mildred's heart went out to her sister.

The square-numeraled clock on the wall said only 6:17. Just about an hour ago, she had been on the bus going home. The crowded bus seemed suddenly dismal and hideous. It was as if another person had been riding on it an hour ago, not herself, not this person who sipped whiskey in a bar where dance music played, this person who awaited a train from Cleveland.

One of the men offered her a high red stool, but she was so

short, she decided just to lean against it. Then all at once it was 6:28. She paid her check, clutched her handbag, and dashed off.

Now, really now, her sister was pulling into the station. She giggled excitedly. A bell went *whang-whang-whang*! A metal gate folded back. People rushed up the slope, people rushed down, among them herself. And there was Edith, walking toward her!

"Edith!"

"Millie!"

They fell upon each other. My own flesh and blood, Mildred thought, patting Edith's back and feeling a little weepy. There was confusion for a few minutes while Edith found her suitcase, Mildred asked questions about the family, and they looked for a cab. With a flash of pain, Mildred remembered the eggs on the stove at home. They would be burning now, aflame probably, the gas was so high. How did burning eggs smell? In the taxi, Mildred braced Edith's suitcase against the jump seat with her foot and tried to listen to everything Edith was telling her, but she couldn't keep track of anything for thinking of the eggs.

"How is Arthur?" Mildred asked, one eye out the window to see if the driver was going right.

"Just as well as can be. He has a new baby."

Mildred hoped every child in the neighborhood wasn't cluttering the front steps. Sometimes they played cards right in the doorway. "Oh, a new baby! Oh, has he?"

"Yes, another little girl," said Edith. "Just last week. I was saving it to tell you."

"So now you're twice a grandmother! I'll have to send Arthur and Helen something right away."

Edith protested she shouldn't.

Mildred paid the driver, then struggled out with the suitcase, waving Edith's assistance aside, and not waiting for the driver to help, because drivers usually didn't. She realized too late that she might have added another dime to the tip, and hoped Edith hadn't noticed. Pinching each other's fingers under the suitcase handle, the sisters climbed the three flights. Mildred felt a rough corner of the suitcase tearing at her good stocking.

"Are you hungry?" she asked cheerily as she felt for her keys, trying not to sound out of breath. She sniffed for burning eggs.

"I had a snack on the train about five o'clock," Edith replied, "so I'm bearing up, as they say."

"Well, here it is, such as it is!" Mildred smiled fearfully as she swung the door open for Edith, braced for any kind of odor.

"It's just lovely," Edith said, even before the light was turned on.

Mildred had flown past her into the kitchen. The eggs were turned off, resting quietly in their water. She stared at them incredulously for a second or two. "It's just the one room and a bit of a kitchen this time," Mildred remarked as she returned to her sister, for Edith, standing in the middle of the room, seemed to be expecting her to show her the rest. "But it's much more convenient to the office than the Bronx apartment was. I know you'll want to wash up, Edie, so just have your coat off and I'll show you where everything is."

But Edith did not want to wash up.

"As Father used to say, 'I propose we have a wee nip in honor of the occasion!'" Mildred said a bit wildly, her voice rising over the roar of a passing truck on Third Avenue. She thought Edith looked at her in a funny way, so she added, "Not that I've become a drinking woman, by any means! I did have one while I was waiting for you in the station, though. Could you tell?"

"No. You mean you went in a bar by yourself and had a drink?"

"Why, yes," Mildred replied, wishing now that she hadn't mentioned it. "Women often go into bars in New York, you know. It's not like Cleveland." Mildred turned a little unsteadily and went into the kitchen. She did want another bit of a drink, just to continue feeling as calm as she did now, for it certainly was helping to calm her. She took a quick nip, then fixed a tray with the bottle and glasses and ice. "Well, down the hatch!" Mildred said as she set the tray down on the coffee table.

Edith had refused the maroon-covered easy chair Mildred had offered her, and now she sat tensely on the couch and sipped her whiskey as if it were poison. She gazed off now and then at the windows—the curtains, Mildred admitted, were not so clean as Cleveland curtains, but at least she had brushed them down last night—and at the brown bureau that was her least attractive piece of furniture. Why didn't Edith look over at the kitchen table where everything was lined up as neatly as a color photograph in a magazine?

"The gladiolas are beautiful, Millie," Edith said, looking at the gladiolas Mildred had set in a blue vase atop the bureau. "I grow gladiolas in the backyard."

Mildred lighted up appreciatively at Edith's compliment. "How long am I to have the pleasure of your company, sister?"

"Oh, just till—" Edith broke off and looked at the windows with an expression of annoyance.

A truck or perhaps a cement mixer was rattling and clanking up the avenue. Suddenly Mildred, whose ears had adjusted long ago to the street noises, realized how it must sound to Edith, and writhed with shame. She had quite forgotten the worst feature of her apartment—the noise. The garbage trucks that started grinding around three A.M. were going to be worse.

"It's a nuisance," Mildred said carelessly, "but one gets used to it. What with the housing—" Something else was passing, backfiring like pistol shots, and Mildred realized she couldn't hear her own voice. She waited, then resumed. "What with the housing being—"

But Edith silenced her with a hopeless shake of her head.

A war of horns was going on now, probably a little traffic jam at the corner. That was the way it went, Mildred tried to convey to Edith with a smile and a shrug, all at once or nothing at all. For a few moments their ears, even Mildred's ears, were filled with the cacophony of car horns, of snarling human voices.

"Really, Millie, I don't see how you stand this noise day after day," Edith said.

Mildred shrugged involuntarily, started to say something, and said nothing after all. She felt inexplicably foolish all at once.

"What were you going to say before?" Edith prompted.

"Oh. Well, what with the housing being what it is today, New Yorkers can't be too picky where they live. I have my budget, and I didn't have any choice but this place and something on Tenth Avenue when I wanted to move from the Bronx. Took me three months to find this." She said it with a little pride that was instantly quelled by her sister's troubled regard of the windows. Well, there weren't any trucks passing now, Mildred thought a bit resentfully, and the traffic jam had evidently cleared up. What was she looking at? Self-consciously, Mildred got up and lowered the window, though she knew it would not help much to lessen the noise. She looked at her geranium. The geranium was nothing but a crooked dry stalk in its pot now, at the extreme left of the windowsill where the sun lingered longest. It must have been three weeks since she'd watered it, and now she felt overcome with remorse. Why was she always rushing so, she forgot all about doing the nice things, all the little things that gave her real pleasure? A wave of self-pity brought tears to her eyes. A lot her sister knew about all she had to contend with, the million and one things she had to think of all by herself, not only at home but at the office, too. You could tell just by looking at Edith she never had to worry or rush about anything, even to take a hard-boiled egg off the stove.

With a smile, Mildred turned to Edith, and under cover of a "Hungry yet?" ducked into the kitchen to see about the hard-boiled eggs. She balanced the three hot eggs on top of the block of ice in the icebox, so they would cool as fast as possible.

"Remember the time we took the raw eggs by mistake on the

picnic, Edie?" Mildred said, laughing as she came back into the living room. It was an old family joke, and one or the other of them mentioned it almost every time they cooked hard-boiled eggs.

"Will I ever forget!" Edith shrieked, bringing her hands down gently on her knees. "I still say Billy Reed switched them on us. He's the same rascal today he always was."

"Those were happy old days, weren't they?" Mildred said vaguely, wondering if she shouldn't perhaps cook the eggs even longer. She made a start for the kitchen and changed her mind.

"Millie, do you think it's really worth it to live in New York?" Edith asked suddenly.

"Worth it? How do you mean worth it?—I suppose I earn fairly good money." She didn't mean to sound superior to her sister, but she was proud of her independence. "I'm able to save a little, too."

"I mean, it's such a hard life you lead and all, being away from the family. New York's so unfriendly, and no trees to look at or anything. I think you're more nervous than you were two years ago."

Mildred stared at her. Maybe New York had made her more nervous, quicker about things. But wasn't she as happy and healthy as Edith? "They're starting trees right here on Third Avenue. They're pretty small yet, but tomorrow you can see them.—I don't think it's such an unfriendly town," she went on defensively. "Why, just this afternoon, I heard the delicatessen man talking with a woman about— And even the plumber—" She broke off, knowing she wouldn't be able to express what she meant.

"Well, I don't know," Edith said, twiddling her hands limply in her lap. "My last trip here, I asked a policeman where the Radio City Music Hall was, and you'd have thought I was asking him to map me a way to the North Pole or something, he seemed so put out about it. Nobody's got time for anybody else—have they?" Her voice trailed off, and she looked at Mildred for an answer.

Mildred moistened her lips. Something in her struggled slowly and painfully to the surface. "I—I've always found our policemen very courteous. Maybe yours was a traffic officer or something. They're pretty busy, of course. But New York policemen are famous for their courtesy, especially to out-of-towners. Why, they even call them New York's Finest!" A tingle of civic pride swept over her. She remembered the morning she had stood in the rain at Forty-second Street and Fifth Avenue and watched the companies of policemen—*New York's Finest*—march down the avenue. And the mounted policemen! How handsome they had looked, row upon row with their horses' hoofs clattering! She had stood there not caring that she was all by herself then, or that the rain was soaking her, she felt so proud of her big city. A man with a little boy perched on his shoulder had turned around in the crowd and smiled at her, she remembered. "New York's *very* friendly," Mildred protested earnestly.

"Well, maybe, but that's not the way it seems to me." Edith slipped off a shoe and rubbed her instep against the heel of her other foot. "And sister," she continued in a more subdued tone, "I hope you're not indulging more than you should."

Mildred's eyes grew wide. "Do you mean drinking? Goodness, no! Why, at least I don't think so. I just took these in your honor, Edie. Gracious, you don't think I do this every night, do you?"

"Oh, I didn't mean I thought *that!*" Edith said, forcing a smile.

Mildred chewed her underlip and wondered whether she should think of some other excuse for herself, or let the matter drop.

"You know, Millie, I'd meant to speak to you about maybe coming back to Cleveland to live. Everybody's talking about the interesting new jobs opening up there, and you're not—well, so deep-fixed in this job that you couldn't leave, are you?"

"Of course, I could leave if I wanted to. But Mr. Sweeney depends a great deal on me. At least he says he does." She swallowed, and tried to collect all that clamored inside her for utterance. "It's not a very big job, I suppose, but it's a good one. And we've all been working together for seven years, you know," she asserted, but she knew this by itself couldn't express to Edith how the four of them—she had written Edith many a time about Louise who handled the books and the files, and Carl their salesman, and Mr. Sweeney, of course—were much more of a family than many families were. "Oh, New York's my home now, Edie."

"You've always got a home with us, Millie."

Mildred was about to say that was very sweet of her, but a truck's brakes were mounting to a piercing crescendo outside. She dropped her eyes from Edith's disappointed face.

"I've got some things I ought to put on hangers overnight," Edith said finally. "And do you mind if I wash my white gloves? They'll just about dry by morning. I'll have to leave early."

"What time?" Mildred asked, in order to be cooperative, but, aware that her worried expression might make her seem eager for Edith's departure, she smiled, which was almost worse.

"The train's at eight-forty-eight," Edith replied, going to her suitcase.

"That's too bad. I'm sorry you're not staying longer, Edith." She really did feel sorry. They'd hardly have time to talk at all. And Edith probably wouldn't notice half the things she had done around the house, the neat closets, the half of the top drawer she had cleared for her in the bureau, the container of soft drinks Edith liked that she had thought of the first thing last evening.

Mildred wiped the back of her hand across her eyes, and went into the kitchen. She got the stew pan of boiled potatoes from the icebox and dumped them into the salad bowl. She separated the celery under running water, bunched it, and sliced it onto the potatoes. The old habit of rushing, of saving split seconds, caught her up in its machinery as if she no longer possessed a volition of her own, and she surrendered to it with a kind of tortured enjoyment. She hardly breathed except to gasp at intervals, and she moved faster and faster. The jar of olives flew into the bowl at one burst, followed by a shower of onion chips and a cloud of paprika that made her cough. Finally, she seized knife and fork and began to slice everything in the bowl every which way. Her muscles grew so taut, it hurt her even to move to the icebox to get the eggs. The eggs had descended three inches or more into the ice, and she could not extract them with her longest fingers. She peered at their murkily enlarged forms through the ice cake, then burst out laughing.

"Edie!" she cried. "Edie, come here and look!"

But her only reply was the flushing of the toilet. Mildred bent over in silent, paroxysmic hilarity. If her sister only knew about the toilet! The toothbrush the plumber had dragged out that hadn't even *looked* like a toothbrush!

Mildred straightened and grimly wrestled the ice cake from the box. She shook the eggs into the sink, holding the ice with hands and forearms. The eggs had bright, gooey orange centers, but they were fairly cold. She hacked them into the salad, listening the while for Edith's coming out of the bathroom. She was racing to have the supper ready when Edith came out, but what did it matter really whether she was ready or not? Why was she in such a hurry? She giggled at herself, then, with her mouth still smiling, set her teeth and stirred the dressing so fast it rose high up the sides of the mixing bowl.

"Can I help you, Millie?"

"Not a thing to do, thank you, Edie." Mildred dragged the coleslaw out of the icebox so hastily, she dropped it facedown on the floor, but Edith had just turned away and didn't see.

Within moments, she was ready, the table laid, the coffee perking, the pumpernickel bread—but there wasn't any butter. She'd forgotten butter for herself yesterday, and forgotten it again today.

"There isn't any butter," Mildred said in an agony of apology. Edith took her place at the table. She thought of running down for some, but felt it would be rude to make Edith wait. "It's the same old-fashioned potato salad Mama used to make at home, though."

"It looks delicious. Don't you ever have hot meals here at home?"

"Why, most of the time. I try to eat a very balanced diet." She knew what her sister was thinking now, that she lived off deli-catessen sandwiches, probably. She passed Edith the coleslaw. "Here's something very healthful, if you like." Her throat closed up. She felt ready to cry again. "I'm sorry, Edie. I suppose you'd have preferred a hot meal."

"No, this tastes very nice. Now, don't you worry," Edith said, poking at the potato salad.

At the end of the supper, Mildred realized she had not put out the dill pickles. Or the rollmops.

"Would you like to step out tonight? Take a look at the big city?" Mildred came in from the kitchen, where she had just fin-ished cleaning up.

Edith was lying on the couch. "Well, maybe. I don't think I can nap after all, with all the traffic going. I suppose it lets up at night, though."

"There's a nice movie a few blocks uptown within walking distance," Mildred said, feeling a sink of defeat. How would she ever break it to Edith that there was some kind of noise on Third Avenue all night long?

They went to a shabby little movie house on Thirty-fourth Street whose gay lights Edith had seen and fixed upon.

"Is this your neighborhood theater?" Edith asked.

"Oh, no. There's any number of better theaters around," Mildred answered rather shortly. Edith had chosen the place. She almost wished Edith had wanted to go up to Broadway. She'd have spent more money, but at least the theater would have been nicer, and Edith couldn't have complained. Mildred was so tired, she dozed during some of the picture.

162

That night, Mildred was aware that Edith got out of bed several times, to get glasses of water or to stand by the window. Mildred suggested that Edith get some cotton from the medicine cabinet to put in her ears. But Mildred slept so hard herself, even on the too-short sofa, most of her impressions might have come from a great distance.

"Are they mixing cement at this hour?" Edith asked.

"No, that's our garbage disposal, I'm afraid," Mildred said with an automatic little smile, though it was too dark for Edith to see her. She had dreaded this: the clatter of ash cans, the uninterrupted moaning of machinery chewing up cans, bottles, cartons, and anything else that was dumped into the truck's open rear. Mildred bared her set teeth and tried to estimate just how awful it sounded to her sister: the clank of bottles now, the metallic bump of an emptied ash can carelessly dropped on the sidewalk, and under it all the relentless *rrrr-rrrr-rrr-rrr.* Quite bad, she decided, and quite ugly, if one wasn't used to it. "They have their job to do," Mildred added. "I don't know what a big city like this would do without them."

"Um-m. Looks to me like they could do it in the daytime when nobody's trying to sleep," said Edith.

"What?"

Edith repeated it more loudly. "I don't see how you stand it, even with the cotton in your ears."

"I don't use cotton anymore," Mildred murmured.

Mildred did not feel too wide awake the next morning, and Edith said she hadn't slept all night and was dead tired, so neither said very much. At the core of Mildred's silence was both her ignominy at having failed as a hostess and a desire not to waste a second, for despite having gotten up early, they were a bit pressed to get off when they should. At eight o'clock sharp, the pneumatic drill burst out like a fanfare of machine guns: a big apartment house was going up directly across the street. Edith just glanced at Mildred and shook her head, but around 8:15, there was an explosion across the street that made Edith jump and drop something she had in her hands.

Mildred smiled. "They have to blast some. New York has rock foundations, you know. You'd be surprised how fast they build things, though."

Edith's suitcase was not closed for the last time until 8:27, and they arrived at the station with no time to spare.

"I hope you can manage a longer visit on your return trip, Edith," Mildred said.

"Well, Arthur did say something about going back to Cleveland with me for a while, but we'll let you know. I can't thank you enough for the lovely time, Millie."

A pressed hand, a brushed cheek, and that was all. Mildred watched the train doors close down the platform, but she had no time to watch the train pull out. What time was it? Eight forty-nine on the dot, her wristwatch said. If she hurried, she might be at the office by nine as usual. Of course, Mr. Sweeney wouldn't mind her being late on such a special morning, but for that very reason, she thought it would be nice to be prompt.

She darted to the corner of Seventh Avenue and Thirty-fourth Street and caught the crosstown bus. She could catch the Third Avenue bus uptown and be at the office on Second Avenue in no time. At the Third Avenue bus stop, an anxious frown came on her face as she estimated the speed and distance of an oncoming truck, then ran. She mustn't forget to buy stockings today during her lunch hour, she thought. And tonight, she ought to drop a note to Edith in Ithaca, telling her how she had enjoyed her stay, and inviting her again when she could make it. And a note to Arthur, of course, about the new baby. Maybe Edith and Arthur both could stay with her awhile, if they went back to Cleveland together. She'd be able to make them comfortable somehow.

THE BEST OF BETTY

Jincy Willett

★ ★ ★

Dear Betty:

I'm only forty-two years old and already going through the Change. I tried for twenty years to get pregnant and now I never will. Also, I get horrible cluster migraines now. The worst ones feel like a huge tarantula is clamped to my head with his legs sticking into my eyes and ears, and I have to scream with the pain. Next Tuesday I'm going to have all my teeth pulled, because the hormones have rotted my gums. I'm forty-two years old and for the rest of my life I'm going to sleep with my teeth in a glass by the bed. I hate being a woman. I hate my life. I hate Iowa. If I didn't be-lieve in hell I'd kill myself.

Hopeless in the Heartland

Dear Hopeless:

What's the question?

Sorry, Readers. It's broken record time again. (1) Seek the aid of a competent therapist or clergyman; (2) Keep busy; (3) Above all, don't think about yourself so much, because (4) WHINING DOESN'T ADVANCE THE BALL.

For starters, Hopeless, why don't you rewrite this letter; only instead of cataloguing your complaints, include everything you have to be grateful for. You'll be amazed at how well this works.

✱ ✱ ✱

Dear Betty:

Calling all Tooth Fairies! Don't throw away your kids' teeth! Save them up until you have a good third cupful, then scatter them around your tulip beds come spring, and you won't lose one bulb to marauding squirrels. Scares the dickens out of them, I guess!

Petunia

Dear Petunia:

I guess it would! Thanks for another of your timely and origi-nal gardening tips.

✱ ✱ ✱

Dear Betty:

Lately, at parties, my husband has started calling me "Lard-bottom." I know he loves me, and he says he doesn't mean anything by it, but he hurts me terribly. Last night, at the bowling alley with some of his trucker buddies, he kept referring to me as "Wide Load." Betty, I cried all night.

We're both big fans of yours. Would you comment on his cruel behavior? He'd pay attention to you. Tell him that I may have put on weight, but I'm still a

Human Being

Dear Human:

Yes, a human being with an enormous behind. Sorry, Toots. If I read correctly between the lines, hubby's worried sick about your health. Try a little self-control. Quit stuffing your face.

★ ★ ★

Dear Betty:

Last winter my sister and I moved out here to Drygulch, Arizona, for her health. She's doing well, but I've developed tic douloureux, of all things, and the spasms are unpredictable and agonizing. Our nearest doctor is fifty miles away, as is, for that matter, our nearest neighbor. I can't help feeling I'd be better off in Tucson or Phoenix, near a large medical center, but my sister, who's quite reclusive, says that if we moved, her emphysema would just kick up again. Should we split up? Do I have the right to leave her, on account of a disease which, though painful, is not life-threatening?

Dolorous in Drygulch

Dear Dolorous:

Why not join a tic douloureux support group? If there isn't already one in the area, why not start one? (The company might bring Sis out of her shell!)

★ ★ ★

Dear Betty:

Isn't it about time for a rerun of "Betty Believes"? I'd love to get a new copy laminated for my niece.

Happiness Is

Dear Happiness:
Of course. Here goes:

BETTY BELIEVES

1. That everything has a funny side to it.
2. That whining doesn't advance the ball.
3. That there's always somebody worse off than you.
4. That there's such a thing as being too smart for your own good.
5. That there are worse things in the world than ignorance and mediocrity.
6. That it takes all kinds.
7. That nobody's opinion is worth more than anybody else's.
8. That the more things stay the same, the better.
9. That everything happens for a good reason.
10. That no one ever died from an insult to the intelligence.

★ ★ ★

Dear Betty:
My grandma Claire used to read your column every morning with her first cup of coffee and cigarette of the day. She called "Ask Betty" the real news. She said that following the progress of your career over the years was her only truly wicked pleasure, and that it was like watching a massacre through a telescope. What did she mean by that? She got throat cancer and died, and the last thing she said to me was, "There are too atheists in foxholes." My mom says she was out of her mind. What do you think?

Fourteen and Wondering

Dear Wondering:
That your grandma Claire will not have died in vain if you will heed the lesson of her life: *Don't smoke.*

★ ★ ★

CONFIDENTIAL to *First Person Singular:*

Is it worth it, kid? Is it really?

Sure, on the one side you have money—obscene amounts of money—not to mention job security, reputation, celebrity. But . . . what about the numbing boredom? What about self-respect? What about, you should pardon the expression, honor? Huh, Toots?

I mean, who's really contemptible here? Them, or you?

Hint: Who's got the ulcer?

Who's got the whim-whams?

Who's got the blues in the night?

✷ ✷ ✷

Dear Betty:

This is going to sound ridiculous, but hear me out. My husband smacks his lips in his sleep and it's driving me batty. If he were only snoring or gnashing his teeth, but this is a licking sound, a lapping, sipping, slurping sound, like a huge baby gumming pureed peas in the dark, and it makes my flesh crawl. I've tried nudging him awake, but he just looks at me so pitifully, and then I feel guilty. Imagine how he'd feel if I told him what I really want, which is my own bed in my own separate bedroom! Help!

Nauseous in Nashville

Dear Nauseous:

Sounds like hubby has some deep dark cravings, or so my sleep disorder experts tell me. Why not fix him up a yummy bowl of butterscotch pudding (from scratch) just before bedtime?

By the way . . . you mean "nauseated," dear.

✷ ✷ ✷

Dear Betty:

You want to know what burns me up? Inconsiderate bozos who jam up the speedy checkout line with grocery carts loaded to the brim, and moronic bimbos who let their children rip open bags of candy and cereal boxes and knock over jelly jars, and don't even have the decency to tell the stockboy to clean up their disgusting mess. I just got back from two hours at the grocery store and my new pumps are covered with mincemeat. What do you think of these lunkheads?

Burned Up

Dear Burned:

These people are not bozos, bimbos, or lunkheads. They are trash.

✷ ✷ ✷

Dear Betty:

I am 135 pounds of screaming muscle in crepe-soled shoes. I groan under enormous trays laden with exotic delicacies I shall never taste, as they are beyond my meager economic means. Having seen your face once I am able to connect it with the food and drink of your choice. I smile when you are rude to me and apologize when the fault lies in the kitchen. I walk the equivalent of five miles each night on throbbing feet to satisfy your every whim, and when you are stuffed and have no further need of me, I act grateful for a substandard tip, if at all. I am

Your Waitress

Dear Waitress:

Thank you.
What's the question?

✷ ✷ ✷

Dear Betty:

You hear from so many unfortunates with serious problems that I feel a bit ashamed to take up your time this way. I am an attractive woman of 59, my thighs are perfectly smooth, my waist unthickened, I still have both my breasts and all my teeth; in fact I am two dress sizes smaller than I was at eighteen. My three grown daughters are intelligent, healthy, and independent. My husband and I are as much in love as when we first were married, despite the depth of our familiarity, and the, by now, considerable conflation of our tastes, political beliefs, preferences in music and art, and, of course, memories. He still interests and pleasures me; miraculously our sexual life remains joyous, inventive, and mutually fulfilling. I continue to adore the challenge and variety of my career as an ethnic dance therapist. We have never had to worry about money. Our country home is lovely, and very old, and solidly set down in a place of incomparable, ever shifting beauty; our many friends, old and new, are delightful people, amusing and wise, and every one of them honorable and a source of strength to us.

And yet, with all of this, and more, I am frequently very sad and cannot rid myself of a growing, formless, yet very real sense of devastating loss, no less hideous for its utter irrationality. Forgive me, but does this make any sense to you?

Niobe

Dear Niobe:

Certainly. You're lying about the sex.

★ ★ ★

Dear Betty:

Why not scissor the cups out of your old brassieres and set them out in your annual garden as little domes to protect fragile seedlings? It looks wacky but it sure does the trick!

Petunia

Dear Petunia:

Why the heck not? And hey, don't throw away those brassiere *straps*! Kids love to carry their schoolbooks in them, especially once you've disguised their embarrassing identity with precision-cut strips of silver mylar cemented front and back with epoxy, then adorned with tiny hand-sewn appliques in animal or rock-star designs. Use your imagination!

☆ ☆ ☆

CONFIDENTIAL to *Smarting and Smiling:*

What you describe is not a "richly deserved comeuppance" but a sexual perversion, which, aside from being your own business and none of mine, is harmless enough and, if I read accurately between the lines, apparently works well for both of you.

You might just try these thought experiments, though: Imagine the effect upon your sex life of: a business failure; the birth of a child; rheumatoid arthritis (his); a positive biopsy (yours); the death of a child; a sudden terrifying sense of vastation that comes to either of you at three in the morning; a Conelrad Alert. In what ways would it differ from the experience of a couple for whom the concepts of integrity, maturity, valor and dignity retained actual relevance and power?

☆ ☆ ☆

Dear Betty:

You deserve a swift kick in the pants for your burn advice to *Fretting in Spokane.* Where do you get off telling that lady to iron her dustcloths? Dollars to doughnuts you've got a maid to keep *your* rags shipshape, but most of us aren't so lucky.

And another thing. These days there's getting to be a snotty, know-it-all, lah-dee-dah, cynical tone to your column. I can't put my finger on it, but I'm not the only one who thinks you're getting "too big for your britches." Don't kid yourself. You need us more than we need you. So bend over, Betty, if you know what's good for you, and get ready for a

Washington Wallop

Dear Wallop:

For what it's worth, I agree with you about the dustcloths. But I sincerely regret having ever unwittingly encouraged your brand of coarse familiarity. And may I suggest that you take yourself to the nearest dictionary—you can find one in any public library—and "put your finger" on the distinction between cynicism and irony. Think about it, Wallop. And tell me how it turns out.

☆ ☆ ☆

Dear Betty:

Many years ago you ran a column that started off "The Other Woman is a sponging parasitic succubus. . . ." I clipped it and kept it magnetized to my freezer, but it finally fell apart. Do you know the one I mean? Would you mind running it again?

Sister Sue

Dear Sis:

Not at all. Here goes:

The Other Woman is a sponging parasitic succubus, a proper role model for young people, a vacuous nitwit, a manic-depressive, a Republican, a good mother, an international terrorist, or what-have-you, depending, of course, upon the facts of her particular character and life.

"Though this much should be obvious, there are those who believe that any woman sexually involved with a man she is not married to can be, for social and moral purposes, reduced to a cheap stereotype. *This is dangerous nonsense. This is a terrible habit of thought.* For who among us has fewer than three dimensions? In the history of the human race, has there ever existed a single per-

son, besides Hitler, who could slip beneath closed doors, disappear
when viewed from the side, and settle comfortably, with room to
spare, between the pages of a bad novel?

"Therefore let us rejoice in our variety! Let every one of us
celebrate the special homeliness of her own history! Let us wonder,
and be surprised, and admit to possibilities, and get on with it, and
stop being so damn stupid!"

✳ ✳ ✳

Dear Betty:

Are you nuts? You can't get away with this. Even if you do,
what's the point?

First Person Singular

Dear F.P.S.:

The point is, watch my smoke.

✳ ✳ ✳

Dear Betty:

I need you to settle an argument. My brother-in-law says
you're not the original Betty and that you're not even a *person.* He
says Betty died two years ago in a car wreck and they covered it up
and this column is being carried on by a committee, hush-hush. I
say he's all wet. (He's one of those conspiracy nuts.) Anyway, what's
the poop? (Hint: There's a lobster dinner riding on this.)

No Skeptic

Dear No:

This is a stumper. I've been staring for so long at the wonderful phrase "original Betty" that the words have become nonsensical
and even the letters look strange. Who, I wonder, is or was the
"original Betty"? I'm not making fun of you, dear. I honestly don't
know what to say. If it's any help to you, I do have the same finger-
prints as the infant born prematurely to Mary Alice Feeney in

1927, and the vivacious coed who won first prize in the national "My Country Because" essay contest of 1946, and the woman who put this column into syndication in 1952. So I suppose you deserve the lobster, although how you're going to convince your brother-in-law is anybody's guess. I wonder what he'd take as proof. I've got to think about this.

✷ ✷ ✷

Dear Betty:

It's *him* I can't stand. In *bed*! And he knows it, too. I just don't want him *touching* me, I can't bear it! And *I still love him*! But there's *nothing* left anymore, and how the hell is homemade butterscotch pudding going to help that? My God! My God! And don't tell me it's just a phase, because I know better and so does he. God, I'm so unhappy.

Nauseated, All Right? in Nashville

Dear N:

That's much better. Awful, isn't it? The death of desire? And you're probably right, there's no help for it. Though if you can stomach the notion that intimacy is nothing more than a perfectable technique, you might try what they call a "reputable sex therapist."

Of all the foolish, ignoble, even evil acts I have committed in my long life, including the "My Country Because" essay, the single event that most shames me, so that I flush from chest to scalp even as I write this, was when I sat, of my own free will, in the offices of one of these technicians, and in the presence of a pink, beaming, gleaming young man, a total stranger, took my husband's hands in mine, and stared into his face, his poor face, crimson like my own, transfixed with humiliation and disbelief, and said—oh, this is dreadful; my husband of twenty-three years!—and said, in public, "I love it when you lick my nipples."

My God! *My God!*

✷ ✷ ✷

Dear Betty:

Our family recently spent a weekend in our nation's Capital. While there we visited the moving Vietnam Memorial. Upon our return home I penned the following lines, which I would like to share with you.

You Could Have Been a Son of Ours

You could have been a son of ours
  If we had ever had a son,
You could have been our pride and joy
  But someone shot you with a gun
    And now your work is done.

You perished in a jungle wild
  So that our freedoms might be insured
You risked your life without complaint
  You laid it down without a word.

And now upon a long black stone
  Are chiseled words that give you fame,
You could have been a son of ours—
  We're proud to say, "We know your name"

Emily

READERS:

Policy change! Policy change! Pay attention, now, because I'm not kidding around. Hereafter this column will continue to run the usual advice letters, recipes, and household hints, but we will no longer publish original verse. There will be no exceptions. Don't even think about it.

★ ★ ★

Dear Betty:

I guess you think you're pretty funny. I guess you think we're all hicks and idiots out here.

Well, maybe you're right, but I'll tell you one thing. That old letter I asked for about "The Other Woman"? It's not the one you ran before, even though you said it was, or you changed it in some way. I may not be super intelligent but I've got a good memory, and what's more I know when I'm being made fun of.

You know what? You really hurt me. Congratulations.

Sister Sue

Dear Sis:

I am ashamed.

I, too, have an excellent memory, and for this reason my record-keeping has never been systematic. And very occasionally I confuse genuine mail with letters I have concocted for one reason or another. This is what happened in your case. I had you down as a fiction.

I can't apologize enough.

★ ★ ★

Dear Betty:

Aren't you taking a big chance, admitting that you make up some of this stuff? Also, you haven't dealt with Sister Sue's real complaint, which is that now, inexplicably, after spending three decades securing the trust and affection of middle American women, you expose yourself as a misanthrope, misogynist, intellectual snob, and cheat. What are you up to, anyway?

F.P.S.

Dear F:

Look, nobody reads this but us gals, so I'm hardly "taking a big chance." And it should be obvious, especially to you, that I'm "up to" no good.

★ ★ ★

Dear Betty:

Do you believe in God? I don't. Also, do you ever sit in front of a mirror and stare at your face? My face is so blobby that I can't figure out how even my own parents can recognize me. Lastly, do you think we should be selling weapons to Jordan?

Fifteen and Wondering

Dear Wondering:

Take five years off after you graduate from high school. Move away from home, get a menial job, fall for as many unworthy young men as it takes to get all that nonsense out of your system. Don't even think about college until your mind is parched and you are frantic to learn. Don't marry in your twenties. Don't be kind to yourself. *Keep in touch.*

★ ★ ★

Dear Betty:

I was not "lying about the sex"; nor do I for a minute imagine that you thought I was. You simply could not resist making a flip wisecrack at my expense.

I was lying about my friends, who have gradually lost their affection for me but continue to socialize with us because they value my husband's company. He is aging well. I am turning into a fool. I'm one of those handsome old beauties with a gravelly, post-menopausal voice and a terrible laugh. I never had much of a sense of humor, but once I had a smoky, provocative laugh, which has now somehow become the sort of theatrical bray that hushes crowds. Strangers, accosted by me at parties, attacked at lunch counters and in elevators, shift and squirm in alarm: Even the most obtuse knows he's about to be mugged, that he will not be allowed to pass until I have exacted my tribute. I am all affectation, obvious need and naked ego: just that kind of horrible woman who imagines herself an unforgettable character. I tell off-color jokes and hold my breath after the punch line, threatening to asphyxiate if you fail to applaud my remarkably emancipated attitude. During the past forty years I have told countless people about the stillbirth of my son, to show that I Have Known Great Sorrow. I parade my political beliefs, all liberal and unexamined, as evidence of my wisdom. I am a deeply boring, fatuous woman, and strangers pity me, friends lose patience with me, and my family loves me because it never occurs to any of them that I know it. I am the emperor in his new clothes, who knew perfectly well he was naked, who just needed a little attention, that's all, merely the transfixed attention of the entire populace, not an unreasonable request, just unlimited lifetime use of the cosmic footlights.

Don't try to tell me I can change. Of course I can't. And don't for an instant presume that I'm not all that bad. I am. Believe it.

Niobe

Dear Niobe:

Yes, but on the other hand your astonishing self-awareness makes you a genuinely tragic figure. And, honey, cling to this: you're not ordinary. Commonplace sufferers find themselves trapped in homely, deformed, or dying bodies; you're trapped in an inferior *soul*. You really *are* a remarkable woman. Bravo!

How about it, Ladies? Isn't she something?

✻ ✻ ✻

Dear Betty:

Just who the hell do you think you are?

Washington Wallop

Dear Wallop:

I am 147 pounds of despair in a fifty-pound mail sack. Though overpaid, I groan with ennui beneath the negligible weight of your all too modest expectations, and when I fail to counter one of your clichés with another twice as mindless, I apologize, even though the fault, God knows, is yours. I am

Betty

* * *

Dear Betty:
   Temper, temper.

F.P.S.

Dear F:
   I can't help it. That broad really frosts my butt.

* * *

Dear Betty:
   Do I have an inner life? I think I read somewhere that women don't. Also, what does it mean? Do you think we're capable of original thought?

Fifteen and Still Wondering

Dear Wondering:
   I love you, and wish you were my own daughter. I have in fact two daughters, but neither of them has an inner life. I am what they call nowadays a "controlling personality." (Believe me, dear, that's not what they used to call it.) I was one of those omniscient mothers—the ones who always claim to know what their children are thinking, what they've just done, what they are planning to do. Not for any sinister reasons, mind you, but I got so good at guessing and predicting that, without intending to, I actually convinced them both of their utter transparency. They are each adrift, goalless and pathetic. They are big soft women, big criers, especially when they spend much time with me. I think I should feel worse about this than I actually do. Do you think this is Darwinian of me? (Hint: Go to a good library, and take out some books on Darwin.)

* * *

Dear Betty:

It's me again! Do you have any suggestions as to what I can do with a ten-foot length of old garden hose?

Petunia

Dear Petunia:

Do you ever just sit still? Do you ever just sit in front of a mirror, for instance, and stare at your face? It's none of my business, but—and I say this with no snide intent; I am trying to be good, so that my teeth are literally clenched as I write this—I seriously think you should calm down. Petunia, even the Athenians threw things away. Let the garden hose be what it is, a piece of garbage. Now sit very very very still and try to think of nothing but the weight of your eyelids. Come to rest. Let your muscles slip and slide. Easy does it, girl. Easy. *Shhhhhhhhhhhh.*

* * *

Dear Betty:

Maybe you should stop "trying to be good" if that's the best you can do. If I were Petunia, I'd rather get a wisecrack than a lot of patronizing advice based upon a snap analysis of my character and the circumstances of my life. You're a fine one to exhort them to wonder, be surprised, and admit to possibilities. On the basis of little evidence you've turned the woman into a cartoon. You don't see her as a person at all, just a type. Early thirties, right? Hyperthyroid, narrow-shouldered, big-bottomed, frantically cheery, classically obsessive-compulsive, a churchgoing, choir-singing, Brownie-troop-mothering Total Woman with a soft sweet high voice, darting panic behind her deep-set eyes, an awful corn-ball sense of humor, and an overbite like a prairie dog. Am I right? Boy, how trite can you get! And how presumptuous you've become! I've tried to see it your way, but it's no go. I say, bring back the Original Betty.

F.P.S.

Dear F:

Look, we know for a fact she's a cornball. No one who asks what she should do with a ten-foot length of hose could possibly have a sense of humor. As for the rest, well, I stayed up half the night trying to imagine another psychological context for her question (which, I must object, is hardly "a little evidence"), so that if I have failed, it isn't for lack of trying.

Oh, all right, I admit it. I did see her as a type. But it becomes so difficult to believe that Petunia, or any of them, has any kind of independent existence. Remember, these folks are just words on a page; of course they're full-fleshed and complex, but I have to take this on faith. Most of them probably think they're revealing their true selves, whereas really they tell me almost nothing, and with every letter I'm supposed to make up a whole person, out of *scraps.*

I don't like to complain, but this doesn't get any easier with practice, and I'm tiring now, and losing my nerve. I can live with not being nice—nobody nice would do what I do—but what if I'm not any *good*?

READERS:

Do you think that failure of the imagination can have moral significance? I mean, is it a character flaw or just an insufficiency of skill? Is triteness a *sin*? Or what?

Dear Betty:

Last night my husband woke me up at 2:00 A.M. with a strange request. Then after a while this old song started going through my head that I hadn't thought about for thirty years. I must have gone through the darn thing ten thousand times. It got so I was following the words with a bouncing ball, so that even when I blocked out the sound, that old ball was still bobbing away in my head and I never did get to sleep until sunrise. The question is, does anybody out there know the missing words?

> Herman the German and Frenchie the Swede
>> Set out for the Alkali Flats—Oh!
> Herman did follow and Frenchie did lead
>> And they carried something in, or on, their hats—Oh!

> Now Herman said, "Frenchie, let's rest for a while,
>> "My pony has something the matter with it—Oh!"
> Now Frenchie said, "Herman, we'll rest in a mile,
>> "On the banks of the River Something—Oh!"*

> Now Hattie McGurk was a sorrowful gal,
>> Something something something.
> She had a dirt camp in the high chaparral
>> And a something as wide as Nebraska.

There's more, but I never did know the other verses, so they don't matter so much.

Betty, we sure do love you out here in Elko.

Sleepytime Sal

Dear Betty:

One time I was at this Tupperware party at my girlfriend's. Actually, it was just like a Tupperware party, only it was marital underwear, but it was run the same way. Anyway, everybody was drinking beer and passing around the items, and cutting up, you know, laughing about the candy pants and whatnot, and having a

(*If I could get the name of the river I'd be all set here)

real good time. Only all of a sudden this feeling came over me. I started feeling real sorry for everybody, even though they were screaming and acting silly. I thought about how much work it was to have fun, and how brave we all were for going to the trouble, since the easiest thing would be to just moan and cry and bite the walls, because we're all going to die anyway, sooner or later. Isn't that sad? I saw how every human life is a story, and the story always ends badly. It came to me that there wasn't any God at all and that we've always known this, but most of us are too polite and kind to talk about it. Finally I got so blue that I had to go into the bathroom and bawl. Then I was all right.

Partly Sunny

★ ★ ★

Dear Betty:

When I was first married you ran a recipe in your column called "How to Preserve Your Mate." It had all kinds of stuff in it like "fold in a generous dollop of forgiveness" and "add plenty of spice." I thought it was so cute that I copied it out on a sampler. Time went by, and I got a divorce, and finished high school, and then I got a university scholarship, and eventually a master's degree in business administration. Now I'm married again, to a corporate tax lawyer, and we live in a charming old pre-Revolutionary farmhouse, and all our pillows are made of goose down, and our pot holders and coffee mugs and the bedspreads and curtains in the children's rooms all have Marimekko prints, and every item of clothing I own is made of natural fiber. But I never threw that old sampler away, and every now and then, when I'm all alone, I take it out and look at it and laugh my head off about what an incredible middle-class jerk I used to be.

Save the Whales

★ ★ ★

Dear Betty:

This is the end of the line for you and the rest of your ilk. We shall no longer seek the counsel of false matriarchs, keepers of the Old Order, quislings whose sole power derives from the continuing bondage of their sisters. Like the dinosaurs, your bodies will fuel the new society, where each woman shall be sovereign, and acknowledge her rage, and validate her neighbor's rage, and rejoice in everybody's rage, and caper and dance widdershins beneath the gibbous moon.

Turning and Turning in the Widening Gyre

★ ★ ★

Dear Betty:

I did what you said and sat real quiet and let myself go. Then you know what happened? I got real nutty and started wondering if I was just an idea in the mind of God. Is this an original thought? 'Cause if it is, you can keep it.

Hey, are you all right?

Petunia

Dear Petunia:

No, since you ask. My mother is dying. My husband's mistress has myesthenia gravis. My younger daughter just gave all of her trust money to the Church of the Famous Maker. And I, like Niobe, am not aging well. My ulcer is bleeding, I can't sleep, and I'm not so much depressed as humiliated, both by slapstick catastrophe and by the minute tragedy of my wasted talents. To tell you the truth, I feel like hell.

★ ★ ★

Dear Betty:

I can see you have problems, dear, but whining doesn't advance the ball. Why not make a list of all your blessings and tape it to your medicine chest? Or send an anonymous houseplant to your oldest enemy? Why not expose yourself to the clergyman of your choice?

Or, you could surprise hubby with a yummy devil's food layer cake, made from scratch in the nude.

Or, if nothing seems to work, you can put your head down and suffer like any other dumb animal. This always does the trick for me.

Ha ha ha. How do you like it, Sister? Ha ha ha ha ha.

Bitterly Laughing in the Heartland

★ ★ ★

Dear Betty:

See? They're closing in. You had to try it, didn't you, you got them going, and now all hell's breaking loose. You took a sweet racket and ruined it, and for what? Honor? Integrity? *Aesthetic principle?* Well, go ahead and martyr yourself, but leave me out of it.

F.P.S.

READERS:

For what it's worth,

BETTY REALLY BELIEVES

1. That God is criminally irresponsible.
2. That nobility is possible.
3. That hope is necessary.
4. That courage is commonplace.
5. That sentimentality is wicked.
6. That cynicism is worse.
7. That most people are surprisingly good sports.
8. That some people are irredeemable idiots.
9. That everybody on the Board of Directors of GM, Ford, Chrysler, and U.S. Steel, and every third member of Congress and the Cabinet, ought to be taken out, lined up against a wall and shot.
10. That whining, though ugly, sometimes advances the ball.

How about it, Readers? What do *you* believe?

⭐ ⭐ ⭐

Dear Betty:

Does anybody have the recipe for Kooky Cake?

Kooky in Dubuque

Dear Kooky:

Forget the cake. The cake is terrible. What we're trying for here is a community of souls, a free exchange of original thoughts, an unrehearsed, raucous, a cappella chorus of Middle American women.

A Symphony of Gals!

Kooky, for God's sake, tell me your fears, your dreams, your awfulest secrets, and I'll tell you mine. Tell me, for instance, why you use that degrading nickname. I'm sending you my private phone number. Use it. Call me, Kooky. Call me anytime. Call collect. *Call soon.*

That goes for everybody else. All my dear readers, the loyal and the hateful, the genuine and the fictional, the rich and the strange. Call me anytime. Or, I'll send you my home address. Drop in. I'm serious. Let's talk.

Serious? You're critical. These people are going to kill you.

These people are my dearest friends. I love them all.

You do not! You don't even know them!

What's the question?

But . . . sentimentality is wicked.

But cynicism is worse.

SONG OF THE SHIRT, 1941

Dorothy Parker

★ ★ ★

It was one of those extraordinarily bright days that make things look somehow bigger. The Avenue seemed to stretch wider and longer, and the buildings to leap higher into the skies. The window-box blooms were not just a mass and a blur; it was as if they had been enlarged, so that you could see the design of the blossoms and even their separate petals. Indeed you could sharply see all sorts of pleasant things that were usually too small for your notice—the lean figurines on radiator caps, and the nice round gold knobs on flagpoles, the flowers and fruits on ladies' hats and the creamy dew applied to the eyelids beneath them. There should be more of such days.

The exceptional brightness must have had its effect upon unseen objects, too, for Mrs. Martindale, as she paused to look up the Avenue, seemed actually to feel her heart grow bigger than ever within her. The size of Mrs. Martindale's heart was renowned among her friends, and they, as friends will, had gone around babbling about it. And so Mrs. Martindale's name was high on the lists of all those organizations that send out appeals to buy tickets and she was frequently obliged to be photographed seated at a table, listening eagerly to her neighbor, at some function for the good of charity. Her big heart did not, as is so sadly often the case, inhabit a big bosom. Mrs. Martindale's breasts were admirable, delicate yet firm, pointing one to the right, one to the left; angry at each other, as the Russians have it.

Her heart was the warmer, now, for the fine sight of the Avenue. All the flags looked brand-new. The red and the white and the blue were so vivid they fairly vibrated, and the crisp stars seemed to dance on their points. Mrs. Martindale had a flag, too, clipped to the lapel of her jacket. She had had quantities of rubies and diamonds and sapphires just knocking about, set in floral designs on evening bags and vanity boxes and cigarette-cases; she had taken the lot of them to her jeweller, and he had assembled them into a charming little Old Glory. There had been enough of them for him to devise a rippled flag, and that was fortunate, for those flat flags looked sharp and stiff. There were numbers of emeralds, formerly figuring as leaves and stems in the floral designs, which were of course of no use to the present scheme and so were left over, in an embossed leather case. Someday, perhaps, Mrs. Martindale would confer with her jeweller about an arrangement to employ them. But there was no time for such matters now.

There were many men in uniform walking along the Avenue under the bright banners. The soldiers strode quickly and surely, each on to a destination. The sailors, two by two, ambled, paused at a corner and looked down a street, gave it up and went slower along their unknown way. Mrs. Martindale's heart grew again as she looked at them. She had a friend who made a practice of stopping uniformed men on the street and thanking them, individually, for what they were doing for *her*. Mrs. Martindale felt that this was going unnecessarily far. Still, she did see, a little bit, what her friend meant.

And surely no soldier or sailor would have objected to being addressed by Mrs. Martindale. For she was lovely, and no other woman was lovely like her. She was tall, and her body streamed like a sonnet. Her face was formed all of triangles, as a cat's is, and her eyes and her hair were blue-gray. Her hair did not taper in its growth about her forehead and temples; it sprang suddenly, in great thick waves, from a straight line across her brow. Its blue-gray was not premature. Mrs. Martindale lingered in her fragrant forties. Has not afternoon been adjudged the fairest time of the day?

To see her, so delicately done, so finely finished, so softly sheltered by her very loveliness, you might have laughed to hear that she was a working-woman. "Go on!" you might have said, had such been your unfortunate manner of expressing disbelief. But you would have been worse than coarse; you would have been wrong. Mrs. Martindale worked, and worked hard. She worked doubly hard, for she was unskilled at what she did, and she disliked the doing of it. But for two months she had worked every afternoon five afternoons of every week, and had shirked no moment. She received no remuneration for her steady services. She gave them because she felt she should do so. She felt that you should do what you could, hard and humbly. She practiced what she felt.

The special office of the war-relief organization where Mrs. Martindale served was known to her and her coworkers as Headquarters; some of them had come to call it H.Q. These last were of the group that kept agitating for the adoption of a uniform—the design had not been thoroughly worked out, but the idea was of something nurselike, only with a fuller skirt and a long blue cape and white gauntlets. Mrs. Martindale was not in agreement with this faction. It had always been hard for her to raise her voice in opposition, but she did, although softly. She said that while of course there was nothing *wrong* about a uniform, certainly nobody could possibly say there was anything *wrong* with the idea, still it seemed—well, it seemed not quite right to make the work an excuse, well, for fancy dress, if they didn't mind her saying so. Naturally, they wore their coifs at Headquarters, and if anybody wanted to take your photograph in your coif, you should go through with it, because it was good for the organization and publicized its work. But please, not whole uniforms, said Mrs. Martindale. Really, *please,* Mrs. Martindale said.

Headquarters was, many said, the stiffest office of all the offices of all the war-relief organizations in the city. It was not a place where you dropped in and knitted. Knitting, once you have caught the hang of it, is agreeable work, a relaxation from what strains life may be putting upon you. When you knit, save when you are at those bits where you must count stitches, there is enough of your mind left over for you to take part in conversations, and for you to be receptive of news and generous with it. But at Headquarters they sewed. They did a particularly difficult and tedious form of sewing. They made those short, shirtlike coats, fastened in back with tapes, that are put on patients in hospitals. Each garment must have two sleeves, and all the edges must be securely bound. The material was harsh to the touch and the smell, and impatient of the needle of the novice. Mrs. Martindale had made three and had another almost half done. She had thought that after the first one the others would be easier and quicker of manufacture. They had not been.

There were sewing machines at Headquarters, but few of the workers understood the running of them. Mrs. Martindale herself was secretly afraid of a machine; there had been a nasty story, never traced to its source, of somebody who put her thumb in the wrong place, and down came the needle, right through nail and all. Besides, there was something—you didn't know quite how to say it—something more of sacrifice, of service, in making things by hand. She kept on at the task that never grew lighter. It was wished that there were more of her caliber.

For many of the workers had given up the whole thing long before their first garment was finished. And many others, pledged to daily attendance, came only now and then. There was but a handful like Mrs. Martindale.

All gave their services, although there were certain doubts about Mrs. Corning, who managed Headquarters. It was she who oversaw the work, who cut out the garments, and explained to the workers what pieces went next to what other pieces. (It did not always come out as intended. One amateur seamstress toiled all the way to the completion of a coat that had one sleeve depending from the middle of the front. It was impossible to keep from laughing; and a sharp tongue suggested that it might be sent in as it was, in case an elephant was brought to bed. Mrs. Martindale was the first to say, "Ah, don't! She worked so hard over it.") Mrs. Corning was a cross woman, hated by all. The high standards of Headquarters were important to the feelings of the workers, but it was agreed that there was no need for Mrs. Corning to scold so shrilly when one of them moistened the end of her thread between her lips before thrusting it into her needle.

"Well, really," one of the most spirited among the rebuked had answered her. "If a little clean spit's the worst they're ever going to get on them . . ."

The spirited one had returned no more to Headquarters, and there were those who felt that she was right. The episode drew new members into the school of thought that insisted Mrs. Corning was paid for what she did.

When Mrs. Martindale paused in the clear light and looked along the Avenue, it was at a moment of earned leisure. She had just left Headquarters. She was not to go back to it for many weeks, nor were any of the other workers. Somewhere the cuckoo had doubtless sung for summer was coming in. And what with everybody leaving town, it was only sensible to shut Headquarters until autumn. Mrs. Martindale, and with no guilt about it, had looked forward to a holiday from all that sewing.

Well, she was to have none, it turned out. While the workers were gaily bidding farewells and calling out appointments for the autumn, Mrs. Corning had cleared her throat hard to induce quiet and had made a short speech. She stood beside a table piled with cut-out sections of hospital coats not yet sewn together. She was a graceless woman, and though it may be assumed that she meant to be appealing, she sounded only disagreeable. There was, she said, a desperate need, a dreadful need, for hospital garments. More were wanted right away, hundreds and thousands of them; the organization had had a cable that morning urging and pleading. Headquarters was closing until September—that meant all work would stop. Certainly they had all earned a vacation. And yet, in the face of the terrible need, she could not help asking—she would like to call for volunteers to take coats with them, to work on at home.

There was a little silence, and then a murmur of voices, gaining in volume and in assurance as the owner of each realized that it was not the only one. Most of the workers, it seemed, would have been perfectly willing, but they felt that they absolutely must give their entire time to their children, whom they had scarcely *seen* because of being at Headquarters so constantly. Others said they were just plain too worn out, and that was all there was to it. It must be admitted that for some moments Mrs. Martindale felt with this latter group. Then shame waved over her like a blush, and swiftly, quietly, with the blue-gray head held high, she went to Mrs. Corning.

"Mrs. Corning," she said. "I should like to take twelve, please."

Mrs. Corning was nicer than Mrs. Martindale had ever seen her. She put out her hand and grasped Mrs. Martindale's.

"Thank you," she said, and her shrill voice was gentle.

But then she had to go and be the way she always had been before. She snatched her hand from Mrs. Martindale's and turned to the table, starting to assemble garments.

"And please, Mrs. Martindale," she said, shrilly, "kindly try and remember to keep the seams straight. Wounded people can be made terribly uncomfortable by crooked seams, you know. And if you could manage to get your stitches even, the coat would look much more professional and give our organization a higher standing. And time is terribly important. They're in an awful hurry for these. So if you could just manage to be a little quicker, it would help a lot."

Really, if Mrs. Martindale hadn't offered to take the things, she would have . . .

The twelve coats still in sections, together with the coat that was half finished, made a formidable bundle. Mrs. Martindale had to send down for her chauffeur to come and carry it to her car for her. While she waited for him, several of the workers came up, rather slowly, and volunteered to sew at home. Four was the highest number of garments promised.

Mrs. Martindale did say good-by to Mrs. Corning, but she expressed no pleasure at the hope of seeing her again in the autumn. You do what you can, and you do it because you should. But all you can do is all you can do.

Out on the Avenue, Mrs. Martindale was herself again. She kept her eyes from the great package the chauffeur had placed in the car. After all, she might, and honorably, allow herself a recess. She need not go home and start sewing again immediately. She would send the chauffeur home with the bundle, and walk in the pretty air, and not think of unfinished coats.

But the men in uniform went along the Avenue under the snapping flags, and in the sharp, true light you could see all their faces; their clean bones and their firm skin and their eyes, the confident eyes of the soldiers and the wistful eyes of the sailors. They were so young, all of them, and all of them doing what they could, doing everything they could, doing it hard and humbly, without question and without credit. Mrs. Martindale put her hand to her heart. Someday, maybe, someday some of them might be lying on hospital cots . . .

Mrs. Martindale squared her delicate shoulders and entered her car.

"Home, please," she told her chauffeur. "And I'm in rather a hurry."

At home, Mrs. Martindale had her maid unpack the clumsy bundle and lay the contents in her upstairs sitting-room. Mrs. Martindale took off her outdoor garments and bound her head, just back of the first great blue-gray wave, in the soft linen coif she had habitually worn at Headquarters. She entered her sitting-room, which had recently been redone in the color of her hair and her eyes; it had taken a deal of mixing and matching, but it was a success. There were touches, splashes rather, of magenta about, for Mrs. Martindale complemented brilliant colors and made them and herself glow sweeter. She looked at the ugly, high pile of unmade coats, and there was a second when her famous heart shrank. But it swelled to its norm again as she felt what she must do. There was no good thinking about those twelve damned new ones. Her job immediately was to get on with the coat she had half made.

She sat down on quilted blue-gray satin and set herself to her task. She was at the most hateful stretch of the garment—the binding of the rounded neck. Everything pulled out of place, and nothing came out even, and a horrid starchy smell rose from the thick material, and the stitches that she struggled to put so prettily appeared all different sizes and all faintly gray. Over and over, she had to rip them out for their imperfection, and load her needle again without moistening the thread between her lips, and see them wild and straggling once more. She felt almost ill from the tussle with the hard, monotonous work.

Her maid came in, mincingly, and told her that Mrs. Wyman wished to speak to her on the telephone; Mrs. Wyman wanted to ask a favor of her. Those were two of the penalties attached to the possession of a heart the size of Mrs. Martindale's—people were constantly telephoning to ask her favors and she was constantly granting them. She put down her sewing, with a sigh that might have been of one thing or of another, and went to the telephone.

Mrs. Wyman, too, had a big heart, but it was not well set. She was a great, hulking, stupidly dressed woman, with flapping cheeks and bee-stung eyes. She spoke with rapid diffidence, inserting apologies before she needed to make them, and so was a bore and invited avoidance.

"Oh, my dear," she said now to Mrs. Martindale, "I'm so sorry to bother you. Please do forgive me. But I do want to ask you to do me the most tremendous favor. Please do excuse me. But I want to ask you, do you possibly happen to know of anybody who could possibly use my little Mrs. Christie?"

"Your Mrs. Christie?" Mrs. Martindale asked. "Now, I don't think—or do I?"

"You know," Mrs. Wyman said. "I wouldn't have bothered you for the world, with all you do and all, but you know my little Mrs. Christie. She has that daughter that had infantile, and she has to support her, and I just don't know *what* she's going to do. I wouldn't have bothered you for the world, only I've been sort of thinking up jobs for her to do for me right along, but next week we're going to the ranch, and I really don't know *what* will become of her. And the crippled daughter and all. They just won't be able to *live!*"

Mrs. Martindale made a soft little moan. "Oh, how awful," she said. "How perfectly awful. Oh, I wish I could—tell me, what can I do?"

"Well, if you could just think of somebody that could use her," Mrs. Wyman said. "I wouldn't have bothered you, honestly I wouldn't, but I just didn't know who to turn to. And Mrs. Christie's really a wonderful little woman—she can do anything. Of course, the thing is, she has to work at home, because she wants to take care of the crippled child—well, you can't blame her, really. But she'll call for things and bring them back. And she's so quick, and so good. Please do forgive me for bothering you, but if you could just think—"

"Oh, there must be somebody!" Mrs. Martindale cried. "I'll think of somebody. I'll rack my brains, truly I will. I'll call you up as soon as I think."

Mrs. Martindale went back to her blue-gray quilted satin. Again she took up the unfinished coat. A shaft of the exceptionally bright sunlight shot past a vase of butterfly orchids and settled upon the waving hair under the gracious coif. But Mrs. Martindale did not turn to meet it. Her blue-gray eyes were bent on the drudgery of her fingers. This coat, and then the twelve others beyond it. The need, the desperate, dreadful need, and the terrible importance of time. She took a stitch and another stitch and another stitch and another stitch; she looked at their wavering line, pulled the thread from her needle, ripped out three of the stitches, rethreaded her needle, and stitched again. And as she stitched, faithful to her promise and to her heart, she racked her brains.

THE GIRL WITH THE BLACKENED EYE

Joyce Carol Oates

★ ★ ★

From *Witness*

This black eye I had, once! Like a clown's eye painted on. Both my eyes were bruised and ugly but the right eye was swollen almost shut, people must've seen me and I wonder what they were thinking. I mean you have to wonder. Nobody said a word—didn't want to get involved, I guess. You have to wonder what went through their minds, though.

Sometimes now I see myself in a mirror, like in the middle of the night getting up to use the bathroom, I see a blurred face, a woman's face I don't recognize. And I see that eye.

Twenty-seven years.

In America, that's a lifetime.

✷ ✷ ✷

This weird thing that happened to me, fifteen years old and a soph-omore at Menlo Park High, living with my family in Menlo Park, California, where Dad was a dental surgeon (which was lucky: I'd need dental and gum surgery, to repair the damage to my mouth). Weird, and wild. Ugly. I've never told anyone who knows me now. Especially my daughters. My husband doesn't know, he couldn't have handled it. We were in our late twenties when we met, no need to drag up the past. I never do. I'm not one of those. I left California forever when I went to college in Vermont. My family moved, too. They live in Seattle now. There's a stiffness between us, we never talk about that time. Never say that man's name. So it's like it never did happen.

Or, if it did, it happened to someone else. A high school girl in the 1970s. A silly little girl who wore tank tops and jeans so tight she had to lie down on her bed to wriggle into them, and teased her hair into a mane. That girl.

When they found me, my hair was wild and tangled like broom sage. It couldn't be combed through, had to be cut from my head in clumps. Something sticky like cobwebs was in it. I'd been wearing it long since ninth grade and after that I kept it cut short for years. Like a guy's hair, the back of my neck shaved and my ears showing.

I'd been forcibly abducted at the age of fifteen. It was some-thing that could happen to you, from the outside, *forcibly abducted*, like being in a plane crash, or struck by lightning. There wouldn't be any human agent, almost. The human agent wouldn't have a name. I'd been walking through the mall parking lot to the bus stop, about 5:30 p.m., a weekday, I'd come to the mall after school with some kids, now I was headed home, and somehow it happened, don't ask me how, a guy was asking me questions, or saying something, mainly I registered he was an adult my dad's age possibly, every adult man looked like my dad's age except obviously old white-haired men. I hadn't any clear impression of this guy except afterward I would recall rings on his fingers which would've caused me to glance up at his face with interest except at that instant something slammed into the back of my head behind my ear, knocking me forward, and down, like he'd thrown a hook at me from in front, I was on my face on the sun-heated vinyl upholstery of a car, or a van, and another blow or blows knocked me out. Like anesthesia, it was. You're out.

This was the *forcible abduction*. How it might be described by a witness who was there, who was also the victim. But who hadn't any memory of what happened because it happened so fast, and she hadn't been personally involved.

It's like they say. You are there, and not-there. He drove to this place in the Sonoma Mountains, I would afterward learn, this cabin it would be called, and he raped me, beat me, and shocked me with electrical cords and he stubbed cigarette butts on my stomach and breasts, and he said things to me like he knew me, he knew all my secrets, what a dirty-minded girl I was, what a nasty girl, and selfish, like everyone of my *privileged class* as he called it. I'm saying these things were done to me but in fact they were done to my body mostly. Like the cabin was in the Sonoma Mountains north of Healdsburg but it was just anywhere for those eight days, and I was anywhere, I was holding on to being alive the way you would hold on to a straw you could breathe through, lying at the bottom of deep water. And that water opaque, you can't see through to the surface.

He was gone, and he came back. He left me tied in the bed, it was a cot with a thin mattress, very dirty. There were only two windows in the cabin and there were blinds over them drawn tight. It was hot during what I guessed was the day. It was cool, and it was very quiet, at night. The lower parts of me were raw and throbbing with pain and other parts of me were in a haze of pain so I wasn't able to think, and I wasn't awake most of the time, not what you'd call actual wakefulness, with a personality.

What you call your personality, you know?—it's not the actual bones, or teeth, something solid. It's more like a flame. A flame can be upright, and a flame can flicker in the wind, a flame can be extinguished so there's no sign of it, like it had never been.

My eyes had been hurt, he'd mashed his fists into my eyes. The eyelids were puffy, I couldn't see very well. It was like I didn't try to see, I was saving my eyesight for when I was stronger. I had not seen the man's face actually. I had felt him but I had not seen him, I could not have identified him. Any more than you could identify yourself if you had never seen yourself in a mirror or in any likeness.

In one of my dreams I was saying to my family I would not be seeing them for a while, I was going away. *I'm going away, I want to say good-bye.* Their faces were blurred. My sister, I was closer to than my parents, she's two years older than me and I adored her, my sister was crying, her face was blurred with tears. She asked where I was going and I said I didn't know, but I wanted to say good-bye, and I wanted to say *I love you.* And this was so vivid it would seem to me to have happened actually, and was more real than other things that happened to me during that time I would learn afterward was eight days.

It might've been the same day repeated, or it might've been eighty days. It was a place, not a day. Like a dimension you could slip into, or be sucked into, by an undertow. And it's there, but no one is aware of it. Until you're in it, you don't know; but when you're in it, it's all that you know. So you have no way of speaking of it except like this. Stammering, and ignorant.

★ ★ ★

Why he brought me water and food, why he decided to let me live, would never be clear. The others he'd killed after a few days. They went stale on him, you have to suppose. One of the bodies was buried in the woods a few hundred yards behind the cabin, others were dumped along Route 101 as far north as Crescent City. And possibly there were others never known, never located or identified. These facts, if they are facts, I would learn later, as I would learn that the other girls and women had been older than me, the oldest was thirty, and the youngest he'd been on record as killing was eighteen. So it was speculated he had mercy on me because he hadn't realized, abducting me in the parking lot, that I was so young, and in my battered condition in the cabin, when I'd started losing weight, I must've looked to him like a child. I was crying a lot, and calling *Mommy! Mom-my!*

Like my own kids, grown, would call *Mom-my!* in some nightmare they were trapped in. But I never think of such things.

The man with the rings on his fingers, saying, There's some reason I don't know yet, that you have been spared.

Later I would look back and think, there was a turn, a shifting of fortune, when he first allowed me to wash. To wash! He could see I was ashamed, I was a naturally shy, clean girl. He allowed this. He might have assisted me, a little. He picked ticks out of my skin where they were invisible and gorged with blood. He hated ticks! They disgusted him. He went away, and came back with food and Hires diet root beer. We are together sitting on the edge of the cot. And once when he allowed me out into the clearing at dusk. Like a picnic. His greasy fingers, and mine. Fried chicken, french fries and runny coleslaw, my hands started shaking and my mouth was on fire. And my stomach convulsing with hunger, cramps that doubled me over like he'd sunk a knife into my guts and twisted. Still, I was able to eat some things, in little bites. I did not starve. Seeing the color come back into my face, he was impressed, stirred. He said, in mild reproach, Hey, a butterfly could eat more'n you.

I would remember these pale-yellow butterflies around the cabin. A swarm of them. And jays screaming, waiting to swoop down to snatch up food.

I guess I was pretty sick. Delirious. My gums were infected. Four of my teeth were broken. Blood kept leaking to the back of my mouth, making me sick, gagging. But I could walk to the car leaning against him, I was able to sit up normally in the passenger's seat, buckled in, he always made sure to buckle me in, and a wire wound tight around my ankles. Driving then out of the forest, and the foothills I could not have identified as the Sonoma hills, and the sun high and gauzy in the sky, and I lost track of time, lapsing in and out of time but noticing that highway traffic was changing to suburban, more traffic lights, we were cruising through parking lots so vast you couldn't see to the edge of them, sun-blinded spaces and rows of glittering cars like grave markers: I saw them suddenly in a cemetery that went on forever.

He wanted me with him all the time now, he said. Keep an eye on you, girl. Maybe I was his trophy? The only female in his abducting/raping/killing spree of an estimated seventeen months to be publicly displayed. Not beaten, strangled, raped to death, kicked to death and buried like animal carrion. (This I would learn later.) Or maybe I was meant to signal to the world, if the world glanced through the windshield of his car, his daughter. A sign of— what? *Hey, I'm normal. I'm a nice guy, see.*

Except the daughter's hair was wild and matted, her eyes were bruised and one of them swollen almost shut. Her mouth was a slack puffy wound. Bruises on her face and throat and arms and her ribs were cracked, skinny body was covered in pus-leaking burns and sores. Yet he'd allowed me to wash, and he'd allowed me to wash out my clothes, I was less filthy now. He'd given me a T-shirt too big for me, already soiled but I was grateful for it. Through acres of parking lots we cruised like sharks seeking prey. I was aware of people glancing into the car, just by accident, seeing me, or maybe not seeing me, there were reflections in the windshield (weren't there?) because of the sun, so maybe they didn't see me, or didn't see me clearly. Yet others, seeing me, looked away. It did not occur to me at the time that there must be a search for me, my face in the papers, on TV. My face as it had been. At the time I'd stopped thinking of that other world. Mostly I'd stopped thinking. It was like anesthesia, you give in to it, there's peace in it, almost. As cruising the parking lots with the man whistling to himself, humming, talking in a low affable monotone, I understood that he wasn't thinking either, as a predator fish would not be thinking cruising beneath the surface of the ocean. The silent gliding of sharks, that never cease their motion. I was concerned mostly with sitting right: my head balanced on my neck, which isn't easy to do, and the wire wound tight around my ankles cutting off circulation. I knew of gangrene, I knew of toes and entire feet going black with rot. From my father I knew of tooth-rot, gum-rot. I was trying not to think of those strangers who must've seen me, sure they saw me, and turned away, uncertain what they'd seen but knowing it was trouble, not wanting to know more.

Just a girl with a blackened eye, you figure she maybe deserved it.

He said: There must be some reason you are spared.

He said, in my daddy's voice from a long time ago, Know what, girl?—you're not like the others. That's why.

They would say he was insane, these were the acts of an insane person. And I would not disagree. Though I knew it was not so.

★ ★ ★

The red-haired woman in the khaki jacket and matching pants. Eventually she would have a name but it was not a name I would wish to know, none of them were. This was a woman, not a girl. He'd put me in the backseat of his car now, so the passenger's seat was empty. He'd buckled me safely in. O.K., girl? You be good, now. We cruised the giant parking lot at dusk. When the lights first come on. (Where was this? Ukiah. Where I'd never been. Except for the red-haired woman I would have no memory of Ukiah.)

He'd removed his rings. He was wearing a white baseball cap.

There came this red-haired woman beside him smiling, talking like they were friends. I stared, I was astonished. They were coming toward the car. Never could I imagine what those two were talking about! I thought, *He will trade me for her* and I was frightened. The man in the baseball cap wearing shiny dark glasses asking the red-haired woman—what? Directions? Yet he had the power to make her smile, there was a sexual ease between them. She was a mature woman with a shapely body, breasts I could envy and hips in the tight-fitting khaki pants that were stylish pants, with a drawstring waist. I felt a rush of anger for this woman, contempt, disgust, how stupid she was, unsuspecting, bending to peer at me where possibly she'd been told the man's daughter was sitting, maybe he'd said his daughter had a question for her? needed an adult female's advice? and in an instant she would find herself shoved forward onto the front seat of the car, down on her face, her chest, helpless, as fast as you might snap your fingers, too fast for her to cry out. So fast, you understand it had happened many times before. The girl in the backseat blinking and staring and unable to speak though she wasn't gagged, no more able to scream for help than the woman struggling for her life a few inches away. She shuddered in sympathy, she moaned as the man pounded the woman with his fists. Furious, grunting! His eyes bulged. Were there no witnesses? No one to see? Deftly he wrapped a blanket around the woman, who'd gone limp, wrapping it tight around her head and chest, he shoved her legs inside the car and shut the door and climbed into the driver's seat and drove away humming, happy. In the backseat the girl was crying. If she'd had tears she would have cried.

Weird how your mind works: I was thinking I was that woman, in the front seat wrapped in the blanket, so the rest of it had not yet happened.

It was that time, I think, I saw my mom. In the parking lot. There were shoppers, mostly women. And my mom was one of them. I knew it couldn't be her, so far from home, I knew I was hundreds of miles from home, so it couldn't be, but I saw her, Mom crossing in front of the car, walking briskly to the entrance of Lord & Taylor.

Yet I couldn't wave to her, my arm was heavy as lead.

✷ ✷ ✷

Yes. In the cabin I was made to witness what he did to the red-haired woman. I saw now that this was my importance to him: I would be a witness to his fury, his indignation, his disgust. Tying the woman's wrists to the iron rails of the bed, spreading her legs and tying her ankles. Naked, the red-haired woman had no power. There was no sexual ease to her now, no confidence. You would not envy her now. You would scorn her now. You would not wish to be her now. She'd become a chicken on a spit.

I had to watch, I could not close my eyes or look away.

For it had happened already, it was completed. There was certitude in this, and peace in certitude. When there is no escape, for what is happening has already happened. Not once but many times.

When you give up struggle, there's a kind of love.

The red-haired woman did not know this, in her terror. But I was the witness, I knew.

They would ask me about him. I saw only parts of him. Like jigsaw puzzle parts. Like quick camera jumps and cuts. His back was pale and flaccid at the waist, more muscular at the shoulders. It was a broad pimply sweating back. It was a part of a man, like my dad, I would not see. Not in this way. Not straining, tensing. And the smell of a man's hair, like congealed oil. His hair was stiff, dark, threaded with silver hairs like wires, at the crown of his head you could see the scalp beneath. On his torso and legs, hairs grew in dense waves and rivulets like water or grasses. He was grunting, he was making a high-pitched moaning sound. When he turned, I saw a fierce blurred face, I didn't recognize that face. And the nipples of a man's breasts, wine-colored like berries. Between his thighs the angry thing swung like the length of rubber, slick and darkened with blood.

I would recall, yes, he had tattoos. Smudged-looking like inkblots. Never did I see them clearly. Never did I see him clearly. I would not have dared as you would not look into the sun in terror of being blinded.

He kept us there together for three days. I mean, the red-haired woman was there for three days, unconscious most of the time. There was a mercy in this. You learn to take note of small mercies and be grateful for them. Nor would he kill her in the cabin. When he was finished with her, disgusted with her, he half-carried her out to the car. I was alone, and frightened. But then he returned and said, O.K., girl, goin for a ride. I was able to walk, just barely. I was very dizzy. I would ride in the backseat of the car like a big rag doll, boneless and unresisting.

He'd shoved the woman down beside him, hidden by a blanket wrapped around her head and upper body. She was not struggling now, her body was limp and unresisting for she, too, had weakened in the cabin, she'd lost weight. You learned to be weak to please him for you did not want to displease him in even the smallest things. Yet the woman managed to speak, this small choked begging voice. Don't kill me, please. I won't tell anybody. I won't tell anybody don't kill me. I have a little daughter, please don't kill me. Please, God. Please.

I wasn't sure if this voice was (somehow) a made-up voice. A voice of my imagination. Or like on TV. Or my own voice, if I'd been older and had a daughter. *Please don't kill me. Please, God.*

For always it's this voice when you're alone and silent you hear it.

* * *

Afterward they would speculate that he'd panicked. Seeing TV spot announcements, the photographs of his "victims." When last seen and where, Menlo Park, Ukiah. There were witnesses' descriptions of *the abductor* and a police sketch of his face, coarser and uglier and older than his face which was now disguised by dark glasses. In the drawing he was clean-shaven but now his jaws were covered in several days' beard, a stubbly beard, his hair was tied in a ponytail and the baseball cap pulled low on his head. Yet you could recognize him in the drawing, that looked as if it had been executed by a blind man. So he'd panicked.

The first car he'd been driving he left at the cabin, he was driving another, a stolen car with switched license plates. You came to see that his life was such maneuvers. He was tireless in invention as a willful child and would seem to have had no purpose beyond such maneuvers and when afterward I would learn details of his background, his family life in San Jose, his early incarcerations as a juvenile, as a youth, as an adult "offender" now on parole from Bakersfield maximum security prison, I would block off such information as not related to me, not related to the man who'd existed exclusively for me as, for a brief while, I'd existed exclusively for him. I was contemptuous of "facts" for I came to know that no accumulation of facts constitutes knowledge, and no impersonal knowledge constitutes the intimacy of knowing.

Know what, girl? You're not like the others. You're special. That's the reason.

* * *

Driving fast, farther into the foothills. The road was even narrower and bumpier. There were few vehicles on the road, all of them minivans or campers. He never spoke to the red-haired woman moaning and whimpering beside him but to me in the backseat, looking at me in the rearview mirror, the way my dad used to do when I rode in the backseat, and Mom was up front with him. He said, How ya doin, girl?

O.K.

Doing O.K., huh?

Yes.

I'm gonna let you go, girl, you know that, huh? Gonna give you your freedom.

To this I could not reply. My swollen lips moved in a kind of smile as you smile out of politeness.

Less you want to trade? With her?

Again I could not reply. I wasn't certain what the question was. My smile ached in my face but it was a sincere smile.

He parked the car on an unpaved lane off the road. He waited, no vehicles approaching. There were no aircraft overhead. It was very quiet except for birds. He said, C'mon, help me, girl. So I moved my legs that were stiff, my legs that felt strange and skinny to me, I climbed out of the car and fought off dizziness helping him with the bound woman, he'd pulled the blanket off her, her discolored swollen face, her face that wasn't attractive now, scabby mouth and panicked eyes, brown eyes they were, I would remember those eyes pleading. For they were my own, but in one who was doomed as I was not. He said then, so strangely: Stay here, girl. Watch the car. Somebody shows up, honk the horn. Two-three times. Got it?

I whispered yes. I was staring at the crumbly earth.

I could not look at the woman now. I would not watch them move away into the woods.

Maybe it was a test, he'd left the key in the ignition. It was to make me think I could drive the car away from there, I could drive to get help, or I could run out onto the road and get help. Maybe I could get help. He had a gun, and he had knives, but I could have driven away. But the sun was beating on my head, I couldn't move.

My legs were heavy like lead. My eye was swollen shut and throbbing. I believed it was a test but I wasn't certain. Afterward they would ask if I'd had any chance to escape in those days he kept me captive and always I said no, no I did not have a chance to escape. Because that was so. That was how it was to me, that I could not explain.

Yet I remember the keys in the ignition, and I remember that the road was close by. He would strangle the woman, that was his way of killing and this I seemed to know. It would require some minutes. It was not an easy way of killing. I could run, I could run along the road and hope that someone would come along, or I could hide, and he wouldn't find me in all that wilderness, if he called me I would not answer. But I stood there beside the car because I could not do these things. He trusted me, and I could not betray that trust. Even if he would kill me, I could not betray him.

Yes, I heard her screams in the woods. I think I heard. It might have been jays. It might have been my own screams I heard. But I heard them.

☆ ☆ ☆

A few days later he would be dead. He would be shot down by police in a motel parking lot in Petaluma. Why he was there, in that place, about fifty miles from the cabin, I don't know. He'd left me in the cabin chained to the bed. It was filthy, flies and ants. The chain was long enough for me to use the toilet. But the toilet was backed up. Blinds were drawn on the windows. I did not dare to take them down or break the windowpanes but I looked out, I saw just the clearing, a haze of green. Overhead there were small planes sometimes. A helicopter. I wanted to think that somebody would rescue me but I knew better, I knew nobody would find me.

But they did find me.

He told them where the cabin was, when he was dying. He did that for me. He drew a rough map and I have that map!—not the actual piece of paper but a copy. He would never see me again, and I would have trouble recalling his face for I never truly saw it.

Photographs of him were not accurate. Even his name, printed out, is misleading. For it could be anyone's name and not *his*.

In my present life I never speak of these things. I have never told anyone. There would be no point to it. Why I've told you, I don't know: you might write about me but you would respect my privacy.

Because if you wrote about me, these things that happened to me so long ago, no one would know it was me. And you would disguise it so that no one could guess, that's why I trust you.

My life afterward is what's unreal. The life then, those eight days, was very real. The two don't seem to be connected, do they? I learned you don't discover the evidence of any cause in its result. Philosophers debate over that but if you know, you know. There is no connection though people wish to think so. When I was recovered I went back to Menlo Park High and I graduated with my class and I went to college in Vermont, I met my husband in New York a few years later and married him and had my babies and none of my life would be different in any way, I believe, if I had not been "abducted" when I was fifteen.

Sure, I see him sometimes. More often lately. On the street, in a passing car. In profile, I see him. In his shiny dark glasses and white baseball cap. A man's forearm, a thick pelt of hair on it, a tattoo, I see him. The shock of it is, he's only thirty-two.

That's so young now. Your life all before you, almost.

PEOPLE LIKE THAT ARE THE ONLY PEOPLE HERE: CANONICAL BABBLING IN PEED ONK

Lorrie Moore

A beginning, an end: there seems to be neither. The whole thing is like a cloud that just lands and everywhere inside it is full of rain. A start: the Mother finds a blood clot in the Baby's diaper. What is the story? Who put this here? It is big and bright, with a broken khaki-colored vein in it. Over the weekend, the Baby had looked listless and spacey, clayey and grim. But today he looks fine—so what is this thing, startling against the white diaper, like a tiny mouse heart packed in snow? Perhaps it belongs to someone else. Perhaps it is something menstrual, something belonging to the

Mother or to the Babysitter, something the Baby has found in a wastebasket and for his own demented baby reasons stowed away here. (Babies they're crazy! What can you do?) In her mind, the Mother takes this away from his body and attaches it to someone else's. There. Doesn't that make more sense?

★ ★ ★

Still, she phones the clinic at the children's hospital. "Blood in the diaper," she says, and, sounding alarmed and perplexed, the woman on the other end says, "Come in now."

Such pleasingly instant service! Just say "blood." Just say "diaper." Look what you get!

In the examination room, pediatrician, nurse, head resident— all seem less alarmed and perplexed than simply perplexed. At first, stupidly, the Mother is calmed by this. But soon, besides peering and saying "Hmmmm," the pediatrician, nurse, and head resident are all drawing their mouths in, bluish and tight—morning glories sensing noon. They fold their arms across their white-coated chests, unfold them again and jot things down. They order an ultrasound. Bladder and kidneys. "Here's the card. Go downstairs; turn left."

★ ★ ★

Radiology, the Baby stands anxiously on the table, naked against the Mother as she holds him still against her legs and waist, the Radiologist's cold scanning disc moving about the Baby's back. The Baby whimpers, looks up at the Mother. *Let's get out of here,* his eyes beg. *Pick me up!* The Radiologist stops, freezes one of the many swirls of oceanic gray, and clicks repeatedly, a single moment within the long, cavernous weather map that is the Baby's insides.

"Are you finding something?" asks the Mother. Last year, her uncle Larry had had a kidney removed for something that turned out to be benign. These imaging machines! They are like dogs, or metal detectors: they find everything, but don't know what they've found. That's where the surgeons come in. They're like the owners of the dogs. "Give me that," they say to the dog. "What the heck is that?"

"The surgeon will speak to you," says the Radiologist.

"Are you finding something?"

"The surgeon will speak to you," the Radiologist says again. "There seems to be something there, but the surgeon will talk to you about it."

"My uncle once had something on his kidney," says the Mother. "So they removed the kidney and it turned out the something was benign."

The Radiologist smiles a broad, ominous smile. "That's always the way it is," he says. "You don't know exactly what it is until it's in the bucket."

" 'In the bucket,'" the Mother repeats.

The Radiologist's grin grows scarily wider—is that even possible? "That's doctor talk," he says.

"It's very appealing," says the Mother. "It's a very appealing way to talk." Swirls of bile and blood, mustard and maroon in a pail, the colors of an African flag or some exuberant salad bar: *in the bucket*—she imagines it all.

"The Surgeon will see you soon," he says again. He tousles the Baby's ringletty hair. "Cute kid," he says.

✳ ✳ ✳

"Let's see now," says the Surgeon in one of his examining rooms. He has stepped in, then stepped out, then come back in again. He has crisp, frowning features, sharp bones, and a tennis-in-Bermuda tan. He crosses his blue-cottoned legs. He is wearing clogs.

The Mother knows her own face is a big white dumpling of worry. She is still wearing her long, dark parka, holding the Baby, who has pulled the hood up over her head because he always thinks it's funny to do that. Though on certain windy mornings she would like to think she could look vaguely romantic like this, like some French Lieutenant's Woman of the Prairie, in all of her saner moments she knows she doesn't. Ever. She knows she looks ridiculous—like one of those animals made out of twisted party balloons. She lowers the hood and slips one arm out of the sleeve. The Baby wants to get up and play with the light switch. He fidgets, fusses, and points.

"He's big on lights these days," explains the Mother.

"That's okay," says the Surgeon, nodding toward the light switch. "Let him play with it." The Mother goes and stands by it, and the Baby begins turning the lights off and on, off and on.

"What we have here is a Wilms' tumor," says the Surgeon, suddenly plunged into darkness. He says "tumor" as if it were the most normal thing in the world.

"Wilms'?" repeats the Mother. The room is quickly on fire again with light, then wiped dark again. Among the three of them here, there is a long silence, as if it were suddenly the middle of the night. "Is that apostrophe s or s apostrophe?" the Mother says finally. She is a writer and a teacher. Spelling can be important— perhaps even at a time like this, though she has never before been at a time like this, so there are barbarisms she could easily commit and not know.

The lights come on: the world is doused and exposed.

"S apostrophe," says the Surgeon. "I think." The lights go back out, but the Surgeon continues speaking in the dark. "A malignant tumor on the left kidney."

Wait a minute. Hold on here. The Baby is only a baby, fed an organic applesauce and soy milk—a little prince!—and he was standing so close to her during the ultrasound. How could he have this terrible thing? It must have been *her* kidney. A fifties kidney. A DDT kidney. The Mother clears her throat. "Is it possible it was my kidney on the scan? I mean, I've never heard of a baby with a tumor, and, frankly, I was standing very close." She would make the blood hers, the tumor hers; it would all be some treacherous, farcical mistake.

"No, that's not possible," says the Surgeon. The light goes back on.

"It's not?" says the Mother. Wait until it's *in the bucket,* she thinks. Don't be so sure. *Do we have to wait until it's in the bucket to find out a mistake has been made?*

"We will start with a radical nephrectomy," says the Surgeon, instantly thrown into darkness again. His voice comes from nowhere and everywhere at once. "And then we'll begin with chemotherapy after that. These tumors usually respond very well to chemo."

"I've never heard of a baby having chemo," the Mother says. *Baby* and *Chemo,* she thinks: they should never even appear in the same sentence together, let alone the same life. In her other life, her life before this day, she had been a believer in alternative medicine. Chemotherapy? Unthinkable. Now, suddenly, alternative medicine seems the wacko maiden aunt to the Nice Big Daddy of Conventional Treatment. How quickly the old girl faints and gives way, leaves one just standing there. Chemo? Of course: chemo! Why by all means: chemo. Absolutely! Chemo!

The Baby flicks the switch back on, and the walls reappear, big wedges of light checkered with small framed watercolors of the local lake. The Mother has begun to cry: all of life has led her here, to this moment. After this, there is no more life. There is something else, something stumbling and unlivable, something mechanical, something for robots, but not life. Life has been taken and broken, quickly, like a stick. The room goes dark again, so that the Mother can cry more freely. How can a baby's body be stolen so fast? How much can one heaven-sent and unsuspecting child endure? Why has he not been spared this inconceivable fate?

Perhaps, she thinks, she is being punished: too many babysitters too early on. ("Come to Mommy! Come to Mommy-Babysitter!" she used to say. But it was a joke!) Her life, perhaps, bore too openly the marks and wigs of deepest drag. Her unmotherly thoughts had all been noted: the panicky hope that his nap would last longer than it did; her occasional desire to kiss him passionately on the mouth (to make out with her baby!); her ongoing complaints about the very vocabulary of motherhood, how it degraded the speaker ("Is this a poopie onesie! Yes, it's a very poopie onesie!"). She had, moreover on three occasions used the formula bottles as flower vases. She twice let the Baby's ears get fudgy with wax. A few afternoons last month, at snacktime, she placed a bowl of Cheerios on the floor for him to eat, like a dog. She let him play with the Dustbuster. Just once, before he was born, she said, "Healthy? I just want the kid to be rich." A joke, for God's sake! After he was born she announced that her life had become a daily sequence of mind-wrecking chores, the same ones over and over again, like a novel by Mrs. Camus. Another joke! These jokes will kill you! She had told too often, and with too much enjoyment, the story of how the Baby had said "Hi" to his high chair, waved at the lake waves, shouted "Goody-goody-goody" in what seemed to be a Russian accent, pointed at his eyes and said "Ice." And all that nonsensical baby talk: wasn't it a stitch? "Canonical babbling," the language experts called it. He recounted whole stories in it—totally made up, she could tell. He embroidered; he fished; he exaggerated. What a card! To friends, she spoke of his eating habits (carrots yes, tuna no). She mentioned, too much, his sidesplitting giggle. Did she have to be so boring? Did she have no consideration for others, for the intellectual demands and courtesies of human society? Would she not even attempt to be more interesting? It was a crime against the human mind not even to try.

Now her baby, for all these reasons—lack of motherly gratitude, motherly judgment, motherly proportion—will be taken away.

The room is fluorescently ablaze again. The Mother digs around in her parka pocket and comes up with a Kleenex. It is old and thin, like a mashed flower saved from a dance; she dabs at her eyes and nose.

The Baby won't suffer as much as you," says the Surgeon.

And who can contradict? Not the Baby, who in his Slavic Betty Boop voice can say only *mama, dada, cheese, ice, bye-bye, outside, boogie-boogie, goody-goody, eddy-eddy,* and *car.* (Who is Eddy? They have no idea.) This will not suffice to express his mortal suffering. Who can say what babies do with their agony and shock? Not they themselves. (Baby talk: isn't it a stitch?) They put it all no place any-one can really see. They are like a different race, a different species: they seem not to experience pain the way *we* do. Yeah, that's it: their nervous systems are not as fully formed, and *they just don't ex-perience pain the way we do.* A tune to keep one humming through the war. "You'll get through it," the Surgeon says.

"How?" asks the Mother. "How does one get through it?"

"You just put your head down and go," says the Surgeon. He picks up his file folder. He is a skilled manual laborer. The tricky emotional stuff is not to his liking. The babies. The babies! What can be said to console the parents about the babies? "I'll go phone the oncologist on duty to let him know," he says, and leaves the room.

"Come here, sweetie," the Mother says to the Baby, who has toddled off toward a gum wrapper on the floor. "We've got to put your jacket on." She picks him up and he reaches for the light switch again. Light, dark. Peekaboo: where's baby? Where did baby go?

★ ★ ★

At home, she leaves a message—"Urgent! Call me!"—for the Husband on his voice mail. Then she takes the Baby upstairs for his nap, rocks him in the rocker. The Baby waves good-bye to his little bears, then looks toward the window and says, "Bye-bye, outside." He has, lately, the habit of waving good-bye to everything, and now it seems as if he senses an imminent departure, and it breaks her heart to hear him. *Bye-bye!* She sings low and monotonously, like a small appliance, which is how he likes it. He is drowsy, dozy, drifting off. He has grown so much in the last year, he hardly fits in her lap anymore; his limbs dangle off like a pietà. His head rolls slightly inside the crook of her arm. She can feel him falling backward into sleep, his mouth round and open like the sweetest of poppies. All the lullabies in the world, all the melodies threaded through with maternal melancholy now become for her— abandoned as a mother can be by working men and napping babies—the songs of hard, hard grief. Sitting there, bowed and bobbing, the Mother feels the entirety of her love as worry and heartbreak. A quick and irrevocable alchemy: there is no longer one unworried scrap left for happiness. "If you go," she keens low into his soapy neck, into the ranunculus coil of his ear, "we are going with you. We are nothing without you. Without you, we are a heap of rocks. We are gravel and mold. Without you, we are two stumps, with nothing any longer in our hearts. Wherever this takes you, we are following. We will be there. Don't be scared. We are going, too. That is that."

✷ ✷ ✷

"Take Notes," says the Husband, after coming straight home from work, midafternoon, hearing the news, and saying all the words out loud—*surgery, metastasis, dialysis, transplant*—then collapsing in a chair in tears. "Take notes. We are going to need the money."

"Good God," cries the Mother. Everything inside her suddenly begins to cower and shrink, a thinning of bones. Perhaps this is a soldier's readiness, but it has the whiff of death and defeat. It feels like a heart attack, a failure of will and courage, a power failure: a failure of everything. Her face, when she glimpses it in a mirror, is cold and bloated with shock, her eyes scarlet and shrunk. She has already started to wear sunglasses indoors, like a celebrity widow. From where will her own strength come? From some philosophy? From some frigid little philosophy? She is neither stalwart nor realistic and has trouble with basic concepts, such as the one that says events move in one direction only and do not jump up, turn around, and take themselves back.

The Husband begins too many of his sentences with "What if." He is trying to piece everything together like a train wreck. He is trying to get the train to town.

"We'll just take all the steps, move through all the stages. We'll go where we have to go. We'll hunt; we'll find; we'll pay what we have to pay. What if we can't pay?"

"Sounds like shopping."

"I cannot believe this is happening to our little boy," he says, and starts to sob again. "Why didn't it happen to one of us? It's so unfair. Just last week, my doctor declared me in perfect health: the prostate of a twenty-year-old, the heart of a ten-year-old, the brain of an insect—or whatever it was he said. What a nightmare this is."

What words can be uttered? You turn just slightly and there it is: the death of your child. It is part symbol, part devil, and in your blind spot all along, until, if you are unlucky, it is completely upon you. Then it is a fierce little country abducting you; it holds you squarely inside itself like a cellar room—the best boundaries of you are the boundaries of it. Are there windows? Sometimes aren't there windows?

✳ ✳ ✳

The Mother is not a shopper. She hates to shop, is generally bad at it, though she does like a good sale. She cannot stroll meaningfully through anger, denial, grief, and acceptance. She goes straight to bargaining and stays there. How much? she calls out to the ceiling, to some makeshift construction of holiness she has desperately, though not uncreatively, assembled in her mind and prayed to; a doubter, never before given to prayer, she must now reap what she has not sown; she must assemble from scratch an entire altar of worship and begging. She tries for noble abstractions, nothing too anthropomorphic, just some Higher Morality, though if this particular Highness looks something like the manager at Marshall Field's, sucking a Frango mint, so be it. Amen. Just tell me what you want, requests the Mother. And how do you want it? More charitable acts? A billion starting now. Charitable thoughts? Harder, but of course! Of course! I'll do the cooking, honey; I'll pay the rent. Just tell me. *Excuse me?* Well, if not to you, to whom do I speak? Hello? To whom do I have to speak around here? A higher-up? A superior? Wait? I can wait. I've got all day. I've got the whole damn day.

The Husband now lies next to her in bed, sighing. "Poor little guy could survive all this, only to be killed in a car crash at the age of sixteen," he says.

The wife, bargaining, considers this. "We'll take the car crash," she says.

"What?"

"Let's Make a Deal! Sixteen Is a Full Life! We'll take the car crash. We'll take the car crash, in front of which Carol Merrill is now standing."

Now the Manager of Marshall Field's reappears. "To take the surprises out is to take the life out of life," he says.

The phone rings. The Husband gets up and leaves the room.

"But I don't want these surprises," says the Mother. "Here! You take these surprises!"

"To know the narrative in advance is to turn yourself into a machine," the Manager continues. "What makes humans human is precisely that they do not know the future. That is why they do the fateful and amusing things they do: who can say how anything will turn out? Therein lies the only hope for redemption, discovery, and—let's be frank—fun, fun, fun! There might be things people will get away with. And not just motel towels. There might be great illicit loves, enduring joy, faith-shaking accidents with farm machinery. But you have to not know in order to see what stories your life's efforts bring you. The mystery is all."

The Mother, though shy, has grown confrontational. "Is this the kind of bogus, random crap they teach at merchandising school? We would like fewer surprises, fewer efforts and mysteries, thank you. K through eight; can we just get K through eight?" It now seems like the luckiest, most beautiful, most musical phrase she's ever heard: K through eight. The very lilt. The very thought.

The Manager continues, trying things out. "I mean, the whole conception of 'the story,' of cause and effect, the whole idea that people have a clue as to how the world works is just a piece of laughable metaphysical colonialism perpetrated upon the wild country of time."

Did they own a gun? The Mother begins looking through drawers.

The Husband comes back into the room and observes her. "Ha! The Great Havoc that is the Puzzle of all Life!" he says of the Marshall Field's management policy. He has just gotten off a conference call with the insurance company and the hospital. The surgery will be Friday. "It's all just some dirty capitalist's idea of a philosophy."

"Maybe it's just a fact of narrative and you really can't politicize it," says the Mother. It is now only the two of them.

"Whose side are you on?"

"I'm on the Baby's side."

"Are you taking notes for this?"

"No."

"You're not?"

"No. I can't. Not this! I write fiction. This isn't fiction."

"Then write nonfiction. Do a piece of journalism. Get two dollars a word."

"Then it has to be true and full of information. I'm not trained. I'm not that skilled. Plus, I have a convenient personal principle about artists not abandoning art. One should never turn one's back on a vivid imagination. Even the whole memoir thing annoys me."

"Well, make things up, but pretend they're real."

"I'm not that insured."

"You're making me nervous."

"Sweetie, darling, I'm not that good. I can't *do this*. I can do—what can I do? I can do quasi-amusing phone dialogue. I can do succinct descriptions of weather. I can do screwball outings with the family pet. Sometimes I can do those. Honey, I only do what I can. I do *the careful ironies of daydream*. I do *the marshy ideas upon which intimate life is built*. But this? Our baby with cancer? I'm sorry. My stop was two stations back. This is irony at its most gaudy and careless. This is a Hieronymus Bosch of facts and figures and blood and graphs. This is a nightmare of narrative slop. This cannot be designed. This cannot even be noted in preparation for a design—"

"We're going to need the money."

"To say nothing of the moral boundaries of pecuniary recompense in a situation such as this—"

"What if the other kidney goes? What if he needs a transplant? Where are the moral boundaries there? What are we going to do, have bake sales?"

"We can sell the house. I hate this house. It makes me crazy."

"And we'll live—where again?"

"The Ronald McDonald place. I hear it's nice. It's the least McDonald's can do."

"You have a keen sense of justice."

"I try. What can I say?" She pauses. "Is all this really happening? I keep thinking that soon it will be over—the life expectancy of a cloud is supposed to be only twelve hours—and then I realize something has occurred that can never ever be over."

The Husband buries his face in his hands: "Our poor baby. How did this happen to him?" He looks over and stares at the bookcase that serves as the nightstand. "And do you think even one of these baby books is any help?" He picks up the Leach, the Spock, the *What to Expect*. "Where in the pages or index of any of these does it say 'chemotherapy' or 'Hickman catheter' or 'renal sarcoma'? Where does it say 'carcinogenesis'? You know what these books are obsessed with? *Holding a fucking spoon*." He begins hurling the books off the night table and against the far wall.

"Hey," says the Mother, trying to soothe. "Hey, hey, hey." But compared to his stormy roar, her words are those of a backup singer—a Shondell, a Pip—a doo-wop ditty. Books, and now more books, continue to fly.

✷ ✷ ✷

Take Notes.

Is *fainthearted* one word or two? Student prose has wrecked her spelling.

It's one word. Two words—*Faint Hearted*—what would that be? The name of a drag queen.

✷ ✷ ✷

Take Notes. In the end, you suffer alone. But at the beginning you suffer with a whole lot of others. When your child has cancer, you are instantly whisked away to another planet: one of bald-headed little boys. Pediatric Oncology. Peed Onk. You wash your hands for thirty seconds in antibacterial soap before you are allowed to enter through the swinging doors. You put paper slippers on your shoes. You keep your voice down. A whole place has been designed and decorated for your nightmare. Here is where your nightmare will occur. We've got a room all ready for you. We have cots. We have refrigerators. "The children are almost entirely boys," says one of the nurses. "No one knows why. It's been documented, but a lot of

225

people out there still don't realize it." The little boys are all from sweet-sounding places—Janesville and Appleton—little heartland towns with giant landfills, agricultural runoff, paper factories, Joe McCarthy's grave (Alone, a site of great toxicity, thinks the Mother. The soil should be tested).

All the bald little boys look like brothers. They wheel their IVs up and down the single corridor of Peed Onk. Some of the lively ones, feeling good for a day, ride the lower bars of the IV while their large, cheerful mothers whiz them along the halls. *Wheee!*

✷ ✷ ✷

The Mother does not feel large and cheerful. In her mind, she is scathing, acid-tongued, wraith-thin, and chain-smoking out on a fire escape somewhere. Beneath her lie the gentle undulations of the Midwest, with all its aspirations to be—to be what? To be Long Island. How it has succeeded! Strip mall upon strip mall. Lurid water, poisoned potatoes. The Mother drags deeply, blowing clouds of smoke out over the disfigured cornfields. When a baby gets cancer, it seems stupid ever to have given up smoking. When a baby gets cancer, you think, Whom are we kidding? Let's all light up. When a baby gets cancer, you think, Who came up with *this* idea? What celestial abandon gave rise to *this*? Pour me a drink, so I can refuse to toast.

The Mother does not know how to be one of these other mothers, with their blond hair and sweatpants and sneakers and determined pleasantness. She does not think that she can be anything similar. She does not feel remotely like them. She knows, for instance, too many people in Greenwich Village. She mail-orders oysters and tiramisu from a shop in SoHo. She is close friends with four actual homosexuals. Her husband is asking her to Take Notes.

Where do these women get their sweatpants? She will find out.

She will start, perhaps, with the costume and work from there.

She will live according to the bromides. Take one day at a time. Take a positive attitude. *Take a hike!* She wishes that there were more interesting things that were useful and true, but it seems now that it's only the boring things that are useful and true. *One day at a time.* And *at least we have our health.* How ordinary. How obvious. One day at a time. You need a brain for that?

✷ ✷ ✷

While the Surgeon is fine-boned, regal, and laconic—they have correctly guessed his game to be doubles—there is a bit of the mad, overcaffeinated scientist to the Oncologist. He speaks quickly. He knows a lot of studies and numbers. He can do the math. Good! Someone should be able to do the math! "It's a fast but wimpy tumor," he explains. "It typically metastasizes to the lung." He rattles off some numbers, time frames, risk statistics. Fast but wimpy: the Mother tries to imagine this combination of traits, tries to think and think, and can only come up with Claudia Osk from the fourth grade, who blushed and almost wept when called on in class, but in gym could outrun everyone in the quarter-mile fire-door-to-fence dash. The Mother thinks now of this tumor as Claudia Osk. They are going to get Claudia Osk, make her sorry. All right! Claudia Osk must die. Though it has never been mentioned before, it now seems clear that Claudia Osk should have died long ago. Who was she, anyway? So conceited: not letting anyone beat her in a race. Well, hey, hey, hey: don't look now, Claudia!

The Husband nudges her. "Are you listening?"

"The chances of this happening even just to one kidney are one in fifteen thousand. Now given all these other factors, the chances on the second kidney are about one in eight."

"One in eight," says the Husband. "Not bad. As long as it's not one in fifteen thousand."

The Mother studies the trees and fish along the ceiling's edge in the Save the Planet wallpaper border. Save the Planet. Yes! But the windows in this very building don't open and diesel fumes are leaking into the ventilating system, near which, outside, a delivery truck is parked. The air is nauseous and stale.

"Really," the Oncologist is saying, "of all the cancers he could get, this is probably the best."

"We win," says the Mother.

"*Best,* I know, hardly seems the right word. Look, you two probably need to get some rest. We'll see how the surgery and histology go. Then we'll start with chemo the week following. A little light chemo: vincristine and—"

"Vincristine?" interrupts the Mother. "Wine of Christ?"

"The names are strange, I know. The other one we use is actinomycin-D. Sometimes called 'dactinomycin.' People move the *D* around to the front."

"They move the *D* around to the front," repeats the Mother.

"Yup!" the Oncologist says. "I don't know why—they just do!"

"Christ didn't survive his wine," says the Husband.

"But of course he did," says the Oncologist, and nods toward the Baby, who has now found a cupboard full of hospital linens and bandages and is yanking them all out onto the floor. "I'll see you guys tomorrow, after the surgery." And with that, the Oncologist leaves.

"Or, rather, Christ *was* his wine," mumbles the Husband. Everything he knows about the New Testament, he has gleaned from the sound track of *Godspell*. "His blood was the wine. What a great beverage idea."

"A little light chemo. Don't you like that one?" says the Mother. "*Eine kleine* dactinomycin. I'd like to see Mozart write that one up for a big wad o' cash."

"Come here, honey," the Husband says to the Baby, who has now pulled off both his shoes.

"It's bad enough when they refer to medical science as 'an inexact science,'" says the Mother. "But when they start referring to it as 'an art,' I get extremely nervous."

"Yeah. If we wanted art, Doc, we'd go to an art museum." The Husband picks up the Baby. "You're an artist," he says to the Mother, with the taint of accusation in his voice. "They probably think you find creativity reassuring."

The Mother sighs. "I just find it inevitable. Let's go get something to eat." And so they take the elevator to the cafeteria, where there is a high chair, and where, not noticing, they all eat a lot of apples with the price tags still on them.

✷ ✷ ✷

Because his surgery is not until tomorrow, the Baby likes the hospital. He likes the long corridors, down which he can run. He likes everything on wheels. The flower carts in the lobby! ("Please keep your boy away from the flowers," says the vendor. "We'll buy the whole display," snaps the Mother, adding, "Actual children in a children's hospital—unbelievable, isn't it?") The Baby likes the other little boys. Places to go! People to see! Rooms to wander into! There is Intensive Care. There is the Trauma Unit. The Baby smiles and waves. What a little Cancer Personality! Bandaged citizens smile and wave back. In Peed Onk, there are the bald little boys to play with. Joey, Eric, Tim, Mort, and Tod (Mort! Tod!). There is the four-year-old, Ned, holding his little deflated rubber ball, the one with the intriguing curling hose. The Baby wants to play with it. "It's mine. Leave it alone," says Ned. "Tell the Baby to leave it alone."

"Baby, you've got to share," says the Mother from a chair some feet away.

Suddenly, from down near the Tiny Tim Lounge, comes Ned's mother, large and blond and sweatpanted. "Stop that! Stop it!" she cries out, dashing toward the Baby and Ned and pushing the Baby away. "Don't touch that!" she barks at the Baby, who is only a Baby and bursts into tears because he has never been yelled at like this before.

Ned's mom glares at everyone. "This is drawing fluid from Neddy's liver!" She pats at the rubber thing and starts to cry a little.

"Oh my God," says the Mother. She comforts the Baby, who is also crying. She and Ned, the only dry-eyed people, look at each other. "I'm so sorry," she says to Ned and then to his mother. "I'm so stupid. I thought they were squabbling over a toy."

"It does look like a toy," agrees Ned. He smiles. He is an angel. All the little boys are angels. Total, sweet, bald little angels, and now God is trying to get them back for himself. Who are they, mere mortal women, in the face of this, this powerful and overwhelming and inscrutable thing, God's will? They are the mothers, that's who. You can't have him! they shout every day. You dirty old man! *Get out of here! Hands off!*

"I'm so sorry," says the Mother again. "I didn't know."

Ned's mother smiles vaguely. "Of course you didn't know," she says, and walks back to the Tiny Tim Lounge.

✷ ✷ ✷

The Tiny Tim Lounge is a little sitting area at the end of the Peed Onk corridor. There are two small sofas, a table, a rocking chair, a television and a VCR. There are various videos: *Speed, Dune,* and *Star Wars.* On one of the lounge walls there is a gold plaque with the singer Tiny Tim's name on it: his son was treated once at this hospital and so, five years ago, he donated money for this lounge. It is a cramped little lounge, which, one suspects, would be larger if Tiny Tim's son had actually lived. Instead, he died here, at this hospital, and now there is this tiny room which is part gratitude, part generosity, part *fuck you.*

Sifting through the videocassettes, the Mother wonders what science fiction could begin to compete with the science fiction of cancer itself—a tumor with its differentiated muscle and bone cells, a clump of wild nothing and its mad, ambitious desire to be something: something inside you, instead of you, another organ-

230

ism, but with a monster's architecture, a demon's sabotage and chaos. Think of leukemia, a tumor diabolically taking liquid form, better to swim about incognito in the blood. George Lucas, direct that!

Sitting with the other parents in the Tiny Tim Lounge, the night before the surgery, having put the Baby to bed in his high steel crib two rooms down, the Mother begins to hear the stories: leukemia in kindergarten, sarcomas in Little League, neuroblastomas discovered at summer camp. "Eric slid into third base, but then the scrape didn't heal." The parents pat one another's forearms and speak of other children's hospitals as if they were resorts. "You were at St. Jude's last winter? So were we. What did you think of it? We loved the staff." Jobs have been quit, marriages hacked up, bank accounts ravaged; the parents have seemingly endured the unendurable. They speak not of the *possibility* of comas brought on by the chemo, but of the *number* of them. "He was in his first coma last July," says Ned's mother. "It was a scary time, but we pulled through."

Pulling through is what people do around here. There is a kind of bravery in their lives that isn't bravery at all. It is automatic, unflinching, a mix of man and machine, consuming and unquestionable obligation meeting illness move for move in a giant even-steven game of chess—an unending round of something that looks like shadowboxing, though between love and death, which is the shadow? "Everyone admires us for our courage," says one man. "They have no idea what they're talking about."

I could get out of here, thinks the Mother. I could just get on a bus and go, never come back. Change my name. A kind of witness relocation thing.

"Courage requires options," the man adds.

The Baby might be better off.

"There are options," says a woman with a thick suede headband. "You could give up. You could fall apart."

"No, you can't. Nobody does. I've never seen it," says the man. "Well, not *really* fall apart." Then the lounge falls quiet. Over the VCR someone has taped the fortune from a fortune cookie. "Optimism," it says, "is what allows a teakettle to sing though up to its neck in hot water." Underneath, someone else has taped a clipping from a summer horoscope. "Cancer rules!" it says. Who would tape this up? Somebody's twelve-year-old brother. One of the fathers—Joey's father—gets up and tears them both off, makes a small wad in his fist.

There is some rustling of magazine pages.

The Mother clears her throat. "Tiny Tim forgot the wet bar," she says.

Ned, who is still up, comes out of his room and down the corridor, whose lights dim at nine. Standing next to her chair, he says to the Mother, "Where are you from? What is wrong with your baby?"

✵ ✵ ✵

In the tiny room that is theirs, she sleeps fitfully in her sweatpants, occasionally leaping up to check on the Baby. This is what the sweatpants are for: leaping. In case of fire. In case of anything. In case the difference between day and night starts to dissolve, and there is no difference at all, so why pretend? In the cot beside her, the Husband, who has taken a sleeping pill, is snoring loudly, his arms folded about his head in a kind of origami. How could either of them have stayed back at the house, with its empty high chair and empty crib? Occassionally the Baby wakes and cries out, and she bolts up, goes to him, rubs his back, rearranges the linens. The clock on the metal dresser shows that it is five after three. Then twenty to five. And then it is really morning, the beginning of this day, nephrectomy day. Will she be glad when it's over, or barely alive, or both? Each day this week has arrived huge, empty, and unknown, like a spaceship, and this one especially is lit a bright gray.

"He'll need to put this on," says John, one of the nurses, bright and early, handing the Mother a thin greenish garment with roses and teddy bears printed on it. A wave of nausea hits her; this smock, she thinks, will soon be splattered with—with what?

The Baby is awake but drowsy. She lifts off his pajamas. "Don't forget, *bubeleh,*" she whispers, undressing and dressing him. "We will be with you every moment, every step. When you think you are asleep and floating off far away from everybody, Mommy will still be there." If she hasn't fled on a bus. "Mommy will take care of you. And Daddy, too." She hopes the Baby does not detect her own fear and uncertainty, which she must hide from him, like a limp. He is hungry, not having been allowed to eat, and he is no longer amused by this new place, but worried about its hardships. Oh, my baby, she thinks. And the room starts to swim a little. The Husband comes in to take over. "Take a break," he says to her. "I'll walk him around for five minutes."

She leaves but doesn't know where to go. In the hallway, she is approached by a kind of social worker, a customer-relations person, who had given them a video to watch about the anesthesia: how the parent accompanies the child into the operating room, and how gently, nicely the drugs are administered.

"Did you watch the video?"

"Yes," says the Mother.

"Wasn't it helpful?"

"I don't know," says the Mother.

"Do you have any questions?" asks the video woman. "Do you have any questions?" asked of someone who has recently landed in this fearful, alien place seems to the Mother an absurd and amazing little courtesy. The very specificity of a question would give a lie to the overwhelming strangeness of everything around her.

"Not right now," says the Mother. "Right now, I think I'm just going to go to the bathroom."

When she returns to the Baby's room, everyone is there: the

surgeon, the anesthesiologist, all the nurses, the social worker. In their blue caps and scrubs, they look like a clutch of forget-me-nots, and forget them, who could? The Baby, in his little teddy-bear smock, seems cold and scared. He reaches out and the Mother lifts him from the Husband's arms, rubs his back to warm him.

"Well, it's time!" says the Surgeon, forcing a smile.

"Shall we go?" says the Anesthesiologist.

What follows is a blur of obedience and bright lights. They take an elevator down to a big concrete room, the anteroom, the greenroom, the backstage of the operating room. Lining the walls are long shelves full of blue surgical outfits. "Children often become afraid of the color blue," says one of the nurses. But of course. Of course! "Now, which one of you would like to come into the operating room for the anesthesia?"

"I will," says the Mother.

"Are you sure?" asks the Husband.

"Yup." She kisses the Baby's hair. "Mr. Curlyhead," people keep calling him here, and it seems both rude and nice. Women look admiringly at his long lashes and exclaim, "Always the boys! Always the boys!"

Two surgical nurses put a blue smock and a blue cotton cap on the Mother. The Baby finds this funny and keeps pulling at the cap. "This way," says another nurse, and the Mother follows. "Just put the Baby down on the table."

In the video, the mother holds the baby and fumes are gently waved under the baby's nose until he falls asleep. Now, out of view of camera or social worker, the Anesthesiologist is anxious to get this under way and not let too much gas leak out into the room generally. The occupational hazard of this, his chosen profession, is gas exposure and nerve damage, and it has started to worry him. No doubt he frets about it to his wife every night! Now he turns the gas on and quickly clamps the plastic mouthpiece over the baby's cheeks and lips.

The Baby is startled. The Mother is startled. The Baby starts to scream and redden behind the plastic, but he cannot be heard. He thrashes. "Tell him it's okay," says the nurse to the Mother.

Okay? "It's okay," repeats the Mother, holding his hand, but she knows he can tell it's not okay, because he can see not only that she is still wearing that stupid paper cap but that her words are mechanical and swallowed, and she is biting her lips to keep them from trembling. Panicked, he attempts to sit. He cannot breathe; his arms reach up. *Bye-bye, outside.* And then, quite quickly, his eyes shut; he untenses and has fallen not *into* sleep but aside to sleep, an odd, kidnapping kind of sleep, his terror now hidden someplace deep inside him.

"How did it go?" asks the social worker, waiting in the concrete outer room. The Mother is hysterical. A nurse has ushered her out.

"It wasn't at all like the filmstrip!" she cries. "It wasn't like the filmstrip at all!"

"The filmstrip? You mean the video?" asks the social worker.

"It wasn't like that at all! It was brutal and unforgivable."

"Why that's terrible," she says, her role now no longer misinformational but janitorial, and she touches the Mother's arm, though the Mother shakes it off and goes to find the Husband.

✷ ✷ ✷

She finds him in the large mulberry Surgery Lounge, where he has been taken and where there is free hot chocolate in small Styrofoam cups. Red cellophane garlands festoon the doorways. She has totally forgotten it is as close to Christmas as this. A pianist in the corner is playing "Carol of the Bells," and it sounds not only unfestive but scary, like the theme from *The Exorcist*.

There is a giant clock on the far wall. It is a kind of porthole into the operating room, a way of assessing the Baby's ordeal: forty-five minutes for the Hickman implant; two and a half hours for the nephrectomy. And then, after that, three months of chemotherapy. The magazine on her lap stays open at a ruby-hued perfume ad.

"Still not taking notes," says the Husband.

"Nope."

"You know, in a way, this is the kind of thing you've *always* written about."

"You are really something, you know that? This is life. This isn't a 'kind of thing.'"

"But this is the kind of thing that fiction is: it's the unlivable life, the strange room tacked onto the house, the extra moon that is circling the earth unbeknownst to science."

"I told you that."

"I'm quoting you."

She looks at her watch, thinking of the Baby. "How long has it been?"

"Not long. Too long. In the end, maybe those're the same things."

"What do you suppose is happening to him right this second?" Infection? Slipping knives? "I don't know. But you know what? I've gotta go. I've gotta just walk a bit." The Husband gets up, walks around the lounge, then comes back and sits down.

The synapses between the minutes are unswimmable. An hour is thick as fudge. The Mother feels depleted; she is a string of empty tin cans attached by wire, something a goat would sniff and chew, something now and then enlivened by a jolt of electricity.

She hears their names being called over the intercom. "Yes? Yes?" She stands up quickly. Her words have flown out before her, an exhalation of birds. The piano music has stopped. The pianist is gone. She and the Husband approach the main desk, where a man looks up at them and smiles. Before him is a xeroxed list of patients' names. "That's our little boy right there," says the Mother, seeing the Baby's name on the list and pointing at it. "Is there some word? Is everything okay?"

"Yes," says the man. "Your boy is doing fine. They've just finished with the catheter, and they are moving on to the kidney."

"But it's been two hours already! Oh my God, did something go wrong? What happened? What went wrong?"

"Did something go wrong?" The Husband tugs at his collar.

"Not really. It just took longer than they expected. I'm told everything is fine. They wanted you to know."

"Thank you," says the Husband. They turn and walk back toward where they were sitting.

"I'm not going to make it." The Mother sighs, sinking into a fake leather chair shaped somewhat like a baseball mitt. "But before I go, I'm taking half this hospital out with me."

"Do you want some coffee?" asks the Husband.

"I don't know," says the Mother. "No, I guess not. No. Do you?"

"Nah, I don't, either, I guess," he says.

"Would you like part of an orange?"

"Oh, maybe, I guess, if you're having one." She takes an orange from her purse and just sits there peeling its difficult skin, the flesh rupturing beneath her fingers, the juice trickling down her hands, stinging the hangnails. She and the Husband chew and swallow, discreetly spit the seeds into Kleenex, and read from photocopies of the latest medical research, which they begged from the intern. They read, and underline, and sigh and close their eyes, and after some time, the surgery is over. A nurse from Peed Onk comes down to tell them.

"Your little boy's in recovery right now. He's doing well. You can see him in about fifteen minutes."

★ ★ ★

How can it be described? How can any of it be described? The trip and the story of the trip are always two different things. The narrator is the one who has stayed home, but then, afterward, presses her mouth upon the traveler's mouth, in order to make the mouth work, to make the mouth say, say, say. One cannot go to a place and speak of it; one cannot both see and say, not really. One can go, and upon returning make a lot of hand motions and indications with the arms. The mouth itself, working at the speed of light, at the eye's instructions, is necessarily struck still; so fast, so much to report, it hangs open and dumb as a gutted bell. All that unsayable life! That's where the narrator comes in. The narrator comes with her kisses and mimicry and tidying up. The narrator comes and makes a slow, fake song of the mouth's eager devastation.

It is a horror and a miracle to see him. He is lying in his crib in his room, tubed up, splayed like a boy on a cross, his arms stiffened into cardboard "no-no's" so that he cannot yank out the tubes. There is the bladder catheter, the nasal-gastric tube, and the Hickman, which, beneath the skin, is plugged into his jugular, then popped out his chest wall and capped with a long plastic cap. There is a large bandage taped over his abdomen. Groggy, on a morphine drip, still he is able to look at her when, maneuvering through all the vinyl wiring, she leans to hold him, and when she does, he begins to cry, but cry silently, without motion or noise. She has never seen a baby cry without motion or noise. It is the crying of an old person: silent, beyond opinion, shattered. In someone so tiny, it is frightening and unnatural. She wants to pick up the Baby and run—out of there, out of there. She wants to whip out a gun: *No-no's, eh? This whole thing is what I call a no-no.* Don't you touch him! she wants to shout at the surgeons and the needle nurses. Not anymore! No more! No more! She would crawl up and lie beside him in the crib if she could. But instead, because of all his intricate wiring, she must lean and cuddle, sing to him, songs of peril and flight: "We gotta get out of this place, if it's the last thing we ever do. We gotta get out of this place . . . there's a better life for me and you."

Very 1967. She was eleven then and impressionable.

The Baby looks at her, pleadingly, his arms splayed out in surrender. To where? Where is there to go? Take me! Take me!

✻ ✻ ✻

That night, postop night, the Mother and Husband lie afloat in the cot together. A fluorescent lamp near the crib is kept on in the dark. The Baby breathes evenly but thinly in his drugged sleep. The morphine in its first flooding doses apparently makes him feel as if he were falling backward—or so the Mother has been told—and it causes the Baby to jerk, to catch himself over and over, as if he were being dropped from a tree. "Is this right? Isn't there something that should be done?" The nurses come in hourly, different ones—the night shifts seem strangely short and frequent. If the Baby stirs or frets, the nurses give him more morphine through the Hickman catheter, then leave to tend to other patients. The Mother rises to check on him in the low light. There is gurgling from the clear plastic suction tube coming out of his mouth. Brownish clumps have collected in the tube. What is going on? The Mother rings for the nurse. Is it Renée or Sarah or Darcy? She's forgotten.

"What, what is it?" murmurs the Husband, waking up.

"Something is wrong," says the Mother. "It looks like blood in his N-G tube."

"What?" The Husband gets out of bed. He, too, is wearing sweatpants.

The nurse—Valerie—pushes open the heavy door to the room and enters quietly. "Everything okay?"

"There's something wrong here. The tube is sucking blood out of his stomach. It looks like it may have perforated his stomach and that now he's bleeding internally. Look!"

Valerie is a saint, but her voice is the standard hospital saint voice: an infuriating, pharmaceutical calm. It says, Everything is normal here. Death is normal. Pain is normal. Nothing is abnormal. So there is nothing to get excited about. "Well now, let's see."

She holds up the plastic tube and tries to see inside it. "Hmmm," she says. "I'll call the attending physician."

Because this is a research and teaching hospital, all the regular doctors are at home sleeping in their Mission-style beds. Tonight, as is apparently the case every weekend night, the attending physician is a medical student. He looks fifteen. The authority he attempts to convey, he cannot remotely inhabit. He is not even in the same building with it. He shakes everyone's hands, then strokes his chin, a gesture no doubt gleaned from some piece of dinner theater his parents took him to once. As if there were an actual beard on that chin! As if beard growth on that chin were even possible! *Our Town! Kiss Me Kate! Barefoot in the Park!* He is attempting to convince, if not to impress.

"We're in trouble," the Mother whispers to the Husband. She is tired, tired of young people grubbing for grades. "We've got Dr. 'Kiss Me Kate,' here."

The Husband looks at her blankly, a mix of disorientation and divorce.

The medical student holds the tubing in his hands. "I don't really see anything," he says.

He flunks! "You don't?" The Mother shoves her way in, holds the clear tubing in both hands. "That," she says. "Right here and here." Just this past semester, she said to one of her own students, "If you don't see how this essay is better than that one, then I want you just to go out into the hallway and stand there until you do." Is it important to keep one's voice down? The Baby stays asleep. He is drugged and dreaming, far away.

"Hmmm," says the medical student. "Perhaps there's a little irritation in the stomach."

"A little irritation?" The Mother grows furious. "This is blood. These are clumps and clots. This stupid thing is sucking the life right out of him!" Life! She is starting to cry.

They turn off the suction and bring in antacids, which they

feed into the Baby through the tube. Then they turn the suction on again. This time on low.

"What was it on before?" asks the Husband.

"High," says Valerie. "Doctor's orders, though I don't know why. I don't know why these doctors do a lot of the things they do."

"Maybe they're . . . not all that bright?" suggests the Mother. She is feeling relief and rage simultaneously: there is a feeling of prayer and litigation in the air. Yet essentially, she is grateful. Isn't she? She thinks she is. And still, and still: look at all the things you have to do to protect a child, a hospital merely an intensification of life's cruel obstacle course.

✵ ✵ ✵

The Surgeon comes to visit on Saturday morning. He steps in and nods at the Baby, who is awake but glazed from the morphine, his eyes two dark unseeing grapes. "The boy looks fine," the Surgeon announces. He peeks under the Baby's bandage. "The stitches look good," he says. The Baby's abdomen is stitched all the way across like a baseball. "And the other kidney, when we looked at it yesterday face-to-face, looked fine. We'll try to wean him off the morphine a little, and see how he's doing on Monday." He clears his throat. "And now," he says, looking about the room at the nurses and medical students, "I would like to speak with the Mother, alone."

The Mother's heart gives a jolt. "Me?"

"Yes," he says, motioning, then turning.

She gets up and steps out into the empty hallway with him, closing the door behind her. What can this be about? She hears the Baby fretting a little in his crib. Her brain fills with pain and alarm. Her voice comes out as a hoarse whisper. "Is there something—"

"There is a particular thing I need from you," says the Surgeon, turning and standing there very seriously.

"Yes?" Her heart is pounding. She does not feel resilient enough for any more bad news.

"I need to ask a favor."

"Certainly," she says, attempting very hard to summon the strength and courage for this occasion, whatever it is; her throat has tightened to a fist.

From inside his white coat, the surgeon removes a thin paperback book and thrusts it toward her. "Will you sign my copy of your novel?"

The Mother looks down and sees that it is indeed a copy of a novel she has written, one about teenaged girls.

She looks up. A big, spirited grin is cutting across his face. "I read this last summer," he says, "and I still remember parts of it! Those girls got into such trouble!"

Of all the surreal moments of the last few days, this, she thinks, might be the most so.

"Okay," she says, and the Surgeon merrily hands her a pen.

"You can just write 'To Dr.— Oh, I don't need to tell you what to write."

The Mother sits down on a bench and shakes ink into the pen. A sigh of relief washes over and out of her. Oh, the pleasure of a sigh of relief, like the finest moments of love; has anyone properly sung the praises of sighs of relief? She opens the book to the title page. She breathes deeply. What is he doing reading novels about teenaged girls, anyway? And why didn't he buy the hardcover? She inscribes something grateful and true, then hands the book back to him.

"Is he going to be okay?"

"The boy? The boy is going to be fine," he says, then taps her stiffly on the shoulder. "Now you take care. It's Saturday. Drink a little wine."

★ ★ ★

Over the weekend, while the Baby sleeps, the Mother and Husband sit together in the Tiny Tim Lounge. The Husband is restless and makes cafeteria and sundry runs, running errands for everyone. In his absence, the other parents regale her further with their sagas. Pediatric cancer and chemo stories: the children's amputations, blood poisoning, teeth flaking like shale, the learning delays and disabilities caused by chemo frying the young, budding brain. But strangely optimistic codas are tacked on—endings as stiff and loopy as carpenter's lace, crisp and empty as lettuce, reticulate as a net—ah, words. "After all that business with the tutor, he's better now, and fitted with new incisors by my wife's cousin's husband, who did dental school in two and a half years, if you can believe that. We hope for the best. We take things as they come. Life is hard."

"Life's a big problem," agrees the Mother. Part of her welcomes and invites all their tales. In the few long days since this nightmare began, part of her has become addicted to disaster and war stories. She wants only to hear about the sadness and emergencies of others. They are the only situations that can join hands with her own; everything else bounces off her shiny shield of resentment and unsympathy. Nothing else can even stay in her brain. From this, no doubt, the philistine world is made, or should one say recruited? Together, the parents huddle all day in the Tiny Tim Lounge—no need to watch *Oprah*. They leave Oprah in the dust. Oprah has nothing on them. They chat matter-of-factly, then fall silent and watch *Dune* or *Star Wars*, in which there are bright and shiny robots, whom the Mother now sees not as robots at all but as human beings who have had terrible things happen to them.

✼ ✼ ✼

Some of their friends visit with stuffed animals and soft greetings of "Looking good" for the dozing baby, though the room is way past the stuffed-animal limit. The Mother arranges, once more, a plateful of Mint Milano cookies and cups of take-out coffee for guests. All her nutso pals stop by—the two on Prozac, the one obsessed with the word *penis* in the word *happiness*, the one who recently had her hair foiled green. "Your friends put the *de* in *fin de siècle*," says the Husband. Overheard, or recorded, all marital conversation sounds as if someone must be joking, though usually no one is.

She loves her friends, especially loves them for coming, since there are times they all fight and don't speak for weeks. Is this friendship? For now and here, it must do and is, and is, she swears it is. For one, they never offer impromptu spiritual lectures about death, how it is part of life, its natural ebb and flow, how we all must accept that, or other such utterances that make her want to scratch out some eyes. Like true friends, they take no hardy or elegant stance loosely choreographed from some broad perspective. They get right in there and mutter "Jesus Christ!" and shake their heads. Plus, they are the only people who not only will laugh at her stupid jokes but offer up stupid ones of their own. *What do you get when you cross Tiny Tim with a pit bull?* A child's illness is a strain on the mind. They know how to laugh in a fluty, desperate way— unlike the people who are more her husband's friends and who seem just to deepen their sorrowful gazes, nodding their heads with Sympathy. How exiling and estranging are everybody's Sympathetic Expressions! When anyone laughs, she thinks, Okay! Hooray: a buddy. In disaster as in show business.

Nurses come and go; their chirpy voices both startle and soothe. Some of the other Peed Onk parents stick their heads in to see how the Baby is and offer encouragement.

Green Hair scratches her head. "Everyone's so friendly here. Is there someone in this place who isn't doing all this airy, scripted optimism—or are people like that the only people here?"

"It's Modern Middle Medicine meets the Modern Middle Family," says the Husband. "In the Modern Middle West."

Someone has brought in take-out lo mein, and they all eat it out in the hall by the elevators.

★ ★ ★

Parents are allowed use of the Courtesy Line.

"You've got to have a second child," says a different friend on the phone, a friend from out of town. "An heir and a spare. That's what we did. We had another child to ensure we wouldn't off ourselves if we lost our first."

"Really?"

"I'm serious."

"A formal suicide? Wouldn't you just drink yourself into a lifelong stupor and let it go at that?"

"Nope. I knew how I would do it even. For a while, until our second came along, I had it all planned."

"What did you plan?"

"I can't go into too much detail, because—Hi, honey!—the kids are here now in the room. But I'll spell out the general idea: R-O-P-E."

✷ ✷ ✷

Sunday evening, she goes and sinks down on the sofa in the Tiny Tim Lounge next to Frank, Joey's father. He is a short, stocky man with the currentless, flatlined look behind the eyes that all the parents eventually get here. He has shaved his head bald in solidarity with his son. His little boy has been battling cancer for five years. It is now in the liver, and the rumor around the corridor is that Joey has three weeks to live. She knows that Joey's mother, Heather, left Frank years ago, two years into the cancer, and has remarried and had another child, a girl named Brittany. The Mother sees Heather here sometimes with her new life—the cute little girl and the new, young, full-haired husband who will never be so maniacally and debilitatingly obsessed with Joey's illness the way Frank, her first husband, was. Heather comes to visit Joey, to say hello and now good-bye, but she is not Joey's main man. Frank is.

Frank is full of stories—about the doctors, about the food, about the nurses, about Joey. Joey, affectless from his meds, sometimes leaves his room and comes out to watch TV in his bathrobe. He is jaundiced and bald, and though he is nine, he looks no older than six. Frank has devoted the last four and a half years to saving

Joey's life. When the cancer was first diagnosed, the doctors gave Joey a 20 percent chance of living six more months. Now here it is, almost five years later, and Joey's still here. It is all due to Frank, who, early on, quit his job as vice president of a consulting firm in order to commit himself totally to his son. He is proud of everything he's given up and done, but he is tired. Part of him now really believes things are coming to a close, that this is the end. He says this without tears. There are no more tears.

"You have probably been through more than anyone else on this corridor," says the Mother.

"I could tell you stories," he says. There is a sour odor between them, and she realizes that neither of them has bathed for days.

"Tell me one. Tell me the worst one." She knows he hates his ex-wife and hates her new husband even more.

"The worst? They're all the worst. Here's one: one morning, I went out for breakfast with my buddy—it was the only time I'd left Joey alone ever; left him for two hours is all—and when I came back, his N-G tube was full of blood. They had the suction on too high, and it was sucking the guts right out of him."

"Oh my God. That just happened to us," said the Mother.

"It did?"

"Friday night."

"You're kidding. They let that happen again? I gave them such a chewing-out about that!"

"I guess our luck is not so good. We get your very worst story on the second night we're here."

"It's not a bad place, though."

"It's not?"

"Naw. I've seen worse. I've taken Joey everywhere."

"He seems very strong." Truth is, at this point, Joey seems like a zombie and frightens her.

"Joey's a fucking genius. A biological genius. They'd given him six months, remember."

The Mother nods.

"Six months is not very long," says Frank. "Six months is nothing. He was four and a half years old."

All the words are like blows. She feels flooded with affection and mourning for this man. She looks away, out the window, out past the hospital parking lot, up toward the black marbled sky and the electric eyelash of the moon. "And now he's nine," she says. "You're his hero."

"And he's mine," says Frank, though the fatigue in his voice seems to overwhelm him. "He'll be that forever. Excuse me," he says, "I've got to go check. His breathing hasn't been good. Excuse me."

★ ★ ★

"Good news and bad," says the Oncologist on Monday. He has knocked, entered the room, and now stands there. Their cots are unmade. One wastebasket is overflowing with coffee cups. "We've got the pathologist's report. The bad news is that the kidney they removed had certain lesions, called 'rests,' which are associated with a higher risk for disease in the other kidney. The good news is that the tumor is stage one, regular cell structure, and under five hundred grams, which qualifies you for a national experiment in which chemotherapy isn't done but your boy is monitored with ultrasound instead. It's not all that risky, given that the patient's watched closely, but here is the literature on it. There are forms to sign, if you decide to do that. Read all this and we can discuss it further. You have to decide within four days."

Lesions? Rests? They dry up and scatter like M&M's on the floor. All she hears is the part about no chemo. Another sigh of relief rises up in her and spills out. In a life where there is only the bearable and the unbearable, a sigh of relief is an ecstasy.

"No chemo?" says the Husband. "Do you recommend that?"

The Oncologist shrugs. What casual gestures these doctors are permitted! "I know chemo. I like chemo," says the Oncologist. "But this is for you to decide. It depends how you feel."

The Husband leans forward. "But don't you think that now

that we have the upper hand with this thing, we should keep going? Shouldn't we stomp on it, beat it, smash it to death with the chemo?"

The Mother swats him angrily and hard. "Honey, you're delirious!" She whispers, but it comes out as a hiss. "This is our lucky break!" Then she adds gently, "We don't want the Baby to have chemo."

The Husband turns back to the Oncologist. "What do *you* think?"

"It could be," he says, shrugging. "It could be that this is your lucky break. But you won't know for sure for five years."

The Husband turns back to the Mother. "Okay," he says. "Okay."

★ ★ ★

The Baby grows happier and strong. He begins to move and sit and eat. Wednesday morning, they are allowed to leave, and leave without chemo. The Oncologist looks a little nervous. "Are you nervous about this?" asks the Mother.

"Of course I'm nervous." But he shrugs and doesn't look that nervous. "See you in six weeks for the ultrasound," he says, waves and then leaves, looking at his big black shoes as he does.

The Baby smiles, even toddles around a little, the sun bursting through the clouds, an angel chorus crescendoing. Nurses arrive. The Hickman is taken out of the Baby's neck and chest; antibiotic lotion is dispensed. The Mother packs up their bags. The Baby sucks on a bottle of juice and does not cry.

"No chemo?" says one of the nurses. "Not even a *little* chemo?"

"We're doing watch and wait," says the Mother.

The other parents look envious but concerned. They have never seen any child get out of there with his hair and white blood cells intact.

"Will you be okay?" asks Ned's mother.

"The worry's going to kill us," says the Husband.

"But if all we have to do is worry," chides the Mother, "every day for a hundred years, it'll be easy. It'll be nothing. I'll take all the worry in the world, if it wards off the thing itself."

"That's right," says Ned's mother. "Compared to everything else, compared to all the actual events, the worry is nothing."

The Husband shakes his head. "I'm such an amateur," he moans.

"You're both doing admirably," says the other mother. "Your baby's lucky, and I wish you all the best."

The Husband shakes her hand warmly. "Thank you," he says. "You've been wonderful."

Another mother, the mother of Eric, comes up to them. "It's all very hard," she says, her head cocked to one side. "But there's a lot of collateral beauty along the way."

Collateral beauty? Who is entitled to such a thing? A child is ill. No one is entitled to any collateral beauty!

"Thank you," says the Husband.

Joey's father, Frank, comes up and embraces them both. "It's a journey," he says. He chucks the Baby on the chin. "Good luck, little man."

"Yes, thank you so much," says the Mother. "We hope things go well with Joey." She knows that Joey had a hard, terrible night.

Frank shrugs and steps back. "Gotta go," he says. "Good-bye!"

"Bye," she says, and then he is gone. She bites the inside of her lip, a bit tearily, then bends down to pick up the diaper bag, which is now stuffed with little animals; helium balloons are tied to its zipper. Shouldering the thing, the Mother feels she has just won a prize. All the parents have now vanished down the hall in the opposite direction. The Husband moves close. With one arm, he takes the Baby from her; with the other, he rubs her back. He can see she is starting to get weepy.

"Aren't these people nice? Don't you feel better hearing about their lives?" he asks.

Why does he do this, form clubs all the time; why does even this society of suffering soothe him? When it comes to death and dying, perhaps someone in this family ought to be more of a snob.

"All these nice people with their brave stories," he continues as they make their way toward the elevator bank, waving good-bye to the nursing staff as they go, even the Baby waving shyly. *Bye-bye! Bye-bye!* "Don't you feel consoled, knowing we're all in the same boat, that we're all in this together?"

But who on earth would want to be in this boat? the Mother thinks. This boat is a nightmare boat. Look where it goes: to a silver-and-white room, where, just before your eyesight and hearing and your ability to touch or be touched disappear entirely, you must watch your child die.

Rope! Bring on the rope.

"Let's make our own way," says the Mother, "and not in this boat."

Woman Overboard! She takes the Baby back from the Husband, cups the Baby's cheek in her hand, kisses his brow and then, quickly, his flowery mouth. The Baby's heart—she can hear it—drums with life. "For as long as I live," says the Mother, pressing the elevator button—up or down, everyone in the end has to leave this way—"I never want to see any of these people again."

☆ ☆ ☆

There are the notes.

Now where is the money?

REVELATION

Flannery O'Connor

★ ★ ★

The doctor's waiting room, which was very small, was almost full when the Turpins entered and Mrs. Turpin, who was very large, made it look even smaller by her presence. She stood looming at the head of the magazine table set in the center of it, a living demonstration that the room was inadequate and ridiculous. Her little bright black eyes took in all the patients as she sized up the seating situation. There was one vacant chair and a place on the sofa occupied by a blond child in a dirty blue romper who should have been told to move over and make room for the lady. He was five or six, but Mrs. Turpin saw at once that no one was going to tell him to move over. He was slumped down in the seat, his arms idle at his sides and his eyes idle in his head; his nose ran unchecked.

Mrs. Turpin put a firm hand on Claud's shoulder and said in a voice that included anyone who wanted to listen, "Claud, you sit in that chair there," and gave him a push down into the vacant one. Claud was florid and bald and sturdy, somewhat shorter than Mrs. Turpin, but he sat down as if he were accustomed to doing what she told him to.

Mrs. Turpin remained standing. The only man in the room besides Claud was a lean stringy old fellow with a rusty hand spread out on each knee, whose eyes were closed as if he were asleep or dead or pretending to be so as not to get up and offer her his seat. Her gaze settled agreeably on a well-dressed gray-haired lady whose eyes met hers and whose expression said: if that child belonged to me, he would have some manners and move over—there's plenty of room there for you and him too.

Claud looked up with a sigh and made as if to rise.

"Sit down," Mrs. Turpin said. "You know you're not supposed to stand on that leg. He has an ulcer on his leg," she explained.

Claud lifted his foot onto the magazine table and rolled his trouser leg up to reveal a purple swelling on a plump marble-white calf.

"My!" the pleasant lady said. "How did you do that?"

"A cow kicked him," Mrs. Turpin said.

"Goodness!" said the lady.

Claud rolled his trouser leg down.

"Maybe the little boy would move over," the lady suggested, but the child did not stir.

"Somebody will be leaving in a minute," Mrs. Turpin said. She could not understand why a doctor—with as much money as they made charging five dollars a day to just stick their head in the hospital door and look at you—couldn't afford a decent-sized waiting room. This one was hardly bigger than a garage. The table was cluttered with limp-looking magazines and at one end of it there was a big green glass ash tray full of cigarette butts and cotton wads with little blood spots on them. If she had had anything to do with the running of the place, that would have been emptied every so often. There were no chairs against the wall at the head of the room. It had a rectangular-shaped panel in it that permitted a view of the office where the nurse came and went and the secretary listened to the radio. A plastic fern in a gold pot sat in the opening and trailed its fronds down almost to the floor. The radio was softly playing gospel music.

Just then the inner door opened and a nurse with the highest stack of yellow hair Mrs. Turpin had ever seen put her face in the crack and called for the next patient. The woman sitting beside Claud grasped the two arms of her chair and hoisted herself up; she pulled her dress free from her legs and lumbered through the door where the nurse had disappeared.

Mrs. Turpin eased into the vacant chair, which held her tight as a corset. "I wish I could reduce," she said, and rolled her eyes and gave a comic sigh.

"Oh, *you* aren't fat," the stylish lady said.

"Ooooo I am too," Mrs. Turpin said. "Claud he eats all he wants to and never weighs over one hundred and seventy-five pounds, but me I just look at something good to eat and I gain some weight," and her stomach and shoulders shook with laughter. "You can eat all you want to, can't you, Claud?" she asked, turning to him.

Claud only grinned.

"Well, as long as you have such a good disposition," the stylish lady said, "I don't think it makes a bit of difference what size you are. You just can't beat a good disposition."

Next to her was a fat girl of eighteen or nineteen, scowling into a thick blue book which Mrs. Turpin saw was entitled *Human Development*. The girl raised her head and directed her scowl at

Mrs. Turpin as if she did not like her looks. She appeared annoyed that anyone should speak while she tried to read. The poor girl's face was blue with acne and Mrs. Turpin thought how pitiful it was to have a face like that at that age. She gave the girl a friendly smile but the girl only scowled the harder. Mrs. Turpin herself was fat but she had always had good skin, and, though she was forty-seven years old, there was not a wrinkle in her face except around her eyes from laughing too much.

Next to the ugly girl was the child, still in exactly the same position, and next to him was a thin leathery old woman in a cotton print dress. She and Claud had three sacks of chicken feed in their pump house that was in the same print. She had seen from the first that the child belonged with the old woman. She could tell by the way they sat—kind of vacant and white-trashy, as if they would sit there until Doomsday if nobody called and told them to get up. And at right angles but next to the well-dressed pleasant lady was a lank-faced woman who was certainly the child's mother. She had on a yellow sweat shirt and wine-colored slacks, both gritty-looking, and the rims of her lips were stained with snuff. Her dirty yellow hair was tied behind with a little piece of red paper ribbon. Worse than niggers any day, Mrs. Turpin thought.

The gospel hymn playing was "When I looked up and He looked down," and Mrs. Turpin, who knew it, supplied the last line mentally, "And wona these days I know I'll we-eara crown."

Without appearing to, Mrs. Turpin always noticed people's feet. The well-dressed lady had on red and gray suede shoes to match her dress. Mrs. Turpin had on her good black patent leather pumps. The ugly girl had on Girl Scout shoes and heavy socks. The old woman had on tennis shoes and the white-trashy mother had on what appeared to be bedroom slippers, black straw with gold braid threaded through them—exactly what you would have expected her to have on.

Sometimes at night when she couldn't go to sleep, Mrs. Turpin would occupy herself with the question of who she would have chosen to be if she couldn't have been herself. If Jesus had said to her before he made her, "There's only two places available for you. You can either be a nigger or white-trash," what would she have said? "Please, Jesus, please," she would have said, "just let me wait until there's another place available," and he would have said, "No, you have to go right now and I have only those two places so make up your mind." She would have wiggled and squirmed and begged and pleaded but it would have been no use and finally she would have said, "All right, make me a nigger then—but that don't mean a trashy one." And he would have made her a neat clean respectable Negro woman, herself but black.

Next to the child's mother was a red-headed youngish woman, reading one of the magazines and working a piece of chewing gum, hell for leather, as Claud would say. Mrs. Turpin could not see the woman's feet. She was not white-trash, just common. Sometimes Mrs. Turpin occupied herself at night naming the classes of people. On the bottom of the heap were most colored people, not the kind she would have been if she had been one, but most of them; then next to them—not above, just away from— were the white-trash; then above them were the home-owners, and above them the home-and-land owners, to which she and Claud belonged. Above she and Claud were people with a lot of money and much bigger houses and much more land. But here the complexity of it would begin to bear in on her, for some of the people with a lot of money were common and ought to be below her and Claud and some of the people who had good blood had lost their money and had to rent and then there were colored people who owned their homes and land as well. There was a colored dentist in town who had two red Lincolns and a swimming pool and a farm with registered white-face cattle on it. Usually by the time she had fallen asleep all the classes of people were moiling and roiling around in her head, and she would dream they were all crammed in together in a box car, being ridden off to be put in a gas oven.

"That's a beautiful clock," she said and nodded to her right. It was a big wall clock, the face encased in a brass sunburst.

"Yes, it's very pretty," the stylish lady said agreeably. "And right on the dot too," she added, glancing at her watch.

The ugly girl beside her cast an eye upward at the clock, smirked, then looked directly at Mrs. Turpin and smirked again. Then she returned her eyes to her book. She was obviously the lady's daughter because, although they didn't look anything alike as to disposition, they both had the same shape of face and the same blue eyes. On the lady they sparkled pleasantly but in the girl's seared face they appeared alternately to smolder and to blaze.

What if Jesus had said, "All right, you can be white-trash or a nigger or ugly"!

Mrs. Turpin felt an awful pity for the girl, though she thought it was one thing to be ugly and another to act ugly.

The woman with the snuff-stained lips turned around in her chair and looked up at the clock. Then she turned back and appeared to look a little to the side of Mrs. Turpin. There was a cast in one of her eyes. "You want to know wher you can get you one of themther clocks?" she asked in a loud voice.

"No, I already have a nice clock," Mrs. Turpin said. Once somebody like her got a leg in the conversation, she would be all over it.

"You can get you one with green stamps," the woman said. "That's most likely wher he got hisn. Save you up enough, you can get you most anythang. I got me some joo'ry."

Ought to have got you a wash rag and some soap, Mrs. Turpin thought.

"I get contour sheets with mine," the pleasant lady said.

The daughter slammed her book shut. She looked straight in front of her, directly through Mrs. Turpin and on through the yellow curtain and the plate glass window which made the wall behind her. The girl's eyes seemed lit all of a sudden with a peculiar light, an unnatural light like night road signs give. Mrs. Turpin turned her head to see if there was anything going on outside that she should see, but she could not see anything. Figures passing cast only a pale shadow through the curtain. There was no reason the girl should single her out for her ugly looks.

"Miss Finley," the nurse said, cracking the door. The gum-chewing woman got up and passed in front of her and Claud and went into the office. She had on red high-heeled shoes.

Directly across the table, the ugly girl's eyes were fixed on Mrs. Turpin as if she had some very special reason for disliking her.

"This is wonderful weather, isn't it?" the girl's mother said.

"It's good weather for cotton if you can get the niggers to pick it," Mrs. Turpin said, "but niggers don't want to pick cotton any more. You can't get the white folks to pick it and now you can't get the niggers—because they got to be right up there with the white folks."

"They gonna try anyways," the white-trash woman said, leaning forward.

"Do you have one of the cotton-picking machines?" the pleasant lady asked.

"No," Mrs. Turpin said, "they leave half the cotton in the field. We don't have much cotton anyway. If you want to make it farming now, you have to have a little of everything. We got a couple of acres of cotton and a few hogs and chickens and just enough white-face that Claud can look after them himself."

"One thang I don't want," the white-trash woman said, wiping her mouth with the back of her hand. "Hogs. Nasty stinking things, a-gruntin and a-rootin all over the place."

Mrs. Turpin gave her the merest edge of her attention. "Our hogs are not dirty and they don't stink," she said. "They're cleaner than some children I've seen. Their feet never touch the ground.

We have a pig-parlor—that's where you raise them on concrete,"
she explained to the pleasant lady, "and Claud scoots them down
with the hose every afternoon and washes off the floor." Cleaner
by far than that child right there, she thought. Poor nasty little
thing. He had not moved except to put the thumb of his dirty
hand into his mouth.

The woman turned her face away from Mrs. Turpin. "I know I
wouldn't scoot down no hog with no hose," she said to the wall.

You wouldn't have no hog to scoot down, Mrs. Turpin said to
herself.

"A-gruntin and a-rootin and a-groanin," the woman muttered.

"We got a little of everything," Mrs. Turpin said to the pleasant
lady. "It's no use in having more than you can handle yourself with
help like it is. We found enough niggers to pick our cotton this
year but Claud he has to go after them and take them home again
in the evening. They can't walk that half a mile. No they can't. I tell
you," she said and laughed merrily, "I sure am tired of buttering up
niggers, but you got to love em if you want em to work for you.
When they come in the morning, I run out and I say, 'Hi yawl this
morning?' and when Claud drives them off to the field I just wave
to beat the band and they just wave back." And she waved her hand
rapidly to illustrate.

"Like you read out of the same book," the lady said, showing
she understood perfectly.

"Child, yes," Mrs. Turpin said. "And when they come in from
the field, I run out with a bucket of icewater. That's the way it's going to be from now on," she said. "You may as well face it."

"One thang I know," the white-trash woman said. "Two thangs
I ain't going to do: love no niggers or scoot down no hog with no
hose." And she let out a bark of contempt.

The look that Mrs. Turpin and the pleasant lady exchanged indicated they both understood that you had to *have* certain things

before you could *know* certain things. But every time Mrs. Turpin exchanged a look with the lady, she was aware that the ugly girl's peculiar eyes were still on her, and she had trouble bringing her attention back to the conversation.

"When you got something," she said, "you got to look after it." And when you ain't got a thing but breath and britches, she added to herself, you can afford to come to town every morning and just sit on the Court House coping and spit.

A grotesque revolving shadow passed across the curtain behind her and was thrown palely on the opposite wall. Then a bicycle clattered down against the outside of the building. The door opened and a colored boy glided in with a tray from the drugstore. It had two large red and white paper cups on it with tops on them. He was a tall, very black boy in discolored white pants and a green nylon shirt. He was chewing gum slowly, as if to music. He set the tray down in the office opening next to the fern and stuck his head through to look for the secretary. She was not in there. He rested his arms on the ledge and waited, his narrow bottom stuck out, swaying to the left and right. He raised a hand over his head and scratched the base of his skull.

"You see that button there, boy?" Mrs. Turpin said. "You can punch that and she'll come. She's probably in the back somewhere."

"Is that right?" the boy said agreeably, as if he had never seen the button before. He leaned to the right and put his finger on it. "She sometime out," he said and twisted around to face his audience, his elbows behind him on the counter. The nurse appeared and he twisted back again. She handed him a dollar and he rooted in his pocket and made the change and counted it out to her. She gave him fifteen cents for a tip and he went out with the empty tray. The heavy door swung to slowly and closed at length with the sound of suction. For a moment no one spoke.

"They ought to send all them niggers back to Africa," the

white-trash woman said. "That's wher they come from in the first place."

"Oh, I couldn't do without my good colored friends," the pleasant lady said.

"There's a heap of things worse than a nigger," Mrs. Turpin agreed. "It's all kinds of them just like it's all kinds of us."

"Yes, and it takes all kinds to make the world go round," the lady said in her musical voice.

As she said it, the raw-complexioned girl snapped her teeth together. Her lower lip turned downwards and inside out, revealing the pale pink inside of her mouth. After a second it rolled back up. It was the ugliest face Mrs. Turpin had ever seen anyone make and for a moment she was certain that the girl had made it at her. She was looking at her as if she had known and disliked her all her life—all of Mrs. Turpin's life, it seemed too, not just all the girl's life. Why, girl, I don't even know you, Mrs. Turpin said silently.

She forced her attention back to the discussion. "It wouldn't be practical to send them back to Africa," she said. "They wouldn't want to go. They got it too good here."

"Wouldn't be what they wanted—if I had anythang to do with it," the woman said.

"It wouldn't be a way in the world you could get all the niggers back over there," Mrs. Turpin said. "They'd be hiding out and lying down and turning sick on you and wailing and hollering and raring and pitching. It wouldn't be a way in the world to get them over there."

"They got over here," the trashy woman said. "Get back like they got over."

"It wasn't so many of them then," Mrs. Turpin explained.

The woman looked at Mrs. Turpin as if here was an idiot indeed but Mrs. Turpin was not bothered by the look, considering where it came from.

"Nooo," she said, "they're going to stay here where they can go to New York and marry white folks and improve their color. That's what they all want to do, every one of them, improve their color."

"You know what comes of that, don't you?" Claud asked.

"No, Claud, what?" Mrs. Turpin said.

Claud's eyes twinkled. "White-faced niggers," he said with never a smile.

Everybody in the office laughed except the white-trash and the ugly girl. The girl gripped the book in her lap with white fingers. The trashy woman looked around her from face to face as if she thought they were all idiots. The old woman in the feed sack dress continued to gaze expressionless across the floor at the high-top shoes of the man opposite her, the one who had been pretending to be asleep when the Turpins came in. He was laughing heartily, his hands still spread out on his knees. The child had fallen to the side and was lying now almost face down in the old woman's lap.

While they recovered from their laughter, the nasal chorus on the radio kept the room from silence.

> *"You go to blank blank*
> *And I'll go to mine*
> *But we'll all blank along*
> *To-geth-ther,*
> *And all along the blank*
> *We'll hep each other out*
> *Smile-ling in any kind of*
> *Weath-ther!"*

Mrs. Turpin didn't catch every word but she caught enough to agree with the spirit of the song and it turned her thoughts sober. To help anybody out that needed it was her philosophy of life. She never spared herself when she found somebody in need, whether they were white or black, trash or decent. And of all she had to be thankful for, she was most thankful that this was so. If Jesus had said, "You can be high society and have all the money you want and be thin and svelte-like, but you can't be a good woman with it," she would have had to say, "Well don't make me that then. Make me a good woman and it don't matter what else, how fat or how ugly or how poor!" Her heart rose. He had not made her a nigger or white-trash or ugly! He had made her herself and given her a little of everything. Jesus, thank you! she said. Thank you thank you thank you! Whenever she counted her blessings she felt as buoyant as if she weighed one hundred and twenty-five pounds instead of one hundred and eighty.

"What's wrong with your little boy?" the pleasant lady asked the white-trashy woman.

"He has a ulcer," the woman said proudly. "He ain't give me a minute's peace since he was born. Him and her are just alike," she said, nodding at the old woman, who was running her leathery fingers through the child's pale hair. "Look like I can't get nothing down them two but Co' Cola and candy."

That's all you try to get down em, Mrs. Turpin said to herself. Too lazy to light the fire. There was nothing you could tell her about people like them that she didn't know already. And it was not just that they didn't have anything. Because if you gave them everything, in two weeks it would all be broken or filthy or they would have chopped it up for lightwood. She knew all this from her own experience. Help them you must, but help them you couldn't.

All at once the ugly girl turned her lips inside out again. Her eyes fixed like two drills on Mrs. Turpin. This time there was no mistaking that there was something urgent behind them.

Girl, Mrs. Turpin exclaimed silently, I haven't done a thing to you! The girl might be confusing her with somebody else. There was no need to sit by and let herself be intimidated. "You must be in college," she said boldly, looking directly at the girl. "I see you reading a book there."

The girl continued to stare and pointedly did not answer.

Her mother blushed at this rudeness. "The lady asked you a question, Mary Grace," she said under her breath.

"I have ears," Mary Grace said.

The poor mother blushed again. "Mary Grace goes to Wellesley College," she explained. She twisted one of the buttons on her dress. "In Massachusetts," she added with a grimace. "And in the summer she just keeps right on studying. Just reads all the time, a real book worm. She's done real well at Wellesley; she's taking English and Math and History and Psychology and Social Studies," she rattled on, "and I think it's too much. I think she ought to get out and have fun."

The girl looked as if she would like to hurl them all through the plate glass window.

"Way up north," Mrs. Turpin murmured and thought, well, it hasn't done much for her manners.

"I'd almost rather to have him sick," the white-trash woman said, wrenching the attention back to herself. "He's so mean when he ain't. Look like some children just take natural to meanness. It's some gets bad when they get sick but he was the opposite. Took sick and turned good. He don't give me no trouble now. It's me waitin to see the doctor," she said.

If I was going to send anybody back to Africa, Mrs. Turpin thought, it would be your kind, woman. "Yes, indeed," she said aloud, but looking up at the ceiling, "it's a heap of things worse than a nigger." And dirtier than a hog, she added to herself.

"I think people with bad dispositions are more to be pitied than anyone on earth," the pleasant lady said in a voice that was decidedly thin.

"I thank the Lord he has blessed me with a good one," Mrs. Turpin said. "The day has never dawned that I couldn't find something to laugh at."

"Not since she married me anyways," Claud said with a comical straight face.

Everybody laughed except the girl and the white-trash.

Mrs. Turpin's stomach shook. "He's such a caution," she said, "that I can't help but laugh at him."

The girl made a loud ugly noise through her teeth.

Her mother's mouth grew thin and tight. "I think the worst thing in the world," she said, "is an ungrateful person. To have everything and not appreciate it. I know a girl," she said, "who has parents who would give her anything, a little brother who loves her dearly, who is getting a good education, who wears the best clothes, but who can never say a kind word to anyone, who never smiles, who just criticizes and complains all day long."

"Is she too old to paddle?" Claud asked.

The girl's face was almost purple.

"Yes," the lady said, "I'm afraid there's nothing to do but leave her to her folly. Some day she'll wake up and it'll be too late."

"It never hurt anyone to smile," Mrs. Turpin said. "It just makes you feel better all over."

"Of course," the lady said sadly, "but there are just some people you can't tell anything to. They can't take criticism."

"If it's one thing I am," Mrs. Turpin said with feeling, "it's grateful. When I think who all I could have been besides myself and what all I got, a little of everything, and a good disposition besides, I just feel like shouting. 'Thank you, Jesus, for making everything the way it is!' It could have been different!" For one thing, somebody else could have got Claud. At the thought of this, she was flooded with gratitude and a terrible pang of joy ran through her. "Oh thank you, Jesus, Jesus, thank you!" she cried aloud.

The book struck her directly over her left eye. It struck almost at the same instant that she realized the girl was about to hurl it. Before she could utter a sound, the raw face came crashing across the table toward her, howling. The girl's fingers sank like clamps into the soft flesh of her neck. She heard the mother cry out and Claud shout, "Whoa!" There was an instant when she was certain that she was about to be in an earthquake.

All at once her vision narrowed and she saw everything as if it were happening in a small room far away, or as if she were looking at it through the wrong end of a telescope. Claud's face crumpled and fell out of sight. The nurse ran in, then out, then in again. Then the gangling figure of the doctor rushed out of the inner door. Magazines flew this way and that as the table turned over. The girl fell with a thud and Mrs. Turpin's vision suddenly reversed itself and she saw everything large instead of small. The eyes of the white-trashy woman were staring hugely at the floor. There the girl, held down on one side by the nurse and on the other by her mother, was wrenching and turning in their grasp. The doctor was kneeling astride her, trying to hold her arm down. He managed after a second to sink a long needle into it.

Mrs. Turpin felt entirely hollow except for her heart which swung from side to side as if it were agitated in a great empty drum of flesh.

"Somebody that's not busy call for the ambulance," the doctor said in the off-hand voice young doctors adopt for terrible occasions.

Mrs. Turpin could not have moved a finger. The old man who had been sitting next to her skipped nimbly into the office and made the call, for the secretary still seemed to be gone.

"Claud!" Mrs. Turpin called.

He was not in his chair. She knew she must jump up and find him but she felt like someone trying to catch a train in a dream, when everything moves in slow motion and the faster you try to run the slower you go.

"Here I am," a suffocated voice, very unlike Claud's, said.

He was doubled up in the corner on the floor, pale as paper, holding his leg. She wanted to get up and go to him but she could not move. Instead, her gaze was drawn slowly downward to the churning face on the floor, which she could see over the doctor's shoulder.

The girl's eyes stopped rolling and focused on her. They

seemed a much lighter blue than before, as if a door that had been tightly closed behind them was now open to admit light and air.

Mrs. Turpin's head cleared and her power of motion returned. She leaned forward until she was looking directly into the fierce brilliant eyes. There was no doubt in her mind that the girl did know her, knew her in some intense and personal way, beyond time and place and condition. "What you got to say to me?" she asked hoarsely and held her breath, waiting, as for a revelation.

The girl raised her head. Her gaze locked with Mrs. Turpin's. "Go back to hell where you came from, you old wart hog," she whispered. Her voice was low but clear. Her eyes burned for a moment as if she saw with pleasure that her message had struck its target.

Mrs. Turpin sank back in her chair.

After a moment the girl's eyes closed and she turned her head wearily to the side.

The doctor rose and handed the nurse the empty syringe. He leaned over and put both hands for a moment on the mother's shoulders, which were shaking. She was sitting on the floor, her lips pressed together, holding Mary Grace's hand in her lap. The girl's fingers were gripped like a baby's around her thumb. "Go on to the hospital," he said. "I'll call and make the arrangements."

"Now let's see that neck," he said in a jovial voice to Mrs. Turpin. He began to inspect her neck with his first two fingers. Two little moon-shaped lines like pink fish bones were indented over her windpipe. There was the beginning of an angry red swelling above her eye. His fingers passed over this also.

"Lea' me be," she said thickly and shook him off. "See about Claud. She kicked him."

"I'll see about him in a minute," he said and felt her pulse. He was a thin gray-haired man, given to pleasantries. "Go home and have yourself a vacation the rest of the day," he said and patted her on the shoulder.

Quit your pattin me, Mrs. Turpin growled to herself.

"And put an ice pack over that eye," he said. Then he went and squatted down beside Claud and looked at his leg. After a moment he pulled him up and Claud limped after him into the office.

Until the ambulance came, the only sounds in the room were the tremulous moans of the girl's mother, who continued to sit on the floor. The white-trash woman did not take her eyes off the girl. Mrs. Turpin looked straight ahead at nothing. Presently the ambulance drew up, a long dark shadow, behind the curtain. The attendants came in and set the stretcher down beside the girl and lifted her expertly onto it and carried her out. The nurse helped the mother gather up her things. The shadow of the ambulance moved silently away and the nurse came back in the office.

"That ther girl is going to be a lunatic, ain't she?" the white-trash woman asked the nurse, but the nurse kept on to the back and never answered her.

"Yes, she's going to be a lunatic," the white-trash woman said to the rest of them.

"Po' critter," the old woman murmured. The child's face was still in her lap. His eyes looked idly out over her knees. He had not moved during the disturbance except to draw one leg up under him.

"I thank Gawd," the white-trash woman said fervently, "I ain't a lunatic."

Claud came limping out and the Turpins went home.

As their pick-up truck turned into their own dirt road and made the crest of the hill, Mrs. Turpin gripped the window ledge and looked out suspiciously. The land sloped gracefully down through a field dotted with lavender weeds and at the start of the rise their small yellow frame house, with its little flower beds spread out around it like a fancy apron, sat primly in its accustomed place between two giant hickory trees. She would not have been startled to see a burnt wound between two blackened chimneys.

Neither of them felt like eating so they put on their house clothes and lowered the shade in the bedroom and lay down, Claud with his leg on a pillow and herself with a damp washcloth over her eye. The instant she was flat on her back, the image of a razor-backed hog with warts on its face and horns coming out behind its ears snorted into her head. She moaned, a low quiet moan.

"I am not," she said tearfully, "a wart hog. From hell." But the denial had no force. The girl's eyes and her words, even the tone of her voice, low but clear, directed only to her, brooked no repudiation. She had been singled out for the message, though there was trash in the room to whom it might justly have been applied. The full force of this fact struck her only now. There was a woman there who was neglecting her own child but she had been overlooked. The message had been given to Ruby Turpin, a respectable, hard-working, church-going woman. The tears dried. Her eyes began to burn instead with wrath.

She rose on her elbow and the washcloth fell into her hand. Claud was lying on his back, snoring. She wanted to tell him what the girl had said. At the same time, she did not wish to put the image of herself as a wart hog from hell into his mind.

"Hey, Claud," she muttered and pushed his shoulder.

Claud opened one pale baby blue eye.

She looked into it warily. He did not think about anything. He just went his way.

"Wha, whasit?" he said and closed the eye again.

"Nothing," she said. "Does your leg pain you?"

"Hurts like hell," Claud said.

"It'll quit terreckly," she said and lay back down. In a moment Claud was snoring again. For the rest of the afternoon they lay there. Claud slept. She scowled at the ceiling. Occasionally she raised her fist and made a small stabbing motion over her chest as if she was defending her innocence to invisible guests who were like the comforters of Job, reasonable-seeming but wrong.

About five-thirty Claud stirred. "Got to go after those niggers," he sighed, not moving.

She was looking straight up as if there were unintelligible handwriting on the ceiling. The protuberance over her eye had turned a greenish-blue. "Listen here," she said.

"What?"

"Kiss me."

Claud leaned over and kissed her loudly on the mouth. He pinched her side and their hands interlocked. Her expression of ferocious concentration did not change. Claud got up, groaning and growling, and limped off. She continued to study the ceiling.

She did not get up until she heard the pick-up truck coming back with the Negroes. Then she rose and thrust her feet in her brown oxfords, which she did not bother to lace, and stumped out onto the back porch and got her red plastic bucket. She emptied a tray of ice cubes into it and filled it half full of water and went out into the back yard. Every afternoon after Claud brought the hands in, one of the boys helped him put out hay and the rest waited in the back of the truck until he was ready to take them home. The truck was parked in the shade under one of the hickory trees.

"Hi yawl this evening?" Mrs. Turpin asked grimly, appearing with the bucket and the dipper. There were three women and a boy in the truck.

"Us doin nicely," the oldest woman said. "Hi you doin?" and her gaze stuck immediately on the dark lump on Mrs. Turpin's forehead. "You done fell down, ain't you?" she asked in a solicitous voice. The old woman was dark and almost toothless. She had on an old felt hat of Claud's set back on her head. The other two women were younger and lighter and they both had new bright green sunhats. One of them had hers on her head; the other had taken hers off and the boy was grinning beneath it.

Mrs. Turpin set the bucket down on the floor of the truck. "Yawl hep yourselves," she said. She looked around to make sure

Claud had gone. "No, I didn't fall down," she said, folding her arms. "It was something worse than that."

"Ain't nothing bad happen to you!" the old woman said. She said it as if they all knew that Mrs. Turpin was protected in some special way by Divine Providence. "You just had you a little fall."

"We were in town at the doctor's office for where the cow kicked Mr. Turpin," Mrs. Turpin said in a flat tone that indicated they could leave off their foolishness. "And there was this girl there. A big fat girl with her face all broke out. I could look at that girl and tell she was peculiar but I couldn't tell how. And me and her mama was just talking and going along and all of a sudden WHAM! She throws this big book she was reading at me and . . ."

"Naw!" the old woman cried out.

"And then she jumps over the table and commences to choke me."

"Naw!" they all exclaimed, "naw!"

"Hi come she do that?" the old woman asked. "What ail her?"

Mrs. Turpin only glared in front of her.

"Somethin ail her," the old woman said.

"They carried her off in an ambulance," Mrs. Turpin continued, "but before she went she was rolling on the floor and they were trying to hold her down to give her a shot and she said something to me." She paused. "You know what she said to me?"

"What she say?" they asked.

"She said," Mrs. Turpin began, and stopped, her face very dark and heavy. The sun was getting whiter and whiter, blanching the sky overhead so that the leaves of the hickory tree were black in the face of it. She could not bring forth the words. "Something real ugly," she muttered.

"She sho shouldn't said nothin ugly to you," the old woman said. "You so sweet. You the sweetest lady I know."

"She pretty too," the one with the hat on said.

"And stout," the other one said. "I never knowed no sweeter white lady."

"That's the truth befo' Jesus," the old woman said. "Amen! You des as sweet and pretty as you can be."

Mrs. Turpin knew exactly how much Negro flattery was worth and it added to her rage. "She said," she began again and finished this time with a fierce rush of breath, "that I was an old wart hog from hell."

There was an astounded silence.

"Where she at?" the youngest woman cried in a piercing voice.

"Lemme see her. I'll kill her!"

"I'll kill her with you!" the other one cried.

"She b'long in the sylum," the old woman said emphatically. "You the sweetest white lady I know."

"She pretty too," the other two said. "Stout as she can be and sweet. Jesus satisfied with her!"

"Deed he is," the old woman declared.

Idiots! Mrs. Turpin growled to herself. You could never say anything intelligent to a nigger. You could talk at them but not with them. "Yawl ain't drunk your water," she said shortly. "Leave the bucket in the truck when you're finished with it. I got more to do than just stand around and pass the time of day," and she moved off and into the house.

She stood for a moment in the middle of the kitchen. The dark protuberance over her eye looked like a miniature tornado cloud which might any moment sweep across the horizon of her brow. Her lower lip protruded dangerously. She squared her massive shoulders. Then she marched into the front of the house and out the side door and started down the road to the pig parlor. She had the look of a woman going single-handed, weaponless, into battle.

The sun was a deep yellow now like a harvest moon and was riding westward very fast over the far tree line as if it meant to reach the hogs before she did. The road was rutted and she kicked several good-sized stones out of her path as she strode along. The pig parlor was on a little knoll at the end of a lane that ran off from the side of the barn. It was a square of concrete as large as a small room, with a board fence about four feet high around it. The concrete floor sloped slightly so that the hog wash could drain off into a trench where it was carried to the field for fertilizer. Claud was standing on the outside, on the edge of the concrete, hanging on to the top board, hosing down the floor inside. The hose was connected to the faucet of a water trough nearby.

Mrs. Turpin climbed up beside him and glowered down at the hogs inside. There were seven long-snouted bristly shoats in it—tan with liver-colored spots—and an old sow a few weeks off from farrowing. She was lying on her side grunting. The shoats were running about shaking themselves like idiot children, their little slit pig eyes searching the floor for anything left. She had read that pigs were the most intelligent animal. She doubted it. They were supposed to be smarter than dogs. There had even been a pig astronaut. He had performed his assignment perfectly but died of a heart attack afterwards because they left him in his electric suit, sitting upright throughout his examination when naturally a hog should be on all fours.

A-gruntin and a-rootin and a-groanin.

"Gimme that hose," she said, yanking it away from Claud. "Go on and carry them niggers home and then get off that leg."

"You look like you might have swallowed a mad dog," Claud observed, but he got down and limped off. He paid no attention to her humors.

Until he was out of earshot, Mrs. Turpin stood on the side of the pen, holding the hose and pointing the stream of water at the hindquarters of any shoat that looked as if it might try to lie down. When he had had time to get over the hill, she turned her head slightly and her wrathful eyes scanned the path. He was nowhere in sight. She turned back again and seemed to gather herself up. Her shoulders rose and she drew in her breath.

"What do you send me a message like that for?" she said in a low fierce voice, barely above a whisper but with the force of a shout in its concentrated fury. "How am I a hog and me both? How am I saved and from hell too?" Her free fist was knotted and with the other she gripped the hose, blindly pointing the stream of water in and out of the eye of the old sow whose outraged squeal she did not hear.

The pig parlor commanded a view of the back pasture where their twenty beef cows were gathered around the hay-bales Claud and the boy had put out. The freshly cut pasture sloped down to the highway. Across it was their cotton field and beyond that a dark green dusty wood which they owned as well. The sun was behind the wood, very red, looking over the paling of trees like a farmer inspecting his own hogs.

"Why me?" she rumbled. "It's no trash around here, black or white, that I haven't given to. And break my back to the bone every day working. And do for the church."

She appeared to be the right size woman to command the arena before her. "How am I a hog?" she demanded. "Exactly how am I like them?" and she jabbed the stream of water at the shoats. "There was plenty of trash there. It didn't have to be me.

"If you like trash better, go get yourself some trash then," she railed. "You could have made me trash. Or a nigger. If trash is what you wanted why didn't you make me trash?" She shook her fist with the hose in it and a watery snake appeared momentarily in the air. "I could quit working and take it easy and be filthy," she growled. "Lounge about the sidewalks all day drinking root beer. Dip snuff and spit in every puddle and have it all over my face. I could be nasty.

"Or you could have made me a nigger. It's too late for me to be a nigger," she said with deep sarcasm, "but I could act like one. Lay down in the middle of the road and stop traffic. Roll on the ground."

In the deepening light everything was taking on a mysterious hue. The pasture was growing a peculiar glassy green and the streak of highway had turned lavender. She braced herself for a final assault and this time her voice rolled out over the pasture. "Go on," she yelled, "call me a hog! Call me a hog again. From hell. Call me a wart hog from hell. Put that bottom rail on top. There'll still be a top and bottom!"

A garbled echo returned to her.

A final surge of fury shook her and she roared, "Who do you think you are?"

The color of everything, field and crimson sky, burned for a moment with a transparent intensity. The question carried over the pasture and across the highway and the cotton field and returned to her clearly like an answer from beyond the wood.

She opened her mouth but no sound came out of it.

A tiny truck, Claud's, appeared on the highway, heading rapidly out of sight. Its gears scraped thinly. It looked like a child's toy. At any moment a bigger truck might smash into it and scatter Claud's and the niggers' brains all over the road.

Mrs. Turpin stood there, her gaze fixed on the highway, all her muscles rigid, until in five or six minutes the truck reappeared, returning. She waited until it had had time to turn into their own road. Then like a monumental statue coming to life, she bent her head slowly and gazed, as if through the very heart of mystery, down into the pig parlor at the hogs. They had settled all in one corner around the old sow who was grunting softly. A red glow suffused them. They appeared to pant with a secret life.

Until the sun slipped finally behind the tree line, Mrs. Turpin remained there with her gaze bent to them as if she were absorbing some abysmal life-giving knowledge. At last she lifted her head. There was only a purple streak in the sky, cutting through a field of crimson and leading, like an extension of the highway, into the descending dusk. She raised her hands from the side of the pen in a gesture hieratic and profound. A visionary light settled in her eyes. She saw the streak as a vast swinging bridge extending upward from the earth through a field of living fire. Upon it a vast horde of souls was rumbling toward heaven. There were whole companies of white-trash, clean for the first time in their lives, and bands of black niggers in white robes, and battalions of freaks and lunatics shouting and clapping and leaping like frogs. And bringing up the end of the procession was a tribe of people whom she recognized at once as those who, like herself and Claud, had always had a little of everything and the God-given wit to use it right. She leaned forward to observe them closer. They were marching behind the others with great dignity, accountable as they had always been for good order and common sense and respectable behavior. They alone were on key. Yet she could see by their shocked and altered faces that even their virtues were being burned away. She lowered her hands and gripped the rail of the hog pen, her eyes small but fixed unblinkingly on what lay ahead. In a moment the vision faded but she remained where she was, immobile.

At length she got down and turned off the faucet and made her slow way on the darkening path to the house. In the woods around her the invisible cricket choruses had struck up, but what she heard were the voices of the souls climbing upward into the starry field and shouting hallelujah.

IN THE CEMETERY WHERE AL JOLSON IS BURIED

Amy Hempel

★ ★ ★

"Tell me things I won't mind forgetting," she said. "Make it use-less stuff or skip it."

I began. I told her insects fly through rain, missing every drop, never getting wet. I told her no one in America owned a tape recorder before Bing Crosby did. I told her the shape of the moon is like a banana—you see it looking full, you're seeing it end-on.

The camera made me self-conscious and I stopped. It was trained on us from a ceiling mount—the kind of camera banks use to photograph robbers. It played us to the nurses down the hall in Intensive Care.

"Go on, girl," she said. "You get used to it."

I had my audience. I went on. Did she know that Tammy Wynette had changed her tune? Really. That now she sings "Stand by Your *Friends*"? That Paul Anka did it too, I said. Does "You're Having *Our* Baby." That he got sick of all that feminist bitching.

"What else?" she said. "Have you got something else?"

Oh, yes.

For her I would always have something else.

"Did you know that when they taught the first chimp to talk, it lied? That when they asked her who did it on the desk, she signed back the name of the janitor. And that when they pressed her, she said she was sorry, that it was really the project director. But she was a mother, so I guess she had her reasons."

"Oh, that's good," she said. "A parable."

"There's more about the chimp," I said. "But it will break your heart."

"No, thanks," she says, and scratches at her mask.

✳ ✳ ✳

We look like good-guy outlaws. Good or bad, I am not used to the mask yet. I keep touching the warm spot where my breath, thank God, comes out. She is used to hers. She only ties the strings on top. The other ones—a pro by now—she lets hang loose.

We call this place the Marcus Welby Hospital. It's the white one with the palm trees under the opening credits of all those shows. A Hollywood hospital, though in fact it is several miles west. Off camera, there is a beach across the street.

✳ ✳ ✳

She introduces me to a nurse as the Best Friend. The impersonal article is more intimate. It tells me that *they* are intimate, the nurse and my friend.

"I was telling her we used to drink Canada Dry ginger ale and pretend we were in Canada."

278

"That's how dumb we were," I say.

"You could be sisters," the nurse says.

So how come, I'll bet they are wondering, it took me so long to get to such a glamorous place? But do they ask?

They do not ask.

Two months, and how long is the drive?

The best I can explain it is this—I have a friend who worked one summer in a mortuary. He used to tell me stories. The one that really got to me was not the grisliest, but it's the one that did. A man wrecked his car on 101 going south. He did not lose consciousness. But his arm was taken down to the wet bone—and when he looked at it—it scared him to death.

I mean, he died.

So I hadn't dared to look any closer. But now I'm doing it—and hoping that I will live through it.

✷ ✷ ✷

She shakes out a summer-weight blanket, showing a leg you did not want to see. Except for that, you look at her and understand the law that requires *two* people to be with the body at all times.

"I thought of something," she says. "I thought of it last night. I think there is a real and present need here. You know," she says, "like for someone to do it for you when you can't do it yourself. You call them up whenever you want—like when push comes to shove."

She grabs the bedside phone and loops the cord around her neck.

"Hey," she says, "the end o' the line."

She keeps on, giddy with something. But I don't know with what.

"I can't remember," she says. "What does Kübler-Ross say comes after Denial?"

It seems to me Anger must be next. Then Bargaining, Depression, and so on and so forth. But I keep my guesses to myself.

"The only thing is," she says, "is where's Resurrection? God knows, I want to do it by the book. But she left out Resurrection."

✷ ✷ ✷

She laughs, and I cling to the sound the way someone dangling above a ravine holds fast to the thrown rope.

"Tell me," she says, "about that chimp with the talking hands. What do they do when the thing ends and the chimp says, 'I don't want to go back to the zoo'?"

When I don't say anything, she says, "Okay—then tell me another animal story. I like animal stories. But not a sick one—I don't want to know about all the seeing-eye dogs going blind."

No, I would not tell her a sick one.

"How about the hearing-ear dogs?" I say. "They're not going deaf, but they are getting very judgmental. For instance, there's this golden retriever in New Jersey, he wakes up the deaf mother and drags her into the daughter's room because the kid has got a flashlight and is reading under the covers."

"Oh, you're killing me," she says. "Yes, you're definitely killing me."

"They say the smart dog obeys, but the smarter dog knows when to disobey."

"Yes," she says, "the smarter anything knows when to disobey. Now, for example."

✷ ✷ ✷

She is flirting with the Good Doctor, who has just appeared. Unlike the Bad Doctor, who checks the IV drip before saying good morning, the Good Doctor says things like "God didn't give epileptics a fair shake." The Good Doctor awards himself points for the cripples he could have hit in the parking lot. Because the Good Doctor is a little in love with her, he says maybe a year. He pulls a chair up to her bed and suggests I might like to spend an hour on the beach.

280

"Bring me something back," she says. "Anything from the beach. Or the gift shop. Taste is no object."

He draws the curtain around her bed.

"Wait!" she cries.

I look in at her.

"Anything," she says, "except a magazine subscription."

The doctor turns away.

I watch her mouth laugh.

☆ ☆ ☆

What seems dangerous often is not—black snakes, for example, or clear-air turbulence. While things that just lie there, like this beach, are loaded with jeopardy. A yellow dust rising from the ground, the heat that ripens melons overnight—this is earthquake weather. You can sit here braiding the fringe on your towel and the sand will all of a sudden suck down like an hourglass. The air roars. In the cheap apartments on-shore, bathtubs fill themselves and gardens roll up and over like green waves. If nothing happens, the dust will drift and the heat deepen till fear turns to desire. Nerves like that are only bought off by catastrophe.

☆ ☆ ☆

"It never happens when you're thinking about it," she once observed. "Earthquake, earthquake, earthquake," she said.

"Earthquake, earthquake, earthquake," I said.

Like the aviaphobe who keeps the plane aloft with prayer, we kept it up until an aftershock cracked the ceiling.

That was after the big one in seventy-two. We were in college; our dormitory was five miles from the epicenter. When the ride was over and my jabbering pulse began to slow, she served five parts champagne to one part orange juice, and joked about living in Ocean View, Kansas. I offered to drive her to Hawaii on the new world psychics predicted would surface the next time, or the next.

I could not say that now—next.
Whose next? she could ask.

☆ ☆ ☆

Was I the only one who noticed that the experts had stopped say-ing *if* and now spoke of *when*? Of course not; the fearful ran to thousands. We watched the traffic of Japanese beetles for deviation. Deviation might mean more natural violence.

I wanted her to be afraid with me. But she said, "I don't know. I'm just not."

She was afraid of nothing, not even of flying.

I have this dream before a flight where we buckle in and the plane moves down the runway. It takes off at thirty-five miles an hour, and then we're airborne, skimming the tree tops. Still, we ar-rive in New York on time.

It is so pleasant.

One night I flew to Moscow this way.

☆ ☆ ☆

She flew with me once. That time she flew with me she ate macadamia nuts while the wings bounced. She knows the wing tips can bend thirty feet up and thirty feet down without coming off. She believes it. She trusts the laws of aerodynamics. My mind stampedes. I can almost accept that a battleship floats when every-body knows steel sinks.

I see fear in her now, and am not going to try to talk her out of it. She is right to be afraid.

After a quake, the six o'clock news airs a film clip of first-graders yelling at the broken playground per their teacher's instruc-tions.

"*Bad* earth!" they shout, because anger is stronger than fear.

☆ ☆ ☆

But the beach is standing still today. Everyone on it is tranquilized, numb, or asleep. Teenaged girls rub coconut oil on each other's hard-to-reach places. They smell like macaroons. They pry open compacts like clamshells; mirrors catch the sun and throw a spray of white rays across glazed shoulders. The girls arrange their wet hair with silk flowers the way they learned in *Seventeen*. They pose.

A formation of low-riders pulls over to watch with a six-pack. They get vocal when the girls check their tan lines. When the beer is gone, so are they—flexing their cars on up the boulevard.

Above this aggressive health are the twin wrought-iron terraces, painted flamingo pink, of the Palm Royale. Someone dies there every time the sheets are changed. There's an ambulance in the driveway, so the remaining residents line the balconies, rocking and not talking, one-upped.

The ocean they stare at is dangerous, and not just the undertow. You can almost see the slapping tails of sand sharks keeping cruising bodies alive.

If she looked, she could see this, some of it, from her window. She would be the first to say how little it takes to make a thing all wrong.

★ ★ ★

There was a second bed in the room when I got back to it!

For two beats I didn't get it. Then it hit me like an open coffin.

She wants every minute, I thought. She wants my life.

"You missed Gussie," she said.

Gussie is her parents' three-hundred-pound narcoleptic maid. Her attacks often come at the ironing board. The pillowcases in that family are all bordered with scorch.

"It's a hard trip for her," I said. "How is she?"

"Well, she didn't fall asleep, if that's what you mean. Gussie's great—you know what she said? She said, 'Darlin', stop this worriation. Just keep prayin', down on your knees'—me, who can't even get out of bed."

She shrugged. "What am I missing?"

"It's earthquake weather," I told her.

"The best thing to do about earthquakes," she said, "is not to live in California."

"That's useful," I said. "You sound like Reverend Ike—'The best thing to do for the poor is not to be one of them.'"

We're crazy about Reverend Ike.

I noticed her face was bloated.

"You know," she said, "I feel like hell. I'm about to stop having fun."

"The ancients have a saying," I said. " 'There are times when the wolves are silent; there are times when the moon howls.' "

"What's that, Navaho?"

"Palm Royale lobby graffiti," I said. "I bought a paper there. I'll read you something."

"Even though I care about nothing?"

I turned to the page with the trivia column. I said, "Did you know the more shrimp flamingo birds eat, the pinker their feathers get?" I said, "Did you know that Eskimos need refrigerators? Do you know *why* Eskimos need refrigerators? Did you know that Eskimos need refrigerators because how else would they keep their food from freezing?"

I turned to page three, to a UPI filler datelined Mexico City. I read her MAN ROBS BANK WITH CHICKEN, about a man who bought a barbecued chicken at a stand down the block from a bank. Passing the bank, he got the idea. He walked in and approached a teller. He pointed the brown paper bag at her and she handed over the day's receipts. It was the smell of barbecue sauce that eventually led to his capture.

☆ ☆ ☆

The story had made her hungry, she said—so I took the elevator down six floors to the cafeteria, and brought back all the ice cream she wanted. We lay side by side, adjustable beds cranked up for optimal TV-viewing, littering the sheets with Good Humor wrappers, picking toasted almonds out of the gauze. We were Lucy and Ethel, Mary and Rhoda in extremis. The blinds were closed to keep light off the screen.

We watched a movie starring men we used to think we wanted to sleep with. Hers was a tough cop out to stop mine, a vicious rapist who went after cocktail waitresses.

"This is a good movie," she said when snipers felled them both.

I missed her already.

✷ ✷ ✷

A Filipino nurse tiptoed in and gave her an injection. The nurse removed the pile of popsicle sticks from the nightstand—enough to splint a small animal.

The injection made us both sleepy. We slept.

I dreamed she was a decorator, come to furnish my house. She worked in secret, singing to herself. When she finished, she guided me proudly to the door. "How do you like it?" she asked, easing me inside.

Every beam and sill and shelf and knob was draped in gay bunting, with streamers of pastel crepe looped around bright mirrors.

✷ ✷ ✷

"I have to go home," I said when she woke up.

She thought I meant home to her house in the Canyon, and I had to say No, *home* home. I twisted my hands in the time-honored fashion of people in pain. I was supposed to offer something. The Best Friend. I could not even offer to come back.

I felt weak and small and failed.

Also exhilarated.

I had a convertible in the parking lot. Once out of that room, I would drive it too fast down the Coast highway through the crab-smelling air. A stop in Malibu for sangria. The music in the place would be sexy and loud. They'd serve papaya and shrimp and watermelon ice. After dinner I would shimmer with lust, buzz with heat, vibrate with life, and stay up all night.

★ ★ ★

Without a word, she yanked off her mask and threw it on the floor. She kicked at the blankets and moved to the door. She must have hated having to pause for breath and balance before slamming out of Isolation, and out of the second room, the one where you scrub and tie on the white masks.

A voice shouted her name in alarm, and people ran down the corridor. The Good Doctor was paged over the intercom. I opened the door and the nurses at the station stared hard, as if this flight had been my idea.

"Where is she?" I asked, and they nodded to the supply closet.

I looked in. Two nurses were kneeling beside her on the floor, talking to her in low voices. One held a mask over her nose and mouth, the other rubbed her back in slow circles. The nurses glanced up to see if I was the doctor—and when I wasn't, they went back to what they were doing.

"There, there, honey," they cooed.

★ ★ ★

On the morning she was moved to the cemetery, the one where Al Jolson is buried, I enrolled in a "Fear of Flying" class. "What is your worst fear?" the instructor asked, and I answered, "That I will finish this course and still be afraid."

★ ★ ★

I sleep with a glass of water on the nightstand so I can see by its level if the coastal earth is trembling or if the shaking is still me.

✷ ✷ ✷

What do I remember?

I remember only the useless things I hear—that Bob Dylan's mother invented Wite-Out, that twenty-three people must be in a room before there is a fifty-fifty chance two will have the same birthday. Who cares whether or not it's true? In my head there are bath towels swaddling this stuff. Nothing else seeps through.

I review those things that will figure in the retelling: a kiss through surgical gauze, the pale hand correcting the position of the wig. I noted these gestures as they happened, not in any retrospect—though I don't know why looking back should show us more than looking *at*.

It is just possible I will say I stayed at night.

And who is there that can say that I did not?

✷ ✷ ✷

I think of the chimp, the one with the talking hands.

In the course of the experiment, that chimp had a baby. Imagine how her trainers must have thrilled when the mother, without prompting, began to sign to her newborn.

Baby, drink milk.

Baby, play ball.

And when the baby died, the mother stood over the body, her wrinkled hands moving with animal grace, forming again and again the words: Baby, come hug, Baby, come hug, fluent now in the language of grief.

for Jessica Wolfson

COSMOPOLITAN

Akhil Sharma

★ ★ ★

A little after ten in the morning Mrs. Shaw walked across Gopal Maurya's lawn to his house. It was Saturday, and Gopal was asleep on the couch. The house was dark. When he first heard the doorbell, the ringing became part of a dream. Only he had been in the house during the four months since his wife had followed his daughter out of his life, and the sound of the bell joined somehow with his dream to make him feel ridiculous. Mrs. Shaw rang the bell again. Gopal woke confused and anxious, the state he was in most mornings. He was wearing only underwear and socks, but his blanket was cold from sweat.

He stood up and hurried to the door. He looked through the peephole. The sky was bright and clear. Mrs. Shaw was standing sideways about a foot from the door, and appeared to be staring out over his lawn at her house. She was short and red-haired and wore a pink sweatshirt and gray jogging pants.

"Hold on! Hold on, Mrs. Shaw!" he shouted, and ran back into the living room to search for a pair of pants and a shirt. The light was dim, and he had difficulty finding them. As he groped under and behind the couch and looked among the clothes crumpled on the floor, he worried that Mrs. Shaw would not wait and was already walking down the steps. He wondered if he had time to turn on the light to make his search easier. This was typical of the details that could baffle him in the morning.

Mrs. Shaw and Gopal had been neighbors for about two years, but Gopal had met her only three or four times in passing. From his wife he had learned that Mrs. Shaw was a guidance counselor at the high school his daughter had attended. He also learned that she had been divorced for a decade. Her husband, a successful orthodontist, had left her. Since then Mrs. Shaw had moved five or six times, though rarely more than a few miles from where she had last lived. She had bought the small mustard-colored house next to Gopal's as part of this restlessness. Although he did not dislike Mrs. Shaw, Gopal was irritated by the peeling paint on her house and the weeds sprouting out of her broken asphalt driveway, as if by association his house were becoming shabbier. The various cars that left her house late at night made him see her as dissolute. But all this Gopal was willing to forget that morning, in exchange for even a minor friendship.

Gopal found the pants and shirt and tugged them on as he returned to open the door. The light and cold air swept in, reminding him of what he must look like. Gopal was a small man, with delicate high cheekbones and long eyelashes. He had always been proud of his looks and had dressed well. Now he feared that the gray stubble and long hair made him appear bereft.

"Hello, Mr. Maurya," Mrs. Shaw said, looking at him and through him into the darkened house and then again at him. The sun shone behind her. The sky was blue dissolving into white. "How are you?" she asked gently.

"Oh, Mrs. Shaw," Gopal said, his voice pitted and rough, "some bad things have happened to me." He had not meant to speak so directly. He stepped out of the doorway.

The front door opened into a vestibule, and one had a clear view from there of the living room and the couch where Gopal slept. He switched on the lights. To the right was the kitchen. The round Formica table and the counters were dusty. Mrs. Shaw appeared startled by this detail. After a moment she said, "I heard." She paused and then quickly added, "I am sorry, Mr. Maurya. It must be hard. You must not feel ashamed; it's no fault of yours."

"Please, sit," Gopal said, motioning to a chair next to the kitchen table. He wanted to tangle her in conversation and keep her there for hours. He wanted to tell her how the loneliness had made him fantasize about calling an ambulance so that he could be touched and prodded, or how for a while he had begun loitering at the Indian grocery store like the old men who have not learned English. What a pretty, good woman, he thought.

Mrs. Shaw stood in the center of the room and looked around her. She was slightly overweight, and her nostrils appeared to be perfect circles, but her small white Reebok sneakers made Gopal see her as fleet with youth and innocence. "I've been thinking of coming over. I'm sorry I didn't."

"That's fine, Mrs. Shaw," Gopal said, standing near the phone on the kitchen wall. "What could anyone do? I am glad, though, that you are visiting." He searched for something else to say. To extend their time together, Gopal walked to the refrigerator and asked her if she wanted anything to drink.

"No, thank you," she said.

"Orange juice, apple juice, or grape, pineapple, guava. I also have some tropical punch," he continued, opening the refrigerator door wide, as if to show he was not lying.

"That's all right," Mrs. Shaw said, and they both became quiet. The sunlight pressed through windows that were laminated with dirt. "You must remember, everybody plays a part in these things, not just the one who is left," she said, and then they were silent again. "Do you need anything?"

"No. Thank you." They stared at each other. "Did you come for something?" Gopal asked, although he did not want to imply that he was trying to end the conversation.

"I wanted to borrow your lawn mower."

"Already?" April was just starting, and the dew did not evaporate until midday.

"Spring fever," she said.

Gopal's mind refused to provide a response to this. "Let me get you the mower."

They went to the garage. The warm sun on the back of his neck made Gopal hopeful. He believed that something would soon be said or done to delay Mrs. Shaw's departure, for certainly God could not leave him alone again. The garage smelled of must and gasoline. The lawn mower was in a shadowy corner with an aluminum ladder resting on it. "I haven't used it in a while," Gopal said, placing the ladder on the ground and smiling at Mrs. Shaw beside him. "But it should be fine." As he stood up, he suddenly felt aroused by Mrs. Shaw's large breasts, boy's haircut, and little-girl sneakers. Even her nostrils suggested a frank sexuality. Gopal wanted to put his hands on her waist and pull her toward him. And then he realized that he had.

"No. No," Mrs. Shaw said, laughing and putting her palms flat against his chest. "Not now." She pushed him away gently.

Gopal did not try kissing her again, but he was excited. *Not now,* he thought. He carefully poured gasoline into the lawn mower, wanting to appear calm, as if the two of them had already made some commitment and there was no need for nervousness. He pushed the lawn mower out onto the gravel driveway and jerked the cord to test the engine. *Not now, not now,* he thought each time he tugged. He let the engine run for a minute. Mrs. Shaw stood silent beside him. Gopal felt like smiling, but wanted to make everything appear casual. "You can have it for as long as you need," he said.

"Thank you," Mrs. Shaw replied, and smiled. They looked at each other for a moment without saying anything. Then she rolled the lawn mower down the driveway and onto the road. She stopped, turned to look at him, and said, "I'll call."

"Good," Gopal answered, and watched her push the lawn mower down the road and up her driveway into the tin shack that huddled at its end. The driveway was separated from her ranch-style house by ten or fifteen feet of grass, and they were connected by a trampled path. Before she entered her house, Mrs. Shaw turned and looked at him as he stood at the top of his driveway. She smiled and waved.

When he went back into his house, Gopal was too excited to sleep. Before Mrs. Shaw, the only woman he had ever embraced was his wife, and a part of him assumed that it was now only a matter of time before he and Mrs. Shaw fell in love and his life resumed its normalcy. Oh, to live again as he had for nearly thirty years! Gopal thought, with such force that he shocked himself. Unable to sit, unable even to think coherently, he walked around his house.

✳ ✳ ✳

His daughter's departure had made Gopal sick at heart for two or three weeks, but then she sank so completely from his thoughts that he questioned whether his pain had been hurt pride rather than grief. Gitu had been a graduate student and spent only a few weeks with them each year, so it was understandable that he would not miss her for long. But the swiftness with which the dense absence on the other side of his bed unknotted and evaporated made him wonder whether he had ever loved his wife. It made him think that his wife's abrupt decision never to return from her visit to India was as much his fault as God's. Anita, he thought, must have decided upon seeing Gitu leave that there was no more reason to stay, and that perhaps after all it was not too late to start again. Anita had gone to India at the end of November—a month after Gitu got on a Lufthansa flight to go live with her boyfriend in Germany—and a week later, over an echoing phone line, she told him of the guru and her enlightenment.

Perhaps if Gopal had not retired early from AT&T, he could have worked long hours and his wife's and daughter's slipping from his thoughts might have been mistaken for healing. But he had nothing to do. Most of his acquaintances had come by way of his wife, and when she left, Gopal did not call them, both because they had always been more Anita's friends than his and because he felt ashamed, as if his wife's departure revealed his inability to love her. At one point, around Christmas, he went to a dinner party, but he did not enjoy it. He found that he was not curious about other people's lives and did not want to talk about his own.

A month after Anita's departure a letter from her arrived—a blue aerogram, telling of the ashram, and of sweeping the courtyard, and of the daily prayers. Gopal responded immediately, but she never wrote again. His pride prevented him from trying to continue the correspondence, though he read her one letter so many times that he inadvertently memorized the Pune address. His brothers sent a flurry of long missives from India, on paper so thin that it was almost translucent, but his contact with them over the decades had been minimal, and the tragedy pushed them apart instead of pulling them closer.

Gitu sent a picture of herself wearing a yellow-and-blue ski jacket in the Swiss Alps. Gopal wrote her back in a stiff, formal way, and she responded with a breezy postcard to which he replied only after a long wait.

Other than this, Gopal had had little personal contact with the world. He was accustomed to getting up early and going to bed late, but now, since he had no work and no friends, after he spent the morning reading the *New York Times* and the *Home News & Tribune* front to back, Gopal felt adrift through the afternoon and evening. For a few weeks he tried to fill his days by showering and shaving twice daily, brushing his teeth after every snack and meal. But the purposelessness of this made him despair, and he stopped bathing altogether and instead began sleeping more and more, sometimes sixteen hours a day. He slept in the living room, long and narrow with high rectangular windows blocked by trees. At some point, in a burst of self-hate, Gopal moved his clothes from the bedroom closet to a corner of the living room, wanting to avoid comforting himself with any illusions that his life was normal.

But he yearned for his old life, the life of a clean kitchen, of a bedroom, of going out into the sun, and on a half-conscious level that morning Gopal decided to use the excitement of clasping Mrs. Shaw to change himself back to the man he had been. She might be spending time at his house, he thought, so he mopped the kitchen floor, moved back into his bedroom, vacuumed and dusted all the rooms. He spent most of the afternoon doing this, aware always of his humming lawn mower in the background. He had only to focus on it to make his heart race. Every now and then he would stop working and go to his bedroom window, where, from behind the curtains, he would stare at Mrs. Shaw. She had a red bandanna tied around her forehead, and he somehow found this appealing. That night he made himself an elaborate dinner with three dishes and a mango shake. For the first time in months Gopal watched the eleven o'clock news. He had the lights off and his feet up on a low table. Lebanon was being bombed again, and Gopal kept bursting into giggles for no reason. He tried to think of what he would do tomorrow. Gopal knew that he was happy and that to avoid depression he must keep himself busy until Mrs. Shaw called. He suddenly realized that he did not know Mrs. Shaw's first name. He padded into the darkened kitchen and looked at the phone diary. "Helen Shaw" was written in the big, loopy handwriting of his wife. Having his wife help him in this way did not bother him at all, and then he felt ashamed that it didn't.

✳ ✳ ✳

The next day was Sunday, and Gopal anticipated it cheerfully, for the Sunday *Times* was frequently so thick that he could spend the whole day reading it. But this time he did not read it all the way through. He left the book review and the other features sections to fill time over the next few days. After eating a large breakfast—the idea of preparing elaborate meals had begun to appeal to him—he went for a haircut. Gopal had not left his house in several days. He rolled down the window of his blue Honda Civic and took the long way, past the lake, to the mall. Instead of going to his usual barber, he went to a hairstylist, where a woman with long nails and large, contented breasts shampooed his hair before cutting it. Then Gopal wandered around the mall, savoring its buttered-popcorn smell and enjoying the sight of the girls with their sometimes odd-colored hair. He went into some of the small shops and looked at clothes, and considered buying a half-pound of cocoa amaretto coffee beans, although he had never cared much for coffee. After walking for nearly two hours, Gopal sat on a bench and ate an ice cream cone while reading an article in *Cosmopolitan* about what makes a good lover. He had seen the magazine in CVS and, noting the article mentioned on the cover, had been reminded how easily one can learn anything in America. Because Mrs. Shaw was an American, Gopal thought, he needed to do research into what might be expected of him. Although the article was about what makes a woman a good lover, it offered clues for men as well.

Gopal felt confident that given time, Mrs. Shaw would love him. The article made attachment appear effortless. All you had to do was listen closely and speak honestly.

He returned home around five, and Mrs. Shaw called soon after. "If you want, you can come over now."

"All right," Gopal answered. He was calm. He showered and put on a blue cotton shirt and khaki slacks. When he stepped outside, the sky was turning pink and the air smelled of wet earth. He felt young, as if he had just arrived in America and the huge scale of things had made him a giant as well.

But when he rang Mrs. Shaw's doorbell, Gopal became nervous. He turned around and looked at the white clouds against the enormous sky. He heard footsteps and then the door swishing open and Mrs. Shaw's voice. "You look handsome," she said. Gopal faced her, smiling and uncomfortable. She wore a different sweatshirt but still had on yesterday's jogging pants. She was barefoot. A yellow light shone behind her.

"Thank you," Gopal said, and then nervously added "Helen," to confirm their new relationship. "You look nice too." She did look pretty to him. Mrs. Shaw stepped aside to let him in. They were in a large room. In the center were two pale couches forming an L, with a television in front of them. Off to the side was a kitchenette—a stove, a refrigerator, and some cabinets over a sink and counter.

Seeing Gopal looking around, Mrs. Shaw said, "There are two bedrooms in the back, and a bathroom. Would you like anything to drink? I have juice, if you want." She walked to the kitchen.

"What are you going to have?" Gopal asked, following her. "If you have something, I'll have something." Then he felt embarrassed. Mrs. Shaw had not dressed up; obviously, "Not now" had been a polite rebuff.

"I was going to have a gin and tonic," she said, opening the refrigerator and standing before it with one hand on her hip.

"I would like that too." Gopal went close to her and with a dart kissed her on the lips. She did not resist, but neither did she respond. Her lips were chapped. Gopal pulled away and let her make the drinks. He had hoped the kiss would tell him something of what to expect.

They sat side by side on a couch and sipped their drinks. A table lamp cast a diffused light over them.

"Thank you for letting me borrow the lawn mower."

"It's nothing." There was a long pause. Gopal could not think of anything to say. *Cosmopolitan* had suggested trying to learn as much as possible about your lover, so he asked, "What's your favorite color?"

"Why?"

"I want to know everything about you."

"That's sweet," Mrs. Shaw said, and patted his hand. Gopal felt embarrassed and looked down. He did not know whether he should have spoken so frankly, but part of his intention had been to flatter her with his interest. "I don't have one," she said. She kept her hand on his.

Gopal suddenly thought that they might make love tonight, and he felt his heart kick. "Tell me about yourself," he said with a voice full of feeling. "Where were you born?"

"I was born in Jersey City on May fifth, but I won't tell you the year." Gopal tried to grin gamely and memorize the date. A part of him was disturbed that she did not feel comfortable enough with him to reveal her age.

"Did you grow up there?" he asked, taking a sip of the gin and tonic. Gopal drank slowly, because he knew that he could not hold his alcohol. He saw that Mrs. Shaw's toes were painted bright red. Anita had never used nail polish, and Gopal wondered what a woman who would paint her toenails might do.

"I moved to Newark when I was three. My parents ran a newspaper and candy shop. We sold greeting cards, stamps." Mrs. Shaw had nearly finished her drink. "They opened at eight in the morning and closed at seven-thirty at night. Six days a week." When she paused between swallows, she rested the glass on her knee.

Gopal had never known anyone who worked in such a shop, and he became genuinely interested in what she was saying. He remembered his lack of interest at the Christmas party and wondered whether it was the possibility of sex that made him fascinated with Mrs. Shaw's story. "Were you a happy child?" he asked, grinning broadly and then bringing the grin to a quick end, because he did not want to appear ironic. The half-glass that Gopal had drunk had already begun to make him feel light-headed and gray.

"Oh, pretty happy," she said, "although I liked to think of myself as serious. I would look at the evening sky and think that no one else had felt what I was feeling." Mrs. Shaw's understanding of her own feelings disconcerted Gopal and made him momentarily think that he wasn't learning anything important, or that she was in some way independent of her past and thus incapable of the sentimental attachments through which he expected her love for him to grow.

Cosmopolitan had recommended that both partners reveal themselves, so Gopal decided to tell a story about himself. He did not believe that being honest about himself would actually change him. Rather, he thought the deliberateness of telling the story would rob it of the power to make him vulnerable. He started to say something, but the words twisted in his mouth, and he said, "You know, I don't really drink much." Gopal felt embarrassed by the non sequitur. He thought he sounded foolish, though he had hoped that the story he would tell would make him appear sensitive.

"I kind of guessed that from the juices," she said, smiling. Gopal laughed.

He tried to say what he had wanted to confess earlier. "I associate drinking with being American, and I haven't been able to truly Americanize. On my daughter's nineteenth birthday we took her to dinner and a movie, but we didn't talk much, and the dinner finished earlier than we had expected it would. The restaurant was in a mall, and we had nothing to do until the movie started, so we wandered around Foodtown." Gopal thought he sounded pathetic, so he tried to shift the story. "After all my years in America, I am still astonished by those huge grocery stores and enjoy walking in them. But my daughter is an American, so our wandering around in Foodtown must have been very strange for her. She doesn't know Hindi, and her parents must seem very strange." Gopal noticed that his heart was racing. He wondered if he was sadder than he knew.

"That's sweet," Mrs. Shaw said. The brevity of her response made Gopal nervous.

Mrs. Shaw kissed his cheek. Her lips were dry, Gopal noticed. He turned slightly so that their lips could touch. They kissed again. Mrs. Shaw opened her lips and closed her eyes. They kissed for a long time. When they pulled apart, they continued their conversation calmly, as if they were accustomed to each other. "I didn't go into a big grocery store until I was in college," she said. "We always went to the small shops around us. When I first saw those long aisles, I wondered what happens to the food if no one buys it. I was living then with a man who was seven or eight years older than I, and when I told him, he laughed at me, and I felt so young." She stopped and then added, "I ended up leaving him because he always made me feel young." Her face was only an inch or two from Gopal's. "Now I'd marry someone who could make me feel that way." Gopal felt his romantic feelings drain away at the idea of how many men she had slept with. But the fact that Mrs. Shaw and he had experienced something removed some of the loneliness he was feeling, and Mrs. Shaw had large breasts. They began kissing again. Soon they were tussling and groping on the floor.

Her bed was large and low to the ground. Behind it was a window, and although the shade was drawn, the lights of passing cars cast patterns on the opposing wall. Gopal lay next to Mrs. Shaw and watched the shadows change. He felt his head and found that his hair was standing up on either side like horns. The shock of seeing a new naked body, so different in its amplitude from his wife's, had been exciting. A part of him was giddy with this, as if he had checked his bank balance and discovered that he had thousands more than he expected. "You are very beautiful," he said, for *Cosmopolitan* had advised saying this after making love. Mrs. Shaw rolled over and kissed his shoulder.

"No, I'm not! I'm kind of fat, and my nose is strange. But thank you," she said. Gopal looked at her and saw that even when her mouth was slack, the lines around it were deep. "You look like you've been rolled around in a dryer," she said, and laughed. Her laughter was sudden and confident. He had not noticed it before, and it made him laugh as well.

They became silent and lay quietly for several minutes, and when Gopal began feeling self-conscious, he said, "Describe the first house you lived in."

Mrs. Shaw sat up. Her stomach bulged, and her breasts drooped. She saw him looking and pulled her knees to her chest. "You're very thoughtful," she said.

Gopal felt flattered. "Oh, it's not thoughtfulness."

"I guess if it weren't for your accent, the questions would sound artificial," she said. Gopal felt his stomach clench. "I lived in a block of small houses that the army built for returning GIs. They were all drab, and the lawns ran into each other. They were near Newark airport. I liked to sit at my window and watch the planes land. That was when Newark was a local airport."

"Your house was two stories?"

"Yes. And my room was on the second floor. Tell me about yourself."

"I am the third of five brothers. We grew up in a small, poor village. I got my first pair of shoes when I left high school." As Gopal was telling her the story, he remembered how he used to make Gitu feel lazy with stories of his childhood, and his voice fell. "Everybody was like us, so I never thought of myself as poor."

They talked this way for half an hour, with Gopal asking most of the questions and trying to discover where Mrs. Shaw was vulnerable and how this vulnerability made him attractive to her. Although she answered his questions candidly, Gopal could not find the unhappy childhood or the trauma of an abandoned wife that might explain the urgency of this moment in bed. "I was planning to leave my husband," she explained casually. "He was crazy. Almost literally. He thought he was going to be a captain of industry or a senator. He wasn't registered to vote. He knew nothing about business. Once, he invested almost everything we had in a hydroponic farm in Southampton. With him I was always scared of being poor. He used to spend two hundred dollars a week on lottery tickets, and he would save the old tickets in shoeboxes in the garage." Gopal did not personally know any Indian who was divorced, and he had never been intimate enough with an American to learn what a divorce was like, but he had expected something more painful—tears and recriminations. The details she gave made the story sound practiced, and he began to think that he would never have a hold over Mrs. Shaw.

Around eight Mrs. Shaw said, "I am going to do my bills tonight." Gopal had been wondering whether she wanted him to have dinner with her and spend the night. He would have liked to, but he did not protest.

As she closed the door behind him, Mrs. Shaw said, "The lawn mower's in the back. If you want it." Night had come, and the stars were out. As Gopal pushed the lawn mower down the road, he wished that he loved Mrs. Shaw and that she loved him.

He had left the kitchen light on by mistake, and its glow was comforting. "Come, come, cheer up," he said aloud, pacing in the kitchen. "You have a lover." He tried to smile and grimaced instead. "You can make love as often as you want. Be happy." He started preparing dinner. He fried okra and steam-cooked lentils. He made both rice and bread.

As he ate, Gopal watched a television movie about a woman who had been in a coma for twenty years and suddenly woke up one day; adding to her confusion, she was pregnant. After washing the dishes he finished the article in *Cosmopolitan* that he had begun reading in the mall. The article was the second of two parts, and it mentioned that when leaving after making love for the first time, one should always arrange the next meeting. Gopal had not done this, and he phoned Mrs. Shaw.

He used the phone in the kitchen, and as he waited for her to pick up, he wondered whether he should introduce himself or assume that she would recognize his voice. "Hi, Helen," he blurted out as soon as she said "Hello." "I was just thinking of you and thought I'd call." He felt more nervous now than he had while he was with her.

"That's sweet," she said, with what Gopal thought was tenderness. "How are you?"

"I just had dinner. Did you eat?" He imagined her sitting on the floor between the couches with a pile of receipts before her. She would have a small pencil in her hand.

"I'm not hungry. I normally make myself an omelet for dinner, but I didn't want to tonight. I'm having another drink." Then, self-conscious, she added, "Otherwise I grind my teeth. I started after my divorce and I didn't have health insurance or enough money to go to a dentist." Gopal wanted to ask if she still ground her teeth, but he did not want to imply anything.

"Would you like to have dinner tomorrow? I'll cook." They agreed to meet at six. The conversation continued for a few minutes longer, and when Gopal hung up, he was pleased at how well he had handled things.

While lying in bed, waiting for sleep, Gopal read another article in *Cosmopolitan*, about job pressure's effects on one's sex life. He had enjoyed both articles and was happy with himself for his efforts at understanding Mrs. Shaw. He fell asleep smiling.

✷ ✷ ✷

The next day, after reading the papers, Gopal went to the library to read the first part of the *Cosmopolitan* article. He ended up reading articles from *Elle, Redbook, Glamour, Mademoiselle,* and *Family Circle,* and one from *Reader's Digest*—"How to Tell If Your Marriage Is on the Rocks." He tried to memorize jokes from the "Laughter Is the Best Medicine" section, so that he would never be at a loss for conversation.

Gopal arrived at home by four and began cooking. Dinner was pleasant, though they ate in the kitchen, which was lit with buzzing fluorescent tubes. Gopal worried that yesterday's lovemaking might have been a fluke. Soon after they finished the meal, however, they were on the couch, struggling with each other's clothing.

Gopal wanted Mrs. Shaw to spend the night, but she refused, saying that she had not slept a full night with anyone since her divorce. At first Gopal was touched by this. They lay on his bed in the dark. The alarm clock on the lampstand said 9:12 in big red figures. "Why?" Gopal asked, rolling over and resting his cheek on her cool shoulder. He wanted to reassure her that he was eager to listen.

"I think I'm a serial monogamist and I don't want to make things too complicated." She twisted a lock of his hair around her middle finger. "It isn't because of you, sweetie. It's with every man."

"Oh," Gopal said, hurt by the idea of other men and disillusioned about her motives. He continued believing, however, that now that they were lovers, the power of his concern would make her love him back. One of the articles he had read that day had suggested that people become dependent in spite of themselves when they are constantly cared for. So he made himself relax and act understanding.

Gopal went to bed an hour after Mrs. Shaw left. Before going to sleep he called her and wished her good night. He began calling her frequently after that, two or three times a day. Over the next few weeks Gopal found himself becoming coy and playful with her. When Mrs. Shaw picked up the phone, he made panting noises, and she laughed at him. She liked his being childlike with her. Sometimes she would point to a spot on his chest, and he would look down, even though he knew nothing was there, so that she could tap his nose. When they made love, she was thoughtful about asking what pleased him, and Gopal learned from this and began asking her the same. They saw each other nearly every day, though sometimes only briefly, for a few minutes in the evening or at night. But Gopal continued to feel nervous around her, as if he were somehow imposing. If she phoned him and invited him over, he was always flattered. As Gopal learned more about Mrs. Shaw, he began thinking she was very smart. She read constantly, primarily history and economics. He was always surprised, therefore, when she became moody and sentimental and talked about how loneliness is incurable. Gopal liked Mrs. Shaw in this mood, because it made him feel needed, but he felt ashamed that he was so insecure. When she did not laugh at a joke, Gopal doubted that she would ever love him. When they were in bed together and he thought she might be looking at him, he kept his stomach sucked in.

★ ★ ★

This sense of precariousness made Gopal try developing other supports for himself. One morning early in his involvement with Mrs. Shaw he phoned an Indian engineer with whom he had worked on a project about corrosion of copper wires and who had also taken early retirement from AT&T. They had met briefly several times since then and had agreed each time to get together again, but neither had made the effort. Gopal waited until eleven before calling, because he felt that any earlier would make him sound needy. A woman picked up the phone. She told him to wait a minute as she called for Rishi. Gopal felt vaguely deceitful, as if he were trying to pass himself off as just like everyone else, although his wife and child had left him.

"I haven't been doing much," he confessed immediately to Rishi. "I read a lot." When Rishi asked what, Gopal answered, "Magazines," with embarrassment. They were silent then. Gopal did not want to ask Rishi immediately if he would like to meet for dinner, so he hunted desperately for a conversational opening. He was sitting in the kitchen. He looked at the sunlight on the newspaper before him and remembered that he could ask Rishi questions. "How are *you* doing?"

"It isn't like India," Rishi responded, complaining. "In India, the older you are, the closer you are to the center of attention. Here, you have to keep going. Your children are away and you have nothing to do. I would go back, but Ratha doesn't want to. America is much better for women."

Gopal felt a rush of relief that Rishi had spoken so much. "Are you just at home or are you doing something part-time?"

"I am the president of the Indian Cultural Association," Rishi said boastfully.

"That's wonderful," Gopal said, and with a leap added, "I want to get involved in that more, now that I have time."

"We always need help. We are going to have a fair," Rishi said. "It's on the twenty-fourth, next month. We need help coordinating things, arranging food, putting up flyers."

"I can help," Gopal said. They decided that he should go to Rishi's house on Wednesday, two days later.

Gopal was about to hang up when Rishi added, "I heard about your family." Gopal felt as if he had been caught in a lie. "I am sorry," Rishi said.

Gopal was quiet for a moment and then said, "Thank you." He did not know whether he should pretend to be sad. "It takes some getting used to," he said, "but you can go on from nearly anything."

Gopal went to see Rishi that Wednesday, and on Sunday he attended a board meeting to plan for the fair. He told jokes about a nearsighted snake and a water hose, and about a golf instructor and God. One of the men he met there invited him to dinner.

Mrs. Shaw, however, continued to dominate his thoughts. The more they made love, the more absorbed Gopal became in the texture of her nipples in his mouth and the heft of her hips in his hands. He thought of this in the shower, while driving, while stirring his cereal. Two or three times over the next month Gopal picked her up during her lunch hour and they hurried home to make love. They would make love and then talk. Mrs. Shaw had once worked at a dry cleaner's, and Gopal found this fascinating. He had met only one person in his life before Mrs. Shaw who had worked in a dry-cleaning business and that was different, because it was in India, where dry-cleaning still had the glamour of advancing technology. Being the lover of someone who had worked in a dry-cleaning business made Gopal feel strange. It made him think that the world was huge beyond comprehension, and to spend his time trying to control his own small world was inefficient. Gopal began thinking that he loved Mrs. Shaw. He started listening to the golden-oldies station in the car, so that he could hear what she had heard in her youth.

Mrs. Shaw would ask about his life, and Gopal tried to tell her everything she wanted to know in as much detail as possible. Once he told her of how he had begun worrying when his daughter was finishing high school that she was going to slip from his life. To show that he loved her, he had arbitrarily forbidden her to ski, claiming that skiing was dangerous. He had hoped that she would find this quaintly immigrant, but she was just angry. At first the words twisted in his mouth, and he spoke to Mrs. Shaw about skiing in general. Only with an effort could he tell her about his fight with Gitu. Mrs. Shaw did not say anything at first. Then she said, "It's all right if you were that way once, as long as you aren't that way now." Listening to her, Gopal suddenly felt angry.

"Why do you talk like this?" he asked.

"What?"

"When you talk about how your breasts fall or how your behind is too wide, I always say that's not true. I always see you with eyes that make you beautiful."

"Because I want the truth," she said, also angry.

Gopal became quiet. Her desire for honesty appeared to refute all his delicate and constant manipulations. Was he actually in love with her, he wondered, or was this love just a way to avoid loneliness? And did it matter that so much of what he did was conscious?

He questioned his love more and more as the day of the Indian festival approached and Gopal realized that he was delaying asking Mrs. Shaw to go with him. She knew about the fair but had not mentioned her feelings. Gopal told himself that she would feel uncomfortable among so many Indians, but he knew that he hadn't asked her because taking her would make him feel awkward. For some reason he was nervous that word of Mrs. Shaw might get to his wife and daughter. He was also anxious about what the Indians with whom he had recently become friendly would think. He had met mixed couples at Indian parties before, and they were always treated with the deference usually reserved for cripples. If Mrs. Shaw had been of any sort of marginalized ethnic group—a first-generation immigrant, for instance—then things might have been easier.

The festival was held in the Edison First Aid Squad's square blue-and-white building. A children's dance troupe performed in red dresses so stiff with gold thread that the girls appeared to hobble as they moved about the center of the concrete floor. A balding comedian in oxblood shoes and a white suit performed. Light folding tables along one wall were precariously laden with large pots, pans, and trays of food. Gopal stood in a corner with several men who had retired from AT&T and, slightly drunk, improvised on jokes he had read in *1,001 Polish Jokes*. The Poles became Sikhs, but he kept most of the rest. He was laughing and feeling proud that he could so easily become the center of attention, but he felt lonely at the thought that when the food was served, the men at his side would drift away to join their families and he would stand alone in line. After listening to talk of someone's marriage, he began thinking about Mrs. Shaw. The men were clustered together, and the women conversed separately. They will go home and make love and not talk, Gopal thought. Then he felt sad and frightened. To make amends for his guilt at not bringing Mrs. Shaw along, he told a bearded man with yellow teeth, "These Sikhs aren't so bad. They are the smartest ones in India, and no one can match a Sikh for courage." Then Gopal felt dazed and ready to leave.

✯ ✯ ✯

When Gopal pulled into his driveway, it was late afternoon. His head felt odd still, as it always did when alcohol started wearing off, but Gopal knew that he was drunk enough to do something foolish. He parked and walked down the road to Mrs. Shaw's. He wondered if she would be in. Pale tulips bloomed in a thin, uneven row in front of her house. The sight of them made him hopeful.

Mrs. Shaw opened the door before he could knock. For a moment Gopal did not say anything. She was wearing a denim skirt and a sleeveless white shirt. She smiled at him. Gopal spoke solemnly and from far off. "I love you," he said to her for the first time. "I am sorry I didn't invite you to the fair." He waited a moment for his statement to sink in and for her to respond with a similar endearment. When she did not, he repeated, "I love you."

Then she said, "Thank you," and told him not to worry about the fair. She invited him in. Gopal was confused and flustered by her reticence. He began feeling awkward about his confession. They kissed briefly, and then Gopal went home.

The next night, as they sat together watching TV in his living room, Mrs. Shaw suddenly turned to Gopal and said, "You really do love me, don't you?" Although Gopal had expected the question, he was momentarily disconcerted by it, because it made him wonder what love was and whether he was capable of it. But he did not think that this was the time to quibble over semantics. After being silent long enough to suggest that he was struggling with his vulnerability, Gopal said yes and waited for Mrs. Shaw's response. Again she did not confess her love. She kissed his forehead tenderly. This show of sentiment made Gopal angry, but he said nothing. He was glad, though, when Mrs. Shaw left that night.

The next day Gopal waited for Mrs. Shaw to return home from work. He had decided that the time had come for the next step in their relationship. As soon as he saw her struggle through her doorway, hugging sacks of groceries, Gopal phoned. He stood on the steps to his house, with the extension cord trailing over one shoulder, and looked at her house and at her rusted and exhausted-looking station wagon, which he had begun to associate strongly and warmly with the broad sweep of Mrs. Shaw's life. Gopal nearly said, "I missed you" when she picked up the phone, but he became embarrassed and asked, "How was your day?"

"Fine," she said, and Gopal imagined her moving about the kitchen, putting away whatever she had bought, placing the tea-kettle on the stove, and sorting her mail on the kitchen table. This image of domesticity and independence moved him deeply. "There's a guidance counselor who is dying of cancer," she said, "and his friends are having a party for him, and they put up a sign saying 'RSVP with your money now! Henry can't wait for the party!'" Gopal and Mrs. Shaw laughed.

"Let's do something," he said.

"What?"

Gopal had not thought this part out. He wanted to do something romantic that would last until bedtime, so that he could pressure her to spend the night. "Would you like to have dinner?"

"Sure," she said. Gopal was pleased. He had gone to a liquor store a few days earlier and bought wine, just in case he had an opportunity to get Mrs. Shaw drunk and get her to fall asleep beside him.

Gopal plied Mrs. Shaw with wine as they ate the linguine he had cooked. They sat in the kitchen, but he had turned off the fluorescent lights and lit a candle. By the third glass Gopal was feeling very brave; he placed his hand on her inner thigh.

"My mother and father," Mrs. Shaw said halfway through the meal, pointing at him with her fork and speaking with the deliberateness of the drunk, "convinced me that people are not meant to live together for long periods of time." She was speaking in response to Gopal's hint earlier that only over time and through living together could people get to know each other properly. "If you know someone that well, you are bound to be disappointed."

"Maybe that's because you haven't met the right person," Gopal answered, feeling awkward for saying something that could be considered arrogant when he was trying to appear vulnerable.

"I don't think there is a right person. Not for me. To fall in love I think you need a certain suspension of disbelief, which I don't think I am capable of."

Gopal wondered whether Mrs. Shaw believed what she was saying or was trying not to hurt his feelings by revealing that she couldn't love him. He stopped eating.

Mrs. Shaw stared at him. She put her fork down and said, "I love you. I love how you care for me and how gentle you are."

Gopal smiled. Perhaps, he thought, the first part of her statement had been a preface to a confession that he mattered so much that she was willing to make an exception for him. "I love you too," Gopal said. "I love how funny and smart and honest you are. You are very beautiful." He leaned over slightly to suggest that he wanted to kiss her, but Mrs. Shaw did not respond.

Her face was stiff. "I love you," she said again, and Gopal became nervous. "But I am not *in* love with you." She stopped and stared at Gopal.

Gopal felt confused. "What's the difference?"

"When you are *in* love, you never think about yourself, because you love the other person so completely. I've lived too long to think anyone is that perfect." Gopal still didn't understand the distinction, but he was too embarrassed to ask more. It was only fair, a part of him thought, that God would punish him this way for driving away his wife and child. How could anyone love him?

Mrs. Shaw took his hands in hers. "I think we should take a little break from each other, so we don't get confused. Being with you, I'm getting confused too. We should see other people."

"Oh." Gopal's chest hurt despite his understanding of the justice of what was happening.

"I don't want to hide anything. I love you. I truly love you. You are the kindest lover I've ever had."

"Oh."

For a week after this Gopal observed that Mrs. Shaw did not bring another man to her house. He went to the Sunday board meeting of the cultural association, where he regaled the members with jokes from *Reader's Digest*. He taught his first Hindi class to children at the temple. He took his car to be serviced. Gopal did all these things. He ate. He slept. He even made love to Mrs. Shaw once, and until she asked him to leave, he thought everything was all right again.

Then one night Gopal was awakened at a little after three by a car pulling out of Mrs. Shaw's driveway. It is just a friend, he thought, standing by his bedroom window and watching the Toyota move down the road. Gopal tried falling asleep again, but he could not, though he was not thinking of anything in particular. His mind was blank, but sleep did not come.

I will not call her, Gopal thought in the morning. And as he was dialing her, he thought he would hang up before all the numbers had been pressed. He heard the receiver being lifted on the other side and Mrs. Shaw saying "Hello." He did not say anything. "Don't do this, Gopal," she said softly. "Don't hurt me."

"Hi," Gopal whispered, wanting very much to hurt her. He leaned his head against the kitchen wall. His face twitched as he whispered, "I'm sorry."

"Don't be that way. I love you. I didn't want to hurt you. That's why I told you."

"I know."

"All right?"

"Yes." They were silent for a long time. Then Gopal hung up. He wondered if she would call back. He waited, and when she didn't, he began jumping up and down in place.

✱ ✱ ✱

For the next few weeks Gopal tried to spend as little time as possible in his house. He read the morning papers in the library and then had lunch at a diner and then went back to the library. On Sundays he spent all day at the mall. His anger at Mrs. Shaw soon disappeared, because he thought that the blame for her leaving lay with him. Gopal continued, however, to avoid home, because he did not want to experience the jealousy that would keep him awake all night. Only if he arrived late enough and tired enough could he fall asleep. In the evening Gopal either went to the temple and helped at the seven o'clock service or visited one of his new acquaintances. But over the weeks he exhausted the kind-heartedness of his acquaintances and had a disagreement with one man's wife, and he was forced to return home.

The first few evenings he spent at home Gopal thought he

would have to flee his house in despair. He slept awkwardly, waking at the barest rustle outside his window, thinking that a car was pulling out of Mrs. Shaw's driveway. The days were easier than the nights, especially when Mrs. Shaw was away at work. Gopal would sleep a few hours at night and then nap during the day, but this left him exhausted and dizzy. In the afternoon he liked to sit on the steps and read the paper, pausing occasionally to look at her house. He liked the sun sliding up its walls. Sometimes he was sitting outside when she drove home from work. Mrs. Shaw waved to him once or twice, but he did not respond, not because he was angry but because he felt himself become so still at the sight of her that he could neither wave nor smile.

A month and a half after they separated, Gopal still could not sleep at night if he thought there were two cars in Mrs. Shaw's driveway. Once, after a series of sleepless nights, he was up until three watching a dark shape behind Mrs. Shaw's station wagon. He waited by his bedroom window, paralyzed with fear and hope, for a car to pass in front of her house and strike the shape with its headlights. After a long time in which no car went by, Gopal decided to check for himself.

He started across his lawn crouched over and running. The air was warm and smelled of jasmine, and Gopal was so tired that he thought he might spill to the ground. After a few steps he stopped and straightened up. The sky was clear, and there were so many stars that Gopal felt as if he were in his village in India. The houses along the street were dark and drawn in on themselves. Even in India, he thought, late at night the houses look like sleeping faces. He remembered how surprised he had been by the pitched roofs of American houses when he had first come here, and how this had made him yearn to return to India, where he could sleep on the roof. He started across the lawn again. Gopal walked slowly, and he felt as if he were crossing a great distance.

The station wagon stood battered and alone, smelling faintly of gasoline and the day's heat. Gopal leaned against its hood. The station wagon was so old that the odometer had gone all the way around. Like me, he thought, and like Helen, too. This is who we are, he thought—dusty, corroded, and dented from our voyages, with our unflagging hearts rattling on inside. We are made who we are by the dust and corrosion and dents and unflagging hearts. Why should we need anything else to fall in love? he wondered. We learn and change and get better. He leaned against the car for a minute or two. Fireflies swung flickering in the breeze. Then he walked home.

Gopal woke early and showered and shaved and made breakfast. He brushed his teeth after eating and felt his cheeks to see whether he should shave again, this time against the grain. At nine he crossed his lawn and rang Mrs. Shaw's doorbell. He had to ring it several times before he heard her footsteps. When she opened the door and saw him, Mrs. Shaw drew back as if she were afraid. Gopal felt sad that she could think he might hurt her. "May I come in?" he asked. She stared at him. He saw mascara stains beneath her eyes and silver strands mingled with her red hair. He thought he had never seen a woman as beautiful or as gallant.

IRISH GIRL

Tim Johnston

The way it began, the way he'd remember it many years later, was a kick to the leg.

He was under the kitchen table playing with army men and somebody kicked him. Not too hard but not too soft, either.

William.

He turned and scowled at corduroys and tube socks, all he could see of his brother. "What?"

"They're waiting for you," William said in an odd voice. "In their bedroom."

And then he walked away.

* * *

Before that, of course, were things Charlie didn't know much about, being eight. He didn't know about Nixon's decision to send troops into Cambodia, or how that led to the shootings at Kent State, or how that led, in turn, to the smashed shop windows in his own hometown. He did know a little about the thirteen boys from the agricultural college arrested for rioting, because his father had been their lawyer. But he didn't know how the trial, which had made the news every night for two weeks, spreading his father's name across the state like goldenrod, had given his father the idea to run for office. He didn't know what the Iowa House of Representatives was, or what people did with all those leaflets he left on their porches, or what it meant to win by a landslide. And he didn't know his father was still riding the high of victory when he decided, a few days before leaving for the state capitol, to have The Talk.

He didn't know that's where William had just come from, he only knew he'd been under the kitchen table, playing with army men, when his brother kicked him.

* * *

It was true: his parents were waiting for him, sitting on the edge of their bed and beaming at him with wet eyes. His father sat him down and explained what adopted meant even though Charlie already knew from school; when you picked on the adopted kid he'd fight and say it was a lie, as if being adopted was the worst thing ever, worse than having no dad at all. Charlie stared at the floor and felt sick to his stomach, waiting for his parents to tell him he was adopted, too. Finally, he had to ask.

His father leaned forward. He was a big man to begin with and when he leaned forward you couldn't see anything else, he was it. "Would you be sad if you were?" his father asked.

Charlie knew what his father wanted to hear—that Charlie wouldn't give a dog's fart because he still had the best parents in the world, who would love him forever.

But all he could do was shrug.

"Well," his father said at last. "You're not adopted, Charlie. You came from your mom and me." He put his hands on Charlie's shoulders. "But that doesn't mean we love you any more or any less than William, or that he's not your real brother. You understand? You boys will be brothers forever."

Charlie understood, but he was so happy not to be adopted he wanted to spread the news, he wanted to put it on a leaflet and hit every porch in the world.

That night, Charlie sat down to dinner like a kid moving underwater, trying to look normal. William was still in the room the boys shared, no light showing under the door. A January wind was in the seams of the back door, moaning eerily. The house, the whole neighborhood, kept its back to open farmland and bore the first, hardest blows of weather. In the spring, the air was soaked in the smell of soil and manure, and at night you heard the cows bawl, and the horn of the freight trains was to warn them, William said, to stay off the tracks or else.

Charlie pushed beans around on his plate and hated himself for being glad he wasn't adopted. He told himself that if anyone ever teased the adopted kid at school again he'd help him fight, he swore to God he would.

"Hey, baby," his mother said, and his father lowered his cup of coffee.

Charlie turned and there was William, hands in his pockets, squinting in the light. He stared at them, and for a second it looked like he might turn and leave, and that's when Charlie moved. Jumped up and ran to him, locked his arms around him so tightly it was hard for William to get his hands out of his pockets. Finally he did, wiggled them out from under Charlie's grip, and got his fingers around Charlie's biceps and moved him, just so, aside. "Lay off, willya?" he said. "I'm hungry."

And that was that. The boys sat down, and Charlie didn't whimper or even rub at the matching dents of pain in his arms where William had sunk his thumbs to the bone.

★ ★ ★

Their father bought a second car for his trips to Des Moines, a green Cougar convertible, and one Sunday early in his term he took William and Charlie with him to show them where he sat in the session chamber, and they spent the night with him in the cramped, untidy trailer he rented near the interstate.

"You think he likes this place more than home?" Charlie asked William that night. Their father had gone to meet someone, and William had his legs stretched out on a nappy brown sofa, studying the pages of a *Playboy* he'd found under the cushions. The trailer smelled like the inside of leather shoes and shower mildew and old pizza boxes, and Charlie could feel the hum of tractor-trailers through a stiff layer of carpet.

"Shit, Charlie," his brother replied, rising and heading for the toilet. "Wouldn't you?"

Their father was home for Christmas but then didn't return for months, and Charlie's mother told them that it was because he was writing bills and had to work extra hard to get them made into laws. William just stared at her, the same look on his face that always let Charlie know he'd said something really stupid, then walked away. He'd stopped cutting his hair and had begun to smell like cigarettes and car engines. At night when he came in, he'd crash into his bed with superhero exhaustion, as if he'd been pushed to the very limit of his powers. In the mornings Charlie watched him plod across the room in his underwear, his boner out before him like the nose of a German shepherd, and felt so puny he wanted to scream. He checked himself daily for signs of growth, but nothing changed, and he worried that something was wrong with him and that when William was a full-grown man, he would still be the hairless little nothing he was right then.

★ ★ ★

William was right about their father preferring a smelly trailer to home, because when his two-year term was over and he went back to his law practice, he moved into another one in their hometown. He picked the boys up on Fridays in the Cougar and the three of them ate pizza and went out for breakfast and saw matinees and sat around the trailer watching TV until Sunday afternoon, when their father would let William, who by now had a driver's permit, drive them back to the house.

During the week, when Charlie got home from school he'd find William and his friends strewn in front of the TV like dead men, drinking Cokes and licking potato chip grease from their fingers. The boys called William Billy, and Charlie knew they had all cut school early, if they'd gone at all. William made sure to clear them out by the time their mother got home, but she could count Cokes and read the air with her nose, and she and William would both start yelling and Charlie would shut himself in his room until he heard the front door slam and he knew William had gone out again.

One night, when she tried to keep William home for dinner, he told her to get off his back and she slapped him. Her handprint spread like a warning light over his face, and for a second Charlie thought he was going to slap her back. "Bitch," he said, and she took a step back like he'd gone ahead and done it. Then he left, and the word "adopted" rose in Charlie's throat like vomit, and he wanted to remind her that's what William was and why he said it, because no real son, no flesh-and-blood son, would ever call his mother that name.

Later that night, Charlie got up to pee and heard her on the phone. She said "Mason," their father's name, with a wobble in her throat, and when he came to get the boys the following Friday, William brought along two pillowcases full of clothes.

✷ ✷ ✷

Charlie didn't miss William until the spring, when he began to hear the cows at night and the moaning trains and he'd remember how he used to fit on William's bed with a flashlight while William made up stories about a gang of killers, whacked-out hippies forever hopping off trains and shooting people. Somehow the hippies always made their way across the fields right up to the living room window where Mason and Connie Whitford sat watching the news of the killing spree. When he told his stories, William's eyes grew brilliant, super-blue, and they lit up a place where he and Charlie were equals, where they snapped into action at the exact same moment and they never failed.

That April, after a month with William, Mason gave up trailers for good. He bought a house, a big old one in the middle of town, and when Charlie arrived for his first weekend he was amazed to learn that the upstairs bedroom with the new bed and the matching dresser and desk and the three windows was all for him. William had his own room on the other side of the wall and Mason's was at the far end of the hall and had its own bathroom. Downstairs, you could reach full speed running from one end of the house to the other, and below that was a basement with a pool table the previous owner had left behind.

His first night in the new house Charlie lay awake for hours, getting used to the shadows of the room and the drone of traffic outside his window. He was finally drifting off when the horn of a freight train, a single short blast, punched through and jerked him back. Warning bells rang in the streets and the horn sounded again, louder this time, so loud he was sure the train was heading right for the house. But the next blast of the horn was weaker, a deflating balloon, and he heard the clacking of the wheels on the rails and it calmed his heart, that rhythm, and he slept.

Mason came downstairs the next night stinking of Brut aftershave and wearing blue jeans that made Charlie laugh. He was going out to dinner with a friend, he told them, and William was in charge.

William stared at the TV. The Six Million Dollar Man was jumping a wall.

"William," his father said.

"Yeah?"

"I said you're going to be in charge for a few hours. Can you handle that?"

"No sweat."

Charlie watched his father standing there squeezing his car keys in his fist, his eyes dark, and for the first time in his life Charlie actually wanted him to go, to leave them alone.

Finally, with a pat to Charlie's head, he did.

"Who's his friend?" Charlie asked when their father was gone.

"What day of the week is it?"

Charlie told him but William just smirked and lit a Camel.

"Dad lets you smoke?"

"Fuck, no." He got up and moved to the open window. "Dad's a fascist."

"What's that?"

"He's the guy who ends up full of bullet holes with old ladies pissing on him in the town square."

Charlie chewed an already raw fingernail. He couldn't believe the things a sixteen-year-old knew, especially one who never went to school.

William eyed him. "You gonna narc on me?"

Charlie shook his head and William took a studious drag on the cigarette. "How 'bout if I split for a while? You gonna be cool with that?"

"If you take me with you."

"Not a chance."

A car horn honked loudly, once, and William flicked his cigarette out the window. Charlie jumped up, but William put a hand on his shoulder, sank his thumb into the flesh above his collarbone. "I can count on you, Charlie, can't I?" The pressure made Charlie feel like a puppet, like William could make his legs buckle with just the right kind of squeeze.

"Yes," he said, refusing to squirm.

"Promise to God and hope to die?"

"Yes."

William let go. "Outstanding," he said, then he left, banging the screen door behind him. Charlie watched him climb behind the wheel of a Chevy Impala the color of an army tank. A girl with straight red hair mashed her lips against his for a full minute, her fingers deep in his hair, before he finally gunned the engine and backed out of the drive, leaving tracks.

Two hours later Mason called, and Charlie picked up.

★ ★ ★

Something was coming down the hallway, fast and loud in the middle of the night.

His bed shook and wood exploded and Charlie flattened himself against the mattress, ready for the floor to drop out from under him. "Get up!" his father yelled.

Not at Charlie. At William, on the other side of the wall. He was in William's room. He'd kicked in the door.

"What for?" William tried to sound tough.

"Because I told you to."

"Christ, Dad. Can't it—"

Bedsprings creaked and something hit the floor, and Charlie heard footsteps like two giant kids practicing a dance. "Get! Up!" Mason yelled. "Get up when I tell you!" The dance thudded out into the hall and something, an elbow or a head, bounced against

Charlie's door. "Open the door when I tell you," his father said. "Watch your brother when I tell you."

"He can watch himself! He's not a baby!"

"I don't care."

They moved down the hall, and Charlie heard William grunt and his father bark back, "Don't you—don't you even try it," and Charlie's bed picked up the shock waves of William slamming into a wall. "Whattaya gonna do, *Dad*?" William's voice rose and came apart. "Gonna hit me? Go ahead! Hit me! Hit me, *Dad*!"

"Don't test me, William, I warn you."

And then the dance moved on, in bursts and thuds, down the stairs and all the way to the opposite end of the house, where it either stopped or merely ceased to distinguish itself, at that distance, from Charlie's banging heart.

✳ ✳ ✳

In the morning, Charlie made an inspection of the door. The jamb was split vertically, and a shard of it lay in the middle of William's room, the brass strike plate still attached and looking stunned, like a mouth knocked from a face.

Charlie spent the rest of the day pretending to read comic books or watch TV, waiting to see William. But he never showed up, and Charlie went back to his mother's thinking William had stayed away because of him—that he never wanted to see Charlie's ugly little narc face again.

He didn't see him again until the following Saturday afternoon. Mason was in the middle of a trial and had gone to the office, so Charlie was alone in the house when William walked in and slugged him in the shoulder. Charlie raised his arms, expecting more, but William was grinning.

"Get your shoes, Charlie Horse."

Outside, Charlie saw the tank-colored Chevy and stopped short. Blood filled his chest. He couldn't breathe right.

"What's with you?" William worked up a gob of spit, sent it

flying. "Look," he said. "I promise you'll be back before he ever knows you were gone. OK?"

The car was full of big teenagers with long hair and army jackets like William's—and the girl Charlie had seen before with the straight red hair. She and one of the boys shifted to let William behind the wheel, and two boys in back made room for Charlie. "Fuckin' A!" a boy with great shining pimples said. "Fresh troops!" He blew smoke in Charlie's face that didn't smell like cigarettes. Charlie coughed, and the girl craned around and stunned him with white teeth and the biggest, greenest eyes he'd ever seen. She looked right at him and kept smiling and said, "Happy birthday, Charlie."

★ ★ ★

The girl's name was Colleen and she was a Foosball wizard. Three times during the game she held the ball in place with one of her men while she put her hand over Charlie's and moved his men just so. Then, with a snap of her wrist he couldn't even see, she scored on William and the boy with pimples. William laughed, but the boy with pimples called her a cheater and she told him to grow up, dickweed. The boy glared at Charlie and asked William, out of the side of his mouth as if Charlie wouldn't hear him that way, "He retarded, or what?"

William stared hard at the boy, then gave Charlie a grin. "You retarded, Charlie?"

Charlie was still floating from Colleen's hand on his, and he couldn't imagine any idiot thing a dickweed with pimples could say to bring him down, so he just shook his head.

"He don't say much, do he," the boy said, and William said, "No, he don't. But he's thinking, man. He thinks more in a day than you do in a year."

"Right," the boy said, and Colleen snapped her wrist and the ball disappeared with a bang.

When it was time to go, William had to drag Charlie from the pinball machines, but Charlie was twelve, too old to make a scene, so he jammed his hands in his pockets and tried to look bored. William hooked an arm around Colleen and dropped his hand on her breast for a quick, secret squeeze. "Back in a flash," he told her. She smiled at Charlie and it was too much, he had to look away.

William drove fast, a grim expression on his face, and when they came to the railroad tracks he locked up the brakes and pounded the steering wheel so hard Charlie couldn't believe it didn't crack. They were at the end of a line of cars waiting for a train to pass. The central hub of the Rock Island Railway was not far away, and the people who lived here, it sometimes seemed, lived in the spaces between its lines like prisoners. Freighters plowed through day and night, trains without head or tail, and there was nothing you could do but sit and wait.

William jammed the Chevy into Park and thumbed in the electric lighter. He pushed his hair back from his face, lit a Camel, and dropped the pack on the seat. Charlie breathed in the first cloud of smoke, always the best-smelling one, and picked up the pack. William didn't seem to notice or care as Charlie pulled out one of the Camels with his lips, the way William did. And he didn't budge when Charlie pushed in the electric lighter. But when the lighter popped and Charlie steered the red coil toward the tip of the Camel, his brother reached over and plucked the cigarette from his mouth.

"You gotta do everything I do? You want Mason breaking down your door at two A.M.?"

Charlie recalled that night and was disgusted with himself—cowering in his room like a pussy while William got the crap beaten out of him, all because Charlie hadn't been smart enough, or brave enough, to come up with a lie on the phone.

He'd tell him he was sorry, he decided. Right now.

He'd tell him before that red boxcar crossed the road . . .

Before the end of the train . . .

But he didn't, and the red lights stopped flashing and the Chevy was moving again and Charlie watched his chance slip away with the caboose.

William whipped into the driveway and braked at the last second, just shy of Mason's Cougar. He shifted into Reverse and tossed Charlie a salute. "Happy birthday, man."

"You're not coming in?"

"Naw. I gotta go get those losers."

Charlie gripped his left hand in his right, remembering the Foosball game. His heart would not slow down.

"I like the girl," he said.

"Colleen?"

He turned and William smiled and Charlie saw a light in his eyes he hadn't seen in so long he'd forgotten it even existed.

"You know what her name means?" William asked.

It was the light, Charlie realized, from the nights when they shared a room and William told stories and they had no idea that one of them was adopted.

"What's it mean?" he asked.

William took a deep drag on the cigarette and stared out the windshield. "Means *Irish girl*."

* * *

Mason was in the kitchen, leaning against the counter with his hands in his pockets, jingling change and keys. "Where'd he take you?" he said quietly.

Charlie glanced into the dining room and saw a chocolate bakery cake with unlit candles and a small pile of gifts on the table. "Nowhere."

"Nowhere?"

He shrugged and felt a wet heat in his armpits, a weakness in his legs that told him what a terrible thing he was about to do. But he did it anyway, and for no good reason except that he hadn't been able to do it the night he should've.

"We went to the movies," he lied. "It was my birthday present." He took a step toward the stairs, but Mason grabbed his arm, pulled him back into the kitchen.

"Don't you walk away from me."

"Let me go!" Charlie wasn't afraid, exactly, his father had never hit him his whole life, but he wanted out of that grip before the tears came and ruined everything.

"You reek of smoke, Charlie. You reek of smoke and pot. Were you smoking pot in that car?"

"What?"

"Did you smoke anything with William?"

"No!"

"Don't you lie to me."

"I'm not!"

Mason had a hold of both arms now, squeezing to the bone, and he was shaking him, a low, rapid jerking that seemed beyond his control. Charlie watched his father's face redden and saw the look in his eyes and thought he was maybe having a heart attack. "Dad," he said. "Dad!" He grabbed his father's wrists and squeezed but his father just held on, staring at him so intensely, so strangely, that Charlie would wonder later if it wasn't at that exact second that William tried to beat the train.

For this to be true he'd have to have driven very fast after dropping Charlie off, in a rush to get back to his friends, back to Colleen, or maybe the light was in his eyes and he drove the only way he knew how when he felt like that, like a man from another planet, like a superhero. Charlie sees him flicking his Camel out the window and gripping the wheel in both hands. He sees his boot stomp the gas pedal and the muscles of his jaw grow hard as the Chevy leaps, and he sees his eyes, the light, the flash of blue wonder, the moment he knows he's not going to make it.

★ ★ ★

Everything after that seems to happen through a cracked window, with Charlie standing outside looking in. There's the police in the house, led there by a driver's license. There's the drive across town and the sound Charlie can hear, sitting in the Cougar in the driveway, of his mother at the kitchen table, her cry a piercing thing, a teapot beginning to boil, a January wind. There's the funeral and William's friends in their cheap ties and army jackets sulking like war buddies. And there's Colleen, wrapping her arms around Charlie so fiercely, so hungrily, that he knows she doesn't know—that she believes Charlie is a true brother, a living blood link to the body in the coffin.

And after that there's just the long withering summer, the weekends with his father, the two of them going out for meals, going to movies, taking long drives at night with the top down. One Saturday, a carpenter comes, an old guy who gets Charlie to help him carry his tools up the stairs and hand him the things he asks for, and when they're done, William's door looks good as new, the brass strike plate, that shocked little mouth, back in place. At the end of the summer, the house is sold and Charlie moves in with Mason for the school year, into a two-bedroom house close to Charlie's new school, and they begin to eat at home in the evenings and Mason begins a new trial and Charlie learns that a pretty girl at school likes him—and still.

Still it's the same town, and when they go somewhere in the Cougar, no matter what streets they take or how they time it, they end up stuck before a passing train. When this happens they don't talk and they don't look at each other, though Charlie would like to know what his father is thinking, if he's thinking about the night he kicked down William's door, or something better, like teaching him to ride a bike, or maybe the day they brought him home, their new son. If his father asked him, Charlie would try to describe the last time he saw William—the look in his eyes, the blue light, the wild secret rush when William said the words "Irish girl."

But his father doesn't ask and the train is a long one, and so they sit there, having no choice, and watch for its end.

BULLET IN THE BRAIN

Tobias Wolff

★ ★ ★

Anders couldn't get to the bank until just before it closed, so of course the line was endless and he got stuck behind two women whose loud, stupid conversation put him in a murderous temper. He was never in the best of tempers anyway, Anders—a book critic known for the weary, elegant savagery with which he dispatched almost everything he reviewed.

With the line still doubled around the rope, one of the tellers stuck a "POSITION CLOSED" sign in her window and walked to the back of the bank, where she leaned against a desk and began to pass the time with a man shuffling papers. The women in front of Anders broke off their conversation and watched the teller with hatred. "Oh, that's nice," one of them said. She turned to Anders and added, confident of his accord, "One of those little human touches that keep us coming back for more."

Anders had conceived his own towering hatred of the teller, but he immediately turned it on the presumptuous crybaby in front of him. "Damned unfair," he said. "Tragic, really. If they're not chopping off the wrong leg, or bombing your ancestral village, they're closing their positions."

She stood her ground. "I didn't say it was tragic," she said. "I just think it's a pretty lousy way to treat your customers."

"Unforgivable," Anders said. "Heaven will take note."

She sucked in her cheeks but stared past him and said nothing. Anders saw that the other woman, her friend, was looking in the same direction. And then the tellers stopped what they were doing, and the customers slowly turned, and silence came over the bank. Two men wearing black ski masks and blue business suits were standing to the side of the door. One of them had a pistol pressed against the guard's neck. The guard's eyes were closed, and his lips were moving. The other man had a sawed-off shotgun. "Keep your big mouth shut!" the man with the pistol said, though no one had spoken a word. "One of you tellers hits the alarm, you're all dead meat. Got it?"

The tellers nodded.

"Oh, bravo," Anders said. *"Dead meat."* He turned to the woman in front of him. "Great script, eh? The stern, brass-knuckled poetry of the dangerous classes."

She looked at him with drowning eyes.

The man with the shotgun pushed the guard to his knees. He handed the shotgun to his partner and yanked the guard's wrists up behind his back and locked them together with a pair of handcuffs. He toppled him onto the floor with a kick between the shoulder blades. Then he took his shotgun back and went over to the security gate at the end of the counter. He was short and heavy and moved with peculiar slowness, even torpor. "Buzz him in," his partner said. The man with the shotgun opened the gate and sauntered along the line of tellers, handing each of them a Hefty bag. When he came to the empty position he looked over at the man with the pistol, who said, "Whose slot is that?"

Anders watched the teller. She put her hand to her throat and turned to the man she'd been talking to. He nodded. "Mine," she said.

"Then get your ugly ass in gear and fill that bag."

"There you go," Anders said to the woman in front of him. "Justice is done."

"Hey! Bright boy! Did I tell you to talk?"

"No," Anders said.

"Then shut your trap."

"Did you hear that?" Anders said. " 'Bright boy.' Right out of *The Killers.*"

"Please be quiet," the woman said.

"Hey, you deaf or what?" The man with the pistol walked over to Anders. He poked the weapon into Anders' gut. "You think I'm playing games?"

"No," Anders said, but the barrel tickled like a stiff finger and he had to fight back the titters. He did this by making himself stare into the man's eyes, which were clearly visible behind the holes in the mask: pale blue and rawly red-rimmed. The man's left eyelid kept twitching. He breathed out a piercing, ammoniac smell that shocked Anders more than anything that had happened, and he was beginning to develop a sense of unease when the man prodded him again with the pistol.

"You like me, bright boy?" he said. "You want to suck my dick?"

"No," Anders said.

"Then stop looking at me."

Anders fixed his gaze on the man's shiny wing-tip shoes.

"Not down there. Up there." He stuck the pistol under Anders' chin and pushed it upward until Anders was looking at the ceiling.

Anders had never paid much attention to that part of the bank, a pompous old building with marble floors and counters and pillars, and gilt scrollwork over the tellers' cages. The domed ceiling had been decorated with mythological figures whose fleshy, toga-draped ugliness Anders had taken in at a glance many years earlier and afterward declined to notice. Now he had no choice but to scrutinize the painter's work. It was even worse than he remembered, and all of it executed with the utmost gravity. The artist had a few tricks up his sleeve and used them again and again—a certain rosy blush on the underside of the clouds, a coy backward glance on the faces of the cupids and fauns. The ceiling was crowded with various dramas, but the one that caught Anders' eye was Zeus and Europa—portrayed, in this rendition, as a bull ogling a cow from behind a haystack. To make the cow sexy, the painter had canted her hips suggestively and given her long, droopy eyelashes through which she gazed back at the bull with sultry welcome. The bull wore a smirk and his eyebrows were arched. If there'd been a bubble coming out of his mouth, it would have said, "Hubba hubba."

"What's so funny, bright boy?"

"Nothing."

"You think I'm comical? You think I'm some kind of clown?"

"No."

"You think you can fuck with me?"

"No."

"Fuck with me again, you're history. *Capiche?*"

Anders burst out laughing. He covered his mouth with both hands and said, "I'm sorry, I'm sorry," then snorted helplessly through his fingers and said, "*Capiche*—oh, God, *capiche,*" and at that the man with the pistol raised the pistol and shot Anders right in the head.

* * *

The bullet smashed Anders' skull and plowed through his brain and exited behind his right ear, scattering shards of bone into the cerebral cortex, the corpus callosum, back toward the basal ganglia, and down into the thalamus. But before all this occurred, the first appearance of the bullet in the cerebrum set off a crackling chain of ion transports and neuro-transmissions. Because of their peculiar origin these traced a peculiar pattern, flukishly calling to life a summer afternoon some forty years past, and long since lost to memory. After striking the cranium the bullet was moving at 900 feet per second, a pathetically sluggish, glacial pace compared to the synaptic lightning that flashed around it. Once in the brain, that is, the bullet came under the mediation of brain time, which gave Anders plenty of leisure to contemplate the scene that, in a phrase he would have abhorred, "passed before his eyes."

It is worth noting what Anders did not remember, given what he did remember. He did not remember his first lover, Sherry, or what he had most madly loved about her, before it came to irritate him—her unembarrassed carnality, and especially the cordial way she had with his unit, which she called Mr. Mole, as in "Uh-oh, looks like Mr. Mole wants to play," and "Let's hide Mr. Mole!" Anders did not remember his wife, whom he had also loved before she exhausted him with her predictability, or his daughter, now a sullen professor of economics at Dartmouth. He did not remember standing just outside his daughter's door as she lectured her bear about his naughtiness and described the truly appalling punishments Paws would receive unless he changed his ways. He did not remember a single line of the hundreds of poems he had committed to memory in his youth so that he could give himself the shivers at will—not "Silent, upon a peak in Darien," or "My God, I heard this day," or "All my pretty ones? Did you say all? O hell-kite! All?" None of these did he remember; not one. Anders did not remember his dying mother saying of his father, "I should have stabbed him in his sleep."

He did not remember Professor Josephs telling his class how Athenian prisoners in Sicily had been released if they could recite Aeschylus, and then reciting Aeschylus himself, right there, in the Greek. Anders did not remember how his eyes had burned at those sounds. He did not remember the surprise of seeing a college classmate's name on the jacket of a novel not long after they graduated, or the respect he had felt after reading the book. He did not remember the pleasure of giving respect.

Nor did Anders remember seeing a woman leap to her death from the building opposite his own just days after his daughter was born. He did not remember shouting, "Lord have mercy!" He did not remember deliberately crashing his father's car into a tree, or having his ribs kicked in by three policemen at an anti-war rally, or waking himself up with laughter. He did not remember when he began to regard the heap of books on his desk with boredom and dread, or when he grew angry at writers for writing them. He did not remember when everything began to remind him of something else.

This is what he remembered. Heat. A baseball field. Yellow grass, the whirr of insects, himself leaning against a tree as the boys of the neighborhood gather for a pickup game. He looks on as the others argue the relative genius of Mantle and Mays. They have been worrying this subject all summer, and it has become tedious to Anders: an oppression, like the heat.

Then the last two boys arrive, Coyle and a cousin of his from Mississippi. Anders has never met Coyle's cousin before and will never see him again. He says hi with the rest but takes no further notice of him until they've chosen sides and someone asks the cousin what position he wants to play. "Shortstop," the boy says. "Short's the best position they is." Anders turns and looks at him. He wants to hear Coyle's cousin repeat what he's just said, but he knows better than to ask. The others will think he's being a jerk, ragging the kid for his grammar. But that isn't it, not at all—it's that Anders is strangely roused, elated, by those final two words, their pure unexpectedness and their music. He takes the field in a trance, repeating them to himself.

The bullet is already in the brain; it won't be outrun forever, or charmed to a halt. In the end it will do its work and leave the troubled skull behind, dragging its comet's tail of memory and hope and talent and love into the marble hall of commerce. That can't be helped. But for now Anders can still make time. Time for the shadows to lengthen on the grass, time for the tethered dog to bark at the flying ball, time for the boy in right field to smack his sweat-blackened mitt and softly chant, *They is, they is, they is.*

EPILOGUE: ABOUT 826NYC

Sarah Vowell

★ ★ ★

You are not holding a book. You happen to have in your hands a desk or two, a couple of computers, untold reams of paper, a photocopier, wood floors, a digital projector, and one new full-time staff member named Ted who weighs 166 pounds. No wonder your arms are sore!

Sure, you were always walking around asking yourself, "I wonder what David Sedaris's favorite works of short fiction are." And then one day you happened in a bookstore and saw this volume, a volume that answers that very crucial question of just what this guy reads when he takes a break from crafting his own hilarious yet wistful tales. (Flannery O'Connor, it turns out. That makes sense, but Patricia Highsmith: Who knew?) That, you were thinking, was enough. Art for art's sake and all that.

I hate to break it to you, but by buying this book, you are helping people. Not just people. Even worse: kids! All the proceeds from *Children Playing Before a Statue of Hercules* go toward 826NYC, a nonprofit organization offering free writing workshops and after-school tutoring to students ages six to eighteen. Things don't get less Patricia Highsmith than that, do they? Though one wonders if Highsmith's most famous character, Tom Ripley, might have turned out less murderous if he had benefited from the one-on-one attention provided by the intelligent, encouraging volunteer tutors like the ones at 826NYC.

826NYC offers free drop-in tutoring for students between the ages of six and eighteen five days a week. As I write this, toward the end of 826's inaugural semester, we average around thirty students a day, almost all of them from public schools. Our regulars include a six-year-old aficionado of dinosaurs and ninjas; a free-spirited twelve-year-old who has learned to sit down and sit still, finishing his homework every day for the first time in his life; a trio of brothers who live around the corner, one of whom, after wrapping up his homework, composes comics in which he saves his favorite tutor from monsters and robbers; and one thirteen-year-old Russian immigrant keen to talk about Dostoyevsky. Volunteer tutors help the students with their homework, which is one of our core services. But just as important to the 826 ethos is the personal attention each child receives. The tutors don't simply help the tutees get better grades, they talk to them, notice them, hear them out.

You're wondering how we are hooking young citizens like the ninja lover with our educational goods day after day? Like any do-gooder, we are forced to use a disguise—in our case, it is the storefront that conceals the tutoring workshop. Unsuspecting citizens believe that the Brooklyn Superhero Supply Co. has moved to the neighborhood and, if they are ever in need of a cape, they'll find the storefront quite a convenience. We sell secret identity kits, anti-matter, a Fog Blaster, a wide variety of grappling hooks and utility belts (vintage to deluxe). It is a wildly successful ploy inspired by 826 Valencia, our predecessor sister organization in San Francisco with its writing center/pirate supply store. Somewhere between half and three quarters of our students started showing up for tutoring after visiting the Superhero Supply Co. They come to try out the cape-tester, they stay to get help writing their social studies reports. Besides being fun and practical—sales at the store support 826NYC's programs—the store is kid-friendly and welcoming. One favorite feature is the secret door that separates the store from the writing lab. Waiting behind it? A secret lair of scholastic improvement! For knowledge is the true superpower.

Along with tutoring, the writing center at 826NYC hosts other free educational events, most notably our workshops and field trips. Upcoming workshops include, for elementary and middle school students, chances to learn how to make pop-up books or write fairy tales ("Elves Under Your Bed," that one is called); and for high school students, in-depth courses on how to write short stories or song lyrics as well as strategies for taking the SATs. That schedule actually paints a fairly accurate portrait of what the organization is about: It is possible and important to help students improve their scores on standardized tests (or write a better college entrance essay) while at the same time remembering that a love of writing and storytelling can come from pondering more whimsical questions about whether elves do or do not live under one's bed and, let's say they do, what would they say and how would they say it?

As of the spring of 2005, we will be sending tutors into local public schools en masse. This will be a huge undertaking, helping potentially thousands of students develop better writing skills on a daily basis. And, because our interest in students' potential extends beyond high school graduation, we hope to start awarding college scholarships.

Our field trips are especially popular. We regularly host entire classes from New York City schools who show up for the day to write and publish a book. The students write the book together, save for the last page, which each student finishes alone. Then the book is illustrated, published, and bound, and each student goes home with his or her own copy complete with author photos and blurbs. Recent titles include *The Swooshys Save the Day!,* about married superheroes made of Swiss cheese, or *Leafy Goes to School,* about a maple tree "in the rainforest of Pennsylvania" who, along with her best friend, a dingo named Morris, encounters "Crabby the boy crab." Toward the end, "Morris and Crabby ran as fast as they could but, out of nowhere, the aquarium keepers grabbed them and threw them in the recycling bin!" What more could one ask from a story than that—friendship, action, and a devotion to conserving natural resources. Perhaps David Sedaris will soon have a new favorite piece of short fiction?

Visit us online at www.826nyc.org. And please stop by if you are in the neighborhood. Look for the Superhero Supply Store at 372 Fifth Avenue in Brooklyn, NY 11215.

Ask Ted for directions to the secret door.

PERMISSIONS ACKNOWLEDGMENTS